THE WOMAN IN THE WOOD

ALSO BY M.K. HILL

Sasha Dawson series
The Bad Place

THE WOMAN IN THE WOOD

M.K. HILL

HEAD
of ZEUS

First published in the UK in 2021 by Head of Zeus Ltd

9 7 5 3 1 2 4 6 8

A catalogue record for this book is available from
the British Library.

ISBN (HB): 9781788548304
ISBN (XTPB): 9781788548311
ISBN (E): 9781788548335

Typeset by Siliconchips Services Ltd UK

Printed and bound in Great Britain by
CPI Group (UK) Ltd, Croydon CRO 4YY

MIX
Paper from
responsible sources
FSC® C020471

Head of Zeus Ltd
First Floor East
5–8 Hardwick Street
London EC1R 4RG

WWW.HEADOFZEUS.COM

For Jamie, with thanks

The charm of fame is so great that we like every
object to which it is attached, even death.

Blaise Pascal

1

'Why don't you leave her alone, mate?'

Deano didn't like the way the prat was looking at him. As if he was better than him, as if he was a cut above. Deano wasn't going to let anybody talk to him like that, not in this pub, not ever. Certainly not this pathetic guy, and his whiny bitch of a girlfriend. He lurched forward to jab the little rat in the chest.

'What the *hell*' – Deano's voice was an aggressive slur – 'has it got to do with you?'

'Please, we don't want any trouble.' The man placed an arm around his girl's shoulder to lead her away, but Deano wasn't about to let the snivelling little prick off the hook. All he had done was try to talk to her. Last time he looked, it wasn't a crime to talk to a girl; they liked it when you chatted them up, and it wasn't even like she was that attractive anyway. But the guy had got all snotty. Telling him to stop bothering her, treating him as if he was the lowest of the low.

As if he could see into the depths of Deano's rotten soul.

'You don't know what I'm capable of.' He pursued the pair of them, elbowing his way through the crowd, causing someone's pint to slop. 'None of you wankers do.'

'Give it a rest and go home,' someone shouted.

'Who said that?' Deano swung round, balling his fists, searching for the culprit. He was a big guy, over six foot, with wide shoulders and a pit-bull face, and knew how to intimidate. 'Come on then, if you want some.'

But then he was grabbed from behind. A pair of bouncers in black bomber jackets twisted his arms high behind his back and bundled him towards the door.

'Get off,' Deano screamed, calling them all sorts. 'Get off me!'

He tried to squirm from their grasp, but he was pissed and slow and clumsy, and the tips of his toes barely touched the ground as he was dragged out the door, the laughs and jeers and shouts of 'See ya' from everyone in the pub ringing in his ears.

'You don't know,' he shouted over his shoulder. 'You people don't know who I am, what I've done.'

'Yeah, yeah, big man,' someone called. 'Bore off.'

And then he was thrown into the cool night. His legs folded beneath him as he fell to the pavement.

One of the bouncers jabbed a finger. 'You're barred.'

Deano sat in a heap in the middle of the street,

the palms of his hands stinging from where they had scraped against the concrete kerb. He was humiliated now, and desperate for a drink, and just wanted to go back inside.

'I'll be quiet, I'll be good,' he told the doormen sullenly. 'I won't bother anyone.'

'Get yourself home, mate,' one of them said with a sneer. 'You're embarrassing yourself.'

Deano tried to convince them he'd mind his own business, he wouldn't make any trouble, but they weren't having any of it. So he climbed unsteadily to his feet – the road and the night sky seemed to tip and sway as he stood upright – and straightened his clothes with as much dignity as he could muster.

Now he knew he wouldn't get back in, he pointed a finger at the two doormen. 'I'll be back.'

'Sure, Arnie.' They both laughed at him.

As soon as he was sure nobody could see him, Deano burst out crying. He wept because every night was the same now. He'd go out drinking and get into a fight, he didn't even know how it happened but it always did, and then he'd go into blackout, and wake up covered in cuts and bruises on a hospital trolley, or in a police cell, full of shame and despair.

He smeared the tears from his cheeks with the back of his hand, licked his sopping lips, and tried to focus on the street signs so he could work out where he was, but he didn't recognize any of the landmarks.

So Deano was relieved to see a train station ahead of him. He looked up at the sign, squinting to force the words to stop vibrating, and saw where he was – Hockley, which was a village a few stops from Southend-on-Sea. He vaguely remembered getting on a train a few hours ago, because that's what he had to do now, just so he could get a drink. In Southend it was becoming more and more difficult to find a pub or bar that would let him in; they all knew his face and refused to serve him, so he was forced to travel out of town.

He had no idea what the time was; all he knew was that it was late and he'd been on the piss all day, and he just wanted to get home and sleep. Deano prayed the trains were still running, but if they weren't he'd find a bench to curl up on till morning. It wouldn't be the first time.

Yeah, drink would be the death of him. Now his tears of frustration had dried in the chill of the night, he kind of knew he was on the escalator to hell. One day he'd drop dead of liver failure, or a heart attack, or more likely he'd pick a fight with some guy who was bigger than him. Quicker, stronger – more sober.

All these years later, he was still trying to live with the guilt of what he'd done. If he didn't do something about it, the knowledge would eat away at him like a cancer.

Sometimes, Deano wished those others *had* called the police on him. He'd be paying the price. In prison right now, lying on his bunk after lights out listening to the wails and night terrors of the other cons, three years into a twenty-year stretch. But a life banged up had to be better than what he had right now, which was a living hell. Because *she* was the first thing he thought about when he woke up every morning and the last thing on his mind before he drifted into a sleep filled with nightmares.

And Deano's drinking was getting worse. He was getting obliterated every night in an attempt to blot out what had happened...

What he did.

Sure, he had a temper when he was sober, but if he hadn't been drinking he'd never have done any of the stupid things he had on his conscience. It was the booze that made him attack that random guy in the street all those years ago, it was the drink that made his ex call the police on him – and it was what finally made him a *murderer*.

Deep down, he understood that he picked fights with strangers in pubs because he had a death wish. He knew that one day he could be felled by a single, sickening punch, he may not even see it coming – and then it would all be over. He was sick of himself, he was tired of being Andrew Dean.

So as he approached the station entrance, Deano came to a decision. He was going to go to the police and confess what he did, and where they could find the body; and finally, all these years later, he would face the consequences of his actions. He'd be punished, locked up for years and years, but at least he could get help for his drinking and depression. That's what he was going to do, he was going to *confess*, and maybe one day when he was released, he'd finally be able to turn his life around.

It's true that there'd been many times like this, when drunk and depressed, he had convinced himself that he was going to turn himself in, but then the next morning did nothing about it. But this time Deano was determined. First thing tomorrow, or most likely when he dragged himself out of bed after lunch, he would go to the police station. And then it would all be over.

Relief washed over him as he stood on the empty platform and wept again. Wracking sobs that made his chest heave so hard he could hardly catch his breath. Tears fell through his big hands, hands that had killed, and onto the floor.

But when he looked up, the sobs still catching in his throat, he saw that he wasn't alone. Someone was watching him from the shadows.

'What are you looking at?' Embarrassed at being caught crying, his anger returned. 'Piss off.'

Deano turned away, determined to ignore them. He wasn't going to let anyone wind him up, not now he had come to a decision. But when he looked back, the figure was still there, standing in the darkness beneath the platform roof. All he could see was their glinting, watchful eyes, and that they held something long and thin, like a walking stick, close to their side.

'You are one creepy weirdo,' Deano said. 'You know that, yeah?'

He heard the rumble of a train in the distance, and not before time. He was shattered, and just wanted to get home. He'd really like to smoke a cigarette on the train, that would help him relax, but when he patted his pockets, he realized he was out, so he swallowed his pride and called to the figure in the shadows.

'Hey, mate, got a fag?'

The stranger reached slowly into a pocket, and Deano knew his luck was in. So he stumbled over – trying not to look too drunk or threatening, in case they freaked out – and stood with his hand out. The train was getting louder in the distance.

'Cheers,' he slurred. 'No hard feelings, yeah?'

He couldn't take his eyes off the hand trying to lift something from the pocket, a cigarette, or maybe the whole packet if the stranger was feeling generous, and Deano was already looking forward to that first hit of smoke filling his lungs. He had already decided he wasn't going to get on this train, he'd sit on the bench and enjoy the cigarette on the platform.

Deano licked his lips in anticipation, but then the stranger took out a bottle with a spray nozzle on it, and lifted it towards him. He barely had time to focus before he heard a hiss – and felt an excruciating pain in his eyes.

'Aaargh!' Deano clutched his face. The agony was indescribable; his eyeballs felt like they were on fire, the pain sizzling all the way behind his sockets and into his skull. His cheeks felt like they were melting, and his nose and ears. He wheeled away, blinded.

Dimly, he heard the train approaching and wanted to wave his arms – *Help me!* – but couldn't bear to tear his hands away from his face. He scratched at his eyes with his nails in a desperate attempt to claw away the pain.

And then – he didn't understand it – there was another sharp sensation in his ribs, a shocking jolt, accompanied by a harsh buzz. He yelped and reared away. Unable to comprehend what it was, or what was happening to him, he stumbled backwards. Twisting an ankle, he only just managed to keep his balance before he felt another burning shock in the soft flesh of his stomach. Confused, helpless, Deano screeched. The pain – in his eyes, in his face and stomach – was beyond anything he had ever imagined.

Another excruciating shock, this time in his left side, made him squirm away – but then he felt another in his ribs. His eyes felt like they were on fire in their sockets, the skin on his face burning.

'No,' he screamed, helpless. 'Stop it!'

There was another buzzing shock in his right side,

then to his chest and stomach, and Deano jumped back, trying to get out of reach of his tormentor.

The roar of the train filled his ears now. He cried for help, for someone to come and help him, and make it stop.

And then he felt another prolonged shock on his belly; the searing pain and the buzz seemed to last forever, and he smelled his own flesh burn. His face was on fire, and now his stomach.

Deano had to get away, he had to make it stop, to get help – and he leaped.

Straight off the platform and into the path of the train.

2

Detective Inspector Sasha Dawson pulled her knackered Spider Veloce into the station car park, negotiating a narrow space between a patrol car and a forensics van. She was carefully nosing the front end forward, using the wing mirrors as she edged into the space with inches to spare on either side, when her phone began to ring in her bag on the passenger seat, causing her unnecessary anxiety during the delicate manoeuvre.

'Wait a minute,' she appealed to the impatient phone. 'Just let me…'

As soon as she was satisfied the front bumper was nestled against the kerb, she cranked the handbrake and killed the engine.

Flustered, Sasha dug the phone from her bag. 'Yes?'

'You do remember we're meeting tonight, don't you, darling?' said her sister, not bothering with any of the usual introductory niceties.

'Hello, Connie, *how are you*?' said Sasha, making a point.

Con ignored her and said, 'You won't let me down again, will you?'

Sasha gave herself a quick once-over in the rear-view mirror, clawing her fingers and dragging them through her white hair. Clamping the phone as best she could between her ear and shoulder, she pulled the long bob into a ponytail, accentuating the perfect point of her widow's peak against her olive skin, and tied it in place. Then she opened the driver's door as far as she could in the tiny space between her Spider and the patrol car – it was incredibly tight, and in hindsight she maybe should have parked somewhere else – ignoring the smirks of the uniforms and forensics team who watched her trying to squeeze into the gap between the vehicles.

'Are you there, darling?' asked her sister impatiently.

Shuffling sideways along the slice of space, Sasha swallowed her irritation. She and Con had been meaning to catch up for weeks now, had several times arranged a time, date and location, but Connie always bailed at the last minute, and blamed Sasha for postponing.

'I'm going to have to play it by ear, Con.' A late night in the office could be on the cards if the death of the man on the rail track proved suspicious. 'But I promise I'll do my best.'

'Good morning, ma'am,' said a uniformed officer, who came over with a clipboard.

'Hello.' She showed him her ID and he signed her into the scene cordon log. 'Good to see you.'

'What did you say?' Connie asked on the phone, but she didn't wait for Sasha to answer. 'I really need to see you… well, the fact is, I need a favour.'

Stepping out of the way of the stream of emergency personnel walking to and from the building, Sasha lifted her eyes to the blue, cloudless sky. Connie's requests for favours usually involved loans or financial support for her boyfriend Barry's doomed business ventures. And besides, Sasha couldn't remember the last time Connie had done her any favours in return, hadn't even offered to babysit her kids when they were younger. Getting help from Con, for anything at all, was like getting blood from a stone.

Perhaps sensing Sasha's reticence, Connie added quickly, 'And of course, I'm so looking forward to seeing you, it's been *ages*.'

'As I say, Con—'

'Shall we say seven at that new bar in Leigh? See you then, Sash. Can't wait.'

And then Connie hung up. Sasha was still staring at her phone when Detective Sergeant Ajay de Vaz, already suited in his forensic coveralls, came over.

'Sorry I'm late, but my son lost his school bag in his tip of a bedroom.' She offered him an amused eye-roll, intended to make light of her tardiness. Sasha's timekeeping wasn't the best; at her most recent work appraisal she had promised to be more punctual. But she also knew that nobody in her Major Incident Team

would drop her in it. She nodded towards the station.
'Tell me now, is it bad?'

'Guy was hit by a train.' The ends of de Vaz's mouth
pulled down in a grimace. 'He's all over the place.'

'Okay, then,' she said stoically as they approached
the inner cordon set up at the station entrance, where
she would be obliged to put on Tyvek coveralls over her
M&S trouser suit, and shoe covers over her brogues.

Her prematurely white hair – Sasha was only just
sliding down the wrong side of forty-five – was already
secure, ready for the hood. But because of her pear-shaped
body, her slim waist tapering to wide hips, and her legs,
which weren't the longest, she always felt self-conscious
walking around in those infernal suits. But then, they
made everyone look like a Teletubby. Everyone except
Ajay, who always managed to look catwalk-ready.

On the way, her gaze swept across the small crowd
that had formed at the entrance of the car park, where
the police outer cordon had been established. People
had come to see what on earth had happened that
would require the attendance of the emergency services,
and the quick arrival of a TV camera crew.

A face in the crowd made Sasha do a double take,
but when she searched for it again she couldn't see
anyone she knew. Instead, she turned her attention
to the nondescript building in front of her. It was as
unremarkable as any of the thousands of train stations
in towns and villages across the UK, stripped of any

character it may have once possessed, the platforms and train tracks sealed off by spiked metal fencing.

Four stops from Southend Victoria on the Shenfield line, the trains that stopped there transported commuters to and from London Liverpool Street, fifty minutes away. But this morning the line was severely disrupted because of the body on the track; it would be out of action for a few hours yet.

'What do we know?' she asked as she climbed into a support van to suit up.

'A man fell in front of a train late last night. The driver said he thought he saw someone else on the platform just before the deceased died. Said he saw them waving about a walking stick. It was dark, of course, and the train flashed past, so he couldn't be sure.'

'A walking stick?' She frowned. 'Have we got the CCTV footage from the driver's compartment yet?'

'We've put in a request with the operator.'

'And how is the driver?'

'Traumatized,' said Ajay, 'as you can well imagine.'

'Poor man. Is anyone from British Transport Police here yet?'

Because the crime had taken place on railway property, there was a strong chance that BTP would have jurisdiction over it, particularly if it involved a random encounter on the platform.

'They're on their way.'

'And the deceased?'

'Name's Andrew Dean. He's a Southend resident, lives... *lived* on York Road.' As she climbed into the Tyvek suit, Ajay held up clear plastic bags containing the victim's debit card, driving licence and other unidentified items. 'His wallet was found trackside. All the contents of his pockets were literally slammed from his body when the train hit him.'

'Do we know what he was doing here in Hockley?'

'Making a nuisance of himself in a local pub, by all accounts.'

Ajay watched her snap the elasticated plastic covers over her shoes. His small, perfectly groomed features were already half-hidden by the polyethylene material and his dark hair, combed so immaculately smooth you'd think it was a piece of Lego, was hidden beneath a hood. 'He became abusive and got thrown out just before closing time.'

'Ah.' If Andrew Dean had got himself into a dispute elsewhere that led to his violent death on the tracks, then transport police wouldn't get involved. 'And we know this how?'

He gestured towards the knot of onlookers. 'I spoke to one of the locals and it was the first thing she remembered about last night. There was a guy causing trouble at a local pub, hassling people, getting increasingly intoxicated and lairy, and he was ejected. I showed her his driver's ID and Bob's your uncle.'

'Did he get into a fight with anyone in particular?'

'He was harassing a young woman, and her boyfriend tried to intervene, but mostly he was obnoxious to everyone.'

'A pub full of suspects,' Sasha said. 'That's a good start.'

'Andrew Dean could barely stand when he left the pub. Could be he fell off the platform by accident.'

Sasha took the plastic bag to get a better look at the driving licence with Andrew Dean's personal details on it. He was a hulking figure in the headshot, bull-necked, with a big square jaw, a broken nose and hooded eyes; he glowered sullenly at the camera.

'Looks a charmer,' she said.

'Ring any bells, Mrs Dawson?'

That caught her attention and she looked up quickly. 'Should he?'

Ajay's eyes flashed mischievously. 'I did a quick search for him on the internet.'

'I love that about you, Ajay,' she told him. 'Your initiative.'

'Him and a group of other men were questioned about the disappearance of a girl a few years back. One of them was some kind of' – his nostrils flared, as if the phrase was distasteful – '*reality star.*'

She pulled the hood of the Tyvek suit over her head and they climbed from the van to duck under the crime tape at the inner cordon, established outside the ticket office. Sasha took a moment to notice the black bulb of the CCTV camera in one corner of the room.

The sun was lifting in the blue sky now. The summers were getting hotter and hotter in this part of south Essex, and as they walked along the platform towards the footbridge that crossed the rail track, Sasha was baking in the coveralls.

'That thing is turned off, right?' She pointed at the electrified track and he grinned, as if to say, *You'd better hope so.* 'Just checking.'

It was disconcerting to see sheets laid along the track to hide a number of different body parts. Sasha had seen numerous corpses in her career as a murder detective. But the effect of a train collision on the human body was catastrophic. The train that mowed down Andrew Dean weighed hundreds of tons and because it wasn't due to stop at Hockley would have passed through the station at over a hundred miles an hour. At the moment of impact, Andrew Dean would have been killed instantaneously, sustaining massive internal and external injuries. His body would have been thrown in the air like a football, the limbs flying off, or sliced to bits beneath the wheels of the train.

Standing beneath the footbridge that spanned the platforms, Sasha could see the rear of the train where it had finally come to a stop a quarter mile further up the track. CSIs moved about the front carriage like ants, swabbing its steel surface. A PolSA team, trained police searchers, moved methodically along the tracks in a tight line.

A single white tent had been erected fifty yards beyond the end of the eastbound platform, which meant the body was at least partially intact. Sasha and Ajay walked down the slope at the end of the platform towards it.

A couple of CSIs stood outside the tent chatting as they approached. Sasha paused at the entrance for a moment, steeling herself to face the body inside. Ajay waited patiently for her to gather her thoughts.

'That girl who disappeared,' she turned to ask him. 'Was she ever found?'

He shook his head. 'No.'

She gestured at the tent, inviting him to go in first. 'Brains before beauty.'

3

'Hey, Abs, thanks for coming.'
          'Sure, no problem.'
'It's not often we get someone as famous as you in one of our retail units. Have you ever opened one of our shops before?'

'No.' Abs looked around QuidStore, with its shelves of products at rock-bottom prices and its automated tills. It smelled of bleach and air freshener. He tried to sound upbeat. 'This is my first... discount store.'

'We're really pleased you're here.' The assistant manager was a young Asian man, who looked like he'd just left school. 'What we'd like you to do is say a few words outside about what you love about QuidStore, and then cut the ribbon, maybe chat to some of our customers.'

'Sure thing.'

Abs gave the guy a big grin, because that's what everyone wanted from him, that's what they expected – a flash of his famous pearly whites – but inside he felt depressed. He had fallen a long way since that time he was flown out by private jet to make a personal appearance at a millionaire's party in Ibiza. Here he was, opening a discount shop – a QuidStore – on Basildon High Street.

'Excuse me.'

A woman with a shopping trolley came up to him and he took out his Sharpie, ready to give her an autograph. In his career, he'd had to sign all kinds of things, even cheeky bits of flesh, although it had been a few years since women had thrust their chests at him.

'Yes, darling?'

He waited for her to ask him to sign something, but she pointed over his shoulder. 'I just want to get to the detergents.'

'Oh,' said Abs, moving out of the way. 'Sorry, love.'

'We got word out to the local press, but to tell you the truth we were expecting more of a crowd,' the assistant manager said, embarrassed.

There were half a dozen people outside with their phones in their hands. But Abs didn't kid himself. Some of those were passers-by who had seen the balloons and ticker tape and had stopped to see what was going on. It was all very different from the days when he arrived in a limo to open luxury apartments, state-of-the-art spas and glitzy nightclubs. He missed those receptions with champagne and canapés on silver platters; he used to love those little prawn things, the biscuits covered in creamy pâté, and pulled pork sliders, served by sexy women in tight black dresses. In those days, everyone was eager to get into his orbit.

But that was when he was one of the biggest celebs in the UK, the star of TV reality show *Laid In Essex!* and voted 'Britain's Sexiest Guy' three years on the trot by readers of the *Daily Star*. It felt like a long time ago now. The crowds had disappeared, along with the TV panel shows, sponsorship deals and party invites.

But, hell, Abs was a professional and he was going to make the best of it, because anyone's fortune could change in an instant. All it took was a lucky break, and if Abs was anything in life, he was a lucky guy.

Yeah, he was just opening a discount store, but those people outside – the teenagers on their phones, that single mum with the double buggy, and those pensioners eating rolls – they had come here to see him, or at least most of them had, and it was his duty to bring a little bit of sunshine into their drab lives. His only talent in life was to make other people happy, to make them smile and giggle, and that's what he was going to do.

'Don't worry about it, it's a bit overcast today,' said Abs, who had always been a people pleaser. 'And there's still time for people to arrive. When do we cut the ribbon?'

The assistant manager looked at his watch. 'We're still waiting for the photographer.'

Paparazzi! Abs liked the sound of that. 'At least the press are coming.'

'He's from our in-house magazine. Shall we go outside?'

Abs didn't need asking twice, and he strode out of the shop. He was wearing his usual hoodie and distressed jeans and white trainers – he was famous for his pristine footwear – and his thick, dark hair was pulled up in a small topknot. His dazzling smile was his trademark, his brand.

'Don't shoot,' he told the crowd. 'I'm coming out.'

'Here's a guy who needs no introduction,' said the assistant manager, holding a wireless microphone so close to his mouth that his voice contorted with flatulent static. 'It's Abs.'

Grabbing the mic, Abs was relieved to see more people were coming to watch.

'Have they found the right man to open their new shop? *Abs, mate!*' Everyone laughed at his catchphrase. On the show, he was always saying *Abs, mate!* as in absolutely, and it was how he got his famous nickname.

'Not a lot of people know that I once worked in a shop, and was—' He glanced over the heads of the crowd and saw a guy on the other side of the pedestrian walkway. Standing perfectly still, hands in his pockets, the man was watching him from behind dark glasses, and it made Abs momentarily lose the thread of what he was saying. 'What was I... oh yeah, I worked in a shop, like I say, and was sacked after five minutes.' There were a few giggles from the crowd because everyone knew

Abs wasn't the sharpest tool in the box, which was why everyone liked him so much. 'A guy came in and told me he wanted to buy a spider, so I told him to pick one up on the web.'

'I miss you on *Laid In Essex!*, Abs,' someone called. 'It's not the same without you, are you going back on it?'

'You never know.' Abs winked. 'Stranger things have happened. And anyway, me and Kelz have got unfinished business.'

'You can get cheap digging equipment here, for the next time you go on a date,' someone shouted, but Abs ignored the distasteful jibe.

'Honestly, I'm over the moon to be here.' He paced on the pavement, as if working the main stage at Glastonbury. 'In one of the best towns in the whole world, in one of my favourite shops.'

He said a few more things about how proud he was to be there, and what good value QuidStore was, and then said he was going to cut the ribbon to officially open the shop. But the assistant manager shook his head because the photographer hadn't turned up, so Abs said he'd sign autographs.

People crowded around. One girl had brought along a copy of his autobiography, called simply *Abs, Mate!* In truth, he'd had nothing to do with the writing of it. They hired this ghostwriter, a nice lady who had asked him lots of questions, teasing out the interesting facts of his life and career, and then turned it all into a book. What he had never told anyone was that, not being much of a reader, he hadn't even read *Abs, Mate!* He took a moment to look at the cover now, with its embossed gold title and topless photo of him looking young and hot, taken by a top fashion photographer.

'Blimey, I haven't seen a copy of this for years,' he told the girl. 'Where did you get it?'

'It was in the bargain bin at the charity shop. I bought it for 10p.'

Abs was about to sign it when he looked up to see the guy was still watching him at the back of the crowd. There was something about the look on his face – grim, almost threatening – that made Abs nervous. He definitely recognized him from somewhere.

Abs forced himself to pay attention to the girl. 'What's your name, love?'

'It's for my mum, Tracey.'

Abs scribbled:

To Tracy, Absolutly my gratest fan. Luv, Abs!!!! xxxxxxx

The girl frowned. 'It's Tracey with an "e".'

'Sorry about that.' He shoved the book back at her just as his phone rang.

Abs felt a chill drop down his spine when he saw who it was: Tony. He gawped at it, thinking he wasn't seeing straight. He hadn't heard from Tony in three years, not since... what happened.

Neither of them had been in a hurry to speak to each other, not after the events of *that* night. So he knew that whatever Tony wanted to talk to him about was going to be important, and that whatever it was, he didn't want to hear it. But Abs couldn't help himself, and he touched the screen of his old iPhone and cradled it between his shoulder and his ear while he continued to sign autographs.

'Tone.' He tried to sound chilled and happy in front of the public. More people had arrived; there was getting to be quite a crowd. Abs did his best to scribble on the pieces of paper they all thrust at him. 'It's been too long,' he lied.

'Deano's dead,' said Tony quickly.

Abs's pen lifted from the till receipt he was signing. 'I'm sorry to hear that, Tone,' he said carefully. If he was honest with himself, he wasn't sorry in the slightest. Tony's mate Deano was a wrong 'un, and Abs would never forgive him for what happened.

'Yeah.' Tony sounded upset. 'He was hit by a train.'

'Ooh.' Abs handed back the slip of paper and edged back from the throng, trying to find some space. 'Nasty way to go.'

'They reckon it could be murder, Abs. The police, I mean.'

'I can't talk right now, Tone.' Abs couldn't hear

himself think above all the people pressing against him on every side.

'I think someone's been following me, Abs.'

'You're just upset, mate.' Abs tried to stay calm. 'I'm in the middle of something right now, but let's have a catch-up, you, me and Jez.'

'Someone's after us, Abs, because of what we did. I'm scared.'

'Calm down, bruv.' Abs was getting the willies now. He was surrounded. People were shoving bits of paper at him to sign, along with DVDs and *Laid In Essex!* memorabilia. 'I'll call you as soon as I get away from here, yeah?'

'They're coming for us, Abs,' said Tony in a panic.

'Who is, Tone?'

'I don't know, but I'm scared.'

Abs was finding it difficult to breathe. 'Just give me half an hour, yeah? I'll call you back, I promise.'

'They're after us.'

'Tony, mate,' said Abs urgently. 'Relax, you're getting—' But then the line went dead. 'Tone, are you still there?'

Abs looked up quickly in the direction of the guy who had been watching him, but he was gone. He whirled in a circle to try and find him. The crowd pressed forward, reaching out. Abs scanned their faces in a panic.

You're a professional, he scolded himself. *Get a grip*.

And then a glinting blade flashed in front of his face – making him flinch in terror.

'Now would be a good time to cut the ribbon,' said the assistant manager, flipping the scissors over and offering them handle first to Abs.

4

Back in the Major Incident Team's suite of offices at the police station on Victoria Avenue in Southend, Sasha flipped off her shoes and fired up her computer. A television fixed to the wall was showing the local news, a report about coastal erosion along the estuary.

'Hi, Sasha.' DC Lolly Chambers gave a little wave from behind her desk.

'Morning, Lols,' Sasha said brightly, trying to get the sight of Andrew Dean's broken torso out of her head. 'Lovely day.'

It was hectic as usual. Phones rang across the office as her team chased lines of inquiry across numerous active investigations. The photocopier chuntered on the other side of the office, paper sliding from its innards, a thin beam of light racing along the edges of its plastic lid.

DC Craig Power tapped gingerly at his computer

keyboard with two fingers, examining each key carefully beforehand, as if hitting the wrong one would result in a nuclear detonation. Lolly, who liked a chinwag, chatted with one of the civilian staff about something she had been forced to send back to ASOS. Wrong colour, wrong size, wrong style; Sasha could never keep up.

In his side office, DCI Vaughn was hunched over his phone, kneading the skin around his eyes with his big fingers. Her boss had been subdued recently, had lost much of his legendary bite, and didn't spend half as much time prowling around the incident room looking over everybody's shoulder. Sasha, who knew him as well as anyone in the MIT, had been meaning to take him aside to ask whether there was anything troubling him, but the right moment hadn't yet presented itself.

Before she did anything else – before she read her emails or prepared for the morning team briefing, before she checked her diary to remind herself of the numerous pointless meetings that would likely punctuate her long day – she clicked open a browser and typed in Andrew Dean's name.

A news article from three years ago appeared instantly, detailing the facts of the disappearance of the girl three years ago in Denbighshire, Wales, which Ajay had told her about.

FATHER PLEADS
FOR NEWS OF MISSING DAUGHTER

Police have renewed their appeal for information about missing teenager Rhiannon Jenkins, who disappeared nine days ago.

In a media briefing organized by North Wales Police in Wrexham, Rhiannon's father, Owen Jenkins, joined Superintendent Sharon Thomas to ask for anyone who has seen nineteen-year-old Rhiannon to come forward with information.

Rhiannon went missing following an evening at The Red Lion pub near the village of Llandrillo on the evening of 4 May. A distraught Mr Jenkins told the assembled press he was extremely concerned for the welfare of his daughter.

Joined by other members of his family – including Rhiannon's aunt Jennie and uncle Davey Jenkins, an independent businessman, with whom Rhiannon was holidaying at the time of her disappearance – widower Mr Jenkins made a direct plea to his daughter to make herself known to police.

'I want you to come home, Rhiannon,' he told the media, before becoming overcome with emotion. 'You're my little girl, you're all I have left in the world, and I just want you back.'

Superintendent Thomas told the press: 'Rhiannon's family and all of us in North Wales Police are very concerned for her safety. Rhiannon is an independent and outgoing young woman, with plenty of friends, but it is totally out of character for her not to make contact with her family. We have a dedicated team of detectives doing everything to locate her, and we will leave no stone unturned.'

Detectives are currently piecing together the teenager's last known movements. She and friends spent much of the evening at The Red Lion, where she met *Laid In Essex!* star Danny 'Abs' Cruikshank, who was holidaying in a cottage nearby with a group of friends, named as Andrew Dean, Jeremy Weston and Tony Gardner. The men, all from Southend-on-Sea in Essex, were questioned by police when an eyewitness reportedly saw them talking to Rhiannon outside the pub in the early hours of the following morning, but they were later released.

'Rhiannon left the pub at half past ten that night and someone must have seen her,' said Superintendent Thomas. 'I'm appealing to members of the public who have information about her whereabouts to get in contact.'

There were plenty of other articles about Rhiannon Jenkins published in the weeks and months following her disappearance. Newspapers followed the twists and turns of the investigation very closely, and the unlikely connection of reality heart-throb Danny 'Abs'

Cruikshank to Rhiannon's last known appearance meant the story picked up a lot of national coverage. There were further appeals for information, a reconstruction of the young woman's last known movements. Hopeful sightings of Rhiannon poured in from all parts of Wales, and the length and breadth of the UK.

Her uncle, Davey Jenkins, made a number of veiled comments in various papers about what he would like to do to the people who were responsible for Rhiannon's disappearance. A *Mail* article published later that year featured an interview with the girl's father.

'I'M AN ALCOHOLIC
AND A GAMBLING ADDICT –
AND I FEAR I FAILED MY DAUGHTER'

Heartbreak of Missing Welsh Lass Rhiannon's Father

Owen Jenkins was photographed in his small Cardiff flat looking pale and unwell, and surrounded by numerous mementoes and photos of Rhiannon. In the interview, he spoke at great length, and with terrible anguish, about how he felt he had not been a good parent since the passing of his wife. Rhiannon's mother had died when his daughter was only a little girl.

But with each passing month the flood of news stories became a trickle, and within a year they dried up completely, along with all viable lines of inquiry.

The case was never solved – the investigation was kept open, but Rhiannon remained missing.

In all of the coverage, Andrew Dean – if he was indeed the same man who was found dead on the train tracks at Hockley – was nothing more than a footnote. But there were plenty of stories about Danny Cruikshank, the man everybody in the country knew simply as Abs.

The celebrity connection to the mystery of Rhiannon's disappearance, as tangential as it appeared, was catnip to journalists, who couldn't resist shochorning the famous star of reality show *Laid In Essex!* into every story about the missing girl. Every single report mentioned the good-looking young celebrity, and every article was inevitably accompanied by a photo of Abs.

In those images, publicity shots from the show, Abs was usually leaning against the bar in a club, looking rakish and charming. Beneath perfect eyebrows, which arched like fighting alley cats, his come-to-bed eyes twinkled mischievously – *look at me*, they said, *I'm full of youth and sex and fun.* He had a thick head of hair, which was swept back over his brow and tied in a knot at the crown, and his tombstone teeth were so dazzling they appeared almost radioactive. Abs had a bit of bumfluff under his chin, which could have been intentional, but Sasha wasn't sure. He wore a stylish jacket over a hoodie, and jeans with fashionable jagged holes at the knees and on the thighs, some of which were so big it was a wonder the jeans didn't disintegrate. On his feet were the whitest trainers Sasha had ever seen.

'Lols.' Enlarging the image on the screen, Sasha hooked a finger at the detective constable. 'What do you know about this Abs person?'

When Lolly saw the photo, she let out a screech, which Sasha thought was a little bit over the top.

'Oh my God.' Lolly's big blue eyes widened. 'I love Abs.'

'Why's he called Abs?' asked Sasha. 'Has he got big muscles, or what?'

'It's his catchphrase,' said Lolly. 'It means absolutely. Whenever someone asks him something on the show – like, are you good in bed? – he'll give this cheeky grin and say, *Abs, mate!*'

On the other side of the room, Ajay lifted an eyebrow. 'Who in polite society would ask a question like that?'

'Wait, you haven't even seen *Laid In Essex!*?' Ajay didn't have a television, and Lolly simply couldn't get her head around the fact. 'You must know *Laid In Essex!*'

'I know of it, but I've never watched it.'

'You're having me on, mate.' Lolly's jaw fell open, as if she was affronted. 'They're always asking stuff like that. Do you fancy me? Do you think my dress is sexy? Will you stay the night?'

A few years back, *Laid In Essex!*, about the lives and loves of a group of socially mobile young people, was all anyone talked about. It was a TV sensation and its young cast became stars overnight.

Some worthies in the county complained that its revolving cast of highly sexed and largely uneducated young men and women, who fell in and out of love and in and out of bed with each other, portrayed Essex in a bad light, and as a result a generation of young women had been forever labelled as airhead 'Essex Girls', and young men as oversexed yobs. But one thing was for certain, it put Essex firmly on the cultural map.

Sasha had watched a couple of episodes with her daughter, Angel – 'You will *so* love it, Mum' – who gave her a running commentary about what was going on. Who was in love with who; which BFFs had fallen out; who was exploring their sexuality; and who was moving in on whose boyfriend/girlfriend. The episodes Sasha watched featured endless scenes of spray-tanned men and women meeting in bars, cafés and nightclubs to talk about why they broke up and to explore the possibility of getting back together, despite the fact they were currently dating other people.

Abs, Sasha knew, was one of the breakout stars of the show, and shared an addictive *will they/won't they* onscreen partnership with *LIE!* vixen Kelsey DeMarco.

For a while, Abs was ubiquitous. He appeared on Saturday night entertainment shows – including that thing with Ant and Dec – and she vaguely remembered seeing him in something on Channel 5. He was all over papers, magazines and the internet; his amiable grin was familiar from adverts and sponsorship deals. For a short while, there was nowhere you could go without seeing Abs grinning at you from posters and billboards.

And then… nothing.

Sasha couldn't remember the last time she saw him on the telly, or had even thought about him, and realized his disappearance from public life coincided with Rhiannon Jenkins going missing. Telly producers, advertisers and sponsors must have dropped him like a hot coal.

Lolly leaned over the screen. 'What's he done?'

'He was questioned about the disappearance of a girl,' Sasha told her. 'Three years ago.'

'I know about that,' said Lolly. 'But I don't care, I still *would*.'

Looking up from his computer, DC Craig Power pulled a face. 'Dear, oh dear.'

'Abs is sex on a stick,' Lolly told him. 'He's the perfect man.'

Craig smirked. 'Each to their own.'

'I'm going to marry him one day,' Lolly told him defensively, and Sasha hoped she was joking. 'He's ten times the man you are, Craig. You're just jealous, mate.'

That must have hit a nerve, because Craig spun in his chair to face her. 'As if I'm jealous of that muppet. He ain't all that. And, anyway, as if he's going to look at you when he can have any woman he likes.'

'Craiiggg,' warned Sasha in a singsong, her eyes drifting up to the television screen on the wall. 'Play nice.'

'Abs, mate!' London born and bred, Craig did what he believed to be a funny estuary accent. 'I'm well jel, what*evah*, yeah?'

'You think you're Idris,' Lolly replied with venom. 'You think you're God's gift, but I'm telling you right now, you *ain't*.'

'Now now, team,' warned Sasha. Lolly and Craig's unspoken burning desire for each other was becoming a problem. 'Let's keep it professional.'

Craig Power shrugged. 'I've had offers, from model agencies and that.'

Lolly snorted. 'You live in a fantasy world.'

The news report changed on the TV and Sasha recognized Hockley station. She saw patrol cars and vans, crime scene tape flapping at the outer cordon, and realized the footage had been taken this morning.

'You know it's the truth.' Craig gave Lolly a sarcastic wink. 'Some of us have the X factor, that special something, know what I mean?'

Lolly rolled a finger beside her temple. 'You're losing it, mate.'

'Right,' snapped Sasha, 'this is all very interesting, but we have things to do.' She made a shooing movement with her hands. 'Off you go, Lols.'

Folding her arms, she sat back in her chair to

watch the news report, interested to see if she could be glimpsed in the footage. Nobody could resist trying to spot themselves on television, although it might be difficult to recognize herself among the many identical forensic suits. The camera panned around the car park to reveal the small crowd of onlookers.

And there it was again – that momentary glimpse of a familiar face in the crowd. Sasha jumped out of her seat and rushed to the table where all three million remote controls that operated the office tech were kept, and began picking them up. She hadn't got a clue what any of them did, and couldn't find the right one.

'Who's got the remote?' she called across the room to nobody in particular. 'For the TV?'

The news report had ended now, and the presenter was introducing the weather person.

'Who's got the remote?' Sasha asked again, walking from desk to desk. 'Honestly, people, it's like being at home.'

'This one?' Craig held it up; it had been on his desk the whole time. Sasha pointed it at the screen. Nothing happened, she was pointing the wrong end, so she turned it over to turn up the volume and then rewind the live television feed back to the news report about Andrew Dean's death. At the moment the crowd appeared in shot and she saw the face, she hit the pause button.

'Right, everybody.' She clapped her hands to get the

attention of the whole room, then reached up to the screen to press her finger to the familiar face in the crowd. 'I know this man. Tell me where from.'

'Remove your finger,' someone suggested, and she stepped out of the way so that people could gather around the screen and study the man's face closely, as if he were a portrait in an art gallery.

'Ring any bells?' Sasha knew the Met Police in London had a crack team of Super Recognizers, people who were able to remember thousands of faces, more than some computerized recognition systems, but she didn't have those kinds of resources here. 'First person to tell me who this man is wins a biscuit.'

'Sasha,' someone called, and she turned to see DCI Vaughn at the door of his office. He was a big man – her mother would delicately describe him as stout – and his broad frame filled the narrow space. 'Got a moment?'

'Of course,' she said, and left her team discussing the man in the crowd.

He stood aside as she walked in, leaving the door ajar. She pinched her toes on his carpet, conscious that once again she was barefooted, because Vaughn didn't approve of her walking about without shoes in the office.

'Where are we with the death in Hockley?'

'The victim's name is Andrew Dean. I've asked for the post-mortem report to be fast-tracked, we should get that this afternoon, but the cause of death looks pretty cut and dried – he was hit by a train.'

'He got into some kind of altercation at a local pub, is that right?'

'The deceased was from Southend – he lived just off York Road – but, yes, he spent the evening in a Hockley pub, antagonizing the other punters. He was very drunk and aggressive to various people, and was thrown out. Dean had a number of previous violent offences under his belt, for assault, affray, making threats.'

'You think he bit off more than he could chew?'

'It's a possibility, or he ran into an unfriendly face from the past.'

Vaughn nodded. 'British Transport Police are definitely stepping back from this. They say the likelihood is that the motivation for his death originated off rail network premises. So you'll be taking the investigation forward.'

'I'll get a couple of detectives to the pub this afternoon to talk to the landlord,' Sasha told Vaughn. 'Hopefully, he'll be able to point us in the direction of some of the other regulars, and we'll get someone to his bedsit. We're expecting the CCTV from the cab on the train soon, but all we have at the moment is the driver's insistence that he saw someone on the platform with a walking stick.'

'A walking stick?' Vaughn made a face. 'Doesn't sound like a fair fight.'

'Andrew Dean would disagree with you,' she told him. 'They're still finding bits of him.'

'Okay.' Vaughn scratched the back of his neck. 'I'm the Senior Investigating Officer, so keep me informed.'

'Of course.'

Sasha nodded, but didn't make any effort to leave. She sensed Vaughn wanted to say something else and after a moment's hesitation he shut the door to the main office.

'I was wondering if you would...' He looked uncomfortable, unwilling to meet her eye, which wasn't like him at all, and she noticed he was slightly dishevelled, too. Her DCI was always so smart, and prided himself on his wardrobe of bespoke suits, fitted shirts and silk ties. But the shirt he was wearing looked unironed, as if he had worn it two days on the trot, and there was a stain at the bottom of his tie, a shadow of stubble on his chin. 'Are you around for a quick drink after work?'

'That shouldn't be a prob—' Sasha winced when she remembered.

'You can't make it,' said Vaughn. 'I understand.'

'It's not that,' she told him quickly. 'It's just that I'm meant to be meeting my sister.'

Vaughn nodded. 'Another time, then.'

But she felt sorry for him – he clearly had something on his mind that he wanted to talk to her about – and said, 'I'm not meeting her till seven. Maybe we could grab a quick drink before that, at six thirty, how does that sound?'

Vaughn looked grateful. 'Sounds good.'

He wasn't the kind of boss who went for a drink after work and, Sasha excepted, certainly not with anyone from the Major Incident Team. Vaughn was a private man, who always headed straight home to the bosom of his family. She had met his intimidating wife, Miranda, a glamorous woman who ran some kind of charity in the City, and his sons were both on track to go to Oxbridge. Vaughn's perfect family life often made her feel embarrassed by her own chaotic household.

So she was shocked when he said, 'The thing is, Miranda and I have split up.'

Sasha bit hard on her bottom lip to stop her jaw dropping open.

'I'm really sorry to hear that, Vaughn.' Of all the couples she expected to break up, Vaughn and Miranda didn't even make the longlist. 'I mean, what... how?'

'I know I haven't been across things in the office lately,' he said, avoiding the question. 'And for that I apologize.'

'You have nothing to apologize for,' she told him quickly.

'It's been hard.'

She reached out and squeezed his arm. 'Of course it has.'

'So, six thirty tonight, then. If you can make it. There's something... I would really like to pick your brains about.'

'Of course.'

'In the meantime,' he said gruffly, and opened the door wide, 'I'm sure there are lots of things you should be doing.'

Back in the incident room, one of her team was leaning over Ajay, who was typing at his desk.

'Stephen with a p-h,' the detective was saying, pointing at the screen. 'There he is.'

'We've got an ID on your face in the crowd,' Ajay told Sasha as she came up behind him, and he clicked on the Police National Computer. 'Stephen Gosling, one of our local drug dealers.'

All the man's details appeared on the screen, including his police mugshot. It was definitely the same man she saw in the crowd. Sasha remembered him now. As a detective sergeant, she'd been involved in a drugs operation that had resulted in Gosling's conviction a few years back. Leaning across Ajay's desk, she read the list of his other offences, which were as long as your proverbial arm.

'So Gosling was just passing by Hockley station, which is miles from his home on Canvey Island,' said Ajay sarcastically. 'He just happened to be in the neighbourhood the morning after Andrew Dean's death, and stopped to see what was going on, as you do. It could be a coincidence.'

'Maybe.' Sasha reached over Ajay's shoulder to manipulate the mouse. He rolled back his chair to give her room to scroll down the screen, skim-reading Gosling's last known address, vehicle registration, his date of birth, convictions, cautions, and the other information they had about him on the database. And her attention was caught by one name on a list of known associates. 'Or maybe not.'

5

Abs had just stepped inside Jez and Bethany's plush double-fronted town house in the Clifftown conservation area when the doorbell rang again and Tony stood on the step, a sagging bunch of geraniums in his fist. There was no paper or cellophane around them, and Abs suspected Tony had picked them from someone's front garden on the way.

It was the first time Abs had seen Tony in three years, and he had to swallow his shock at the sight of his former mate. Tony was never the best-looking of men, but he had aged badly. His face was red and blotchy and his deep-set eyes were almost lost in a web of creases that streaked down his cheeks and back into his receding hairline. His weak chin dropped into his short neck and he wore the same cheap denim jacket he had on the last time Abs had seen him. The pot belly which bulged over his tatty jeans, and the battered trainers he wore, only added to the general sense that Tony hadn't been looking after himself in the intervening years.

It was difficult to believe he was in his early thirties, the same as Abs and Jez. And judging from the awkward silence in the hallway, Abs knew Jez was thinking the same thing.

'Tone, come in.' Abs pulled him inside, even though it wasn't his house. 'Look at us, the old squad back together again.'

Tony looked warily around the reception of Jez's big house, which had been tastefully designed and decorated at great expense by his wife, Bethany. As far as Abs knew, Tony was still living in that bungalow the size of a shoebox up in Hadleigh. Jez had gone up in the world since Tony had last seen him, on the day they came home from the disastrous holiday in Wales.

'Are these for me?' Abs reached for the flowers. 'Bruv, you didn't have to.'

'They're for Bethany,' said Tony, in that reedy voice of his.

'I was joking, fella.' Abs held out his arms. 'Come here.'

He didn't like it when people were unhappy, and he moved in for a hug as if he had missed Tony every single day. The fact that he and Jez had avoided Tony and Deano like the plague for three years was beside the point. He didn't want any bad blood, definitely not now. But beneath the aftershave, there was a proper pong coming off his former friend, of body odour and Dettol, and he stepped smartly back.

'You got a nice place here,' Tony told Jez, but his voice betrayed resentment. 'You've certainly fallen on your feet.'

'Thanks, Tone,' said Jez modestly.

Then they heard a clopping sound and looked behind them to see a pair of strappy heels coming down the hardwood stairs into the large reception, revealing a trim woman in an expensive summer dress. Faced with the arrival of Bethany, Tony seemed to become even more diminished. Jez had a nice house *and* a beautiful wife.

Back when Jez and Bethany first started dating, Abs was one of the biggest stars on the telly. Everyone loved him – *everyone*. But Bethany had taken an instant dislike to him, an attitude that had only hardened down the years. It was like she had a force field around her that repelled all his charm, and the more he tried to get her to like him, the more she treated him with disdain.

After they came back from the Welsh trip, her dislike of him intensified. It was like she knew something bad had happened. Maybe she sensed a change in Jez, felt his simmering guilt and anxiety, despite the fact that he swore blind to Abs that he'd never tell her what happened: 'I would never, Abs, it would be the *end*.'

The way Bethany acted, with airs and graces, you'd think she had been born with a silver spoon in her mouth. But her old man was an old East End geezer who earned all his money selling knock-off motors, and if the

47

rumours were true he had a few unsavoury associates. Her parents, who lived out of town in a massive mansion surrounded by acres of private land, treated their only daughter like a princess, showering her with money and *stuff*. They had paid for this big town house, for the sports car in the garage, and the many exotic holidays that she and Jez enjoyed every year.

But the main thing was that she adored Jez, and Abs was over the moon for his mate. Even as kids, Abs and Jez had been like chalk and cheese – Jez was as quiet and unassuming as Abs was loud and cheeky – but maybe they hit it off because they both had shitty mums. And despite growing up in care together, they had both in their own ways made something of themselves. Jez had definitely fallen on his feet hooking up with Bethany.

Abs, who never left the house without spending hours deciding what he was going to wear, envied his mate's low-key style. Jez had always been a good-looking fella with his diamond-shaped face, self-effacing smile and neat, dark hair, but this morning he looked a proper man about the house, too, in his slim fit Ted Baker trousers and black Reiss V-neck which accentuated his compact body, suede loafers and claret red socks. It was high street stuff, sure, but good quality.

'How you doing, Beth?' Abs said, and she pointed a cheek in his direction for him to kiss, careful to keep the rest of her body as far from him as possible. Bethany tolerated Abs because he was Jez's lifelong friend, but her icy smile suggested she definitely didn't care for Tony, with his scruffy double-denim and careworn face. Like Abs, he was also tainted by the mysterious events in Wales. Bethany blamed them both for Jez getting questioned by the police after the disappearance of that girl.

'It's good to see you again, Tony,' she said in a voice that suggested the complete opposite.

'You too, Bethany.' Eyes lowered as if in the presence of royalty, he shoved the wilting geraniums at her. 'These are for you.'

Bethany accepted them with the grace of someone who had just been gifted potato peelings. 'I'm sure we can find somewhere to put these.'

She looked at Abs and Tony closely, like she was wondering for the first time what they were doing in her home.

'We're just catching up on old times,' said Jez quickly. 'They won't be staying long.'

'Pauline's going to be cleaning in the main room, so please take your friends into the library.'

'Will do,' said Jez, and Bethany walked briskly away towards the back of the house.

Abs raised an eyebrow. 'Pauline?'

'We've got a live-in housekeeper now, because Bethany insisted,' said Jez, embarrassed. 'She said there's no point in owning a three-million-pound house and getting down on our knees like skivvies to clean it ourselves.'

Tony's eyes bulged at the price tag of the house.

'In here.' Jez opened the door to a small room, which was absolutely stuffed with furniture. Two big leather sofas faced each other. Cabinets were covered with bulky knick-knacks like lamps and candelabras, and an antique globe of the world squatted in one corner.

One wall was filled with a large fireplace and the other three by bookcases full of very grand-looking leather books. Abs read some of the titles. *Wuthering Heights*, *The Mayor of Casterbridge, Pride and Prejudice*. He'd never heard of any of them, and he was willing to bet that none of them had been opened.

Standing at the door as if he was afraid to touch anything, Tony looked like he was going to be sick. 'Shall I take my shoes off?'

'Course not,' said Jez gently, closing the door. 'Come and sit down.'

Tony sat gingerly, making the leather crack. Abs thought about making a fart joke, but Tony didn't look in the mood.

'So how are you, Tone?' he asked. 'It's been a while, mate.'

They all knew exactly how long it had been. It had been three years since the four of them had gone on that fateful trip to Wales.

'I've been good, Abs,' said Tony. 'The kids are in junior school now, would you believe?'

'How's Angie?'

'We ain't together no more.'

'Sorry to hear that, mate,' said Abs, and meant it. He liked Ange. Tony rubbed his hands anxiously between his knees.

'So, look,' said Abs. The tension was unbearable; they may as well get around to why they were there. 'Deano, he was—'

'*Murdered*,' said Tony sharply. 'Thrown in front of a train.'

'Deano was a bad drunk,' said Abs. 'If he was killed, it was because he got mouthy with the wrong fella. The main thing is, it changes nothing. I mean no disrespect to you, Tone, because Deano, God rest his soul, was your mate, but this can only be a good thing for us. He was a bit of a loose cannon, and now he's gone, he can't... drop us all in it.'

'The police were there, I saw it on the news. He was murdered, I know he was.' Tony leaned forward. 'The only question is, who killed him?'

'Tone, listen to me, you have to dial back the paranoia.'

'Someone's watching me,' Tony said. 'And I'm scared.'

Abs thought about the man with the scowling face outside QuidStore that morning, and fear spiked in his veins. 'You're seeing things.'

'I'm being followed,' Tony insisted.

He tried to laugh it off. 'Who's following you, exactly?'

Tony shook his head. 'It's just a feeling I get when I'm walking down the street.'

Abs turned to Jez. 'Anyone following you?'

Jez shook his head. 'Not that I know of.'

'You've got yourself into a state, that's all,' Abs said.

'All these years later,' Tony said miserably, 'and I still can't get out of my mind what... we did. It keeps me awake at night. And this is all because of you, Abs.'

'Hang on a sec.' Abs was affronted. 'How do you figure that?'

'Because you *made* us do it.'

'I didn't make you do *anything*.' He felt his chest tighten in panic. He didn't want to think about that night, about that place, about what happened – not now, not ever. Abs's attitude was that if you keep your face to the sunshine, you can't see the shadows. He had to press the reset button on this conversation before it got out of hand. 'Lads, just remember what I always say, teamwork makes the dream work. We're the three amigos now, we just have to hold our nerve.'

'Deano is dead,' cried Tony. 'And we're next.'

'Do us a favour.' Jez glanced at the closed door. 'Keep your voice down.'

'Bruv,' Abs said in a fierce whisper. 'You are totally overreacting.'

'Look me in the eye,' hissed Tony. 'Tell me you believe Deano's death has nothing to do with what we did.'

Abs was clutching at straws now. 'Maybe he took his own life.'

'It's possible,' said Jez. 'Deano came here a couple of weeks back. He told me he was going to the police to confess.'

Abs couldn't believe what he was hearing. 'Why didn't you tell me?'

'I didn't want to scare anyone,' Jez told him.

'And what happened?' asked Tony, who was as white as a sheet of A4.

'I persuaded him not to, gave him a couple of hundred quid, and sent him on his way.'

'Why didn't he come to see me?' Tony looked annoyed. 'He was my mate.'

'I think he wanted to be persuaded not to go to the police, and the money helped him make up his mind. No offence, Tony, but you don't have two pound coins to rub together. It's not the only time he's come here, neither.'

'How many times did he come round with his hand out?' asked Abs.

'Two or three times, maybe more.' Jez shrugged. 'It doesn't matter now, does it? The point is, he was struggling with his conscience.'

'There you go, he probably did himself in.' But if Abs was being honest with himself, he didn't believe his own words. 'So we're good?'

Jez stared at the floor and Tony gave the faintest of nods. *We're good.*

'I tell you what I'm going to do,' said Abs. 'I'm going to go to the police to find out whether they think it was an accident or suicide. See if I can find out what's going on with the, whatsit, the investigation.'

'What if you give us away?' said Tony miserably.

'Mate, I'm deeply offended.' Abs slapped himself on the chest. 'It's me you're talking to, Abs, you're in safe—'

But then there was an almighty smash outside the room, making the three of them jump to their feet. A moment later they heard a shriek. Jez rushed to the door and swung it open to reveal Bethany standing with an old woman in an apron. At their feet was a broken vase, a puddle of water and the geraniums spread across the sopping parquet floor.

'You *fool*.' Bethany's voice was shrill. 'Look what you've done.'

'I'm sorry, I slipped,' said the woman.

'This isn't the first time, though, is it, Pauline?' Bethany's face was puce with anger. 'You are the clumsiest woman I've ever met.'

The housekeeper stared down at the floor, humiliated, and Abs felt sorry for her. He'd worked with a lot of bullies in television, divas who liked nothing more than to lord it over others, and he'd always been careful to treat people with respect. Jez looked embarrassed by Bethany's behaviour, too.

'Just remember, housekeepers are ten-a-penny around here. I could let you go just like that.' Bethany snapped her fingers. 'Go and get a dustpan and brush, and a cloth, and clean it up. I promise you, if there's any damage to the parquet, it will come out of your pay.'

'She didn't mean it, Bethany,' Jez told her softly. 'It was an accident.'

Bethany glared at her. 'You're a very lucky woman, do you know that? You're lucky that my husband, who is a far more understanding person than me, has intervened.' She looked at Jez, her face still contorted with fury. 'God knows where you found this woman. You hired her, *you* sort it out.'

Then she walked off, heels clicking briskly on the wood. Jez turned to the housekeeper and told her gently, 'I'm sorry she spoke to you like that.'

'I understand, sir,' she said. 'I apologize for what happened.'

'You don't have to...' Jez winced. 'Please don't call me sir.'

'I had better clear this up.'

The woman glanced morosely at Abs and Tony and went off to get the equipment.

Abs whistled. 'Bethany has got a temper on her, mate.'

'Her family have always had staff, so she can sometimes be... brisk.'

'That's one way of putting it.'

'She's very particular about how things are done,' said Jez defensively. 'And very house-proud.'

'I've got to go,' said Tony. 'Things to do.'

'So listen, I'll go and see the feds,' Abs said as they walked to the front door. 'In the meantime, we just have to hold our nerve, yeah? I'll say it again, lads, *teamwork makes the dream work.*'

Tony nodded, but it was Jez who worried Abs. He'd been quiet in the library, and Abs noticed the dark circles beneath his eyes, the tension in his face. What Jez needed was a good night out. There was a glitzy *LIE!* production bash that evening. Abs had been invited as a former cast member and had offered to take him, but his mate didn't like noisy parties and said he would rather stay home with Bethany.

'We did a bad thing,' said Tony. 'And I'll never forgive myself.'

'We did.' Abs couldn't disagree with that. He squeezed Tony's shoulder. 'We did a bad thing, Tone, but we're not bad people. We're really not.'

Abs had never hurt a fly in his life – he was a lover, not a fighter. Until that awful night when his life was turned upside down, he had lived a good life, a blameless life.

All he had wanted to do was enjoy a banging night out.

6

Three years ago

And he did. It was the best night, it really was, until the following morning when everything went to shit.

That first evening, they had enjoyed a few drinks at the holiday cottage they were renting – there was nothing else to do, it was literally in the middle of nowhere – and then decided to find a pub where they could enjoy some local hospitality.

Tony's mate, Deano, had brought a load of beers and spirits – there was bourbon and tequila, and vodka in the freezer – and everyone was pissing themselves laughing because Abs hadn't brought any suitable clothes. It got cold at night in the countryside, and all he had packed was a thin cotton jacket and a couple of posy tee-shirts. He wore a pair of white trainers that had already got filthy from walking the few steps between the rental car and the door of the cottage. All the others had brought big coats, but Abs was a metrosexual, and he didn't know the first thing about the countryside.

'I've got some wellies you can wear,' Tony told him.

'I don't wear wellies,' Abs said. 'I wouldn't be seen dead wearing wellies, bruv, it would totally destroy my image.'

'We'll buy you a nice cagoule,' said Jez.

'Yeah?' Tony laughed. 'Good luck finding a shop within a hundred miles.'

Tony had found the cottage on the internet. It was cold and damp, there was a drizzle of hot water, the toilet seat was broken, the flagstones on the kitchen floor were like ice against the soles of your feet. The furniture was old and knackered and smelled of cat piss – at least, Abs *hoped* it was cat piss. The worst thing was, there were only three bedrooms – there were meant to be four – so Tony and Deano had bagsied single bedrooms for themselves and Abs and Jez, who went way back, agreed to share.

'You've really outdone yourself here, bruv,' said Abs, looking around. This wasn't the kind of place he was used to staying in, not at all.

'It was a bargain,' protested Tony.

'Course it was.' Abs pressed his fingers into a rip in an armchair and pulled out the foam stuffing. 'They must have seen a mug like you coming.'

'Better leave some choice words on TripAdvisor,' said Jez.

Tony frowned. 'What's TripAdvisor?'

They had thought a long weekend miles from

anywhere would be a laugh, and it had seemed like a good idea at the time. But Abs already felt cut off from the world. He couldn't get any internet, and everything was so still, so quiet; it gave him the creeps when what he was used to was people and noise and all the mod cons of urban life. He missed all his usual haunts back in Essex, the bars and clubs. And the truth was, he was used to being recognized in the street, and made a fuss of by strangers. He liked to pick up the red tops of a morning to find his face on the showbiz pages. Out here, with just Tony and Jez and Tony's boorish mate Deano for company, he was a nobody.

'Let's get out of here,' he suggested.

So they all went in search of a good time, just as the sun started to drop behind the trees. The idea of sitting around that cottage for the next four days without any mobile reception made Abs feel miserable, particularly as he was waiting to find out if the spin-off from *Laid In Essex!* that a production company was pitching was going to get the green light. If a network picked up *All About Abs*, Kelsey might even agree to become his fiancée.

In the twilight, the four of them walked along endless lanes, which all looked the same. The Welsh place names on the occasional signs they saw just confused them. On top of that, the sky was clouding over quickly, it was going to rain at any minute, and all Abs was wearing was his flimsy jacket. After half an hour, he felt like they had been walking for miles, and they still hadn't seen a soul.

'I hope someone's making a note of the direction,' said Tony. 'Because I don't have a clue how to get back.'

'Where's this effing pub, then?' Deano asked.

He swigged from a bottle he'd brought out with him and was already half pissed. Abs didn't like Deano much. He was Tony's mate, who had only come along to make up the numbers, and Abs found him an arrogant big mouth.

One moment Deano was treating Abs like his best mate and the next he was making some sarcastic remark about him or the show. Abs knew plenty of people like that in the telly business, the kind who were all over you like a rash one minute, pretending you were amigos, and slagging you off the next. They were users and manipulators, and sooner or later they always ended up asking for favours; for money or an introduction to someone in the business. Abs had learned the hard way that these people weren't to be trusted.

After walking for what seemed like forever, they saw a village on the other side of a field. And not a moment too soon, because it had begun to rain. Fat drops splashed on the ground. Abs protested that his trainers were going to get absolutely wrecked walking across the mud. 'That can't be the only way.'

'Come on, you tart,' joked Tony. 'If we don't cut across, we could be walking around all night.'

'I'll carry you over, princess,' said Deano. 'If you don't want to get your glass slippers dirty.'

Abs ignored him and they all climbed over a stile – the metal was freezing between his legs – and onto the field, which was covered in cowpats. That's the other thing about the countryside, thought Abs – it stank. Mud sucked greedily at his trainers as he gingerly made his way across, trying not to slip. Beside him, Tony nearly took a tumble, and Abs had to grab his arm to stop him going face first into shit. By the time they got halfway across the field, they were all pissing themselves laughing, which was just as well, because suddenly it was raining cats and dogs.

'Run for it,' shouted Jez, and they stumbled across the last few yards of slick, muddy field towards the little pub at the edge of the village. It was a pretty little place, with flowers in hanging baskets above the windows, a welcome bloom of colour in the grey deluge of rain, and the warm glow of a flickering fire coming from inside. Soaked to the skin, they raced beneath the porch at the front door. Abs was soaked to the bone. His trainers were caked in mud and cow shit, and his legs, too.

Then his phone rang. It had been so long since he'd had any reception that he'd almost forgotten he had it. He groped for it and despite the driving rain that plastered his hair to his head and made him look like a drowned rat, his heart leaped with excitement when he saw the name on the screen.

'It's my agent,' he said, and the others tensed, because they knew he'd been waiting for this call.

'Abs, son,' said a faint voice. 'It's Vince.'

'I can't hear you properly, Vince.' Abs stuck a finger in his other ear to try to block out the sound of the rain thundering on the tiny porch roof, and off the pavement at his feet. 'We're in the middle of nowhere.'

'It's happening,' shouted his agent. 'Channel 5 has commissioned the spin-off. *All About Abs* is go.'

The guys were laughing and joking, so he had to walk into the pouring rain to give himself a moment to take in what Vince had said. His chest clogged with emotion at the thought of it. His own spin-off show, and on a terrestrial channel, too.

'They want to get on with it quickly,' Vince said. 'They're talking about filming the pilot within weeks, so we're going to have to clear your diary.'

'Oh, Vince.' Abs lifted his face to the rain, enjoying the feel of it on his face. 'Cheers, mate.'

'It's all down to you,' said Vince. 'The public can't get enough of you, Abs. I suggest a little drink to celebrate.'

'You can count on me.'

'Well?' asked Jez, when Abs came back under the porch.

'I got my own series.'

'Hell, yeah!'

They all grabbed each other and jumped up and down in celebration like little kids, cheering and screeching, and Abs really liked being there at that moment with his mates. Far away from the world that he knew, hundreds of miles from the Essex streets and suburbs where he was treated like a king. Even better than that, they were standing outside a pub. Abs wasn't much of a drinker, and his personal trainer would burst a blood vessel if Abs had more than half a lager, but he felt like celebrating tonight.

Deano clapped his hands together. 'Drinks are on me.'

In the euphoria of the moment, Abs liked the man immensely, despite his lairy manner. Maybe he had been too quick to judge him.

But Deano needn't have bothered offering, because as soon as they all walked inside, the heat from the roaring fire already warming their soaking clothes, Abs was recognized.

And that's when everything got a little bit crazy. Because even here, in the wilds of Denbighshire, far from anywhere, nobody would leave him alone. All the locals wanted to meet him and get an autograph or a selfie, and the pub got more rammed as word got out that he was there. All night he was signing beer mats and scraps of paper, whatever people could get their hands on.

'Mate.' He held up his hands when one man brought him over another drink, because the table beside him was littered with pints. 'I should be buying you one.'

'Don't you worry, Abs,' the man said in a gentle Welsh accent. 'We don't get many celebrities around here. I'd love a photo to show the wife. She's visiting her sister tonight and she's going to be gutted she missed you.'

'No problem.' Abs put his arm around the guy and grinned into the camera phone.

You'd think he'd saved the planet the way everyone acted around him, and wasn't just some chump who got lucky appearing on a telly show. And his fame, he knew, was only going to grow now he was going to star in his own series.

Abs was already drowning in offers, and knew that Vince didn't even bother to tell him half of them. He took part in telly panel games and quiz shows, and made personal appearances all over the country. He gave out business awards at gala evenings – what did Abs know about business? *Nothing*. He'd been offered panto at Christmas for silly money, and not in some fleapit local theatre, but at the London Palladium. His diary was full months in advance.

His life was exhausting, and he loved every single minute of it.

Because that was the thing about Abs: he didn't take it for granted. Some of the other guys on *Laid In Essex!* had let it all go to their heads. Sooner or later they got a reputation for being difficult and were let go from the show, and they went back to being labourers and electricians and hairdressers. There were thousands of good-looking Essex lads aching for a shot at stardom, and Abs knew that the only way to stay at the top was to work hard and be nice.

But he also knew that he had that little something extra. Call it charisma, or stardust, but there was something about Abs that people loved, and made *Daily Star* readers vote him the Britain's Sexiest Guy *three years running*. Women wanted to bed him, and men wanted to be like him. His positivity, his enthusiasm and friendliness, was infectious.

'Mate, I don't think I can drink any more,' he said when another guy came over with a pint.

'The night is young, Abs, there's plenty more where that came from.'

It was all becoming a bit of a blur. When he got back to Essex, he'd have to phone his personal trainer to book in extra workouts. Abs kept in good shape, he had to, because he was getting a lot of modelling work now.

And then someone started playing a piano in the corner of the pub and all the locals started singing, some old-time song he'd never heard of, and he wanted to join in. This little pub with its low-beamed ceiling was a world away from the bars and clubs of Essex, with their harsh neon, glittering chrome furnishings, flashing mirror balls, and the music that crashed against your insides. Everything here was old and knackered, and the decor surely hadn't been changed for decades. The ceiling, with its knotted beams and cranky corners, was low and cosy, and it was stifling hot now because the fire had been burning all night in the crowded room.

'Like it here, Abs?' someone roared across the pub, and Abs knew what was expected of him. He winked and shouted back, 'Abs, mate!'

Everyone cheered and Abs was choked with emotion. Because he looked around the pub at all these people, these strangers, who had gone out of their way to make him so welcome. They were happy to be with him, not like his mother, who couldn't wait to be shot of him and put him into care when he was just a little lad, like she was leaving an unwanted puppy at the pound. Tonight, these people were his family, they had invited him into their lives, and Abs felt like the luckiest son of a bitch who ever lived.

But he saw Deano being loud and obnoxious at the other end of the bar – he was taking the piss out of the Welsh accents and generally being disrespectful to people – and Abs pulled Tony close.

'Tell your mate to calm down, yeah?' he suggested. 'He's being a bit of a prick.'

Tony didn't need asking twice and went off to speak to Deano, just as someone behind him said, 'Hey Abs.'

He turned to see a young woman. She was short and pretty, with a wide mouth and curly hair.

'What's your name, babes?' he asked her.

'Rhiannon,' she told him with a smirk.

'That's a cool name.'

She didn't take her eyes off him. 'It's Welsh.'

'Yeah.' Abs grinned. 'Even I could work that one out. Where you from, Rhiannon?'

'Not from around here.' She looked around the pub with distaste. 'I'm on holiday with my aunt and uncle.' She rolled her eyes. 'It's been *so* boring... until now.'

Abs saw that her make-up was over-applied and the dress she wore, a knock-off of something popular in all the London stores, was a size too big for her skinny body. She looked like a little girl from the sticks trying to look older, but she had none of the style or sophistication of Kelsey; she wasn't in the same league. The way her hazel eyes never left his made him uncomfortable.

'How old are you?' he asked.

'Twenty-two.'

He narrowed his eyes. 'How *old* are you?'

'I'm nineteen, but guys tell me I look older. Don't worry...' She slid her tongue along her top teeth, and the edges were smeared with lipstick. 'I'm old enough to kiss.'

'It's nice to meet you, Rhiannon.'

Abs held out a hand for her to shake, but she made a face. 'Is that all I get?'

'I save all my kisses for Kelsey,' he said, making a point of mentioning his on-screen girlfriend.

She rolled her eyes. 'Shame.'

Abs had been in this situation many times, and he knew to be careful. He was used to women coming on to him, excited at the prospect of bedding him and then running to the tabs to tell the tale. The gutter press would eat it up if there was even a hint of infidelity.

And the simple fact was, he wasn't interested. Kelsey was the only girl for him.

Glancing over her shoulder, Abs saw Deano leering at him. Winking, as if to say, *you're in*.

So Abs was grateful when another pub regular came over to ask for a selfie.

'Of course, mate,' Abs said, and turned away from the girl quickly. He sensed her hanging around behind him, waiting patiently for him to give her all his attention, but Abs made a point of chatting to the guy. And when he finally looked round, he was relieved to see Rhiannon had gone. He couldn't see her anywhere.

The laughter and chat continued into the early hours because the landlord had a lock-in. Against his better judgement, Abs was convinced to do some shots – half the time he didn't even know what was in the glass – and he had no idea what the time was when he, Jez, Tony and Deano finally stumbled into the cold night.

'Jesus, it's freezing,' complained Jez, pulling his coat around him. It was pitch-black because there was no street lighting, and it was spitting rain again.

They squinted up the lane towards the village and then across the field. Abs was pissed, he wasn't cut out for drinking, and couldn't make head nor tail of where he was. If it was somewhere in Essex or London, he'd just stick his arm out and hail a cab, or call an Uber. Most probably he'd get a big discount, or let off the fare completely, because of who he was.

'Any ideas how to get back?' asked Jez.

'Haven't got a scooby,' said Tony.

'What a shithole.' Deano gave a drunken sneer. He was swaying, but still swigging from a bottle of Scotch he'd nicked from behind the bar, to Abs's annoyance.

'I don't know how you can still drink,' he said, incredulous.

'All this fresh air has sobered me up, innit.' Deano let out a big belch. 'And I don't have to diet like some celeb tart.'

They trudged along a grassy verge, which was wet and slippery. When he looked up at the night sky, Abs saw a blanket of stars and tried to find the Great Bear, which was the only constellation he knew. Trouble is, the more he looked, the more the stars started to scatter and drift.

Jez stopped in the middle of the road. 'It's not this way.'

'It definitely is.'

'It bloody ain't,' insisted Deano.

'I can show you,' said a voice from the darkness, and they saw the dark outline of a figure sitting on a stile.

Abs stepped forward and recognized Rhiannon, the girl from the pub.

'I'll get you home,' she said. 'And then we can all party.'

7

Sasha was all elbows after lunch and knocked an M&S bottle of orange juice all over her desk.

'Sugar,' she hissed, tearing open a packet of tissues in a frantic race against time to stop the sticky liquid from reaching her keyboard and paperwork. She moved folders and documents, mopping up the spill as best she could, but was unable to stop the juice dripping over the edge of the desk.

'We've got those post-mortem results back.' Ajay de Vaz planted one buttock on the sticky side of the desk. 'You're going to want to hear this.'

'Uh.' Sasha pointed vaguely at his bum. 'I wouldn't—'

Eager to share the forensic pathologist's conclusions, Ajay didn't hear her. 'Andrew Dean died instantly from massive internal injuries consistent with being hit by a train, no great surprise there. And he was very intoxicated – his blood alcohol level was nearly 300 milligrams. He was a big lad, six foot tall and over a hundred and fifteen kilos, but it's pretty amazing that he even managed to get to the station.'

'A hardened drinker.'

Detectives from Sasha's team had gone to the Hockley pub where Andrew Dean had spent the hours before his death. The landlord had provided names and addresses of regulars who had witnessed Dean being abusive to various people. He'd pestered a couple of women, the landlord said, and increasingly made a nuisance of himself with everyone, which is why he was eventually thrown out.

'So in all likelihood Dean drunkenly fell into the path of the train,' said Sasha. 'Despite the mysterious person on the platform.'

'No,' said Ajay. 'He had hydrochloric acid in his eyes. He was blinded.'

Sasha sat back in her chair. 'Holy cow.'

'And, wait, that's not all.' Ajay was enjoying his big reveal. 'There were burns on his forearms, neck and lower stomach.'

'Burns?'

'Scorch marks, very localized, in several places. I'll send the images to you. The train driver said the figure on the platform was holding a walking stick, remember? What if it wasn't a walking stick, what if it was something else?'

Sasha realized she was still clutching the soggy clump

of tissue in her fist and dropped it discreetly in the bin at her feet. 'Go on.'

'Dean was drunk, very drunk, and most likely unsteady on his feet. Then he was blinded.' Ajay made vicious movements with one arm, as if he was prodding with a pointy thing. 'And herded into the path of the train.'

'With a cattle prod.' Sasha sat up quickly. 'Okay, then. Let's go over his flat, speak to friends and family. As of this moment, we treat his death as a homicide.'

She thought again about the man she had glimpsed in the crowd at Hockley station. Stephen Gosling was a petty criminal who had done time for numerous offences, including dealing drugs and shifting stolen goods. It could be a pure coincidence that he was passing Hockley station this morning, but the name she had seen on his list of known associates on the PNC had immediately rung alarm bells.

'Let's find our nosy friend Stephen Gosling and speak to him.'

Detective Constable Craig Power came over and stood behind Ajay, waiting to speak to her.

'You don't have to queue up, Craig,' she told him. 'I'm not an ATM.'

He dropped photos on the desk. 'Do you want the bad news or the bad news?'

Sasha folded her arms. 'What's the bad news?'

'The CCTV in the driver's compartment of the train was faulty.'

'You're joking. And what's the bad news?'

'That's the platform CCTV.' He nodded at the printouts and she picked them up, frowning at the murky images of a figure wearing a long overcoat, wide trousers, trainers and a floppy hat, walking stiffly to the extreme bottom of the time-stamped image, and staying there. 'Our mystery person is of average height, maybe a touch smaller, I'd say five foot eight, but the face is hidden under the brim of the hat.'

'Clever,' said Ajay, as Sasha shuffled through the photos. 'They're standing in the only place on the entire platform they're not able to be seen clearly.'

'Wait,' Sasha told Craig. 'There's a camera in the ticket office, we can get a much clearer shot from that.'

'There is, but the side gate that leads directly from the car park onto the platform is left open late at night when the ticket office is unattended. Our suspect – or witness – used that instead.'

'I can't see a walking stick or a cattle prod.'

'A cattle prod?' asked Craig in surprise.

'Look, the arms are pressed straight down at the sides.' Ajay pointed at the figure. 'I bet they're holding it against their body underneath their coat.'

'And the confrontation?' Sasha asked Craig in exasperation.

'Happens off-screen, directly below the camera.'

'Fiddlesticks,' she said, annoyed.

'Careful with the language, Mrs Dawson,' said Ajay

drily and lifted himself from the edge of the desk. Craig and Sasha saw the wet stain on the seat of Ajay's pristinely pressed trousers, but she shook her head tightly at the DC. *Please don't tell him.*

'I'll come and look at that footage in a minute,' she said quickly. 'We'll go through it as many times as it takes. There must be *something* we can use.'

'By the way,' smirked Craig, 'there's someone downstairs who wants to speak to a senior officer about Andrew Dean.'

'Who?'

He kept his voice down. 'That guy Abs, the one we were talking about.'

Lolly's head popped up above her monitor. 'Abs is here?'

'Do we know why?' Sasha asked Craig, but he shrugged. 'Okay, let's put him in one of the offices downstairs.'

Sasha fumbled her feet into her brogues, stamping her heels so she didn't have to untie the laces. She mopped up the last of the juice, cleaned her hands with wet wipes, then took the stairs to the ground floor. Outside the room, she found the celebrity surrounded by police and civilian staff.

He was chatting and laughing as he moved from person to person, the bracelets on his wrists jangling loudly as he shook hands and posed good-naturedly for selfies. Sasha made a mental note to remind everybody by email *not* to put those photos up on social media.

Lolly Chambers stood at the front of the huddle of people, looking up at Abs with the focused excitement of a small child waiting at an ice-cream van.

'Abs,' Lolly said, 'This is Detective Inspector Sasha Dawson.'

'The boss lady.' His handshake was strong and long, and accompanied by a dazzling flash of perfect white teeth. 'Sweet.'

Sasha smiled back. 'Mr Cruikshank.'

'Man...' He winced. 'Only my bank manager calls me that. I'm Abs.'

Most of the group had dispersed now, but Lolly remained in front of him, transfixed.

'Stand back a bit, DC Chambers,' Sasha told her. 'Give the poor man some air.'

'Sorry.' Lolly reversed quickly, stepping on Sasha's foot in the process. 'I'm so sorry.'

'You ever done any TV?' Abs asked Lolly. 'Because, if you don't mind me saying, you're a stunner. I can see you on *Laid In Essex!*'

She blinked. 'Really?'

'With your looks, you'd put a lot of the girls on there to shame. Or you should apply to be on *Love Island.*'

Lolly's overwhelmed response came out as a little noise.

'Yeah.' Abs nodded. 'Deffo.'

'Detective Constable Chambers,' said Sasha, breaking the spell, 'I can take it from here. Head back to the office now, we've plenty to do.'

Lolly nodded, but didn't appear to hear what Sasha had said because she didn't move an inch.

'You'd better go, Detective Constable Chambers.' Abs laughed. 'We don't want to get you in trouble.'

Lolly reluctantly walked away down the corridor, looking back over her shoulder the whole way.

'Sweet girl,' he said.

'And a very good police officer,' Sasha made a point of saying.

Abs stroked the bumfluff on his chin, thoughtfully appraising Sasha like an artist sizing up a favourite life model. He nodded at her shock of silver hair. 'That out of a bottle, is it?'

'No,' she told him. 'It's all my own.'

'It doesn't make you look old at all. When I'm your age, I hope I've got hair like that.'

Sasha leaned past him to open the door of the room. 'I'll take that as a win.'

This, she realized, was Abs's modus operandi. He immediately complimented each and every person he met. Some of those compliments hit the target and some of them... maybe not so much. But she appreciated the intention. Sasha's hair went white in her mid-twenties – long story – and she had long ago made a decision not to dye it. She was used to all the stares and underhand comments.

'It's good of you to come in, Abs,' she said, offering him a chair. 'What can I do for you?'

'A friend of mine has been... well, not a friend.' The grin on his face lengthened with anxiety. 'He was more of a guy I knew a little bit.'

'Andrew Dean,' she said.

'Deano, yeah.' Abs looked surprised, and less than happy that she immediately knew who he was talking about. He gazed around the small room. It was just an administrative office, but coming to a police station probably brought back sour memories. 'I was gutted to hear what happened to him, but I only met him the once. He was more the friend of a mate of mine. Tony.'

'Tony Gardner,' she said.

'Yeah, that's him.' He tugged at the frayed end of a cloth bracelet on his right wrist. 'Thing is, Tony's upset about his death.'

'Tony couldn't come in himself?'

'He lives a bit out of town, up in Hadleigh, and I'm central, so, you know, I said I'd pop in.'

He watched tensely as Sasha flicked through her notebook.

'So while you're here, Abs, I wonder if you're able to give us some information.' Sasha smiled amiably. 'After all, you and Tony and Andrew Dean and...'

She stared at her notes, momentarily unable to make

sense of her own writing, and Abs said, 'Jez Weston – Jeremy – my best mate.'

'Yes, the four of you were questioned about the disappearance of Rhiannon Jenkins several years ago.'

Abs made a sucking sound with his teeth. 'I regret to say we was. But of course we had nothing to do with that.' He smiled anxiously. 'Why, do you think Deano was…?'

'A murder investigation has begun into Mr Dean's death,' Sasha said, and Abs swallowed. 'Would you like some water?'

'I'm good, Detective Silver.'

'Dawson,' she said.

'Detective Dawson, yeah,' he said. 'Thing is, as I say, I didn't know Deano that well. He was Tony's mate. I only met him the once, on the trip to Wales. We didn't get on, me and him. He wasn't a… charming individual.'

'Do you know if he had any enemies?'

Abs laughed grimly. 'Loads, I'd imagine. Deano couldn't hold his drink, he was a lairy fella, and he'd had a few run-ins with the feds… the police, I mean.'

Andrew Dean's criminal record stretched back to his teenage years and included custodial sentences for assault, affray and threatening behaviour, as well as driving under the influence. He'd also been cautioned a number of times for alcohol-related incidents.

'Look.' Abs took out his phone to look at the time on the screen. 'I'd love to help, but I've got to go soon.

I'm going out tonight. It's the annual *Laid In Essex!* production party.'

He grinned, perhaps waiting for her to ask him all about it, but all she said was, 'That's nice.'

'Yeah, they've invited some of the old faces from the show. Not that any of us are old, I mean former cast members. A lot of famous people are going to be there, some mates of mine you'd probably recognize. I'm really looking forward to it.' Sasha could tell just by the way his grin lifted to his ears. 'And my best girl Kelsey's gonna be there.'

'Sounds great. So just to clarify, do you have any information you think would be useful to us in our investigation?'

Abs's fingers fluttered impatiently on the table. 'No, why would I? I ain't seen Deano in years. I wouldn't wish him harm or anything, but I really didn't have anything in common with him, except...'

Sasha waited for him to finish the thought.

Except for that time we were both questioned about the disappearance of a young woman.

But instead he stood. 'Anyway, better go, got to look fabulous for tonight.'

'I don't mind taking him down, ma'am,' said a voice behind her, and Sasha turned to see Lolly Chambers in the doorway. Her icy-blonde hair, which was usually hitched up in a ponytail at work, tumbled attractively across her shoulders, and she had applied more lipstick, and blusher to her ski-jump nose and high cheekbones.

'Thank you, DC Chambers,' said Sasha. 'That's very thoughtful of you.'

'I'll sign it if you want.' Abs said amiably, and when Sasha looked confused, he nodded at her notebook. 'If you want my autograph.'

She snapped the notebook closed. 'That's very kind of you, Abs, but it won't be necessary.'

'Nice to meet you, Silver Lady.' Abs shook her hand again and walked out of the door. Lolly shot Sasha a look, as if to say *OMG*, and then followed him out.

'Abs.' Sasha came into the corridor, and he turned. 'If you do think of anything about Andrew Dean that would help us, anything at all, here's my number.' She gave him a card. 'Call me any time.'

'Sure thing.' He tucked it in the breast pocket of his jacket and grinned. 'We can have some bantz.'

Sasha gave him a big smile in return. 'That, too.'

She watched him saunter away with Lolly. Wide shoulders rolling, slim hips sliding, he walked with the studied confidence of a man who knew that the eyes of the world were most likely watching him, and when she glanced into the open doors of the offices that lined the corridor, she saw that everyone was.

'Who on earth was that?' asked Vaughn, coming up behind her.

'Danny Cruikshank. Abs from *Laid In Essex!*' He

looked at her as if she was speaking Latin. 'I'll explain later,' she said.

'You still okay for that drink after work?' he asked.

'Of course,' she said, remembering her promise of earlier. 'Just a quick one.'

8

Times were tough, there was no doubt about it. Abs was getting ever more worried that he wouldn't be able to make ends meet, and because he was the kind of guy who stuck his head in the sand, he didn't even know how much money he had left in his account.

At the height of his fame, when the money was rolling in, he didn't stop to think about saving for a rainy day – who did at his age? – and he spent like there was no tomorrow. He splashed out on an expensive seafront apartment, a classic car, and thousands of pounds worth of clothes, most of which he hadn't even worn. He loved to impress his celebrity mates when they were out on the town together, the comedians and TV presenters and rap stars, by paying for everything. It was stupid, really, because a lot of those famous people earned far more than he did, and none of them returned his calls any more.

He also made a number of bad investments following dodgy advice. The investments made a huge loss and the accountant was gone now. The classic car had turned out to be a money pit, and as fashions had changed, he'd bagged up most of the clothes and taken them to Oxfam. All he had left now was his beloved seafront apartment. He was clinging on to that, but the mortgage was crippling.

Someone like him, with a reputation as a sharp dresser, was expected to maintain appearances. Sooner or later, one of the tabloids was going to write something about his falling on hard times. He could imagine the headline: ABSOLUTELY BRASSIC, MATE!

Some paps were already trying to get photos of him looking scruffy. Abs did his best to keep up his grooming regime, he was still getting facials and his hair done at the salon of a celebrity hairdresser in London, and he was still going to the gym – the membership was off-peak these days – but he couldn't afford it for much longer.

Trouble is, Abs wouldn't last five minutes doing a proper job in an office, a shop or even – he shuddered – a factory. All he knew how to do was be Abs. He was good at that.

It all went wrong after someone in the Welsh police tipped off the press that he was questioned in connection with the disappearance of Rhiannon Jenkins.

Plans for his spin-off show were immediately canned, and then Tobias, who was the producer of *Laid In Essex!*

in those days, took him to lunch – not at some expensive place, but a café down a side street in Chelmsford – and told him they weren't renewing his contract.

'We just want to try out some fresh faces.'

'I can be the bad boy on the show,' Abs pleaded, while Tobias checked his phone as if he had other places to be. 'Make me the bad boy.'

'We've got bad boys on the show, Abs. We've got Wayne and we have AJ.'

'It'll be a great twist.' Abs spread his arms, trying to paint a picture. 'Everyone thinks I'm cool, a nice guy, but I turn out to be a love rat.'

Tobias put down his phone and said gravely, 'You're implicated in the disappearance of a woman, Abs. That's not the kind of bad boy we're after on the show. *Laid In Essex!* is family entertainment.'

It wasn't long till the big-name sponsorship deals dried up, and fashion companies and charities dropped him like a rock. Advertisers quietly removed him from their campaigns.

Worse, much worse than that, was that it ended his relationship with the love of his life, Kelsey DeMarco. He didn't even care about his lifestyle or the money; the only thing he wanted was to get back on the show so he could be with Kelz. She wouldn't give him the time of day unless he was as famous as she was.

Walking towards the party venue in Brentwood, Abs took out his phone. Hoping for good news from his agent, praying this would be the day when the work started coming in again.

'Abs.' Vince answered after six rings, but at least he'd picked up this time. 'Nice to hear from you.'

'I was just ringing to find out if there was anything on the horizon?' As if he didn't ring every day, every single day, to ask the exact same thing.

He was desperate for telly work, of course, but he'd take anything within reason. He'd heard on the grapevine there was a sidekick role available on an overnight show on Three Counties Radio.

'I've got a few irons in the fire,' Vince said cheerfully. It was a phrase he used a lot, *a few irons in the fire*, as if any number of hot opportunities were about to drop into Abs's lap.

'What about *I'm A Celebrity*? Did you pitch me for that?' It was the prime-time show Abs really wanted to get on because of its reputation for re-energizing the careers of the people who took part. If he had to eat a few kangaroo scrotums, so be it.

Vince let out a long breath. 'That's a tough call, Abs. There's a lot of competition to appear on *I'm A Celeb*.'

'What about *Love Island*?'

'I'll be honest with you, you're probably too old for that.' Abs heard him flicking the pages of a desk diary. 'Listen, there is one offer of a personal appearance...'

Abs stopped dead in the street, holding his breath. He dreamed of a bit of foreign travel, like in the old days.

The opening of a club or resort in Ayia Napa. Kelsey would be knocked out by that.

'That new burger place wants you to appear at the first anniversary of their opening.'

'The posh burger restaurant?' It wasn't much, but Abs still felt momentarily excited. 'The one in Chelmsford?'

Vince was quiet for a moment. 'The one on Southend seafront, Abs.'

'The burger *stall*? The one next to the stand that sells doughnuts and fizzy pop?'

'It's an organic burger concession, Abs, it's quality stuff.'

Abs pressed his fingers into his eyes. It all seemed so hopeless.

'There's something else, Vince. And it's making me anxious.'

Vince sounded concerned. 'What is it, Abs?'

A van drove past, horn blaring.

'Hey, Abs.' A driver hung out of the window and he waved back – *How you doing?* – but the guy gave him the wanker sign and the car sped off down the road.

He was around the corner from the club now and just wanted to get inside. 'There was this guy at the QuidStore, who was looking at me funny, like he wanted to do me harm. I think I recognize him, I think he's—'

'That's Basildon for you,' said Vince. 'People look at you funny.'

Abs swallowed. 'You heard about Deano's death, right?'

Vince sounded uncomfortable. 'Yeah, it's a shock, so it's understandable you're jumpy. It'll pass, Abs, it'll pass.'

'I think I need some kind of protection, Vince.'

'Protection?'

'A personal bodyguard.'

Vince was incredulous. 'And where do you think I'm going to get the money for that?'

'I'm your client,' said Abs. 'I'm, like, one of your biggest names—'

'You *were*, Abs. Past tense.'

'I thought you would want to make sure I'm safe and sound.'

'I don't have that kind of money, not even for my successful clients.' There was a tense silence on the line. 'Look, Abs, it's not like you're earning at the moment. Your star has dimmed, that's the truth of it. I love you like a younger brother, a *son* even, but I'm not going to get you muscle because some fella looked at you funny at Basildon QuidStore.'

'After what happened to Deano…'

Vince's response was brisk. 'I've got to go, I've a new client on the other line, she's one of them vloggers. You take care, Abs.'

And then he was gone. Abs pressed his thumb against the cracked glass casing of his iPhone – it wasn't the latest model; once upon a time he would have had one of those as soon as it was released – and was hit by a wave of nausea. His legs wobbled. The street seemed to spin, tumbling over and over in his vision. A kaleidoscope of images twisted in his head.

He was once again in the bedroom of that cottage in the wood, waking up drunk in the early morning. The bedroom churned, its contents tipping over and over in his mind. He saw the glass of water at his feet, the hot shaft of blinding light burning between the closed curtains, the damp-stain on the ceiling, the mattress on the floor. All sliding and swooping. His breathing quickened. He knew where it was leading. Whenever he thought about that room, that place, he felt a panic attack coming on.

'What have I told you?' He slapped his own cheek again and again, until the stinging blows took his mind off all the other thoughts and feelings. 'No looking back,' he told himself over and over. 'Not now, not ever.'

Abs gave himself a moment to breathe deeply. It wasn't in his nature to be overwhelmed, that's not who he was, and he wasn't a quitter. There was still every chance he could pull his career around, get back on the show – and back with Kelsey.

And he had a golden opportunity tonight. All he had to do was be himself, and there was nobody in the world who was better at being Abs than Abs was.

The club where they were holding the *LIE!* party

was just around the corner, but he opened up the Uber app on his phone and called a cab, then stepped into a doorway to watch the tiny vehicle icon swivel and slide closer to his location on the screen. The car arrived minutes later, and he jumped in the back.

'Where we going, mate?' asked the driver, accelerating up the street.

'Turn left here,' said Abs, and the entrance to the club, with its small gaggle of paparazzi and reporters behind a barrier, appeared just ahead. 'And you can pull over.'

'Seriously?' asked the driver. 'You just got in.'

'Thanks, mate.' Abs climbed from the cab. This business was all about appearances and he didn't want to be seen approaching the club on foot, as if he hadn't been sent a complimentary cab by the production team. As soon as he stepped onto the pavement, the paps swung in his direction. Flashes went off, cameras whirred, they called his name. 'Over here, Abs. Abs, mate!'

He grinned, he posed, he gave the thumbs up and held his arms above his head, forefingers pointing to the heavens in a cool rock-star pose. He soaked up all the attention – God, how he missed this life – and the moment was made all the sweeter for knowing that Kelsey was inside. In a few short minutes they would be reunited.

'You returning to the show, Abs?' asked a reporter, shoving a phone over the barrier to record his answer.

'We'll see, mate.' Abs tried to be enigmatic, but knew the chances were slim. But then everyone started asking him about what he was doing, his current projects, and it spooked him. 'Got to go, fellas.'

Moving quickly towards the door, he was shocked to see Jez standing outside. 'Bruv, I thought you weren't gonna come?'

But Jez didn't smile. 'I've got to talk to you.'

Abs didn't like the sound of that. The last thing he needed was for Jez to go to the police and 'fess up about what happened in Wales. Inside were a load of TV production people, influencers, execs and celebrities, the love of his life was in there, and a full-scale alien invasion wasn't going to stop him networking, not tonight.

'Is there somewhere we can go?' asked Jez. 'Just for a few minutes.'

'You're here now, let's have a good time.' Abs threw his arm over Jez's shoulder and led him to the red rope that blocked the entrance to the club.

A trendy young girl with a milkmaid plait and a clipboard nodded terse confirmation to the hulking doorman – *That's Abs and his +1, let them in* – and he unhooked the rope.

It felt so good to be back in the game, but Abs couldn't help but look back over his shoulder at the photographers, journos and the small crowd of onlookers. Searching for an angry face, for someone who wanted to do him harm. A car drove past slowly; a guy was hanging out of it looking at him, but then it accelerated away. Vince was right, he was paranoid. Who wouldn't hang out of a car to catch an eyeful of a famous celeb like Abs?

'It's important, Abs,' insisted Jez, looking miserable.

With every step they took into the bowels of the club, Abs became more excited. The brash neon lighting, the overpowering smell of perfume, cologne and hairspray, all the guests milling. The venue had been had hired out by the *LIE!* producers and was teeming with glamorous people. Women with long, flowing hair extensions, tight dresses and scarlet toes; men in casual suits and expensive trainers, with razor-thin lines of beard framing their chins. Abs felt like he was back where he belonged. Everyone was young, successful and beautiful, and they all expected the world on a stick. These were his people, his tribe.

Straight ahead was the dance floor. Strobing mirror balls scattered colour across the room. To one side was a long, winding bar with flashing lights on the front. He felt the blood pump in his veins, the bass shake his organs. A DJ hunched over decks on a stage, moving in time to the banging tunes he spun on vinyl. Smart serving staff walked among the guests with trays of champagne and canapes.

And the best thing was that when Abs walked in, everyone turned to look. He was greeted with smiles and winks and nods from all around the room. From the TV exec who auditioned him for that property show, that guy who won *Big Brother* back in ancient times, and a cluster of his former co-stars. They were glad he was there, they respected him, and it made him want to cry with joy.

Jez said, 'I've got to tell you—'

'Mate, please,' Abs pleaded. 'Not tonight. Whatever it is, we can talk about it tomorrow. I promise, bruv, but just not tonight, yeah?'

Jez looked at him for a long moment. 'Sure, Abs,' he said quietly. 'We'll talk tomorrow.'

Whatever it was Jez wanted to say, it could wait. Tonight, Abs was on a mission. He was going to win back Kelsey, and the only way to do that was to get back on the show.

'Just stay close to me,' he told his wingman as he strutted into the room.

9

Sasha placed a pint of real ale, some microbrewed thing with a strange name, in front of Vaughn. They were sitting on stools around an upturned beer barrel made into a table, in a new bar that had recently opened in Leigh. It was dark and cool inside; the sun had slipped over the canopy but still shone fiercely on the shopfronts on the other side of the street.

Vaughn took a sip of his beer, and she saw by the way his chin wobbled just how much weight he had put on. He'd always been a big man, rugby-player solid, but now his shirt and jacket strained at the seams. He shifted his bulk on the stool, looking vaguely discomforted, and then his hand slipped below the table to discreetly loosen his belt and give his stomach some breathing space.

They sat tensely for a few moments while he summoned the courage to talk to Sasha, who placed her phone at the periphery of her vision so she could keep an eye on the time. They were late getting out of the office, so Connie would be arriving in less than fifteen minutes. Sasha wanted to make sure she'd sent Vaughn packing before then.

'We'll have one quick drink,' she'd told him as they left the station and again as they arrived. 'Just a quick one.'

'I'm so sorry again,' Sasha said now, to break the awkward silence. 'I always thought you and Miranda were such a happy couple. Can I ask what happened?'

Vaughn took another sip. 'It's complicated.'

She was eager for him to add more detail, but he didn't elaborate. He'd reveal all in his own good time and right now he needed her support.

'How long have you been married, it must be over—'

'Twenty-three years,' he told her. 'For better or for worse. I've moved out. I'll get somewhere to rent eventually, but right now I'm staying at a hotel down the road. Miranda and the boys are still at home.' He winced at the word. 'It's only right, but it's hard.'

'Of course it is,' said Sasha, and because she couldn't help but fish, said, 'I'm really at a loss to understand why you've split up.'

But all he said was, 'It's coming up to three weeks now.'

'Your emotions are still very raw, Vaughn, you're going to be hurting. You're grieving for your marriage, for the most important relationship of your life.' Sasha sipped her wine while he tapped his fingers on the tabletop in an agitated rhythm. 'Do you think there's any chance...'

'No,' he said gruffly. 'Not after everything that's happened.'

'Okay,' she said, still dying to get all the facts.

'So I've come to a decision.' He knocked his knuckles on the wood. 'Miranda's moving on, she's made that clear, and I've decided I've had enough of moping about in a hotel. I've got to get on with my own life.'

'Quite right.' She gave his wrist a squeeze. 'You really should.'

He took his phone from a pocket. 'But it's been so long since I've been on a date.'

'A date?' she asked in surprise. 'Do you think that's what you really need right now?'

'At my age, it's not likely I'm even going to meet anyone socially.' She watched him prod at the screen with his thick fingers and swipe open an app. She didn't like the way the conversation was heading, not at all.

'If there's anything I can do,' she said, trying to distract him from the phone. 'You know you can ask me, or if it would help to talk to a chap, I'm sure Kev would be willing to chat.'

'That's very kind, but I thought I'd try this.' He held up the phone so she could see the screen. 'What do you think of these women?'

He was showing her a dating app, holding it in front of her face. Sasha tried to disguise her discomfort. She wanted to tell Vaughn that it wasn't really appropriate for her to help her boss, her DCI, choose a potential partner to ask on a date. But he looked so crestfallen, so hurt by recent events, that she didn't want to embarrass him further. She gulped down a mouthful of Pinot to gather her thoughts.

'What do you think?' Vaughn showed her a photo of a middle-aged woman, and her profile. 'Does she look fun?'

Sasha cleared her throat. 'I don't think—'

'You have to swipe left,' he said.

But then the door to the bar opened and her sister flounced in. Despite the heat, Connie was wearing a heavy leopard-print coat over a wrap dress patterned with yellow flowers, which accentuated the curves of her hourglass figure. The long toes of her wide feet dropped over the front of her white flip-flops. Her broad, ruddy face was red and filmed with sweat from rushing about in the evening sun. Con lifted a large pair of Jackie Os to reveal her pale green eyes, shoving the glasses hard into the dirty roots of her long, bleached-blonde hair.

'You wouldn't *believe* how long it's taken me to get here,' she said irritably, and thumped an old tan handbag, which looked as heavy as an anvil, onto the table. 'You're lucky I came.'

Vaughn quickly slipped his phone back in his pocket and stood to hold out his hand. 'DCI Vaughn.'

'Vaughn.' Connie held her hand just out of his reach

so that he was obliged to lean closer, then slipped her fingers into his and held them for several moments too long. Sasha felt a spike of anxiety already. This was exactly the kind of situation she wanted to avoid with her flirtatious sister. 'That's a nice name. Very masculine. Vaughn *what?*'

'It's my surname,' he told her.

'What's your first name?'

'Everyone just calls me Vaughn.'

Connie frowned. 'But what's your first name?'

'Claude,' he said shyly.

'That's such a classy name.' Connie smiled as if a strong suspicion had been confirmed in her mind. 'Classy Claude.'

'Vaughn likes people to use his surname,' Sasha told her.

Her DCI hated being called Claude, and Sasha had known him to blow his top in the office when someone had been careless enough to mention it. But now he just smiled.

'Well.' Vaughn stood to bring over a stool and Connie plonked herself down, placing her chin on the heel of her hand. A lock of long hair bounced over one eye as she gazed at him. 'You're always going to be Claude to me.'

'Vaughn is my boss,' Sasha warned her sister.

'Well, Claude, I'm Constance, but you can call me Connie.'

As she reached into her massive bag to take out a tissue and dab her perspiring face, Vaughn finished his pint, much to Sasha's relief.

'Anyway,' he said, rising. 'I had better shoot.'

Connie reached out, aghast. 'You can't go yet, we haven't spoken properly.'

'I've things to do,' said Vaughn vaguely, although Sasha knew he was probably going to sit in his hotel room and be miserable.

'What important things do you have to do?' demanded Connie. 'Tell me one thing.'

Vaughn considered the question, but, it seemed to Sasha, not very hard, because he was unable to come up with a reply.

'I've just got here, and if you don't mind me saying, I think it's very rude that you're going.'

'He's got to go, Con,' insisted Sasha with a tense smile.

'*I* think you should have another drink. In fact' – Connie tapped the top of his hand – 'if you were a gentleman, you would buy me one.'

'Connie,' snapped Sasha. 'He wants to go.'

'I'm going to have a glass of wine and you should have another...' She flapped at his empty glass. 'Whatever that is you're drinking. Better still, you have wine so we can split a bottle.' She gestured at Sasha. 'My sister is welcome to join us, but I'll take a guess that she's probably going to sit there with a face like a slapped arse – I expect you know that face *very* well from work – and tut at everything I do or say. So I could really do with some decent company, Claude.'

Vaughn glanced at Sasha, looking for guidance, and she gave him a tense look, as if to say, *Please go.*

'I'll get a bottle then,' Vaughn said, and Sasha pretended to look pleased. 'Sasha?'

She put her hand over her small glass. 'Not for me, I'm driving.'

'Of course you are,' said Connie with great forbearance, and touched Vaughn's hand again. 'They do a very nice Cab Sav here.'

As soon as he had gone to the bar, Sasha asked her sister as calmly as possible – their mother had always urged her not to get aggressive with her older sister, because, she said, Connie was *sensitive* – 'I thought we were going to go eat?'

'He seems a nice man. It would be rude to just get up and leave.'

'Vaughn is vulnerable right now, Con. He's just split with his wife. So please don't barge in like a bull in a china shop.'

'Has he?' Connie put a hand to her chest. 'That poor man. Then I'd say he definitely needs a drink.'

'But we're going after this bottle, yes? We're going to get something to eat?'

'Of course we are.' Connie rolled her eyes. 'Don't get into such a flap about everything.'

'And don't tell him I told you about the break-up. He's a private man and he wouldn't like it if—'

Connie stood immediately when Vaughn returned with an ice bucket containing a bottle of white wine. 'You poor man, I just heard. You must be devastated.'

Vaughn placed down the bucket and three glasses. Embarrassed, he poured from the bottle. 'These things happen.'

'It's awful,' said Connie. 'And I should know.'

Sasha frowned. 'What are you talking about?'

'Oh, me and Barry split up,' said Connie sadly.

'Wait.' Sasha didn't believe a word of it. 'Since when?'

But Connie ignored her, making eye contact with Vaughn as he poured her a glass of wine. 'We're in the same boat, my love. Two lonely people forced to begin again. It's not going to be easy, not at our age.' She wiped something from her eye with her little finger. 'What will become of us?'

'There's plenty of time for you, Connie,' said Vaughn with a hesitant smile. 'You must be in your twenties.'

Connie squeezed his wrist. 'Oh, you charmer.'

'Tell me, Con,' insisted Sasha. 'When did you split up with Barry, exactly?'

Sasha had never liked Connie's partner, who was dishonest and a bit creepy, but this split was totally out of the blue.

Connie waved a hand, like she didn't want to talk about it. 'A week or so ago. It's still very upsetting, to be honest.' Connie held up her glass so that Vaughn could clink his against it. 'We'll just have to drown our sorrows.'

'We're going to have to go soon if we want to get something to eat.' Sasha had seen that focused look before on her sister's face, and knew she had to remove her from the building as soon as possible.

But the minutes dragged on as Connie asked Vaughn question after question about his career as a Detective Chief Inspector, despite having never shown the slightest interest in Sasha's own long career in Essex Police.

'So as Sasha's boss, you get to tell her what to do.' Connie touched his hand. 'I bet that's a thankless task.'

'Sasha is...' Glass poised at his mouth, Vaughn gave the question genuine thought. 'Sasha is Sasha.'

It wasn't the total repudiation of Connie's impudent remark that Sasha had been hoping for. She knocked back the dregs of her glass. 'Come on, Connie, we have to go.'

'You should get something to eat,' Vaughn agreed. 'I'll finish this wine and get back to the hotel.'

'You can't go back to... wherever you're staying. Oh my God, I bet it's grim.' Sasha shot Connie a fierce look, but her sister reached across the table to squeeze Vaughn's hand. 'I'm having fun here. Aren't you having fun, Claude?'

He smiled. 'Yes, I think I am.'

'I've got to be in early, so I had better get on,' said

Sasha, trying to goad her sister into leaving with her. 'It's getting late.'

Connie's gaze didn't leave Vaughn's. 'See you, then.'

'You're staying?'

'I'll keep Claude company. He shouldn't be alone, not after what's happened, and we're getting on like a house on fire.'

Sasha's gaze slid quickly to Vaughn, but he didn't meet her eye. She was conscious that her face, neck and chest were flushed with indignation.

'Okay, then.' Sasha lifted her bag. 'I'll leave you both to it.'

She gave Connie a meaningful stare, a warning not to lead her boss up the garden path – Connie could drink anyone under the table – and her sister smiled sweetly in reply.

'Oh, Sash. Excuse me a moment, Claude.' The way one of Con's fingers lightly stroked the top of his hand made Sasha want to plonk her bag back down and stay. God knows what Connie could do or say when she was gone. 'Don't forget about tomorrow.'

Sasha blinked. 'What are you talking about?'

'We're coming to see you, darling, me and the old folks.'

'What?'

'Duh.' Connie looked at Sasha as if she wasn't very bright, undermining her in front of Vaughn, and spoke very slowly. 'We're coming for a little soiree.' She enjoyed enunciating the word so much that she said it again. 'A *soiree*. Don't you remember? It's been in the diary for weeks.'

'Oh God.' Sasha did actually remember now – she had invited her family round for drinks and snacks – and said quickly, 'It slipped my mind.'

Con smiled. 'I'll see you then, darling.'

'Is that what you wanted to ask me about?'

'Excuse me?'

'You said on the phone you needed a favour.'

'Oh that.' Connie waved a hand. 'It's nothing, forget about it.'

During this exchange, Vaughn kept a low profile by reading the label on the bottle of wine, and he didn't look like he was in any hurry to leave. Sasha hesitated, wondering if it was wise to leave them both here unsupervised.

But Connie folded her fingers over her palm and released them once, twice, as if her hand was a spring-loaded letter box snapping open and shut.

'Ta-ta, Sasha,' she said in a singsong. 'Ta-ta.'

10

Abs was engulfed by a sea of familiar faces. They hugged him and clapped him on the back, and he handed out a ton of cool and complicated handshakes. Pulled deeper into the crowd, he nodded and grinned at everyone he met.

'Alright, geezer?' said Kurt, who was on the show in season one but who left to try his luck in Hollywood as an actor, and who now worked in his old man's roofing business. 'Good to see ya.'

The only person Abs wanted to see was Kelsey, but he couldn't find her anywhere, and had to ask a production assistant.

'She's probably having a fag out the back.'

It took him a few minutes to realize Jez wasn't with him, and he saw him sitting alone at the end of the bar. Worried about his state of mind, Abs was about to go over, but then he heard a familiar throaty laugh and in an instant he forgot all about his mate.

The crowd miraculously parted like the Red Sea in

that old movie, to reveal Kelsey standing there. She wore a shimmering low-cut dress that showed off her voluptuous figure and bronzed thighs, and Perspex shoes with heel spikes as thin as knitting needles, which allowed you to see her painted toes all scrunched together. Her eyes were big and blue behind lashes heavy with mascara, and her skin sparkled with glittery moisturizer. She flicked back her hair extensions, which fell to her waist, and, planting one hand on a broad hip, lifted the other to point at him with one long acrylic nail.

'What are you waiting for, you silly boy,' she commanded him in a voice made husky by menthol cigarettes. 'Come and give me a cuddle.'

Abs felt the eyes of everyone on them both, and maybe he was imagining it, but even the volume of the music seemed to dim. He lifted her up and spun her in the air.

'You made it.' Laughing with delight, Kelsey threw back her head and tossed her hair for the benefit of the room. 'You came.'

'Hello, Kelz,' Abs said, trying to play it cool in front of everyone.

She fluttered her long eyelashes, which were the length of spider legs. He couldn't believe they were together again. What a woman she was; *what a woman*. They were soulmates, him and Kelsey, Abs truly believed that, and he'd do anything to get back with her.

'I've been thinking about you,' she said, running a nail down his chest. 'Lots.'

His response came out in a croak. 'Yeah?'

'I miss the old days, Abs,' she said in her familiar estuary twang, as the music lifted and everyone got on with their own conversations. 'I love the show still, you know I do, it's been good to me, but a lot of the old gang have gone now – Emma G, Tabitha, Justyn, Chase – and the new cast members are so young.' She rolled her eyes. 'I'm feeling *old*, sweets.'

'You're the what-do-they-call-it, the *matriarch* on the show now,' he told her.

'I don't even know what that means.' She pulled a face. 'But I don't like the sound of it. Point is, I think you should come back. To *Laid In Essex!* We'd get the biggest ratings ever, no word of a lie.'

Her invitation was beyond his wildest dreams and he couldn't help but be excited. Back in the day, Abs and Kelz *were* the show; their relationship was the foundation on which the success of *Laid In Essex!* was built. It was their chemistry that turned it quickly into a cultural phenomenon. Together, they had graced the cover of *TV Choice* a record six times.

He couldn't believe it. 'You can really get me back on the show?'

'I reckon I can, babes.' She leaned forward and he got a delirious lungful of her perfume. 'I've got serious pull there now and reckon I can work something out.'

'You'd do that for me?'

'It ain't the same without you, Abs.' She sniffed. 'Viewing figures are in the toilet. If I approach the producer in the right way, I think I can get you something.'

Abs grinned like an idiot. He was conscious of the little island of space he and Kelz had in the middle of the floor, as everyone else kept a respectful distance. She slipped her hand into his. Maybe a paparazzo would sneak in, or some random would snap this special moment on their phone and sell it to the tabs he hoped so. He could see the story now: Abs and Kelz are spotted getting cosy at a showbiz party, the romance is rekindled. He'd never given up hope that she loved him, not just on the show but in real life, but knew he didn't have a chance of winning her back unless he was as famous and successful as she was.

That was the thing about Kelsey. She loved being a celeb; doing the magazine covers, going to the parties, appearing on the entertainment shows. She called people who weren't on TV *civilians*. Abs understood her all-consuming drive to stay at the top of the celebrity ladder. Once you tasted fame, there was no going back. Maybe, just maybe, getting back on the show would convince her to give him a second chance.

All he wanted to say to her now was, 'I love you, Kelz. I've always loved you.'

But he didn't, because he knew she'd prod his arm and

tell him not to be such a silly sod. 'You crack me up, Abs,' she'd say, and he'd have to pretend it was all a big joke.

'The new producer on the show is here tonight,' she told him now, 'and I'm going to go over and ask him.'

'Wait,' Abs said. 'He's here to enjoy himself. Maybe it's better if you speak to him tomorrow.'

'Babes.' Kelz gave an arrogant pout. 'I'm the last jewel in the crown of that show, so I've got clout. When I talk, he'll listen.' She glanced around the room at all the people pretending not to look at them. 'Everyone's talking about us, Abs. Just imagine what they're gonna say when we get you back on – where you belong.' She ran the tip of her tongue along her top set of perfectly straight, white teeth. 'So how do I look?'

'Like a million dollars, doll,' he said.

'Wrong answer, babes.' She tapped his chest with an acrylic. 'It's a *billion*.'

Throwing her head back so her long mane of hair flew up over her head, she roared with laughter. Abs felt pathetically grateful to be with her.

'I hear people talk about you all the time, Abs.' Her thick curved lashes batted slowly. 'But I always stand up for you. I know you couldn't do anything like what they said, babes. That you had something to do with that… girl. I've never doubted you.'

Behind his back, he pressed his nails into the palm of his hand, feeling an intense shame. 'You don't know what it means for me to hear you say that.'

'It's all been a silly misunderstanding.'

'Yeah.' He couldn't look her in the eye. 'That's exactly what it is.'

'I'm going to speak to the producer now. Wish me luck.'

He watched her sashay across the floor, her bum rolling slowly in the shimmering dress. It took Kelsey forever to get to the other side of the dance floor because so many people wanted her attention; she had to kiss countless cheeks and give out a ton of stiff hugs. Abs could hardly bear to watch. But then, after one particularly long conversation with a couple of women, she looked over her shoulder at him and winked, as if to say, *I bet you thought I'd forgotten*. Moments later she was speaking to the producer, a guy who looked about twelve years old.

'Enjoying yourself, sir?' asked a waiter with a tray of drinks.

'Abs, mate,' he said, feeling chipper. He took a flute of champagne. Then a couple of his former castmates came over to say hello. He tried to be friendly, but he couldn't keep his gaze from straying to Kelsey's intense conversation on the other side of the room. The music changed, heavy bass filled the room, the first chords of a hit tune, and people filled the dance floor. Abs lost sight of Kelz and the producer.

He turned towards the bar to see Jez staring morosely into a bottle of beer and wished intensely that he wasn't here, but then he remembered that in all likelihood Jez wanted to confess to the feds about what happened in Wales. Abs couldn't let it happen, particularly not now he had a chance to get back on the show, and back with Kelsey.

He clapped him on the back. 'How you doing, mate?'

'It's a bit noisy for me,' said Jez, gazing round the bar.

'People would kill to get into this party,' said Abs, and Jez winced. 'Who would ever have believed me and you would be at something like this, a couple of scrotes who grew up in care. Back then, we had each other's backs, Jez, we protected each other. Your mum wasn't around, my mum didn't want me, so it was you and me against the world.'

'You're my best mate, always will be.' Jez looked at him thoughtfully. 'But we're so different.'

'There's me, all mouth and trousers, with not a brain in my head, and you quiet and thoughtful. But opposites attract, that's what they say, right?'

'You remember when we first met, Abs, back when we were, what, nine years old?' said Jez. 'Mum had gone away, and I was separated from my sister, and I came to the foster home – and ran off straight away. You came and found me, and stopped me getting beaten up by those two bigger boys and their sister, do you remember?'

'I do, yeah,' said Abs. 'They were giving you a right kicking, the toerags.'

Distracted, Abs couldn't help but glance in the mirror behind the bar to see if he could find Kelsey. He didn't want to miss any of the party, but nor did he want Jez to make any rash decisions.

'You came up and you chased them off.' Jez scraped off bits of the damp label from his bottle of beer. 'You walked me back to the house and I cried my eyes out all the way.'

Abs vaguely recalled what happened. Those kids were really pummelling Jez, he remembered that, but it all happened a long time ago now. 'It's history, mate.'

'And then you got us out of that fix in Wales,' said Jez. 'If it weren't for you, we would all be in jail.'

'Yeah.' Abs didn't want to talk about that, he didn't want to think about it, and closed his mind to it. Abs liked to stay cheerful, he was Mr Positivity, but Deano's death had also spooked him, and he couldn't shake the memory of that menacing guy at QuidStore.

'You've always protected me.' Jez lifted his bottle and Abs picked up his glass of champagne, and they clinked. 'And I thank you for everything you've done.'

Abs tried to make light of it. 'Stop it, you're making me well up.'

Jez gripped his arm so tightly that he winced in momentary pain.

'I've got to tell someone, Abs.' Jez's face twisted in misery. 'It's gnawing away at me.'

'You don't have to tell anyone,' Abs said forcefully.

'Deano is responsible for what happened, he *did* it, and now he's gone, so let's just get on with our lives.'

'No, I need to tell—'

'Mate, you're hurting me.' Abs pulled his arm from Jez's fierce grip.

'I'm sorry.'

Abs clicked his fingers at the barman, nodded at Jez's empty bottle. 'Another beer over here, as quick as you can. This man needs a drink.'

'Danny...' whined Jez.

Abs was shocked, because it had been many years since Jez had used his real name. It reminded him of when they were two lonely kids at the home and Jez used to sneak into Abs's bed at night for comfort, and it sent a chill down his spine.

Jez was in a bad way, that was clear, and Abs had to turn the situation around. He would take Jez home, sit him down and use all his powers of persuasion to make sure he didn't go to the police to confess what they did.

'We don't need that any more,' Abs told the barman when he plonked the beer down, and then turned to Jez. 'You've got to hold in there, bruv. What do I always say? Come on, repeat after me, teamwork...'

'Makes the dream work,' said Jez reluctantly.

'We're going to get through this.' He clapped Jez on the shoulder. 'I've got your back, buddy. Let's go home.'

But then he heard a voice, loud and raucous. An

ear-splitting shriek filled the room, feedback as Kelsey took the microphone too near speakers.

'There's a very special person here who means the world to me.' She stood in the middle of the dance floor and, shielding her eyes against the glare of the lights, peered around the room. 'Me and him shared something special on *Laid In Essex!* but things haven't been going too well for him lately.'

Abs winced inside. He wished she hadn't said that, not in front of all these people.

'Where are you, Abs?' she called into the crowd. 'I can't see you, babes.'

'Over here, Kelz.' He lifted his hand modestly and everyone turned to look at him.

'There you are.' Kelz blew a kiss. 'I want you to know, babes, that I'm always here for you. Because we're soulmates.'

The audience went *awwww* and watched Abs closely for his reaction. He placed his hands together, as in heavenly devotion.

'I'm sure you've all seen our little show, yeah?' said Kelsey, and everyone whooped, like, *Of course we have.* 'Back in the first episode all those years ago, me and Abs sung a song together at a karaoke bar, remember that, babes? You're The One That I Want.'

Abs pretended to grease his hair. 'Highlight of my life, Kelz.'

Everyone laughed. And Kelsey produced another

microphone from behind her back. 'What do you say, babes, wanna sing it again?'

This was more than Abs could have hoped for. Performing with Kelsey in front of a packed audience of industry folk – producers, commissioners, directors. But he didn't want to leave Jez, unhappy and ready to run to the police.

'Please stay there,' he urged him in a frantic whisper, and then walked on to the dance floor.

'DJ, please.' Kelsey struck a pose and the familiar tune from *Grease* began to play.

They were both lousy singers – neither of them could hold a tune to save their lives – but they hammed it up. Abs doing the Travolta moves, and everyone in the crowd pissing themselves laughing, enjoying seeing the Golden Couple back together. He and Kelz went round the room, getting people to sing into the mic like they were bossing Lovebox. And who knew where it could lead, he thought, as someone tossed him a comb to rake through his hair like Danny Zuko.

Abs felt wanted. For the first time in a long time, he felt *loved*.

But as he was singing, he tried to spot Jez at the bar – and couldn't find him. The beer bottle was there, but his stool was empty. There was nothing Abs could do about it now. He would just have to speak to Jez first thing in the morning, and stop him from ruining both their lives.

11

Slamming the front door shut, Sasha kicked off her shoes and threw her jacket over the banister. It missed and fell on the bottom stair. She could hear zombies tearing people apart on the television in the living room.

'Hiya,' called her husband, Kev, over the screams of terror.

'Hi,' she said, taking out her phone and heading to the kitchen.

It had been a mistake to leave Vaughn in the clutches of Connie; she was still annoyed about it, she didn't know what she had been thinking. In normal circumstances, Vaughn would have made his excuses and left as soon as Connie swanned in the door, but he was in a vulnerable state of mind, and it wasn't beyond the realms of possibility that her greedy sister would take advantage of his sensitive state by attempting to borrow money. At the very least, she would expect him to pay for all the drinks.

She tapped a quick message:

Sorry about tonight! Connie can be v pushy!!!

She stared at the screen, uncertain whether to add an x, an X, or even two xxs. Sasha liked to think of Vaughn as a friend and the circumstances were unusual, but it surely wasn't professional to add kisses on a text to her boss. However, neither was it appropriate for her DCI to share his online dating profile with her. Vaughn, who was always so clear-headed and professional, wasn't thinking straight. She couldn't help herself and added another line, with a single token kiss to underline the extraordinary situation.

Sorry again! x

Sasha fired it off before she could change it again and then stared at the phone, hoping he would reply quickly to say he had left the bar, but no text arrived.

'Everything okay?'

She looked up to see Kev in the doorway. Sasha slapped the phone down on the kitchen island and went to the sink. Ignoring the mountain of plates and dishes stacked there, she ran the cold tap, waiting for the stream of water to chill.

'Sorry,' she said. 'Long day, busy day.'

'You saw your sister tonight. That always puts you in a good mood.'

'Oh, you have no idea,' she told him, and gulped from the glass.

'I've some news,' he said.

He was standing in a pair of pyjama bottoms and a tee-shirt and she hoped he hadn't been dressed like that all day. Kev had recently suffered a bout of depression, fallen into a spiral of despair – a delayed reaction to the death of their youngest child, Jake – and quit his job. He was on the mend now, he seemed happier, more resilient, but was apparently in no hurry to rush back to work. Which was fine, she didn't want to put any pressure on him. But, eyeing the washing-up in the sink, she wondered what he did all day. Whatever it was, it didn't involve a lot of housework.

Whenever she got home, he rushed to greet her, eager for conversation and companionship. But it could be awkward to compare their days; Kev got a vicarious pleasure from hearing about her work, but she was wary of burdening him with any upsetting stuff.

I saw the shattered body parts of a man hit by a train today, how was Bargain Hunt?

'I saved you dinner,' he said, nodding at a casserole dish on the hob. The way he said it, you'd think he'd just presented her with a diamond ring.

'I'm not hungry.' She worried that sounded rude, so

she pulled the lid off the dish and made a big show of stirring it. 'Smells delicious, maybe I'll have some later. Is that what you wanted to tell me?'

'You first,' he said. 'Tell me about your day.'

'It was kind of boring, really.' Put on the spot, she didn't want to discuss it. 'Wait, I've ordered a Tesco delivery for tomorrow afternoon, are you...'

'Am I what?'

She was going to ask whether he'd be home, but knew he was hardly likely to be anywhere else.

'Never mind. Mum and Dad are coming tomorrow night, and Connie. I'm sorry I didn't tell you, but I stupidly invited them all a while back. I could really do without it right now.'

'Then cancel it,' he said.

'They'll just turn up anyway. You know Mum, once she puts something in her diary, nothing short of Armageddon will stop it happening.' Something occurred to her. 'Where are the kids?'

'Denny is at a mate's round the corner.'

'When's he back?' she asked in alarm. She'd recently had one child snatched by a maniac, and despite the fact that she knew it was as likely to happen again as an asteroid landing on their house, she felt her anxiety spike. 'He can't come back on his—'

'I told him to ring me and I'd walk him home,' Kev told her.

She looked at what he was wearing. 'In your pyjamas?'

'It'll be dark by then,' he said with a shrug. 'So, listen—'

She wanted all her ducks in a row before they changed the subject. 'And where's Angel?'

'Angel's here,' said her daughter, coming into the kitchen. She was wearing a pink onesie and a pair of enormous slippers in the shape of cuddly dogs. The soles slapped on the kitchen tile.

'Hello, darling,' said Sasha. 'How was your—'

'I'd like to talk to you both,' Angel told them tensely, and she pulled out a couple of stools from under the kitchen island and patted them, as if to say, *Sit*.

Sasha and Kev glanced at each other. They had no idea what Angel wanted to say. Getting her to communicate about anything these days was a struggle, so this situation was totally unprecedented. They both knew the trauma of her abduction would affect her for years. If anything, the experience had made her even more sullen, secretive and unpredictable. More than once when Sasha had picked Angel up from the houses of friends, she suspected her daughter had been drinking, or smoking weed.

The way her daughter pointed gravely to the stools made Sasha nervous, but she did as she was told and sat. 'Is there something wrong?'

'And you too, Dad, please,' Angel told Kev, and he sat beside his wife.

Sasha said uneasily, 'What is it, darling?'

Angel held up a hand. 'Please, Mum, just listen.'

Sasha and Kev waited to hear what she had to say. It had to be something big, something dramatic, for her to demand their attention like this.

'I'm sorry about what happened at school, and what you did for me and everything.'

Angel was talking about how she had got involved with a group of girls who were bullying a former friend. Sasha had gone ballistic at the time, but now Angel seemed to have stepped back from some of the more toxic friendships she had formed.

'Oh, Angel, we're your mum and dad, and you don't have to—'

Kev elbowed her in the arm, *Let her finish*.

'I totally understand why you were angry with me, and I wanted to, you know…' She dragged her bottom lip between her teeth. 'Show my appreciation.'

'Great.' Kev clapped his hands. 'Milk, one sugar, please.'

Angel fumbled in the pocket of her onesie, took out a folded piece of paper and handed it to Sasha.

'What is it?'

'It's a reservation for a night at a posh hotel. It's for one of their biggest rooms – it's got a four-poster bed and a really big bath, and there's a spa and a nice restaurant and everything.' The image on the paper was of a big Victorian hotel, tall and stately in neat landscaped grounds. Sasha knew the hotel by reputation; it was swanky and very expensive.

Sasha handed the paper to Kev. 'I don't know what to say.'

Their daughter shrugged as if it were no big deal. 'You don't have to thank me, just go and enjoy yourself, you both deserve it.'

'Okay, don't get angry, but I have to ask...' After a difficult day, Sasha was full of gratitude, but needed to get something straight in her mind. 'Where did you get the money?'

Angel anxiously twisted the sagging cuff of her onesie. 'I still had some money left over from Christmas and Nan and Grandad helped me out with the rest. They paid quite a lot, really.' She looked nervous that her parents would be angry. 'But I didn't pressure them or anything.'

'It's been a long day and I was feeling a little down tonight, so this is a lovely and unexpected gesture. Come here.' Sasha gave Angel a hug, her heart swelling with love. 'I'm proud of you, sweetheart.'

'I just thought, what with everything that's happened, and Dad's... funny turn and everything, it would be good for you to get away, just the two of you, like, even if it was just for one night. I'm sorry I couldn't afford for you to stay longer.'

'I can't wait.' Kev kissed Angel's forehead and then turned to Sasha and jiggled his eyebrows.

'What?' asked Angel.

'Nothing.' He quickly wiped the look off his face. 'It's nothing.'

But Angel wouldn't let it go. 'What's going on?'

'Your dad is just being silly,' said Sasha.

'Why aren't you telling me?'

Sasha sighed. 'Back when we were younger, me and your dad would go on a night out, or stay overnight somewhere, and we'd play a game.' Angel shook her head, like, *I don't know what you're talking about.* 'We'd, er, pretend to be other people.'

'Why would you do that?'

They role-played because it was fun and exciting – and because they got a thrill out of it. But Sasha didn't really want to explain that to Angel and wished she'd never brought it up. Kev was smirking at her now, as if to say, *Get out of this one.*

'I don't know why we did it, really. It was a silly thing to do.'

'Aaargh.' Angel winced, suddenly realizing. 'It was a sex thing, wasn't it? *Yuck.* You wore a French maid's outfit and stuff like that?'

'No,' said Sasha, shocked. 'I didn't. It wasn't that kind of—'

'Your mother absolutely didn't,' Kev said in a deadpan. 'But I did, once or twice.'

Angel looked terrified for a moment and then Kev laughed, which made Sasha laugh, too. But their daughter made a disgusted face. 'You're both sick. You really shouldn't be talking about this kind of stuff around me.'

'We'll have to check our diaries for the next few

weeks,' Sasha told Kev, as if his schedule was bulging with events and responsibilities.

'It's for Friday night,' said Angel, taken aback. 'I've already booked the room.'

'Oh.' Sasha didn't want to seem ungrateful, but she didn't want to take time out, even a single night, while the investigation into the death of Andrew Dean's murder was at a critical stage. 'You really should have checked with us first.'

Angel looked crestfallen. 'It was the only night they had available.'

'Would you believe it, I'm going to London on Friday for an interview.'

'What interview?' asked Sasha.

'That's what I was going to tell you, I've got an interview for a job as a shipping administrator. It's not till half five.' When Angel made a strangled noise of frustration, Kev said quickly, 'But I should be able to get back quickly enough.'

Sasha remembered Denny was going for a sleepover that night, which meant her daughter would be alone in the house. She didn't like the sound of that – what if she panicked?

But Angel smiled, as if she could read her mother's mind. 'I'll be totally fine.'

'You could go to a friend's house,' Sasha suggested. 'Or spend the night with your grandparents.'

'I'll stay here and Netflix and chill in my PJs with

all the doors and windows locked,' said Angel. 'I'll be on the other end of the phone. You can call me as much as you like, and I can call you. And Nan and Grandad aren't very far away if I need them.'

'You're right,' said Sasha, not totally convinced. 'It's only for a few hours.'

She looked at Kev, who tapped his temple. 'She's got it all worked out.'

'It's very kind of you, Angel,' said Sasha, who was close to tears at the thought that her daughter would do such a nice thing. And it *was* kind. Angel had been a handful in the past, in trouble at school and mixed up with a crowd Sasha didn't much care for, but maybe her daughter was beginning to feel more comfortable in her own skin. She hoped so. This thoughtful gesture gave Sasha hope that Angel was moving in the right direction.

And her daughter was right. A night away was exactly what Sasha and Kev needed. It had been a long time since they'd spent any quality time together alone. The spark had gone, recently. Sasha instinctively reached out to touch Kev's fingers and he responded, and she knew he felt the same way.

Angel pointed at the door. 'I'm going now, because I've given you more than enough of my valuable time.'

Kev saluted. 'Missing you already.'

When Angel had gone, they admired the photo of the posh hotel, and looked up its long list of luxury amenities.

'A four-poster bed, huh?' A smile played across his lips. 'Remember when we broke that four-poster in Rome?'

She gave him a challenging look. 'You'll have to wine and dine me first, just to be in with a chance.'

He drifted towards the door. 'Maybe she's turning a corner.'

'Yeah,' Sasha agreed. 'Maybe she is.'

When Kev was gone, she stayed in the kitchen putting all the dirty pots and pans in the dishwasher and turning it on, and then checked her phone.

No reply from Vaughn.

12

Abs left the party on top of the world. Kelsey was still at the club – she always stayed till the bitter end of a party – but he slipped away, telling everyone that he was off to meet some mates elsewhere.

The truth was, Abs needed a good night's sleep so that he could get up early to convince Jez not to ruin everything by going to the police.

He couldn't afford a minicab home from Brentwood to Southend, but as soon as he was outside he felt immediately vulnerable. All the hacks and paps had drifted away, and the streets were dark and empty. He took a baseball cap from his back pocket, pulled it low over his face, and walked as fast as he could along the pavement, hands thrust deep in his pockets.

It occurred to Abs that it was at this time of night when Deano was killed, and he told himself off for even thinking about it. But it was no wonder he was spooked by events, and Jez's dark mood, his mate's seeming intention to confess, played on his mind. For all Abs knew, Jez could be at a police station at this very moment, spilling the truth about that disastrous weekend in Wales.

The crash of a bin startled Abs and he spun to see a fox leap across the street, the red mirrors of its eyes regarding him reproachfully. He considered going back to the club to blag a lift, because right now he was totally freaking himself out. But then he recognized the street he was on – it wasn't too far from the bus station – and picked up his pace. Moments later he sensed a car keeping pace with him on the road.

'Mate,' someone called. 'Oi, mate.'

Abs adjusted the cap and hurried on. He just wanted to get back to his apartment and lock the door, but he was unable to resist glancing over to the car. He saw there were three fellas in it; the two in the front were hidden in shadow, but the one in the back had wound down the window to poke his head out.

Abs couldn't help but reply, an instinctive reaction: 'How you doing?'

'Is it you?' said the man in the back. 'You're that bloke off the telly called, whatsit, Pecs.'

'Abs,' he replied, but didn't slow his pace.

'It is you.' The man in the car laughed. 'My girl loves you, she's always going on about you, it's all Abs this and Abs that. I can't compete, mate.'

'Sorry about that,' said Abs, walking quickly.

'Come on, Abs, help me out. I'm going to get it in the

neck if I say I've seen you and I don't come home with an autograph.'

Abs didn't slow. 'Sorry, mate, I'm in a hurry.'

'Do me a favour.' The guy waved a pen and paper out of the window. 'Or my head is going to be in a noose.'

'Sorry.' Abs didn't like the way the car kept pace with him, or the fact that he couldn't see who was in the front. But it was also true that he could do with some money to get home. Maybe he'd be able to get the guy to pay for an autograph, even enough for a cab home. So he stopped walking, and the car slowed to a stop.

'Mate.' Abs walked to the window, where the man grinned up at him. 'It's late and I just want to get home, but I've no cash on me, so if you want an autograph I'm going to have to ask you for a tenner.'

'Hop in,' suggested the man helpfully. 'We'll give you a lift.'

Abs leaned into the window to get a better view of the men in the front but all he could see was the back of their heads. 'Nah, I don't want to bother you.'

'It ain't no bother.' The guy grinned. 'You're a celebrity.'

'No, it's okay.' The whole situation didn't feel right to Abs. 'I'll give you an autograph and then I'll get on my way.'

Abs reached for the pen and paper, but the man

pulled them away and said nastily, 'I'm going to have to insist.'

And in that instant, he grabbed Abs's arms and pulled him through the window. Abs screamed in shock and tried to break free from his grasp, but he was grabbed from behind – he glimpsed the front doors were wide open, heard the *ding ding ding* of the seat-belt alert – and his head was forced down as he was bundled into the back seat.

'Help,' he screamed. 'Help me!'

But the street was empty; there was nobody to hear him. He took a punch in the ribs from the man beside him, who raised his fist again.

'Not the face!'

The two men climbed back in the front, the doors slammed and the car roared up the street. Then the guy in the front passenger seat turned to glare at him, and it was with a sickening realization that he recognized him as the man who had been watching outside the QuidStore yesterday.

'What do you want?' Abs stammered in terror, but the man didn't say a word, just stared. The guy beside him in the back casually reached into Abs's pocket, took out his phone and chucked it out the window. Then he pulled a packet of cigarettes from his own pocket, lit one and turned away to look out at the streets speeding past, as if his job was done and he could now relax.

'Where are we going?' Abs asked the man in the front.

'Shut up,' the guy said with a sneer. They were going at such a speed that the man's hair whipped in the breeze billowing through the open window.

'What are you going to do with me?' Abs had seen a movie where this happened, where a guy was kidnapped and taken to some godforsaken place in the middle of nowhere and killed. Then he thought of that poor girl, Rhiannon, and felt sick. 'Tell me what this is about.'

'You know what this is about,' the man told him in a Welsh accent.

'No, I don't,' Abs said. 'Honest I don't.'

'You killed my niece,' said the man. Abs tried to think of the name of the girl's uncle. He remembered he was all over the papers back when it happened, calling for justice, making threats.

'You're…' Abs clicked his fingers, trying desperately to remember his name. 'Davey… Jenkins.'

The man growled. 'I said shut up.'

Jenkins had boasted in the press that he had gangster connections and, oh God, he had threatened to get retribution one day for Rhiannon's death. That was the word he used, *retribution*. Abs knew what that word meant, because he had made a point of looking it up. It meant vengeance. *Revenge*.

'Mate.' Abs held up his hands, ready to say anything to get these men to let him go, but Jenkins turned forward in his seat and Abs could only appeal to his back. 'Davey, I can pay you money, I don't have any on me right now, but I'll make everything okay, because you've made a terrible mistake, yeah? We can sort this out, mate, it's not too late.'

Davey Jenkins snarled over his shoulder, 'Pipe down.'

And then they drove in silence, the faceless driver accelerating along the empty streets. Very soon they would leave town altogether, and then God knows where they would take him. To some abandoned factory where he would be tied to a chair and set alight, or to a reservoir where he'd be weighted down with rocks, or into the desert – wait, there wasn't a desert in the UK, but somewhere *like* that. Somewhere his body would never be found. His mind was going crazy with all the violent possibilities. Abs knew he had to do something. He looked at the man beside him, who was gazing out the window and smoking, as if he were on a casual moonlight drive. The car screeched round corners, the interior filled with the roar of the engine and the blowing wind, and only slowed at junctions.

But Abs knew there was only one thing he could do. He had to wait for the car to slow – they would surely hit a red light soon – and then open the door and throw himself out. People did it all the time in films, or the stuntmen did, and they escaped with barely a scratch. But this wasn't the movies, and Abs knew that if he got it wrong, he could be very badly injured. He could be paralysed or knocked out, and all they had to do was turn the car around and aim for him...

Abs let out a little sob. He had to be brave – but the thought of hurling himself out of the car was terrifying. And he knew that if he didn't make a decision about what to do now, *right now*, they would drive him somewhere and torture him, kill him – just like they did to Deano.

He didn't know what to do; he wished someone would please tell him what to do. There was no way he could take on these guys. All three of them looked like they could take care of themselves, and Abs was a lover, not a fighter. But if he didn't, or if he didn't escape the car soon, he was going to die in a car crusher somewhere or be dropped off the side of a yacht or his bones melted in an acid bath...

And now they were slowing at some lights and –

Oh, *fuck* it.

Abs grabbed the handle and shoved his shoulder into the door and threw himself out while the car was still moving. He hit the ground hard, had never felt such pain – his brain was literally vibrating in his head. He rolled across the tarmac, over and over, the sleeves of his jacket and hoodie tearing and the road scraping the skin off his wrists and hands – and finally came to a stop. He wondered for a split second if he was dead, but he could hear his heart thumping in his chest, and it felt like every bit of him was on fire, so he guessed he wasn't.

There was a screech of brakes. The car had come to a stop up ahead. The engine was idling, smoke puttering from the exhaust. Right now was the time to get the registration number, but it was almost upside down in his vision, and Abs wasn't thinking straight; his brain felt like it was still ricocheting around his skull like a pinball.

He had to get up right away. Every molecule in his body was screaming for him to flee, but instead he lay in the road totally still, hoping they might think he was dead. The car's engine growled, smoke from the exhaust lifting into the night sky.

He prayed that any moment now the car was going to drive off. Any moment now…

But instead the car doors swung open and Abs knew that his nightmare wasn't over. He climbed to his feet and stumbled along the road, desperately trying to get his bearings. The footsteps of the men thundered on the road behind him. He cut left into a narrow alley, panic rising in him, and nearly lost his footing on a dumped bin bag of rubbish.

Looking over his shoulder, Abs saw the black silhouettes of his pursuers racing into the alley. At the other end, he came into a street where all the shops were shuttered. All he had to do was find someone, anyone, and scream his head off. But then he saw a late-night bar on the corner of the street and ran towards it, had never run so fast in his life, despite the stinging pain he felt.

He threw himself through the door and raced into the middle of a small group of people, pointing at his own face. 'Do you know me?'

'Oh my days.' A girl's face lit up. Her eyes were slack with drunkenness, and a pint slopped in her hand. 'It's Abs, from *Laid In Essex!*'

'That's right, darling,' he told her, trying not to sound petrified. 'And right now I'm doing this show in which I'm chased.'

'*Celebrity Manhunt*,' she said. 'I love that.'

'That's it. And there's going to be a couple of fellas coming through that door at any moment.'

'Are we going to be on the telly?' she asked, incredulous.

'Do me a favour, love, and tell them I went out the back.'

'We could just give you away and claim the reward.' A guy draped his arm over her shoulder to show Abs she was his girl. 'They give away reward money on that show if you turn the celebrities in.'

'Why would you do something so mean?' The woman was annoyed with her boyfriend. 'The celebs do it for charity.'

'Yeah,' said Abs desperately. 'It's for the kids.'

The boyfriend looked around. 'Where's the camera?'

'Where's the what?' Abs didn't know what he was talking about.

'Where's the camera crew doing the filming?'

Abs pointed to the zip on the front of his hoodie. 'It's a micro-camera.'

Staring at his chest, the woman subtly rearranged her hair. 'Course we'll do it.' She held up her phone. 'If you give us a selfie.'

'They're coming.' Abs tried not to explode in dribbling panic. 'Any second now.'

'It'll only take a moment.' She and her boyfriend squeezed into the shot and Abs hunched in with them, grinning hideously into her phone. As soon as it flashed, he threw himself over the end of the empty bar and huddled behind it, shutting his eyes to make himself extra invisible, just as someone came in the door of the bar.

Abs clamped a hand over his mouth, convinced his own frantic breathing would give him away. He heard the girl's boyfriend say, 'Are you looking for the guy who ran in here?'

'Yeah.' The Welsh accent made Abs tremble.

'He ran out the back exit, didn't he, Gary?' Abs heard the girl say.

'Yeah,' said the boyfriend reluctantly. 'By the toilets.'

A moment later, footsteps ran past the bar. Abs heard a door slam at the rear. Thanking his lucky stars, he climbed to his feet.

'Wait,' called the girl as Abs flew out the front. 'When's the show on?'

13

'Danny Cruikshank is waiting to see you,' Ajay told Sasha as soon as she arrived, later than she had intended, in the office. 'He claims he was kidnapped last night and his life threatened.'

'Abs? Is he hurt?'

'A few cuts and bruises from escaping out of a moving car. He's in shock, but otherwise unharmed.'

Sasha dropped her bag and took off her jacket. She couldn't help but glance over at Vaughn's office, and saw with alarm that it was empty. Vaughn was never late. You could set your watch by him.

'Is the DCI in?' she asked, hoping he had gone to a meeting or something.

Ajay shrugged. 'I haven't seen him.'

'Put Abs in Interview Room 1,' she said, firing up her computer and moving things about on her desk. 'Just let me get a couple of things sorted.'

'Sure thing.'

'And what's this?' She snatched a Post-it note with a number on it off her computer screen.

'It's the cost of the dry cleaning for my trousers,' he said over his shoulder.

She waved him away, but then called him back. 'And Ajay, get someone to speak to North Wales Police about the Rhiannon Jenkins case. They obviously had cause to interview Abs and Andrew Dean and those others about their contact with her on the night she vanished, so let's find out as much as we can.'

'On it,' he told her.

'One more thing.' Her DS waited with a patient smile. 'Do me a favour and print off a photo of Stephen Gosling and the man we found on his list of known associates.'

'Anything else?' he asked, and she thought about it.

'No.' She gestured sweetly for him to go. 'You may toddle off.'

As soon as he had gone, she took out her mobile and rang Connie's number. It was probably too much to ask that her sister be up at 9 a.m. Con was a night owl. Because of the nature of her job, doing PR for pubs and bars along the Essex coastline – which somehow entailed drinking complimentary booze provided by her clients into the early hours – she often slept in till lunchtime. But that fact didn't help ease Sasha's anxiety when the call dropped straight to voicemail.

'Con.' Sasha pinched the bridge of her nose. 'It's *me*, give me a ring as soon as you're up. Please tell me you didn't... tell me you didn't keep DCI Vaughn out too late. Anyway...' She thought it politic to lighten the tone a little. 'It was lovely to see you last night.'

She shoved the phone in a drawer, grabbed her notebook and yanked off the lid of a Bic with her teeth. Sasha was about to head to the interview room when Vaughn walked in the door with a coffee cup in his hand. But when he looked over, for some reason she didn't even understand – maybe it was her alarm that he was unshaved and wore the same suit and tie as yesterday – she ducked behind the monitor. Peeking around the side, she watched him go into his office and slump tiredly behind his desk. The first thing he did was take out his phone and start texting. Craig Power wandered over while Sasha was still hunched like a troll beneath a bridge.

'Craig,' she said brightly. 'Good morning.'

'You alright?' he asked.

'Bit of a stiff shoulder from sleeping awkwardly last night.' She rubbed her collarbone and slowly straightened in her seat, as if the massage was miraculously curing it. 'What can I do for you?'

'A young woman has been reported missing in Brentwood,' he said. 'Name of Sarah Tovey. Went out clubbing last night with her cousin and a couple of friends. She left them at eleven to look for a cab, but never arrived home. She's a carer for her disabled mum, so it's totally out of character.'

'Is it on the system?' she asked. 'I'll take a look at it this morning.'

'They're handling it at Chelmsford nick,' he said, 'but they want us to be made aware. A couple of other women have gone missing in similar circumstances in the county over the last couple of years. If she doesn't turn up today, they've asked if we'll interview the cousin.'

'Thank you, Power Man,' she told him. 'Keep me up to speed.'

'Sasha, got a moment?'

The sound of Vaughn's voice made her reluctantly peep over the top of her monitor. He was standing in his office doorway, so she did a surprised face for his benefit, as if she didn't know he'd come in.

'Excuse me,' she told Craig, and followed Vaughn into his office.

He sat behind his desk, prodding at his computer keyboard with one hand, clinging to the cup of coffee with the other as if it were a life raft on a stormy sea. Up close, he looked very hungover and dishevelled.

He said, 'I owe you an explanation.'

'No, you don't.' She held up her hands in protest. 'It's none of my business.'

'I've...' His fingers drummed on his desk. 'Behaved very badly.'

She didn't know where this conversation was going and didn't *want* to know. 'Vaughn, really—'

'It's delicate.' He went to the door she had left ajar and closed it. 'This is not something I want you to hear from… your sister. And I don't want her to be embarrassed.'

Oh, she won't be, Sasha thought. Through the glass, she saw more of her team sharing a laugh as they arrived in the office and wished she could be out there with them, joining in the joke.

'It was a crazy night. It's been a long time since I've had such a hangover. We had another couple of bottles at the bar, me and Connie.' He grimaced. 'And then we went back to her place for more and, well…'

Sasha shuddered. 'Vaughn, please—'

He sipped his coffee. 'Well, let's just say one thing led to another.'

She held up a hand: *Stop there*. 'It's really none of my business.'

This whole conversation was a nightmare. Just the idea of Vaughn spending the night at Connie's little flat in Eastwood – it was so untidy it looked like a bomb had hit it – made Sasha squirm.

'But…' He flicked a thumb thoughtfully against the plastic lid of the coffee. 'She made me laugh, she made me feel good, and I haven't felt like that for a long time. I'd like to see her again, Sasha, but only if you're comfortable with that.'

No, Vaughn, I'm not comfortable with that.

'Of course I am,' she said, with as much fake sincerity as she could muster. 'If you want to spend time with each other, then I'm happy for you both, really I am. You don't have to run things past me.'

'I feel terrible. It's not been long since I split with Miranda.'

'No, it hasn't,' she agreed quickly.

'I want you to know that's it's not like I've been looking for romance or fun, but when someone like your sister comes along...' Despite his embarrassment, he chuckled as he remembered something that had happened last night. 'She's a hell of a woman. I've never met anybody like her before.'

Sasha cursed herself for stupidly allowing Vaughn and Connie to meet in the first place. But then she would never have guessed that the urbane, sensible Vaughn could fall for her chancer of a sister. The more Con found out about Vaughn's background, his lifestyle and wealth, the more her sister's eyes must have bulged in her head. If Connie sensed Vaughn was an easy target, and the breakdown of his marriage had left him reeling and vulnerable, she'd be all over him like a velociraptor.

But Sasha knew that if she confronted Connie about her intentions, her sister would be sure to tell Vaughn that she was sticking her nose in.

'Just...' Sasha really wanted to warn him to tread carefully where Connie was concerned, but instead she said, 'It's early days for you, Vaughn. You're still hurting and perhaps you're not in the best frame of mind, just... don't rush into anything.'

'Thanks,' he said, and she didn't know if he had heard her at all.

Ajay knocked on the door and popped his head inside – he'd probably seen through the glass how uncomfortable Sasha looked and knew she needed saving – and said, 'Abs is in the interview room as you requested.'

'Thanks, Ajay.' She made an apologetic face to Vaughn. 'I'd better get back to work.'

14

He was relieved when the detective inspector he liked, the one with the granny hair, walked into the room and said, 'How are you, Abs?'

He stood, uncertain of what to do. His instinctive response when he saw a familiar face was to move in for a friendly hug or kiss – God knows he needed comfort right now – but he knew that in the circumstances it may not be the proper thing to do. Another man, a young Asian guy who looked like he should be gracing the cover of *GQ*, sat beside her, a slim folder in his hand.

'You're looking great, Detective Lawson,' he said, nodding vaguely at her hair.

'Thank you, Abs. It's Dawson. This is my colleague, Detective Sergeant Ajay de Vaz.' Flipping open a notebook, she gave him a sympathetic look. 'So, Abs, it sounds like you've had a terrible shock.'

Abs blew out his cheeks. 'I'm shook up about it, to be honest.'

'Please.' Sasha gestured for him to sit and he dropped

into the chair, flattening his hands between his clenched legs because he didn't know what else to do with them. He was shattered from a lack of sleep and dosed up on painkillers because of the stinging pains in his arms and legs. Abs didn't go to hospital for treatment because he didn't want his ordeal to hit the papers, not now a big comeback was on the cards. He was just thankful he hadn't suffered any loss of skin on his face, where people could properly see it.

Instead, he'd tried to get some shut-eye. But every time he closed his eyes, he saw behind his lids the spinning room in the cottage in Wales. That blade of early morning light knifing through the gap in the curtains, the glass of water at his feet, the damp-stain on the ceiling, the mattress on the floor, all of it whirling around in his head.

Part of him wanted to just forget the kidnap last night even happened, put it down to some random attack, people playing a nasty joke on a celeb, but he knew that wasn't the case. Davey Jenkins and his mates wanted to kill him, just like they killed Deano.

'Can you tell me that happened?' asked Sasha Dawson gently.

And so he did, changing the odd fact here and there. He didn't want to admit that he couldn't afford a cab, so he told her he left the party on foot to clear his head. 'I'm a total lightweight, I can't take my drink.'

Abs said he was bundled into the car by three men.

No, he didn't know the make of the vehicle, or get the registration, he wasn't thinking straight. But when the car slowed, he managed to jump out. He showed her the friction burns on his arms. After that, he'd gone home in shock.

'Did you know any of the men?' said Sasha, and his heart began to clatter in his chest.

'I didn't, no,' he lied, but then added, 'but I've seen one of them before, the one with the Welsh accent.' The detective looked up from her notes. 'He was hanging around at an event I did yesterday morning.'

'We've a couple of photos we want to show you,' said Sasha, and nodded at the other detective, who opened the file and placed a pair of images on the table in front of him. Abs didn't want to look, but knew he had to.

'Yeah, that's him.' He pressed his finger to one of the police mugshots. The man in the photo was younger, but it was the same guy. 'That's the fella in the back of the car, the one who pulled me inside.'

Sasha Dawson placed a fingertip at the top of the other image. 'And what about this man, Abs?'

He didn't want to look at that photo, but he shifted forward to hide the fact that he was squirming in his seat, and recognized him instantly as the man watching him at the QuidStore in Basildon, Davey Jenkins.

'Yeah,' he admitted. 'That's the one sat in the front.'

'Do you remember anything else about him, Abs?' she asked. 'Maybe about the way he spoke?'

Abs's throat was very dry, as if it had also been scraped raw on the road last night. 'He was Welsh, he had an accent.'

'Do you recognize him from anywhere else?' She gave him an encouraging smile. 'Besides from the QuidStore, I mean?'

He shook his head. Abs knew why he had been abducted – and nearly killed – but he didn't want to tell the detective that, because he definitely didn't want to open that can of worms. It was a big mistake coming here.

'The man who sat in the back of the car is Stephen Gosling,' said the detective called Ajay. 'He's local to the area, he lives on Canvey Island, but grew up in Cardiff.'

Sasha Dawson tapped the second image. 'And the man who sat in the front is a known associate of his – his name is Davey Jenkins, do you recognise him?' She waited for him to respond, but he barely trusted himself to speak. 'You do, don't you, Abs?'

'He's the uncle of Rhiannon Jenkins. How...' Abs cleared his throat. 'How did you get these photos?'

'I saw Gosling in the car park at Hockley station the morning after Andrew Dean's death. A check on our database revealed a connection between the two men. Many years ago, they were both charged with public order offences. They were football hooligans, Cardiff City supporters.'

'So you think that Rhiannon's uncle killed Deano?'

Sasha smiled sadly. 'At this stage we have no evidence, but it's certainly a possibility.'

Abs felt dizzy and tried to modulate his breathing, afraid he was going to have a panic attack. 'Why... why would they want to kill me?'

'You were questioned about the disappearance of Jenkins's niece,' said the detective inspector.

'So were a lot of people,' he said quickly.

'On the night she went missing, Rhiannon Jenkins made a phone call to her uncle in which she said she was going to see you again. As you know, Mr Jenkins has always been convinced you and your friends were somehow involved in her disappearance.'

In the weeks and months after Rhiannon vanished, Jenkins was all over the tabs pointing the finger at Abs. Making pointed remarks, veiled threats, suggesting that there had been some kind of police conspiracy to protect the famous celebrity. His angry accusations were one of the reasons why Abs's career had gone down the toilet.

'How did they know where you were last night, do you think?' asked Sasha's colleague.

'The *Laid In Essex!* party was all over the media. It's a big deal every year and they probably guessed I'd be there. Or they could have followed me.' Abs felt all the terror of last night returning. Jenkins's angry face, Gosling smoking a fag as if he didn't have a care in the world, the wind billowing through the interior of the car as they raced through the streets, driving out of town to kill him. He was finding it hard to breathe. 'He's come here for revenge. Because he thinks we had something to do with... with...'

'What?' asked Sasha. Her gentle gaze was full of compassion, and right at that moment he wanted to tell her everything. He ached to lift the enormous weight of guilt off his shoulders once and for all.

Abs imagined that Sasha was his mum, not that she was a bit like his own mother, who he only remembered in flashes of memory that made him wince. When he was a little kid, just a toddler, he remembered her cruel and harsh words. He remembered her when she was pissed-up, shouting at him, calling him names, telling him how worthless he was, how he would amount to nothing.

All Abs had ever wanted was for her to love him and protect him and hold him in her arms, and all she had wanted to do was to get him out of her hair so she could carry on drinking and drugging herself into an early grave. It was no wonder that he craved to be famous, so he could be loved by as many people as possible; so that the whole country would love him, the whole world.

All his life, he could never get enough love.

'We...' He thought of Rhiannon Jenkins and felt shame and revulsion at what happened – disgust for the part he played – and he was going to tell the Silver

Lady the truth, because she was kind and sympathetic and she would understand. His voice was a croak. 'We did...'

But Abs had a shot at reuniting with Kelz and getting his career back on track, and it would be madness to give up now. Plus, there was Jez to consider, and Tony. He didn't have the right to ruin their lives. He was being selfish. His ego wasn't his amigo.

Besides, if he confessed, nobody would love him any more. The world would turn its back on him, he would be disliked, and he couldn't face that. He couldn't bear that at all.

'What, Abs?' asked Sasha softly. 'What did you do?'

'We did nothing wrong,' he told her with emotion. 'Davey Jenkins is wrong, is what he is. Please don't go to the press with this, they'll crucify me.'

'We just want to get to the bottom of why Jenkins would want to attack you,' she said, looking disappointed.

'I've had stalkers before, yeah, disturbed people who write crazy, hateful letters in purple ink, or who stalk me on the internet. People get this weird stuff in their head about famous people like me, it comes with the job. The truth is, Rhiannon left the pub we were in and we never saw her again.'

'And you have no idea what became of her?'

He grunted something, because if he spoke he was afraid of what would come out of his mouth.

'I'm sorry, Abs.' Sasha cocked her head. 'I didn't catch that.'

'No,' he said with feeling. 'We told all this to the police in Wales, me and Tony and Jez, and dearly departed Deano. Look, it's not good that this is happening right now, because I'm going back on the show.'

'Congratulations,' she said.

'Yeah, I'm going back to *Laid In Essex!*' He grinned, but the smile died on his face when he thought about what might happen to him. 'But what if he tries again to murder me? What if this Jenkins fella decides to finish the job? I need police protection.'

Now it was the detective's turn to blow out her cheeks. 'I'm afraid we don't have the resources to provide round-the-clock protection, but we can give you the best possible advice about taking the necessary precautions. We've identified suspects and that gives us the opportunity to find them quickly.' She tapped a plastic pen, one of those ones with a hole in the middle, against her chin. 'So Rhiannon Jenkins went missing three years ago.'

Abs thought he was going to burst with frustration; he didn't understand why he kept having to talk about what happened in Wales. He was a normal guy, a nice guy, a *lovable* guy, and he wasn't equipped to deal with… the truth. He didn't know anything about culture or politics or climate change, he was happy being himself,

being Abs, and conversations about serious stuff like...
the *truth* and *facts* made him confused and fearful.

He'd spent three long years trying not to think about
that terrible night, and about his part in it, and he didn't
want to keep getting reminded about it.

Not now, not ever.

Abs shoved his hands back beneath his thighs to stop
them shaking. 'Yeah, so?'

'Why now?' Sasha shrugged. 'Why wait three years
to get revenge?

'That necklace is beautiful,' he told her. 'It really suits
you.'

Sasha's hand drifted to the chain around her neck and
she smiled, and it made him stupidly happy because he
liked to make other people happy, and maybe it would
stop her talking about that effing night.

'Thank you,' she said. 'Why didn't you report the
attack on you last night, Abs?'

'I don't know,' he said miserably. 'I was in shock,
confused. I'm always confused, to be honest.'

He laughed, playing up to his image of a happy
chappy who was always a bit out of his depth, and the
thought made him laugh even harder, because right now
he was so out of his depth that it wasn't even funny.

And the detective called Sasha smiled gently as she
watched him laughing. And Abs didn't like the look of
that smile at all, not one little bit.

⋆⋆

Minutes later, he stumbled with relief out of the police station and headed towards the seafront in the early morning sun, which was already baking hot. Sometimes just looking at the churning water, with its steady, dependable rhythm, helped centre him. It was the same at night. At the end of a difficult day, Abs liked to sit on the balcony of his apartment watching the water turn gold in the last burning moments of sunset, enjoying the way its surface glittered as if it was on fire. And when it was dark he'd stay there, breathing in the sea air, listening to the surf on the beach, sensing the seething mass of it.

A faint breeze was coming in from the estuary, but Abs sweated in his hoodie as he strode quickly, trying to get as much distance as he could between him and the station. A car horn blared – someone shouted 'Abs, mate!' – and he nearly jumped out of his skin.

He headed onto Marine Parade, where the world-famous pleasure pier pushed across the water, a train transporting visitors along the length of it, its struts stretching into infinity. The arcades were already open for business, and the garbled electronic sounds and music of the games and speaker systems filled the air, competing with the traffic growling on the road and the squawks of the swooping, whirling gulls.

Last night, when Abs was absolutely certain he

wasn't being pursued anymore, he'd retraced the
terrifying journey he'd taken through the streets of
Brentwood in Jenkins's car and miraculously managed
to find his phone. It was smashed to bits, but at least he
could retrieve the SIM card – his entire life was on that
piddling bit of silicon – and he'd put it in an old phone
he found in a drawer. It rang now and he took it out.

'Mate,' he said, trying to sound chipper. 'How's it
going?'

'Hey, Abs.' Jez sounded excited. 'What are you doing
this afternoon?'

'Uh.' Abs was shattered. He was planning on going
back to his flat to kip. Maybe he'd go to the gym later
– it was days since he'd been – and then get an early
night. But he really didn't want to be alone. 'Nothing
mate, why?'

'We're having a bit of a celebration,' said Jez. 'At
Bethany's parents'.'

Beth's mum and dad had a place up near Danbury.
It wasn't quite as big as a mansion, but it came close.
'Yeah? That's nice, what's the occasion?'

Jez took a deep breath. 'Beth's pregnant, Abs. We're
gonna have a baby.'

'Oh, mate.' Abs stopped in his tracks to take in the
good news. Jez and Bethany had been trying for ages to
have a kid. 'I'm made up for you both, that's brilliant
news.'

Jez sounded so happy, his mood completely

transformed from the previous evening. 'We're over the moon, Abs.'

'Course you are. It's the best news ever, bruv.'

'You're gonna be a godparent.'

'Bethany ain't gonna stand for that.'

'I'm putting my foot down, Abs. You're gonna be a godparent, whether she likes it or not.'

It was true Abs was tired and emotional, his nerves were on edge, but he was welling up. Jez's news felt like a sign of better days to come. Abs often felt that his friend could be undermined by Bethany, henpecked even, and his becoming a dad could help put their relationship on an equal footing. Jez still had family out there somewhere, a mother and a sister – not that he'd want to go near either of those nutcases with a bargepole, from what Abs had heard – but now he'd have a brood of his own, a dynasty of little Westons.

And to think Abs had come *this close* to ruining Jez's life by blurting out a confession to the Silver Lady, just as his mate was about to embark on a wonderful new phase of his life.

'So that's what you wanted to tell me last night, yeah? That's why you were acting all funny.'

Jez said after a moment, 'I only found out this morning. You're the first person I've told.'

Abs would love to have kids, he supposed it wasn't too late, but he couldn't see Kelsey agreeing to it, not while she was still the Queen of Reality TV. He'd mentioned it to her once, dropped the possibility into conversation, and she'd thought he was angling for a spin-off show about their life bringing up a showbiz baby.

'Let me run it past my agent, babes,' she'd told him doubtfully, and they never spoke about it again.

But when he was back on the show, and once again as famous as she was, the universe would be in balance, the stars aligned, and they could get back together. They'd be the Golden Couple once again, and the world would be their oyster. Maybe then they'd have a kid of their own, which they could dress in cute designer baby gear.

'I'd love to come, mate, nothing would keep me away. And look...' He felt he had to say something about the party. 'I'm sorry about last night. We never got to have that talk. If you still want to discuss whatever it is...'

Abs held his breath.

'No, it wasn't important.' Relief washed over Abs and he hoped that now Bethany was expecting, Jez had put to bed any silly ideas he may have had about turning himself in to the police. 'Sorry I didn't stay longer. I'll see you later, yeah?'

'Wouldn't miss it for the world, geezer,' said Abs. 'Laters.'

But even as he finished the call, his positivity, the feeling that everything was going to turn out for the best, began to evaporate. Because there was still the little matter that someone was trying to kill Abs, and if they were trying to kill him, they were likely trying to kill Jez and Tony too.

Because of what happened on that night, the worst of his life, when everything went horribly wrong.

15

Three years ago

The girl clung to him all the way back to the cottage. Every time Abs removed her arm from his waist, it would creep back, or she would try to hold his hand as if they were sweethearts, and it made him feel very uncomfortable.

'Looks like you're going to have to sleep in my room tonight, Jez.' There was a nasty smirk on Deano's face, and his words were slurred. 'Abs has pulled. Bloody celebrities, they get all the luck, so there's none left for the rest of us real men.'

The girl giggled.

Swigging the last dregs of his Scotch from the bottle, Deano threw it into the dark. They heard it land somewhere with a thud. 'They should call your own show *Laid In Taffland!*'

'Which way is it now?' Abs tried to change the subject. He was feeling uncomfortable about the whole situation. He didn't want the girl to come back to the cottage, but it was pitch black and if she didn't help them find their way, he knew they could be wandering around all night.

As soon as they got back, he would go straight to bed, and there was no way she was going to climb in with him. One of the lads must have mobile reception – he'd call her a cab and shove her in, and he wouldn't take no for an answer.

They came to a lane that Abs vaguely recognized, despite the fact there were no street lights and even the light of the stars was blotted out by the canopy of trees pressing in on every side, and despite the fact that he felt very drunk and tired.

'It's this way,' Rhiannon told them.

'How do you know where we're staying, anyway?' asked Tony.

'I've been here before, with my aunt and uncle,' she told him. 'When you described the holiday home, it was obvious the one you meant.'

Deano hung an arm around Abs's shoulders. The big man's weight made him stumble, and when Deano leaned close to his ear, his breath stank. 'I'll have some of those leftovers if you're not hungry.'

'She needs to go home,' Abs told him.

'Here it is.' Rhiannon ran into the wood. Abs could just about make out the familiar outline of a cottage in the trees. 'Told you I could get you home.'

When they got inside it was freezing, and once again Abs wished he was back home in his lovely flat, with its central heating and silky bedsheets, changed twice a week by a woman who came in to clean. Jez fiddled with the boiler, which made a lot of noise but didn't generate much heat.

The first thing Deano did was turn on the porch lights, to illuminate a garden bench and a muddy clearing. 'Let there be light.'

Then he started raiding the fridge-freezer, taking out vodka and mixers and bottles of beer, and banging them on the counter. He switched the radio on, playing club classic remixes, and turned it up loud.

Abs couldn't hear himself think and turned it off. 'We need to get the girl home, yeah?'

But Rhiannon grabbed the bottle of vodka and swigged. 'You're joking, we haven't partied yet.'

Deano put the music back on and turned up the volume, then threw open a cupboard. 'Everyone grab a glass.'

'I'm hitting the sack,' said Tony with a yawn, and he headed towards his bedroom.

And with one concerned look in the direction of the girl, Jez agreed. 'Me, too.'

Abs knew his mate didn't want her there any more than he did, and tried to reason with Deano. 'It's late, mate, everyone just wants to get to sleep.'

'You're lightweights,' said the girl resentfully. 'I thought you Essex lads liked to party.'

'I know when I've had enough, sweetheart,' said Abs.

'Forget those boring wankers,' said Deano in disgust, and he started doing dance moves in front of her, a bottle of beer swinging in his fist. 'I'll party hard with ya.'

But Rhiannon looked over his shoulder, fixing her big eyes once again on Abs. 'It's not going to be fun if he ain't here,' she said with a pout.

'I know my limits, yeah?' Abs was conscious of the noise they were making in the kitchen – the bedrooms were all off the main room – and turned off the music. 'Let's go outside.'

So Rhiannon and Deano slammed out of the door and onto the porch and Abs followed them out just in time to see the big man fall off the bottom step and onto the soft earth. Deano was so pissed he probably didn't even feel it. He lay there, staring up at the night sky, laughing his head off. 'Someone moved the steps.'

The girl sidled up to Abs and took his hand, pressing her warm body against his.

'Come on, Abs,' she said, and her face lifted to his. 'How about you and me have some fun? I've come all this way now, I'm not going to be able to get home. Have one more drink with me.'

He thought of Kelsey and all his mates. He could be with them now, in one of his favourite bars or clubs, or curled up on the sofa in his apartment watching Netflix. Curled up against Kelz as she searched social media for mentions of her name.

'You're a lovely girl and everything, Rhiannon, but there's someone who wouldn't be happy.' He removed his hand from her hot grasp. 'And I love her.'

'She don't love you, Abs.' She rolled her eyes. 'It's all just for show.'

Her statement surprised him. 'Of course she does. We're soulmates.'

'If you say so.' Abs didn't like the way her eyes were fastened on his. She tugged at her bottom lip with her teeth. 'But what she don't know, don't hurt her, right?'

'That's very deep coming from someone of your age.'

'Oh, I am, Abs.' Rhiannon stared at him with an intense look of longing and he felt his resolve weakening. 'Why don't you find out how deep?'

He was so drunk that she seemed to split in two in front of him, her image separating into the distance, and he knew he badly needed to get some zeds.

'Not tonight,' he told her quietly.

She tutted. 'Shame.'

'Help me up, you bastards,' cried Deano. He was still rolling around on the ground.

It gave Abs the excuse he needed, and he went over to Deano and pulled him to his feet. They both stumbled about a bit, trying to get their balance.

'Guys.' Abs held up his hands. 'I'm going to say goodnight because I really need to get my head down.'

Deano winked at the girl. 'Yeah, you get yourself off, petal, we'll be alright, won't we, love?' He waved the bottle and Rhiannon, sensing that Abs had made up his mind, grabbed it and took a swig.

'Too right,' she said with annoyance, and went to Abs. 'What about a bedtime kiss, then?'

He craned his cheek forward. 'Just there'll be fine.'

She made a face. 'What am I meant to do with that?'

'It's the best you're going to get, doll,' he said, and twisted his mouth away.

Rhiannon sighed and planted a big, sarcastic kiss on his cheek. 'But you better give me a selfie tomorrow morning, Mister Big Sexy Celebrity.'

'It's a deal,' said Abs, relieved, and nodded at Deano. 'Take care of her.'

Deano winked. He was so pissed his facial expressions were changing every moment. 'Abs, mate,' he said with a leer.

'I mean it,' Abs told him. 'Look after her, and don't let her wander off on her own, yeah? We're in the middle of nowhere.'

Deano gave a military salute. 'You can rely on me, sah.' He sneered, like he was tired of being told what to do. No doubt keen to try his luck with the girl, he clearly wanted Abs to sod off. 'She ain't gonna go nowhere, are ya, darlin'?'

And then he put his hand around her shoulder and pulled her to his chest, smiling nastily at Abs.

Abs left them to it. When he went inside, he hesitated

in the kitchen to watch Deano and the girl sharing the bottle as they staggered towards the clearing in the wood.

Abs wondered whether he should stay up a bit longer, maybe insist that the girl got into a cab. But even if he any had reception, he didn't know if they had cabs out here in the middle of nowhere, or how long it would take for one to arrive. The sun could be rising by the time it got here.

Outside, the girl laughed at something Deano said and he took out a packet of cigarettes. It was none of his business what they got up to next, Abs decided.

They were both adults and it wasn't his place to tell either of them what to do, or how to act. So he stumbled towards the bedroom, slipping in the door as quietly as possible, feeling his way along the wall.

Leaning on the bed, he flicked off his trainers in the dark. Then he stomped out of his jeans, leaving them flattened on the carpet – he was so drunk he didn't have the strength or the will to fold them carefully like he usually would. And then his knees gave way and he toppled face down onto the bed. His mouth was scrunched up against the musty bedsheet as he listened to the drunken rattle of his own breathing in his throat. The hoot of an owl reminded him briefly where he was. This wasn't his world, this place of mud and midges and darkness.

In the dark, Abs saw Jez's body hunched under a

blanket on the mattress on the floor. Outside, the girl was giggling and Deano was roaring with laughter.

And within a matter of moments the dark room began to turn in his vision, picking up speed like a carousel, and he groaned.

16

'What do you think of this one?' Sasha asked Lolly, nodding at a dress on an online store. If she was having a romantic night away at a posh hotel, then she'd need something sophisticated and sexy to wear, but she didn't have time to hit the high street.

'Yeah.' Lolly tipped her head, considering it. 'That's nice.'

Sasha scrolled down the images on her phone, hoping for something dazzling to leap out at her and shout, *Buy me!* 'What about this one, with the long sleeves?'

'Hmm, that's nice, too.' Lolly's pursed lips suggested she thought the same about that one as she did about the others, which wasn't much, but then she gasped and excitedly grabbed the phone from Sasha's fingers to enlarge an image of an impossibly thin woman with legs up to her armpits, wearing what the ad described as a cocktail dress, but which looked more like a baby doll nightie. 'Now, I can see you in *that*.'

Sasha stared at Lolly, wondering just what she thought Sasha wore while she was doing the housework.

'Thanks, Lols,' she said diplomatically and took back the phone. 'I'll take another look later.'

'Where are we on interviewing the cousin of that missing girl?' asked DCI Vaughn, coming over.

'Girl?' asked Sasha, momentarily confused.

'Sarah Tovey, the nineteen-year-old who went missing in Brentwood the other night. Chelmsford are chasing that statement from her cousin.'

'Yes.' Sasha checked her notes and realized it hadn't been actioned. 'I'm sorry, Vaughn, I—'

'Make sure you do. Three other young women have gone missing in the past two years, similar age and profiles, both vanished after leaving friends late at night, and the investigating team is jumpy.'

'I'm on it,' she said, as if it was all under control.

'And where are we with the Andrew Dean murder?'

'Abs has positively ID'd two of the men who abducted him last night,' she told him as his phone buzzed.

Vaughn checked the screen immediately, and when he looked up, seemed distracted. 'Abs?'

'Danny Cruikshank, the reality star. He identified one of the men as Davey Jenkins, the uncle of Rhiannon Jenkins, the girl who went missing in Wales three years ago. Abs, Dean and two other men were questioned by the local police about the disappearance of the girl.'

'Sure,' he said, looking down when his phone buzzed

again. Sasha caught a glimpse of the screen as he lifted it to look at the message.

'And there was someone else in the vehicle we've identified as a local man called Stephen Gosling.'

'Uh huh.' A ghost of a smile appeared on Vaughn's face as his fingers dabbed at the screen, replying to the message.

'Gosling is a petty criminal, he's got a record for drugs offences, burglary, selling stolen goods, fraud, a lot of small-time stuff. I remember him from a case I worked on a few years back. And he's a known associate of our other suspect, Davey Jenkins.' She added, 'We believe the third suspect is a small porcupine called Gavin.'

Vaughn's reply flew away with a *whoosh* and he put the phone away. 'Good work,' he said.

This was as bad as talking to her kids. 'Gosling works at a caravan park near Shoeburyness. I'm going to see him now and I'll take Craig.'

'Keep me in the loop,' he told her.

'I'll definitely try to do that,' she said drily as he walked off.

When Vaughn had gone, she fumbled in her bag for her own phone. This time Connie deigned to pick up.

'How old are you?' Sasha asked her.

'Excuse me?'

'Vaughn has a lot on his plate at the moment, Con. We're all very busy here, we're always very busy, and the last thing he needs is you sending him silly texts every two seconds.' When she saw Lolly and Craig watching, she slunk deeper into her chair, trying once again to shield herself behind her computer monitor.

'How do you know it's me?'

'I saw the aubergine emoji, Con.'

'Me and Claude share a bond,' Connie told her indignantly. 'I think he may be it, Sash. The *One*.'

'Don't be ridiculous,' said Sasha.

'Are we going?' DC Power appeared at the side of her desk and Sasha placed the phone to her shoulder. 'One second, Craig.'

'...think the worst of me, you always have, and maybe' – Connie was already in full flow when Sasha resumed the call – 'sometimes in the past, I've even deserved that distrust, but—'

'Con,' Sasha sighed. 'It's been one night.'

'Yes, and I'm as surprised – so wonderfully, delightfully, romantically surprised – as you are, Sash. I know it's been a long time since you've felt that way with Kev – after all, you've been together practically *forever* – but sometimes you just know straight away. This could be it.'

'He's my boss, Connie, and my friend.'

There was a meaningful pause on the other end, and then Connie said, 'I understand.'

Sasha rubbed her eyes hard and when the undulating stars and shapes finally floated from her vision, she became aware that Craig was still standing beside her. 'I've got to go, Con.'

'See you tonight, darling,' said Connie softly, and Sasha groaned inwardly at the thought of her sister and parents arriving at her house, but it was too late to cancel now. She killed the call and scribbled a note to remind Kev about the supermarket delivery arriving this afternoon, and maybe get him to pop to the shops if they needed more nibbles and wine. He'd know what to get – after all, they'd been together practically *forever*.

'Everything alright?' asked Craig.

Sasha rearranged her irritated expression into what she hoped was a dazzling smile. 'Of course I am, Craig, everything's just *lovely*. Are you ready?'

'I was born ready,' he said.

'Right.' She stood, eager to get out of the office and into the fresh air. 'Let's go, Power Man.'

17

Sasha drove with the top down on her Spider Veloce, taking the A13 to the edge of Southend where the former garrison town of Shoeburyness sat at the mouth of the Thames estuary. It was only a short journey, but it was a relief to get out of the office and enjoy the wind in her face on another blazing hot day.

'Put this on.' She offered Craig a floppy hat imprinted with flowers. Sasha knew how easy it was to get burned on the top of the head driving about under the hot sun, and had taken to wearing one herself. 'Go on.'

He took the hat and placed it on his head, morosely adjusting it in the side mirror, but whipped it off almost immediately.

'I can't,' he said, and she knew he didn't want to look uncool.

'Suit yourself,' she told him, pushing her sunnies up her nose.

The caravan park was buzzing when they got there. It was the height of the season and was packed. As Sasha parked – the suffocating heat enveloping the vehicle as soon as she cranked the handbrake – she saw kids screaming and splashing about in a swimming pool outside the main building. The glittering aquamarine water danced and leaped as the children cannonballed into the middle of the pool or fought for ownership of the lilos that ricocheted about on the surface. The area around the pool – the concrete surround and the faded brown lawn – was full of holidaymakers slathered in sun cream and walking about in bikinis and trunks and flip-flops. They sat in fold-up chairs staring at their phones, or sprawled on sunbeds.

In every direction were rows of caravans. There were long static ones the size of small homes, with porches and pot plants, and some had little white picket fences around them, with tiny gardens of fake grass; and there were tow caravans of all shapes and sizes, short and stubby, long and thin.

The snaking silver hose of a portable air-conditioning unit poked out of the door of the reception building. The unit made a lot of noise, as if it was working hard, but it was still as hot as a sauna inside. Sasha's skin was damp at the hairline from where she'd worn the hat, but Craig looked like he'd been dragged through a blast furnace, and he walked straight out again, saying, 'I'll wait outside.'

She brought the heel of her hand down sharply on a small bell and a thin, harassed-looking woman appeared from a small office behind the desk.

'I'm sorry, we're full,' she said in a voice that suggested she wasn't very sorry at all.

'Detective Inspector Dawson, Essex Police.' Sasha placed her warrant card on the counter and pushed it towards the woman. 'I'm looking for Stephen Gosling.'

'You mean Steve Gosling?'

'That would be him.' Sasha smiled. 'I understand he works here.'

'Hah, you would think that,' said the woman sardonically. 'Although it's not like he actually does eff all.'

'Is he here right now?'

'Yeah.' She jerked a thumb. 'You can usually find him in the bar.'

The tables outside the park's social club were crammed with semi-naked people with burned shoulders, who watched curiously over their pints as Sasha and Craig walked past in their jackets and long trousers – she felt very hot and overdressed – and into the bar. Stephen Gosling sat at a table near the toilets, sipping a pint of lager in a tee-shirt cut off at the arms, a pair of cargo shorts and heavy boots.

'Stephen Gosling?' Sasha sat on the stool opposite him and pushed a second half-empty pint glass to the side. 'I'm Detective Inspector Sasha Dawson and this is my colleague, Detective Constable Power. You probably don't remember me, but we met a number of years ago.'

He blinked at her, and then glanced up at Craig, who leaned with his arms folded against a fruit machine. 'How you doing?'

'It's scorchio out there.' Sasha blew sharply upwards and her damp fringe lifted limply off her forehead. 'I hope you're wearing sunscreen.'

He gave her a nasty smile, his gaze drifting behind her. 'What have I done?'

'Stephen Gosling,' she told him. 'I am arresting you for kidnapping. You do not have to say anything, but it may harm your defence if you do not mention when questioned something which you later rely on in court. Anything you do say may be given in evidence. Do you understand?'

'Oh, come on,' he said very loudly, and his eyes darted over her shoulder again. 'I'm being arrested?'

'Stand up please, Stephen.' She nodded at Craig, who took out a pair of handcuffs.

Gosling pushed his drink away, and stood quickly, 'Let's go, then, and get this over with.' Sasha saw his eyes flick urgently past her again as he held out his wrists to be cuffed.

'You're keen, Stephen, and speaking very loudly.'

'Come on, I haven't got all day,' he said, just as she heard the blast of a hand-dryer.

She nodded at the second glass on the table. 'Did we interrupt anything?'

The door of the men's toilets behind her opened and

a man stepped out. Davey Jenkins stopped dead in his tracks when he saw Sasha and Craig.

'Good morning.' She hoped he would immediately see sense, but Jenkins looked around wildly. 'Davey, don't—'

He raced towards Craig, twisting away from him at the last moment and shoving him hard into the machine, making him lose his footing. Jenkins rushed out of the door, but Craig was on his feet in a heartbeat and chased after him. Sasha took a moment to finish handcuffing Gosling to a bracket on the wall, then flew to the door. Jenkins was running around the edge of the swimming pool, leaping over the people sprawled out on the concrete, with Craig in hot pursuit.

Sasha was about to shout to Craig to stop. The last thing she needed was for him to throw himself onto Jenkins and for the both of them to fall into the pool, which was teeming with kids. Then Craig slipped on the wet surface, both his feet left the ground and for one terrible moment she thought he was going to tumble, but he managed to keep going, disappearing out of the gate, following Jenkins across the grass towards the caravans.

Sasha raced through the crowd as best she could, weaving in and out of all the half-naked men and women wandering about – 'Excuse me, excuse me, coming through!' – and out of the gate. Up ahead, Craig was moving like a steam train towards the older man. Jenkins headed deeper into the park, hoping perhaps to lose his pursuers in the numerous grass alleys between the caravans, and then disappeared behind one of the units, followed by Craig.

Once upon a time, before her kids were born, Sasha had been fit and sporty. She ran long distances, swam regularly at a local pool and played badminton, but she felt out of shape now. Sweat poured down her forehead and neck. It occurred to her that she was wearing a jacket during the hottest part of the day and tried to shrug it off as she ran, but the damp lining turned inside out and the jacket clung stubbornly to one arm. She yanked it off and let it fall to the ground.

And then ahead of her, Craig came back into view, circling one particular caravan, cupping his eyes against the windows, which were covered with thick net curtains. A car, a Nissan, was parked on the grass between the caravan and its neighbour on the far side.

'He's inside.' Craig was panting as she came trotting towards him, bracing her hands on her hips to try to get her breath back, her sopping shirt clinging to the small of her back.

'Are you sure?'

'He went in there and slammed the door shut,' he told her, triumphantly banging his hand against the metal shell of the caravan. 'We've got him, trapped like a rat in a can.'

18

'We know you're in there, Davey, we saw you go inside.' Sasha banged her fist on the door as Craig walked around the caravan, calling for backup on his phone. 'Please come out. You should know that more officers are on the way.'

Holidaymakers had gathered to watch, in shorts and tee-shirts and swimsuits, standing barefoot on the grass, drinking bottles of beer and licking ice creams. Someone was holding up a phone, filming the goings-on.

'Don't do that, please.' Sasha pointed at the party in question. The last thing she needed was for the scene to be posted all over YouTube or whatever, particularly as she was looking very sweaty and bedraggled.

'What's going on?' asked the woman from reception, walking towards her.

'Whose caravan is this?'

'It's one of the ones we use to accommodate staff overnight,' said the woman.

'Gosling uses it?'

'He'll have access, yes.'

Craig came over, putting away his phone. 'Help's on its way.'

'Do you hear that, Davey?' Sasha shouted at the door. 'There's no way out, so why don't you just come out?'

But there was no response from inside and Sasha looked questioningly at Craig.

'I saw him run in there.' He pressed one hand against the metal surround of the door. 'I could probably get this door open easily enough. All it'll take is one good kick.'

'You'll break your ankle.' Sasha told him. 'Let's wait till we have more bodies on the scene.'

'You can't break down the door,' said the woman. 'That's private property.'

Sasha held out her hand. 'Do you have a key?'

'I don't have the authority to give you a key,' said the woman.

'The person we believe is inside—'

'He *is* inside,' Craig insisted.

'Is wanted for questioning about the murder of one man and the abduction of another.' Sasha clawed back her fringe in the unbearable midday sun. 'So you talk to whoever you have to, get a spare from the office. Or we can get a key off Gosling, or force entry. Either way, as soon as we have more bodies here, we're going inside that caravan.'

'The park owners will be livid.'

'And we're probably going to have to search all these caravans,' Sasha told her, in no mood for games.

'What?' The woman was shocked. 'It's the height of the season, there are hundreds of people staying here, you can't just search everyone's caravan.'

'We're investigating a murder,' said Sasha, making a big show of looking around. 'Now let me see, if we're being thorough, the search will take a few days, maybe up to a week. Getting a warrant won't be easy, but I'll do everything in my power to get one, and I promise you I'll get as many police vehicles, specialist units and sniffer dogs as I can fit through that gate. You'll be surprised what turns up in a search. And, oh, we'll have to interview all your occupants.' Sasha smiled. 'Your TripAdvisor reviews will make *very* interesting reading.'

'I'll get a key,' said the woman, stomping off.

When she had gone, Sasha watched Craig restlessly circling the caravan. She could see how tense and impatient he was. 'We're not going to go in till backup arrives.'

He snorted. 'It's just one guy.'

'Craig,' she said quietly. 'Both of us have nearly got killed jumping into unpredictable situations feet first, so we're going to wait. He's inside, he's not going anywhere.'

Then she stepped away to call the office and when she had done that, she wrangled the crowd further back across the grass.

'Step back please, sir, for your own safety,' Sasha said to one man who came forward to ask what was going on, and she told one little boy, 'I love your tee-shirt,' before asking his mother to move him away.

She didn't notice the admin woman arrive with a key on the end of a heavy wooden peg until she heard a shout behind her. Craig had taken the key and was shouldering his way inside.

'David Jenkins, get on the floor,' he shouted.

Sasha ran to the caravan and jumped up the step. Squeezing in beside him at the door, she was stunned to find nobody inside.

'But he was in here,' insisted Craig angrily.

He moved further into the caravan to slap open the toilet door opposite and reveal an empty cubicle. It was impossible for Jenkins to hide. The space was small, twenty foot or so from one end to the other, and the windows were shut; there was simply no way he could have climbed out. And then Sasha saw that the corner of a piece of carpet was partially folded over at the kitchen end. Pulling the carpet up, she revealed a trapdoor – and a dark patch of grass beneath the caravan. The space was narrow, but Jenkins could have crawled underneath and out while they were both at the door.

'Damn it.' Craig punched the wall in frustration as Sasha hopped down the step, into the blinding sunlight and sweltering heat, just as a pair of patrol cars, lights flashing, appeared at the entrance of the park. Jenkins could still be close, hiding somewhere on site, or in the surrounding area.

And then she heard the loud roar of an engine, and the Nissan swung out between the two caravans and into her path. The crowd reared back as it turned sharply towards the entrance and accelerated, its back wheels sliding on the dry grass. Sasha caught a glimpse of Jenkins behind the wheel, but then the car hit a hard ridge of mud, the underside crunched, and he lost control.

The car came straight towards her. Sasha was paralysed with indecision as it bore down on her, but then she was flung off her feet and thrown clear. She hit the grass hard, felt chips of hard mud whip her face, a sharp pain in her shoulder as Craig's heavy body landed on top of her.

Hurtling past, the Nissan veered left and right as Jenkins tried to gain control of it, clipping a water standpipe and then swerving into the path of a police car coming the other way. It crashed through a picket fence and crunched into the side of a caravan, coming to a shuddering halt.

Sasha watched it all happen – the whole thing seemed to last as long as a single heartbeat – and then dropped her head back to the ground, breathing hard, barely able to see for the stinging sweat pouring into her eyes.

19

Just as they were about to go in, Sasha pulled Craig aside outside the interview room at Victoria Avenue. 'What part of wait-for-backup did you not understand?'

He held up his hands. 'I heard a noise coming from inside and thought Jenkins was opening a window.'

'Jenkins is a murder suspect, and I wasn't prepared to go inside until we had more officers there. I don't know how many times I have to tell you, Craig, you don't have to make every arrest single-handed. Please don't make me put you on report.'

'I thought he was escaping,' said the DC in annoyance. Craig was using the so-called noise he said he heard coming from the caravan as a convenient excuse to gain entrance, but she had to admit he was right about Jenkins not being inside. 'And I did push you out of the way of that car, I *did* save your life.'

'Well, there is that,' she conceded, and turned the handle of the door. 'Don't do it again.'

Inside the small, nondescript room, she went to

the table arranged against the near wall and took a chair opposite the duty solicitor, motioning for Davey Jenkins, who stood waiting against the far wall, to do the same. He fell into the chair beside the lawyer as Sasha arranged her notes in front of her.

'Davey Jenkins, you do not have to say anything, but it may harm your defence if you do not mention when questioned something which you later rely on in court. Anything you do say may be given in evidence.' She got him to confirm his name and address, and then said, 'You know why you're here, Mr Jenkins?'

'I didn't have anything to do with Andrew Dean's death, if that's what I'm being accused of.'

'We'll get to that in a moment,' she said, watching him fold his arms tightly across his chest.

In the photos of Jenkins on the police database, which were taken a number of years ago, he was a handsome man with chiselled features and a full head of salt-and-pepper hair. But now he was in his mid-fifties and sliding down the slippery slope of late middle age. His blue eyes were still clear, but his cheeks and nose were ruddy and his jowls thickened beneath his chin, obliterating the sharp line of a once strong jaw.

'What about the abduction of Abs,' she asked him. 'I suppose that wasn't you either?'

'Listen to you calling him Abs, like it's his real name,' he said with a smirk. 'You've bought into his celebrity bullshit, like all those other plebs.'

'That is his name, isn't it, to all intents and purposes? Everyone calls him that.'

Jenkins shoved the heel of a hand into his eye. 'Let's just get on with it. Ask your questions.'

'Abs... Mr Cruikshank identified you and Stephen Gosling as two of the men who forced him into a car last night in Brentwood. He said you abducted him and that he was afraid for his life. He says you threatened to kill him.'

'I never did that.' Davey Jenkins shook his head. 'I mean, yes, we intended to take him somewhere, but we had no intention of killing him.'

'Then what was your intention?' asked Sasha.

Jenkins leaned forward on his elbows. 'We were going to have some fun with the little man.'

'What does that mean?'

'We were going to take him somewhere and rough him up a bit. There, I said it. We were going to give him a bit of a slap, a kicking, but kill him?' He made a face. 'Nah.'

'Why?' said Sasha. 'For what reason would you want to assault him?'

He nodded at the slim file in front of her. 'You know why, I've got unfinished business with that mincing prat. Because of what happened to Rhiannon, because of what they did to her.'

A vein in his neck pulsed when he said his niece's name.

'Okay, then. You've threatened Andrew Dean, Abs, Jeremy Weston and Tony Gardner on more than one occasion. You were quoted in the press soon after they were interviewed about the disappearance of your niece and released *without charge*, as saying that they would…' She took from the folder a photocopy of a newspaper article and read from it. 'Face retribution.'

'In the anger of the moment, my phrasing was… unfortunate. I was grieving.'

'But what did you mean?' said Sasha.

'I meant justice in a court of law.' Jenkins swallowed. 'I was angry, I felt powerless, but it doesn't mean I'd kill four people.' He looked her in the eye. 'Even if they're as guilty as hell.'

'You think she's dead?'

'After all this time?' Jenkins snorted in contempt. 'What do *you* think happened to her?'

'But that wasn't the only time you made threats about those men, Davey. You've made other veiled remarks in the press about how they'll get what's coming to them.'

'That's *Mr* Jenkins to you,' he told her, and she nodded in apology. 'Journalists love a juicy quote and they know how to manipulate you into giving them one.'

'Tell me about the night Rhiannon disappeared,' said Sasha.

'What's the point?' he snapped. 'I told you cops at the time and nothing was done.'

'It'll help me understand a little bit better what's going on here.'

Davey Jenkins wearily pulled his hands down his face.

'What you have to know about Rhiannon is that she had a difficult upbringing. Her mother died when she was a little 'un, and she was brought up by her dad. I love him, of course I do, but if there was ever a man ill-equipped to be a parent, it's my brother Owen. He's spent his life down the bookies, or pissing away his earnings, and was never home. And so Rhiannon went a bit wild, she could be a bit of a handful. Me and the wife tried to help out as much as we could, and took her on holiday with us every year. We didn't have kids, it just never happened for us, and we treated Rhiannon as if she was our own. We'd go somewhere sunny, a resort in Greece or Spain, and she loved that. But that last year we decided to have one of those staycations.' His voice cracked with emotion. 'Worst decision I ever made.'

'My client is upset,' interrupted the lawyer. 'Maybe we should break.'

'No.' Jenkins held up a hand. 'I want to say this.' He stared down at the table, and Sasha and Craig waited for him to gather his thoughts. 'Things weren't great at home at that time. We all knew what she got up to in Cardiff, clubbing and getting off her face. She was just a young girl, they all do that I suppose. So we went up to Edeyrnion, in Denbighshire. It's beautiful up there, we'd taken Rhiannon there when she was a little girl. The wife and I thought we'd all do healthy stuff like go for long walks and outward bound centres, and eat nice meals in the evenings, get some early nights. The idea was to give Rhiannon peace and quiet, a bit of time to chill out, but, of course, she hated every moment of it. She was bored and restless, and sat on her phone the whole time, texting mates.

'And that one night, just that night, she asked to go out on her own. Just to the local pub, she said, because she was bored of sitting in the B&B of an evening. And I said…' He sighed. 'I said yes. Rhiannon was so pleased and relieved, and she put on a nice dress and all her make-up like she was going to the biggest nightclub in town rather than a shitty little pub in the middle of nowhere. She looked a million dollars, she took our breath away.' His eyes lifted to Sasha's. 'And we never saw her again.'

Davey Jenkins sat back and folded his arms. 'Her dad, Owen, has got no one in his final days. The cancer's got him now and I reckon he's got six months left in him, tops. We're not close now, because of what happened.' Jenkins cleared his throat. 'I can't give him back his daughter, but I can find out the truth before he dies. And that's why I grabbed the *celebrity* off the street, because I wanted to find out what he did with Rhiannon. Not to kill him, more's the pity, but just to find out the truth.'

'Why do you blame them still?' asked Sasha, absently

moving her pen between her fingers. 'Abs and Andrew Dean, Jeremy Weston and Tony Gardner were all released without charge. They were just four of many people in the pub that night. Rhiannon was seen leaving at ten o'clock, more than two hours before they left the premises. Why do you think it was them?'

'That night, after she left the pub, she rang me from a payphone,' he said. 'We'd agreed that she'd come back to the hotel at eleven, that was the deal, so me and the wife could go to sleep and not worry about where she was. I'd made it very clear to Rhiannon before she left, but she called me at half ten to tell me she was going to be back late. I was fuming, but she told me not to worry. We had words about it, we argued.

'What I should have done is tell her to stay where she was, and go and pick her up. But I was lying on the bed with a brandy in one hand and the TV remote in the other, and I didn't. I asked her to tell us where she was going, at least. She wouldn't, but her last words to me before she put down the phone were that she was going to be famous. *You'll read about me in the papers, Uncle Davey*. I didn't know what she was talking about at the time, what on earth did that mean, but afterwards it all became clear. She was going to wait for the celebrity, and his gang. She intended to sleep with him, and I think she got her wish. The police dismissed the call at the time, of course, because they assumed someone snatched her while she was waiting.'

He leaned forward so suddenly that Sasha had to force herself not to flinch. 'Cruikshank, that *Abs*—' He spat out the name. 'He thinks that because he's famous he can get away with anything, even murder.'

'The cottage where the four men were staying was examined, and no trace of her was found.'

'Yeah.' Jenkins snorted in disgust. 'It was spotless, from what I heard. When was the last time you heard of a holiday home rented out by four young men that was left sparkling clean and tidy afterwards? I'm expected to believe that some random came along and took her? Rhiannon would never have gone with a stranger, but she wanted to be famous more than anything, she wanted to be on TV, and that wish got her killed.'

'Where were you on Tuesday—'

'Oh, give over,' said Jenkins angrily. 'I didn't come all this way to kill Andrew Dean. I've been a bad boy, I know people, and it wouldn't be difficult for someone with my connections to find someone to do it for me. Why are you asking me all these questions when you should be talking to those three men? To Cruikshank and Weston and Gardner? Do your job, *do – your – job!*'

He leaped suddenly to his feet, fists bunched, making his chair tip back behind him. The duty lawyer gawped. Craig Power was about to hit the emergency button on the wall – the interview was being captured on a live

video feed and officers would already be on their way –
but Sasha touched his wrist. *Wait.*

Jenkins stood in the middle of the room, breathing
hard, his face twisted in misery and anger.

'Mr Jenkins.' Sasha stood slowly. 'Sit down, please.'

'I shouldn't be here. They should be here. *They* should
be rotting in prison.'

The door opened and three officers flew inside, but
Sasha held up an arm. *Stay back.*

'They killed her, they killed Rhiannon,' shouted
Davey Jenkins. 'And you people have done nothing.'

'Are you finished?' Sasha asked him softly.

Jenkins covered his face and began to cry. 'And it's all
my fault because I let her go to that pub.'

'It's not your fault.' Sasha nodded at the officers –
We're fine – and they reluctantly backed out of the
room. Jenkins staggered to the wall and sobbed into his
hands, tears pouring through his fingers.

Sasha picked up the chair, placed it upright. 'Davey,
please.'

He returned to his seat and crumpled into it miserably.

'I took Abs for a ride, yes, so throw the book at me,
it's what I deserve.' He wiped a sleeve across his nose.
'But I didn't kill Andrew Dean.'

'Where were you, Davey?' Sasha asked.

'I was in town, having a meal at a restaurant,' he said.
'Catching up with some mates from around here.'

Sasha clicked the top of her pen. 'What's it called?'

'No idea, but it's a place in Westcliff. Steve will know, he took us all there. We were there from about ten to midnight.'

'You have witnesses, of course.'

'A whole restaurant full.' He shrugged, all the anger in him burned out. 'And I can do better than that, because I paid by credit card.'

'Why was Stephen Gosling at Hockley train station the morning after Andrew Dean was killed?'

'We got word from someone we knew around there about what happened, someone who was helping us out. I couldn't believe Dean was dead, so I sent Steve to take a look.' He sniffed. 'It's not going to happen, is it?'

'What isn't, Davey?'

'I'm not going to find out what happened to Rhiannon before my brother dies.'

'We'll be charging you with kidnap,' she told him.

'All Rhiannon wanted is to be *someone*, all she wanted was to be famous. She was intending to bed him, that Abs, and she was never seen again.' He lifted his red, swollen eyes to Sasha's. 'So I say it again, *do your job*.'

20

In the incident room later that afternoon, Sasha rolled her chair across the office when Lolly called her over. 'What have you got?'

Lolly clicked open a video file on her desktop and the image expanded across the screen: the interior of the Westcliff restaurant where Davey Jenkins said he was dining at the time of Andrew Dean's death.

'He was there alright. He had a meal with his mates and paid for it, and it's all on CCTV.'

They sat and watched the footage taken from a camera high on the ceiling. Jenkins was sitting eating a meal on the far side of the room with four friends, Stephen Gosling included. There didn't look to be much in the way of sparkling conversation; the meal progressed in virtual silence. Sasha and Lolly watched Gosling pick up some ribs with his fingers.

'He could have paid for someone else to do it,' said Lolly. 'It could be a contract killing.'

'But then why come all the way to the scene of the

crime, when he could be two hundred miles away in Cardiff while the deed is done.' They watched the men pass the salt shaker around the table, and because no other question occurred to her, Sasha asked, 'What did Jenkins have?'

'According to the restaurant bill, plaice and chips and three pints of Stella. I've been there, actually, they do a decent chicken burger.'

'Very good.' Sasha dug her heels into the floor, ready to roll her chair back to her desk, but Lolly touched her arm.

'Wait a minute, Sash, you'll want to see this.'

A moment later, a small square of light flashed on the table beside Jenkins – a text arriving on his phone – and he looked down at it, then climbed out of his chair.

'Where's he going, to the toilet?'

'Man of his age, it's a wonder he lasted that long,' said Ajay, standing behind them.

'He went to the loo twice, earlier,' Lolly told him.

She closed the file and opened another. This time the CCTV came from a camera positioned above the door outside the restaurant, where the light was murkier. They saw a small sliver of the car park. Davey Jenkins came out and stood smoking at the edge of the frame, as other customers went in and out. When he'd finished, he ground the fag beneath his foot, and waited with his hands in his pockets.

'Why doesn't he go back in?'

Lolly pointed at the screen. 'Wait for it.'

Sasha rolled her chair closer to the desk in anticipation, clashing knees with Lolly. A few moments later on the screen, Jenkins was caught in the glare of headlights. The nose of a car appeared at the edge of the CCTV image as the vehicle pulled up in front of him. The headlights died. Then Davey stepped off the pavement and walked just out of shot to speak with whoever was in the car. A couple of minutes later, he walked back into the restaurant, caught once again in the glare of the reversing headlights.

'Run it back a smidgen,' said Sasha and Lolly rewound the footage.

'No, that's too much.' Sasha twirled her finger frantically in front of the screen. 'I said a smidgen.'

'I don't know what a smidgen is.'

'It's a tiny bit,' said Ajay.

When they finally got the right segment – Jenkins walking back into the restaurant – Sasha brought her fingers down hard on the space bar, pausing the image.

'There.' She pressed the screen to indicate Jenkins slipping something cylindrical into his pocket. 'What's that?'

'It looks like a lot of rolled-up money.'

'What's that all about?' asked Lolly.

Sasha turned to Ajay behind her to ask him to get Jenkins back into an interview room, but he was already walking away.

'On it,' he said, with a wave over his shoulder.

21

'Bethany Weston?' Sasha flashed her warrant card on the doorstep. 'I'm Detective Inspector Sasha Dawson, Essex Police, and this is my colleague, Detective Constable Lolly Chambers.'

The woman blinked. 'Is this about Jez?'

Seeing Bethany's husband standing on the first-floor landing, Sasha smiled gently. 'Actually, we're here to speak to you.'

Checking up and down the street to see if any of the neighbours had seen the police officers, Bethany stepped back from the entrance of her Clifftown home, motioning for them to step quickly inside. She wore a Diane von Furstenberg wrap dress – Sasha clocked how expensive it was – with tall heels, and a full mask of make-up.

'Me and Jez are just on the way out,' she said, flustered.

'We won't keep you long.'

'You have a lovely house.' Lolly gazed around the large reception. 'And lots of lovely things.'

'Thank you,' said Bethany with an unfriendly smile, and looked over her shoulder in irritation. 'I'd get my housekeeper to take your coats, but I don't know where she is right now.'

'What's this about?' Jez Weston came down the stairs. 'Why do you want to speak to my wife?'

'Is there somewhere private we can speak?' Sasha asked Bethany.

'No,' Bethany said tersely. 'Jez might as well hear whatever you have to say. Come into the library.'

'Wow,' said Lolly, walking into the room, with its bookcases full of leather-bound books. 'I've never seen so many books in my life. How many of these have you read?'

Bethany ignored the question. 'Please, sit.'

Sasha perched on a sofa in the middle of the room and felt her bum immediately slide down the back of the slippery leather, forcing her legs up in the air. To keep her dignity, she heaved herself forward to perch on the edge of the cushion.

Standing at the mantelpiece, Bethany glanced nervously at Jez, who followed them into the room and shut the door.

'We've just found out I'm pregnant,' she told Sasha and Lolly quickly. 'Which is why we're going out this afternoon. My parents are having a gathering for family and friends.'

'Congratulations,' Sasha told them both. 'We won't keep you very long. Where were you on Tuesday night, Mrs Weston?'

'You can't believe I killed Andrew Dean?' Bethany's voice was shrill. 'I would never—'

'You're not a suspect,' said Sasha with a reassuring smile.

Bethany didn't know where to look. 'If you're here already, then it seems to me that you know where I went.'

'What is she talking about? I thought you said you were staying in.' Jez frowned at his wife. 'Bethany?'

'I've done nothing wrong.' She met his concerned gaze. 'I was merely... protecting you, the both of us.'

They heard the front door bell ring, but neither Jez nor Bethany moved. Instead, the housekeeper's footsteps clipped along the hallway.

'What did you do?' said Jez.

When Bethany spoke, she addressed her answer to her husband. 'I went to see that Jenkins person, the uncle of the girl who... the one you were questioned about.'

'What did you go to see him about?' asked Sasha.

Bethany took a steadying breath. 'I paid him money to leave us alone.'

Jez shook his head, confused. 'You did what?'

The door to the library swung open and Abs leaped inside, wearing a white hoodie with an ostentatious brand logo covering the entire chest, skinny jeans and his usual dazzling white trainers.

'She's done it, Kelz has got me back on the show!' He dropped to his knees and lifted his arms to the heavens like a striker celebrating a winning goal in front of an adoring crowd. 'I just heard from Vince, we're filming tomorrow morning. I'm back on *Laid In Essex!*, guys, Abs is back!' He jumped up, whooping and clapping. 'Let's get this party started!'

But Abs froze when he saw Sasha and Lolly on the chesterfield, and Jez and Bethany standing grimly at the mantelpiece. 'What's up?'

'Do you mind waiting outside, please, Abs?' said Bethany shortly.

'No,' Jez told her. 'He stays, I want him to hear this.'

Abs looked at them. 'Will somebody tell me what's going on?'

'The reason Davey Jenkins hasn't been following me,' Jez told him, 'the reason I haven't been attacked or threatened, is because Bethany paid him not to.'

'He turned up here one night,' Bethany told the room. 'This was a week ago or so now, but you were out. Jenkins said he wanted to get to the truth about what happened to that girl and wouldn't stop until he got it. I told him to go away, but he was very insistent and intimidating, and I was afraid.' Bethany reached for

Jez's hand, but he moved it down to his side. 'The last thing I wanted to do was worry you, Jez, but I'm afraid I panicked and phoned Daddy. I didn't know what else to do.' She appealed to Sasha. 'Daddy's been in business for a long time and it just so happens that he and this Jenkins had business acquaintances in common.'

Sasha knew that Bethany's father had been convicted for various offences as a young man and had unsavoury connections in the murky hinterland where business meets crime.

'Daddy reached out to him and suggested we... give Davey Jenkins money to make him go away. Mr Jenkins was happy to take our money, and I was happy to give it, to ensure that he left us alone.'

'I thought you were at home on Tuesday?' Jez said.

'I slipped out to give him the money at a restaurant in Westcliff while you were playing cards with your friends.'

'Wait a minute,' said Abs. 'Why didn't you say anything to the cops? If you told them Davey Jenkins came here and threatened you, he may not have come after *me*, and Deano may still be alive.'

Bethany rested an elbow on the mantelpiece. Above her hung a large portrait photo of her and Jez on their wedding day. Sasha was fascinated by the photo, in which the happy couple faced each other holding hands in front of a gnarled old oak tree. Jez was in his tailcoat and Bethany wore the biggest, puffiest wedding dress Sasha had ever seen; she looked like an enormous marshmallow. The train snaked around the trunk of the tree and into the distance. Sasha had no idea how Bethany had managed to get the dress to fit into the limo, or more likely the pony and trap, to the church.

'Davey Jenkins has an alibi for the night of Andrew Dean's death,' she said, peeling her eyes away from the portrait. 'Mrs Weston met him at the restaurant barely half an hour before his death. That's not to say that he's not involved in Dean's death, he's still a person of interest to us, but we don't have any evidence at this stage to suggest he's responsible.'

'I knew nothing about this, I swear,' Jez told Abs. 'And if I did, I would have put a stop to it and made sure it was reported to the police straight away.'

'That Welsh thug kidnapped me,' said Abs, blinking in disbelief. 'He was going to *murder* me.'

'He said that wasn't his intention,' Sasha told him.

'Oh,' said Abs sarcastically. 'Well, I'm glad we got that cleared up, the Silver Lady says he wouldn't have killed me, so let's pop the champagne. At the very least, he was going to take me somewhere and torture me, go all Marathon Man on my mouth.' He gave everyone a good look at his perfect choppers. 'I paid good money for these.'

'When Mr Jenkins came here,' said Bethany, bristling, 'he was very emotional and I convinced him that Jez knows nothing about the disappearance of that poor girl.'

'But I do, right?'

'Will you let me finish?' Bethany snapped. 'He was very insistent in his accusations and to smooth the way, to convince him of mine and Jez's good faith, I gave him money. I had no idea he would come after you next.'

Abs snorted.

'How much?' Jez demanded of his wife. 'What did you give him?'

'Twenty,' she said quietly. 'Twenty thousand.'

Abs whistled. 'Twenty grand.'

'It came from my father and what he chooses to do with his money is up to him.'

Abs threw up his arms in anger. 'You fed me to the wolves.'

'We're having a child, my darling,' Bethany told Jez impatiently. 'I can't... I will not... have this kind of stress in my life. I will not have what happened to that girl, God rest her soul, hanging over us for the rest of our lives. I did it for me, for you – for our baby.'

'You left the restaurant almost immediately after you met Davey Jenkins,' Sasha said to her. 'Did you go anywhere else that night where you would have been seen?'

'I bought petrol from a station on the way home, and picked up a bottle of wine. It's only ten minutes from here, and I have a receipt.'

'We can check the CCTV if you give us the name of the station, and can we see that receipt?'

'I think it's still in my bag. I'll get Pauline to bring it.' Bethany looked in frustration at her watch. 'We're going to be late for the party. Mummy and Daddy will be worried.'

'We won't keep you much longer.'

As Sasha heaved herself off the sofa, Bethany opened the door to shout for the housekeeper. 'Pauline, can you bring my bag from the kitchen, please?' She listened and got no response. 'Oh, for God's sake, I'll get it myself.'

When she left the room, Abs said to Sasha, 'You don't think it's Davey Jenkins, then, who killed Deano?'

'He has an alibi for the evening,' she told him. 'But our investigation is ongoing.'

'Glad to hear it.'

'He's been charged with kidnapping and we'll be asking him about the money he took from Mrs Weston.'

'Has Beth committed any crime?' asked Jez.

'In other circumstances she'd be in danger of perverting the course of justice, but it sounds like she was put in an impossible position. We'll speak to Davey Jenkins again and maybe add extortion to his charge sheet, but we'll need Mrs Weston to come to the station to make an official statement.'

Jez nodded.

'What if he comes for me again, or for Tony?' asked Abs. 'What if he wants to take this further?'

'Mr Jenkins will remain in custody for the foreseeable,' she assured him.

'Have you spoken to Tony?' Jez asked Abs. 'I haven't heard from him.'

'Nor me.'

'It's time we went to see him,' Sasha said, glancing at Lolly.

The door opened. Bethany came back in with her purse and gave Sasha a receipt.

'I filled the tank on the way back from the restaurant. You can see the time,' she said, pointing at the slip. 'Jez and I have GPS trackers fitted to our cars, in case they're stolen, so you'll be able to see exactly the route I took.'

'You don't like me much, Bethany, do ya?' said Abs, moving restlessly about the room.

'Don't be ridiculous,' she said shortly.

'I don't get it. What have I ever done to you?'

'Abs.' Jez reached out to calm his friend, but Abs yanked his elbow away and went over to her.

'You've always looked down on me. Was it because I'm on the telly?'

'Were,' said Bethany with a venomous smile. 'You *were* on the telly.'

'Or because I'm a bit common, and I've got a big mouth.'

'Abs, please,' she hissed. 'You're embarrassing yourself.'

Jez sighed. 'Abs...'

'No, I want to hear it. What have I ever done to you?' He gestured at Lolly. 'I mean, everyone loves Abs.'

'You're pathetic.' Bethany whirled on him. 'You think it's everybody's duty to love you. You think all you have to do is walk into a room and everybody will fall at your feet, that if you just smile you'll get everything you want. Why are you still hanging around Jez, anyway? He's moved on, he's made something of himself, he's going to be a father. Start acting like a grown-up, for pity's sake.'

'You blame me for Wales, that's what this is all about.'

'Yes, I do,' she shouted. 'That girl's disappearance was the worst thing that ever happened to Jez. He got dragged into all that bad publicity, and it's all because of you.'

Abs looked in panic at the police officers. 'I had nothing to do with—'

'I wish you had never taken Jez with you to that place. Why can't you just leave us be, why can't you just let us get on with our lives?'

'Wow,' Abs said quietly. 'I'd better go.'

'Aren't you coming to celebrate with us?' said Jez.

'You know what, stuff your celebration.' Abs headed to the door.

'Good,' hissed Bethany.

'Congratulations to you both, yeah?'

But Jez grabbed him at the door. 'No, Abs, wait.' He turned to his wife. 'Abs is my friend. He looked after me when I was a kid, he protected me. He was there when nobody else wanted to know, when nobody cared. Abs is my family, Beth. The only family I've got.'

Sasha saw Abs look in surprise at his friend.

Bethany lifted her chin, indignant. 'I'm your family now, Jez.'

'You both are.' Jez stood between Abs and Bethany, desperately trying to bridge the gap between them. 'He's coming with us this afternoon, because I want him there.'

Abs shook his head. 'I'm not—'

'I would very much like it if you came to the party this afternoon,' Jez said with emotion. '*Please*, for me.'

Abs made a big show of thinking about it, but he looked relieved. 'Sure thing,' he said. 'I'd like that.'

'Well.' Sasha made a face to Lolly – *We should get out of here* – and moved towards the door. 'Congratulations again on the baby.'

'It's going to be an adventure,' said Bethany, grateful for the distraction from the tense conversation.

'Oh yes,' Sasha confirmed with a sympathetic smile. 'It'll certainly be that.'

22

While they were already out of the office, they drove to see Tony Gardner at his home in Hadleigh, to discover whether he had been followed or threatened by Davey Jenkins, as Abs had been.

They motored up Leigh Hill, heading towards the A13. In the distance stood the thirteenth-century Hadleigh Castle, the ruined drums of its two remaining towers stubbornly persisting above the country park surrounding it. Unlike Craig, Lolly accepted the offer of the floppy hat to protect her head, and spent the journey admiring herself in the side mirror. Sasha's phone rang in her bag on the back seat.

'Do you mind getting that?' she said. 'It may be work.'

Lolly grabbed her bag, took out the phone and checked the screen. 'It's Connie.'

Sasha cursed under her breath. 'Tell her I'll call her back.'

'Hiya, Connie, it's DC Chambers... Lolly Chambers... DI Dawson is driving right now and said she'll get back to—' She listened into the phone with her eyes clamped on Sasha, then placed the phone to her shoulder. 'She says what time tonight?'

'Oh hell.' Her family were visiting that evening and she still hadn't asked Kev to get food in. Chicken wings, ham, cheese, crusty bread, a few dips, and salad, that should do it, and of course, wine and beer.

'Seven o'clock,' Sasha told Lolly. 'No, make it seven thirty, but tell her it's not going to be a late one.'

'Connie, she says seven thirty,' Lolly said into the phone. 'Yes, and it's not going to be a late one.'

'Do you hear that, Con,' called Sasha as she dropped down a gear. 'I need an early night.'

'I'm sorry,' Lolly said into the phone, 'I can't hand you over, she's driving.' She turned to Sasha. 'She wants to talk to you.'

'Tell her I'll call her back later,' insisted Sasha.

'I can't do that, Connie, she's—'

Eyes glued to the road, Sasha leaned over into Lolly's airspace to shout. 'I'll call you later, Con.'

The phone still to her ear, Lolly looked with apology at Sasha. 'She says she just wants a quick word.'

'Hang up, Lols, she won't take no for an answer.'

'I'm sorry, Connie, but Sasha can't—'

'Hang up,' Sasha told her in exasperation. 'Just end the call.'

Lolly was still trying to reason with Sasha's sister. 'She says she'll—'

The car jerked a little when Sasha grabbed the phone, turned it off and threw it in the back. 'You just have to hang up, there's no reasoning with her.'

Arriving in Hadleigh, they turned into a quiet cul-de-sac and pulled up to the kerb. Tony Gardner's small detached bungalow had seen better days. One of the uPVC windows had a crack running the length of it and the rendered brickwork was crumbling in patches. There was an old garden bench against the front wall, fag ends littering the ground beneath it. Weeds pushed up between the numerous cracks in the paved over front garden, where an old Fiat was parked. At the side of the property, furniture was dumped beside a pair of smelly bins in front of a sagging wooden fence.

Climbing from the Spider, Sasha and Lolly stretched. Sasha was leaning back in to get her bag when a large woman in a tee-shirt, a denim skirt and sliders came slapping along the street towards them, a cigarette in one hand.

'Is he in there?' the woman asked them.

'Excuse me?'

'Is Tony in there?'

Sasha smiled. 'And you are?'

'I'm his wife, is who I am, Angie Gardner. Well, ex-wife, I did my time.' She scratched the stud in the side of her nose. 'Is he in there? I came earlier and got no response. That's his car, but he ain't answering the door. Usually he's watching Tipping Point all day.'

'I've no idea, we've only just arrived.' said Sasha. 'I'm Detective Inspector Sasha Dawson, this is Detective Constable Lolly Chambers.'

Angie sucked on her fag. 'What's the silly sod gone and done now?'

Sasha sidestepped the question with one of her own. 'You came earlier, you said?'

'He's not been returning my calls,' said Angie, 'and we're desperate right now. There's rent to pay and food to put on the table. Getting money out of Tone is like getting blood out of a stone. I know he was laid off from work, but he still has responsibilities.'

Sasha shared a glance with Lolly. 'When was the last time you spoke to him?'

'Yesterday morning. We speak every day, usually. Not because he wants to speak to me, as if I care, but he likes to talk to the kids.'

'So you don't live here, Angie?'

'Nah, we're up the road.' She nodded back the way she had come. 'Tone moved out of our place a couple of years back.'

'And you don't have a key?'

Angie made a face. 'Why would I want a key to that shithole, he'll only have me in there cleaning.' She squinted at them through the smoke. 'Why did you say you were here again? It's not about that girl, is it? Tone is many things, but he ain't no murderer.'

'You mean Rhiannon Jenkins.'

'That was when our marriage really started going down the toilet. Being accused of something like that really knocked the wind out of him.' Angie made a face. 'I wish he never went on that trip, or knew any of those people, even that charming sod from TV. Tony had this cloud hanging over him afterwards, he really took it to heart, and it was the end for us.'

'He was never charged,' said Sasha, fishing. 'Why would it have such an effect on him?'

'Tone's sensitive like that, he lives on his nerves.' Angie ground the stub of her cigarette beneath a foot. 'Because of that mate of his, that Abs, the papers were all over it. Tony's name got dragged through the mud. It ruined his friendship with Deano, that's no great loss, but also Abs and Jez. They all used to be great mates. Abs used to take him to glitzy parties. I even went to a couple.'

'I thought Abs and Tony were still friends?'

'Hah.' Angie shook her head. 'Abs dropped him like a rock. I'll never forgive him for that. I used to complain to Tone about it, but he told me he'd get his own back one day, said he had dirt on Abs that was dynamite.'

Sasha cocked her head. 'Did he say what?'

'I don't think Tone meant anything by it, he was just hurt.' She sniffed. 'What's that smell?'

'How well did you know Andrew Dean, Angie?'

'Deano?' She made a face. 'I never liked him either, he was a right Billy Big Bollocks. Tony was a good mate of his once. They used to get into all kinds of scrapes together when they were young.'

'Scrapes?' asked Sasha.

'Nicking stuff, cars and bikes, fighting with gangs. All the usual stuff you do before you grow up. But even Tony eventually realized Deano was trouble and got shot of him. That's why you're here, is it, because Deano's in the shit?'

'He's died,' Sasha said.

Angie's lips puckered. 'What happened?'

Sasha didn't want to go into detail about how Deano's body was torn apart. But Lolly said with a helpful bluntness, 'He was hit by a train.'

'You don't think Tony's got anything to do with it? He ain't got a nasty bone in his body. He's a good-for-nothing waster, but he couldn't hurt a fly. And anyway,' Angie added, 'he wouldn't know how to operate a train.'

'We just want to speak to Tony about Mr Dean.'

Angie took out another cigarette and tapped it against the packet. 'Well, you talk to Tony, it's none of my business, but first I need to get money from him so his two boys can have something for their tea tonight, so if you'll excuse me.'

Angie walked towards Tony's front door, and Lolly looked at Sasha. *What do we do?*

'Let her speak to him first,' Sasha said. 'There's no rush.'

There was no knocker or doorbell, so Angie banged on the door. She took out a lighter.

'Tone.' Angie crouched at the letter box, lifting the flap, the unlit fag bobbing in her mouth. 'Are you in there?'

'She's right.' Lolly turned in a circle on the pavement, sniffing the air. 'There's a smell.'

Sasha lifted her nose.

'Angie,' she called urgently, running towards the bungalow. 'Get back from—'

But when Angie flicked on the lighter in front of her face, the curtains inside jumped, and then the front windows flew out of the bungalow, and a blast blew them all off their feet.

23

Sasha sat in the ambulance at the entrance to the cul-de-sac. The street was full of emergency services vehicles: police cars, science support vans and a pair of fire engines. The fire raging in Tony Gardner's home had been put out, and the concrete forecourt and pavement outside his house was sopping wet, channels of water racing along the uneven paving and into the gutter; the walls of the bungalow were blackened by smoke.

The front door had been blown off its hinges and landed right on top of Angie Gardner. But she'd had a lucky escape, as it had stopped her from getting caught directly in the blast and showered with the glass that flew everywhere when the windows blew out.

Further away, Sasha and Lolly were thrown to the ground, and mostly shielded by the Fiat and the fence. Glass rained down all around them as they lay curled up on the pavement, and pinged against the metal body of Sasha's open-topped sports car. Other debris – bits of window frame, the tiles ripped from the roof – seemed to take forever to crash to earth, even though everything happened in a matter of moments. The noise of the blast was deafening, making Sasha's ears ring.

And as flames licked around inside the bungalow, and acrid smoke began to billow from the gaping holes where the door and windows used to be, Sasha and Lolly lifted the door off Angie and carried her to safety on the other side of the street, before calling 999. She had been taken to Southend University Hospital, suffering from concussion, along with Lolly, who sustained a number of deep cuts to her neck and shoulders.

'Why the long face?' Ajay asked Sasha as she sat getting her own superficial cuts and bruises treated by a paramedic. 'You don't look like a woman who just escaped getting blown to kingdom come.'

'Mum and Dad and Con are coming round tonight,' she said, picking a shard of glass from inside one of the cuffs of her shirt. 'And I was just thinking how I could really do without it.'

'I think you have a good excuse,' he told her. 'Although it seems to me, the best thing you could do right now is go home and drink a glass or two of wine.'

'I don't see why not,' agreed the paramedic. 'You don't have concussion.'

'Looks like it's going to be a long night.' DC Craig Power came to the door of the ambulance and looked up at them. 'The firemen have just confirmed it. There's a body in the house.'

Sasha gave Ajay a look, as if to say, *There goes that plan.* 'Is it Tony Gardner?'

'The deceased hasn't been ID'd, but it's a white male. The fire investigators won't let us inside until they give us the all-clear that it's safe to do so.'

'Maybe we're looking at this all wrong.' Sasha stood, brushing away the paramedic. 'Angie Gardner said Tony and Deano were close when they were younger, stealing, fighting, getting involved in gang stuff. Maybe this has nothing to do with what did or didn't happen in Wales. Maybe it's always been about Dean and Tony.'

Ajay shared an *uh-oh* glance with Craig. They both knew what happened when Sasha got the bit between her teeth; she worked herself into the ground. 'Honestly, Sash, even if you don't have concussion, I suggest you go home and make sure you're fighting fit for tomorrow.'

'I'm needed here,' she insisted.

'You see these people?' Ajay gestured at all the emergency services personnel moving up and down the street. The firemen in all their heavy gear standing outside Tony's wrecked bungalow; the forensic investigators unloading equipment from a van; her police colleagues securing the scene. Ajay, she knew, had already organized a team of officers to go house-to-house to attempt to piece together Tony Gardner's movements, and to find out if any neighbours had seen anything unusual in the cul-de-sac that day. 'They're all professionals, they all know what they're doing, and not a single one of them needs you here to tell them how to do their work.'

'You know, Ajay,' – Sasha gave him a sideways look – 'I can never quite shake the feeling that you're eyeing up my job.'

'I'm very interested in doing your job, but only when you're a white-haired old lady.' His eyes lifted to her shock of silver hair. 'When you're old, at least.'

'Angie,' said Sasha suddenly. 'She has kids.'

'She's got minor injuries, including a nasty crack on the head from the door.' Craig stepped back as she climbed down from the ambulance. 'They're keeping her in hospital tonight, just in case, and a relative is going to look after her boys until she's back.'

'Okay, good.' Sasha was actually more stressed by the prospect of her family visiting than the fact that she could have been killed or badly injured. 'Fast-track the forensic examination and post-mortem on the body. I want to know the results as soon as they come in.'

'It's going to be a few hours yet,' said Ajay. 'Probably tomorrow.'

'As soon as they come in,' she repeated, and he nodded.

'Get yourself home, Mrs Dawson.' Frowning, he reached into her hair to pick out a fragment of glass. 'Missed a bit.'

Sasha's mind whirled with the possibilities. They had smelled gas earlier. If Tony Gardner was inside, then the likelihood was that he had been there for hours while it filled the house. At which point, he was either incapacitated, unconscious – or already dead.

First Andrew Dean was murdered, and now, in all probability, Tony Gardner. Two friends who had got up to no good as young men, and both implicated in the disappearance of a woman three years ago. The explosion could have been an accident, but what were the chances that their deaths, within forty-eight hours of each other, were a coincidence? Plus, Davey Jenkins was in custody at the station.

'If that's Tony Gardner inside, we should inform Abs and Jeremy Weston that there's a killer still at large,' she said.

They stood watching the proceedings. Firemen wearing breathing apparatus and heavy protective suits gathered up their equipment and rolled up limp hoses, but it could be hours before the building was deemed structurally safe for police and a forensics team to go inside, and for a pathologist to examine the body.

Sasha's car had been moved further along the street and she went over to look inside. There were scratches all over the paintwork and the leather seats were studded with glass; jagged shards were scattered in the footwell. Her beloved Spider was already on its last legs and this indignity was the last thing it needed.

'Poor thing,' Sasha muttered.

Sensing her upset, Ajay said, 'We'll get you home in a patrol car, and I'll get someone to give your car a vacuum. You can pick up the old girl from the station in the morning. Go home, Sasha, and we'll see you tomorrow.'

24

They drove along the coast in stony silence, Jez gunning the open-topped BMW along the winding lanes with Bethany beside him, her eyes hidden behind a big pair of white sunglasses. In the back, Abs watched the way her red hair spilled from the edges of her scarf and whipped about in the wind, trembling against the long slope of her neck. She didn't turn around once, didn't even attempt to communicate with him, and Abs wished he'd never come.

He tried not to bear a grudge against her for what she did – he supposed she believed she was acting in Jez's best interests – but he couldn't help but feel that she would have been totally unconcerned if he had been beaten up, or even killed, by Jenkins and his dodgy mates.

Abs could tell Jez was annoyed that Bethany had gone behind his back in order to protect him from Davey Jenkins, and he drove too fast. They zoomed around bends, the velocity making Abs brace against the back seat, and he heard Bethany tell Jez to slow down. 'You're going to get us killed.'

But after forty minutes or so, Jez took a sharp corner into a narrow lane hidden from the road by shrubs and bushes and flew up a twisting gravel drive towards Bethany's parents' country house.

The house loomed into view as Jez drove onto a circular drive full of cars. It was long and stately, with tall windows on either side of a big black door. Red and yellow roses crept up the brickwork. And the sprawling property was old, Victorian or Edwardian, every inch the home of a man who had earned millions from business. Trying to find the toilet here once, Abs learned that it was one of those buildings where you could easily get lost if you didn't know your way around.

To one side of the house was a converted stable, in which Bethany's old man had built his own bar, and added a games room with a full-sized snooker table, and a gym. There was an indoor swimming pool; Abs had even used it. Bethany may not like him much, but her parents were keen to show off their son-in-law's celebrity mate to their friends. Behind the house and the stable building was a long, neat lawn, and beyond that a dense wood.

Jez spun the wheels on the gravel, making stones spurt and clack against all the cars parked there, as he pulled up in front of the house.

Bethany tutted. 'You've left a tyre mark on the drive.'

She climbed out quickly, slamming the passenger door, and walked to the house, but Jez killed the engine and ran after her.

'Beth, a word. And you too, Abs.'

'Yeah, mate?' Abs and Bethany could barely look each other in the eye as Jez brought them together. The reception room on the other side of the window was full of guests.

'This is meant to be a happy afternoon,' Jez told them both. 'And I won't have it spoiled by a sour atmosphere. You're the two most important people in my life and the last thing I want is for there to be any bad blood between you.' Bethany gazed at the gravel. 'I mean it, Beth, or I'm going to get back in the car and drive back home right this minute.'

It wasn't often that Abs heard Jez raise his voice to Bethany – he was usually a doting and courteous husband – but she must have known she'd gone too far because she offered a limp hand. 'No hard feelings, Abs.'

Abs didn't understand what Bethany had to be annoyed about – she was the one who had thrown *him* to the lions – but he was ready to let bygones be bygones if that's what Jez wanted.

'Same here.' He shook her hand. 'Your fingers are cold.'

'I have bad circulation,' she told him.

'Come here,' he said, and although she didn't wholeheartedly respond, she at least tolerated his hug. In

Abs's mind, there wasn't a problem in the world that couldn't be solved by a cuddle.

It cleared the air a little bit, and Abs felt better as they knocked on the front door, Jez giving him a discreet pat on the back, as if to say, *Thanks, mate*. And everything was instantly forgotten when they went inside. The reception was all panelled walls and oak flooring and antique furniture, similar to the way Bethany had decorated her own home. There was a comfortable-looking velvet armchair in one corner, a grandfather clock, even a chandelier. Abs had stayed in hotels that weren't as plush as this.

People poured out of the big double doors to the reception room to congratulate the happy couple. Surrounded by family and friends, Bethany's mood changed; she was all gushing smiles and joy, and she threw her head back in delighted laughter, hugging and kissing everyone. Her parents made sure Bethany greeted all her elderly relatives first – Abs had never seen so many old people in one place – and then all the nieces and nephews gave her flowers, and she picked up the littlest kids to kiss.

Abs tried to melt into the background, which was difficult because he wasn't used to walking into a room and not being the centre of attention, but everyone knew who he was, and loads of people, young and old, came over to meet him.

'You're shorter than you look on the telly.'

'The things you got up to on that show.'

'I was so hoping you and Kelsey would stay together.'

Abs grinned. He was desperate to let them all know he was filming *Laid In Essex!* again the next morning, and that maybe, just maybe, if he played his cards right, he and Kelsey would get back together, for good this time. But Vince had sworn him to secrecy until it actually happened, so all he could do was wink and say, 'You watch this space.'

Serving people moved through the crowded room with drinks and trays of food.

'How many calories?' Starving, Abs liked the look of the mini-burgers, but when the girl didn't know how fattening they were, he declined.

He signed plenty of autographs, of course, although there was no way he was going to ask for money here, and was careful to keep to the edge of the room. This was Jez and Bethany's special afternoon and he didn't want to take the limelight away from them.

About an hour after they arrived, Bethany's old man banged a gong, an actual gong. The noise reverberated through the room and when everyone fell silent he made a speech about how much he and his wife loved their daughter and admired Jez, and how he was like a son to them. And then her dad announced to the room – of relatives, business associates and old family friends – that his little girl was pregnant. Everyone clapped and cheered, and Abs whistled. And then Bethany's parents raised their flutes of champagne and asked everyone in the room to toast the happy couple. Bethany beamed and placed a protective hand on her stomach, which was still as flat and hard as a piece of chipboard.

Within moments of the speech ending, Jez and Bethany were once again surrounded. People wanted to hug them and make a fuss of them all over again, and it gave Bethany's old man an opportunity to slip out of the room and return with the biggest bouquet of flowers Abs had ever seen. Everyone gasped at the beautiful blooms.

Standing by one of the tall windows, Abs smiled at his friend's good fortune. Bethany's parents had paid for virtually everything they had, the house, the flash car, all the luxury holidays, and Jez would want for nothing in his life. Abs was filled with happiness for his best mate, and for his own success in getting back on the show.

They were both living the dream.

His phone rang and he took it out, but didn't recognize the number.

'Yeah?' he said.

'Mr Cruikshank, this is Detective Sergeant Ajay de Vaz. We met this morning.'

'Course we did,' said Abs, who met a lot of people and didn't remember him at all.

'I'm afraid I have some bad news.'

25

When Sasha got back to her Thorpe Bay home, she heard Kev talking to her mother in the kitchen, and her nerves spiked. Absolutely the last thing she wanted to do was play Happy Families with her nearest and dearest. She whipped off her jacket and shoved it at the banister, kicked her shoes to the skirting, thinking of all the things she had to do. Denny was sitting on the stairs playing on his phone, the tinny music of the game already making her ears bleed.

'Have you said hello to Gran and Grandad?' she asked him. His elbows danced this way and that, reacting to the life-and-death struggle playing out in the game, but he didn't answer.

'This is the *Mother*ship to Deep Space Denny,' she said through the banister. 'Come in, Denny.'

'Not yet,' he said in irritation, his eyes never lifting from the screen.

'Don't you think you should?'

'In a minute.' It was the answer he gave her at least

a dozen times a day. *Are you going to get dressed for school?* In a minute. *Have you tidied your room?* In a minute. *Denny, the house is on fire, run for your life.* In a minute!

'Denny—'

'Don't talk to me,' he shouted. 'You're putting me off.'

'Just so you know, I was nearly blown up today.' She gripped the banisters and thrust her face into the tiny gap. 'For realz!'

'Yeah, right.' He made an incredulous face. 'As if.'

She headed into the kitchen, where her mother, Ursula, was busy emptying dips out of plastic tubs into dishes. Her father, Alec, his skinny knees poking out from cargo shorts and his face as brown as a berry, was perched on a high stool like a sunburned vulture, drinking from a can of lager. She kissed him on one bronzed cheek.

'Hi, Dad.'

'Finally,' Ursula tutted. 'What kept you?'

Sasha couldn't possibly tell her mother that she had narrowly escaped getting blown to smithereens when Tony Gardner's bungalow exploded. She didn't fancy getting another lecture about how dangerous her job was, and how instead she should stay home and concentrate on becoming the new Nigella. Despite the fact that she had never been, and never would be, a very good cook, and despite the fact that right now, and for the foreseeable future, she was the only person bringing money into the house.

But she also didn't want to contemplate just how close she had come to getting seriously injured, or even killed, in Hadleigh. The news was playing silently on a wall-mounted telly, and she saw the front of Gardner's house, with its gaping spaces where the door and windows used to be, and turned it off.

'Sorry I'm late.' She clapped her hands together. 'What can I do to help?'

'What's happened to your trousers?' Standing with a buttered bap in her hand, Ursula stared at them. Sasha looked down to see that one leg had been torn along the thigh.

'Someone smashed a glass at work.'

Kev, who knew all about the explosion, gave her a kiss on the cheek and a discreet squeeze of the arm. What she really wanted was a long, tender hug, but she gave him a warning glance, as if to say, *Not a word*, and he knew better than to mention it. He handed her a glass of Prosecco.

Alec sipped from his can and said, 'It's just as well she's got lovely legs.'

'Thanks, Dad.' Sasha looked around. 'Where's Con?'

Ursula was taking the silver foil off a whole salmon she had brought with her. 'Not here yet,' she said, visibly annoyed. 'And both your children are conspicuous by their absence too. I hope they're going to join us.'

'Good luck with that.' Sasha sipped the Prosecco and glanced at her husband as he took the bottle from the fridge, ready to top her up. 'And thanks for helping Angel pay for our hotel stay. We're both very excited.'

'Ah.' Kev closed the fridge door gingerly. 'About that.'

'What about it?' she asked, alarmed.

'That job interview I told you about has been moved to six o'clock,' he said. 'So I may be a bit late.'

'It shouldn't be a problem, should it?' Her heart sank a little; she'd been looking forward to making the most of their single romantic night away in a swish hotel.

'I can't imagine the interview will last more than half an hour, forty-five minutes.' He topped up his own drink. 'With the wind behind me, I'll be there by eight.'

'Okay, then.' She lifted her glass to her mouth, feeling the bubbles of the Prosecco pop faintly against her chin. And when Angel appeared in the doorway, she added, 'And here's the thoughtful lady who's responsible for our night of luxury.'

'There's a spa there, Mum, and a Michelin-star restaurant.'

'I don't go for all that overpriced Michelin nonsense.' Ursula wrinkled her nose. 'Give me chicken-in-a-basket any day.'

'I think it's a lovely gesture, Angel,' said Sasha. 'Very thoughtful.'

Angel nodded at the glass in Sasha's hand. 'Can I have one?'

'No, you can't,' Sasha told her sweetly.

'I've had a lot worse than a piddling little glass of wine.' Her daughter rolled her eyes. 'Me and my squad have drunk all sorts.'

'Good for you,' said Alec, lifting his can in salute.

'There's lemonade in the fridge,' said Sasha, refusing to rise to the bait.

Her daughter's fingers danced over the screen of her phone and then a text whooshed away. 'I'm going out anyway.'

'Where?'

'To Gabby's.'

'Text me when you get there and when you're coming home. Dad will pick you up.'

Kev, who was about to drink his second Prosecco, put the glass down on the counter. 'Of course I will.'

'Okay,' said Angel, and turned away.

'Angel,' said Sasha, concerned. 'When we're away tomorrow night, you're not going to sneak off some-where, are you?'

'Course I'm not.' Her daughter looked outraged. 'I'm going to be right here. On Nan's life, I will.'

'Oh.' Ursula pressed a hand to her chest, as if someone had walked over her grave. 'I'm not sure I like the sound of that.'

'Denny's going for a sleepover at one of his mates, so it'll be good for her to spend an evening on her own,' said Sasha when Angel left the room. 'After what happened.'

'We're just down the road if she needs us,' Ursula said. 'So you don't have to worry. We'll come by earlier in the evening, just to make sure she's okay, and drop off some treats, won't we, Alec?'

'Oh, yes,' said Alec, who didn't look hugely thrilled at the prospect.

'Don't worry about that,' said Sasha, who didn't want her daughter to think she was under surveillance.

'How is she?' asked Alec, as they heard the front door slam.

'She's good, Dad, she's getting more confident every day, as you can see. Again, thank you both for helping her pay for the hotel, it's very kind of you.'

'We know how hard you both work, particularly you, Sasha.' Ursula glanced with disapproval at Kev. 'Things have been chaotic around here recently. It's the least you deserve... the both of you.'

Her family could be maddening – Ursula and Alec, Kev, her children, *Connie* – they drove her to distraction sometimes. Let's face it, she thought, families are exhausting. But as a police officer, Sasha saw every day how death came suddenly and often violently to random people, fracturing loving relationships. Wives, husbands, children and parents suddenly lost the people closest to them – worlds were upturned, lives destroyed

– and she considered how lucky she was that her family she loved were healthy, happy – and safe. They could be maddening, they all got exasperated with one another, but they were all blessed to have each other.

Sasha lifted her glass in a toast. 'Bottoms up, everybody. Thanks for coming.'

And as everyone sipped from their glasses, and Ursula took plates from the cupboard, there was a ring on the bell. She said, 'That'll be Con. I'll get it.'

Sasha poured her sister a glass of Prosecco in readiness and said, 'Help yourself to some dips, Dad.'

'You're alright, Con,' he said. 'I'm fine.'

'It's Sasha, Dad,' she corrected him, and glanced at Kev, who raised an eyebrow. They heard voices at the door and Ursula came back into the room with her eyes on stalks.

'Connie's brought someone,' she said, and mouthed dramatically, 'it's a *man*.'

Sasha felt her stomach lurch, just as Connie came into the room to kiss and hug everybody, rushing around like a whirlwind, and behind her Vaughn appeared at the door, a bottle of wine in his hand.

'Hello,' he said.

'Look who I've brought with me. Mum, Dad, this is Claude.'

Kev stepped forward to shake his hand. 'Good to see you, Vaughn.'

Alec nodded and offered a hand. 'Nice one, son.'

While Connie and Ursula began to argue about how the chicken wings should have been marinated, Vaughn came over to Sasha to ask her quietly, 'Are you alright?'

'I'm good, Vaughn, really I am,' she told him, trying to sound grateful for his concern and discretion, but, in truth, absolutely seething that he was here in her kitchen, with her sister and parents. 'I got barely a scratch.'

'The body has been confirmed as Tony Gardner,' he told her.

'How do you know that?'

'DS de Vaz told me.'

'He called you?' She was a little bit put out. 'I asked him to call me.'

'The post-mortem is being done tonight. The body was pretty badly burned, but there were localized scorch marks on his stomach and arms, same as Andrew Dean. He was attacked with a cattle prod.'

'What about his eyes?' she asked. 'Was he blinded by acid?'

'We don't know at this stage. We'll have a better picture by tomorrow morning.'

'I'm surprised that Ajay called you, as—'

'I called him,' he told her. 'He's got it all under control. He's a very capable detective.'

'Yes,' said Sasha flatly. Ajay was diligent and capable, but it wasn't what she wanted to hear right then. 'Yes, he is.'

'Oh now, come on.' Connie's voice cut across the kitchen. 'No whispering, no talking shop. We're all here to enjoy ourselves.'

Connie topped up her glass and pulled Vaughn to her. 'Claude is Sasha's superior at work, so I'm sure we're all going to be in for some eye-opening revelations about my little sis.'

'You're Sasha's boss?' asked Ursula, a little slow on the uptake.

Vaughn smiled. 'For my sins.'

'All I can say is, you must be a *very* patient man,' said her mother, and Sasha felt her anger surge at being put in such an awkward situation. 'But you've only just split with Barry, Connie. Isn't it a bit quick to be leaping into bed with another man?'

Sasha winced. 'Mum.'

Connie grabbed a glass and filled it to the brim, and then practically draped herself over Vaughn.

'Trust me, Mum,' she said. 'There's really no comparison in that department.'

'He's a big boy, isn't he?' said Ursula, appraising Vaughn's bulk.

'Oh he is, Mum,' Connie smirked. 'Take it from me.'

'Connie,' snapped Sasha in a flustered singsong. 'A word.'

She grabbed her sister by the arm and pushed her into the hallway, shutting the door behind them.

'What do you think you're doing?' she asked, trying to keep a lid on her temper.

Connie blinked. 'I don't understand.'

'This was meant to be a family get-together. For family. Nobody said anything about bringing guests.'

'But you know Claude,' said Connie. 'And he is family now, surely, in a fashion?'

'Con, you've just met him, and he's my—'

Sasha took a deep breath before she said something she would regret. Their mother was somehow under the impression that Connie was a delicate flower, and had always urged Sasha never to speak harshly for fear of upsetting her. Ursula had the strange idea, nurtured and encouraged by Connie herself, that her sister was afraid of confrontation, and often had to retreat to her bed for days afterwards. But Connie was always fighting with Barry, and more than once Sasha had been forced to break up their screaming rows. Shouting obscenities at the top of her voice, Connie had been anything but meek and traumatized as Sasha dragged her away.

Right now, Sasha was keen to give her sister both barrels. But there was her mother to consider. And her boss, who was in her house and having some kind of fling with Connie – God, Sasha hoped it was no more than that – on the rebound from the end of his long marriage.

'Don't you think it's all going a bit fast?'

'Claude is hurting, Sash, as I am.' Connie rubbed the thick gold chain around her neck. 'We've both been through terrible times. You could say we're kindred spirits.'

Sasha couldn't help herself and asked, 'As a matter of interest, why did he and Miranda split up?'

Connie gave her a patronizing smile. 'It's kind of private. Claude wouldn't like me to tell people.'

Sasha, who had played straight into her sister's hands, blushed. She was intensely annoyed that Con had crashed together like a pair of noisy cymbals the two parts of Sasha's life, work and home, that she had always kept separate.

'Can you at least try to keep your hands off him while you're in my kitchen. It's embarrassing.'

'Oh, Sash, bless.' Connie made a sad face. 'Is that why you're upset? I'm sorry, I forget how long you and Kev have been together. It's been donkey's, yes? I imagine it's been a long time since there's been any spark between you, particularly after Kev's... *episode*. You won't remember the raw sexual urgency in the white heat of a new relationship. I'd quite forgotten myself.' Connie spread her fingers wide, as if mimicking an explosion. 'The physical desire, Sasha, the energy, it's incredible.'

'Things are fine between me and Kev,' protested Sasha.

'Of course they are.' Connie gave her a smile of pity and compassion. 'I've been swept away by something elemental, something...' She searched for the right word. '*Primal*. Believe me, Claude is a hurricane, a tsunami, he's a sexual force. I've never known anything like it.'

'Ugh,' said a voice, and Sasha looked between the banisters to see Denny was still sitting on the stairs.

'Upstairs, Denny – now,' Sasha told him.

Her son rolled his eyes. 'I'm fine here.'

'I'm not going to tell you ag—'

But then there was a sudden, ferocious banging on the front door and a voice wailed, 'Let me in.'

Sasha and Connie looked at each other in surprise.

26

The last thing Abs wanted to do was ruin Jez's happy afternoon by telling him Tony was dead, killed in a fire, but he didn't know what else to do.

'Was it on purpose?' he'd asked the policeman on the phone. 'Was he...' He could barely bring himself to say the word out loud, although it was all he could think about. 'Was he *murdered*?'

'That's not something I can confirm at this stage. The investigation is ongoing and we're now gathering evidence.'

'You said his house blew up.'

'The fire damage is extensive, yes, but we have our forensic experts combing the premises and Mr Gardner's body will be examined. Until we get both sets of results back, it's too early to make assumptions.'

Abs had seen those CSI shows where good-looking geeks examined test tubes while rock music pounded on the soundtrack. 'The forensics people.'

'Exactly, and the pathologist will examine the deceased.'

'The deceased,' repeated Abs. 'You mean Tony.'

'Yes, Mr Gardner. I want to stress that his death could be nothing more than a tragic accident.'

Abs had the feeling this Ajay guy wasn't telling him everything, he wasn't offering the information Abs needed to make sense of it all. Houses didn't just blow up in this day and age, despite what the policeman said. And if that was the case, if the explosion was just an accident, then why was he calling Abs to tell him?

Standing behind a curtain in order to get some privacy, he looked out at all the people in the room. 'I want to speak to Sasha Lawson.'

'Detective Inspector *Dawson* is out of the office. I can get her to phone you first thing tomorrow.'

'I need to speak to her right now,' insisted Abs. 'Because I'm scared.'

The policeman offered advice on how Abs could stay safe, and how he should call if he believed he was in danger, but Abs struggled to concentrate on what he was saying. All he could think about was the fact that Tony was dead. First Deano, and now Tony. He peeked out to see Jez standing with a group of people, one hand placed on the small of Bethany's back, as his father-in-law talked about something. But as everyone listened, Jez slipped out of the room, and Abs saw his chance to speak to him in private.

He said into the phone, 'I've got to go.'

'Don't take any chances,' said DS de Vaz. 'If you have any concerns for your own safety—'

'Sure,' said Abs, and killed the call.

He came out from behind the curtain and bumped straight into an elderly man, who told him, 'I thought you'd have a snazzier phone.'

'Excuse me a moment, yeah?' Abs literally moved the old fella aside. 'Got to visit the little boy's room.'

He followed Jez out of the door, expecting to see him in the hallway, but he wasn't there. This big house was such a maze of corridors and connecting rooms – the dining room led into a study, which led to a sitting room, which had another door that led down a little corridor and into a room with a piano – that Abs got totally lost. He walked around for minutes before he bumped into a young woman who told him where Jez was, near the rear of the house.

But then through a window, Abs spotted him striding across the lawn towards the trees.

'Jez.' He rapped on the window. 'Jez, wait.'

But his friend didn't hear him and soon he had disappeared into the wood.

Abs found the kitchen and ran out the back, and across the lawn. He called Jez's name again, but he was nowhere to be seen.

Bethany's parents boasted they had acres of woodland behind their house. Despite the mud and mulch and the uneven ground, Abs raced into the trees. Under the dark canopy of leaves, it was cool and quiet, but he felt very alone and anxious. Abs's natural environment was a bar, a club, a spa, places with recessed lighting. He had never been, and never would be, a fan of Mother Nature, with her wildlife, bugs and filth. Walking further into the dense wood, he looked around frantically, but couldn't see Jez anywhere. He tried to identify some features – a tree stump, a slope in the ground, a clump of mushrooms on a log – that he could use to find his way back.

'Jez,' he called, wondering if maybe his friend had doubled back around the side of the stables.

And then he saw the chalet. It was a dilapidated old hut that he remembered Jez telling him about, which had once been used as a summer house for guests, but which had long been abandoned. Jez said that when he visited Bethany's parents, he often came to this place to smoke a spliff in peace. He liked to sit on the porch, he said, and gaze at the light shimmering at the top of the trees.

Approaching the chalet, Abs saw how the wooden structure was rotting and warped, and the windows were all boarded up. It was utterly quiet now, except for the squirrels scuttling along the branch of a tree, and the hoots and calls of various birds.

But Jez wasn't sitting on the porch, and when Abs walked towards the building he heard a voice inside. He put his ear to the door and heard the soft lilt of Jez's voice, but not what he was saying. Abs stayed like that for a moment, trying hard to listen, and then the voice suddenly came nearer; it was just on the other side of the door.

'...again tomorrow,' he heard Jez say, and Abs scrambled away from the door and around the corner of the hut to press himself against the wall. When Jez came out, Abs flew around the corner with his hands raised and clawed, growling. 'Grrrrrrrr.'

Jez nearly pissed himself. He almost jumped out of his skin and keys flew out of his hand and hit the dirty wooden porch with a thunk. Abs laughed as Jez slammed the door shut behind him. He looked sick.

'Gotcha,' Abs said. 'Made you jump.'

'What do you think you're doing?' Jez snapped. He put a hand to his chest, and for a moment looked really angry. 'You nearly scared me to death.'

Abs couldn't stop giggling. 'Your face, mate.'

And then even Jez had a little laugh, as he picked up the keys.

Abs nodded. 'Who you got in there?'

Jez frowned as he turned a key in the lock. 'What are you talking about?'

'I heard you talking.'

'Oh, someone phoned me from work.' Jez sighed. 'Some bloody admin problem I'm going to have to sort out.'

'So this is the place you told me about.' Abs stepped off the porch to look at the small wooden building.

'Yeah, it was a summer house type of thing.' Jez began to walk back towards the house. 'But Bethany's parents haven't used it for years. I was thinking of doing it up, bit of a side project.'

'Good luck with that, it's in a right state.' Abs hurried to catch up with his friend, careful not to step on the dampest, mossiest parts of the ground. His white trainers were already scuffed. 'Never knew you were good with your hands, Jez?'

'There's a lot of things you don't know about me.' Jez smiled as he ducked beneath a low-hanging branch. 'What are you skulking around out here for, anyway?'

Abs had almost forgotten about his horrible news. 'You ain't gonna like it, mate.'

'I'm dying for a drink,' said Jez, moving quickly back towards the house. 'Tell me inside.'

'Wait.' Abs caught up with him at the edge of the lawn. 'Listen to me.'

He must have looked upset, because Jez was concerned. 'What is it, mate?'

'They got Tony.' Abs did his best to suck down his anxiety. 'He's dead, Jez.'

'Who got Tony? What are you talking about?'

'There was some kind of explosion at his house. He's been killed, and it's just you and me now.'

Jez stared in shock. 'I don't know what to say.'

'First Deano and now Tone. The feds say it could have been an accident, but it's too much of a coincidence, ain't it? Someone knows what happened in Wales, Jez.'

'It's a coincidence.' Jez shook his head. 'It's got to be.'

'Look me in the eye and tell me you believe that. We're next.'

'No, Abs.' Jez squeezed his arm. 'We're not going to be—'

Someone came to the back door, calling Jez's name. His mother-in-law waved. 'Oh, there you are, Jez. Your phone has been ringing. I've left it in the kitchen.'

'Thanks, Lynn,' Jez called, and when she had gone, he turned back to Abs. 'It's probably the police calling me.'

'Yeah, must be.'

Abs watched Jez walk towards the house, and then looked back into the wood, peering into the darkness between the trees in the direction of the chalet where Jez had said he had been speaking on the phone.

27

'Oh hell,' said Connie, peering around the curtain in the bay window.

'Who is it?' asked Sasha in alarm, and saw Connie's ex, Barry, staggering around outside, waving his arms about.

'I can see you in there.' He pressed his face and hands to the window, leaving finger smears and the condensation of his hot breath on the glass. 'Let me in, Con, please.'

Sasha jumped out of sight behind the curtain and tugged Connie with her. 'What on earth is he doing here?'

'Connie.' Barry banged on the glass. 'Give me a chance, doll. I love you!'

'He's going to smash the window, Con.'

'It's over, Barry,' Connie shouted. 'Just leave me alone.'

'Get rid of him, please,' Sasha hissed at her sister.

Barry took a bottle of Scotch from his jacket pocket

to swig from it. He was clearly drunk, which was no surprise to Sasha, who could count on one hand the number of times she had met him when he was sober. She couldn't understand what her sister ever saw in the guy. She had never liked him, Kev had never liked him, and her parents only tolerated him. Despite considering himself to be Southend's own Richard Branson, Barry never had a penny to his name; he was always ducking and diving. Every month he launched some questionable new business: selling bits of plastic tat on the seafront, investing in a burger van – that enterprise was quickly closed down by the hygiene people – and even becoming a sports agent. And every time he tried to get a new scheme off the ground, he approached Sasha and Kev and her parents with another 'once in a lifetime investment opportunity', or got Connie to do it for him. Once bitten, twice shy, they learned very quickly that throwing a bagful of tenners off the end of Southend pier would probably get them a better return on their investment.

But Connie and Barry's sudden split was a shock. Sasha genuinely believed they were in it for the long haul, and she didn't understand it at all. For all their screaming arguments, they were devoted to each other. And despite her distaste for Barry, there was another reason Sasha wished dearly that he and Con were still together – her sister wouldn't have got her claws into Vaughn.

Her DCI came into the room with Kev and her parents to see what the commotion was.

'What a waster that man is.' Alec gulped from his can of lager. 'He's never worked a day in his life.'

Connie looked sharply at her father.

'I can see you all.' Barry stood at the window with his hands pressed together, as if in prayer. 'Please, Con, don't end it like this, I'm begging you, talk to me.'

'He's making a scene,' said Ursula.

'Go away, Barry,' Connie shouted. 'You're embarrassing yourself.'

'Is that your ex?' Vaughn asked Connie quietly.

Barry cupped his hands against the pane to get a better look at Vaughn, and his bottle banged against the glass. 'Is that him, Con? Is that the guy you're with, the pig?'

'Just go away, Barry,' Connie called in exasperation. 'You're spoiling everything.'

'I love you, Con.' He pounded on the glass. 'I can't live without you.'

'He's going to break the window.' Sasha was losing patience. 'Go and say something to him, Connie, or I will.'

'You're not helping,' retorted her sister. 'Barry is hurting.'

'It's not always this exciting here, Mr Vaughn,' Ursula assured him. 'We're all quite boring really.'

'Speak for yourself,' said her husband.

Sasha followed Connie to the front door, but her

sister held up a hand. 'Do you mind, Sash? You can be like a bull in a china shop.'

Sasha told her in a low voice, 'Just make sure he leaves.'

'I don't think I can do it.' Connie shook her head. 'If I go out, he'll just get more upset.'

'Right.' Kev walked towards the door. 'I've had enough of this.'

'Kev, no.' Sasha intercepted him. The last time they'd had a party at the house, he'd ended up thumping their former neighbour. 'Let me handle it.'

Connie placed a proprietorial arm around Vaughn, which was sure to inflame Barry, who was now hunched at the letter box.

'Barry.' Sasha opened the front door. 'You have to go.'

'She's in there with him.' He stumbled towards her. 'Why's she done it, Sasha? What's that copper got that I ain't?'

A few qualities occurred to her straight away, and then a few more.

'You need to go home and sober up.' She saw curtains twitching in the houses across the street and wished he would sod off. 'I'll get her to call you.'

'I'm sleeping on a mate's couch,' he told her dismally. 'I've got nowhere to go. I thought she was the one, Sash, I was going to ask her to marry me. I was finally going to make an honest woman of her.'

Barry's shoulders slumped, and she sensed some of the panic and manic energy leave him. Given another couple of minutes, she was confident she could have encouraged him to go, which is why her heart sank when Vaughn came up behind her.

'You're not welcome,' he told Barry. 'Connie doesn't want you here, or Sasha or anybody else. Go away, or I'll make sure you leave.'

'Oh yeah, you'll do what, filth?' Barry's upper lip lifted in an angry snarl. 'Arrest me?'

'For breach of the peace, if necessary,' Vaughn told him, his eyes drilling into Barry's. 'Yes.'

Barry swigged from the bottle and lurched forward to poke him in the chest. 'All I want is to see the love of my life, my soulmate, my *rock*. The one you're shagging.'

'I'm not going to tell you again,' said Vaughn, brushing away the finger. 'If you're sensible, you'll leave right now.'

'Typical pig,' said Barry with a sneer. 'Playing the Big I-Am, throwing your weight around. And there's a lot of it to throw around, fat boy.'

Neighbours had come out of their houses to watch what was going on and Sasha gave them a small wave of apology, as if to say that everything was under control, and would they *please* not think too badly of her.

'Connie.' Barry's eyes swivelled. 'Give me another chance.'

Connie told him quietly, 'You have to *trust* me, Barry.'

Sasha didn't know what she meant by that. But she was immediately distracted when Barry raised the bottle over his head. For one terrible moment she thought he was going to throw it at them, but instead he brought his arm down hard and dashed the bottle onto the step. Glass shattered everywhere, splashing their legs with alcohol. Connie let out a little yelp, and Vaughn went to her quickly.

'Are you alright?' He ran his hands over her hair and face. 'Did you get hit by glass?'

'No,' Connie said, a tremor in her voice. 'I'm fine.'

Kev pushed past them to get to Barry, who knew, even in his drunken state, that he'd gone too far and was already backing away down the path. 'Go.'

'Alright.' Barry held up his hands: *I'm off.* But he curled his fingers into the shape of a heart in front of his chest. 'You hurt me, Con. I'm heartbroken and I'll never love again.'

And then he staggered off down the street.

'All finished,' Sasha called to the neighbours. Smiling, trying to make light of it. 'Nothing to see now.'

'Well,' said Connie, as Vaughn led her inside. 'Come on, everybody, I think we all need a drink.'

'I'll clear it up,' Kev said, nodding at the broken glass.

'*I'll* do it,' Sasha told him with a simmering anger, and he knew better than to argue. 'Just look after everybody.'

Within a moment, she heard Connie's braying

laughter in the kitchen, saw her sister pressing her fingers to Vaughn's lower back, chatting away as if nothing had happened. Sasha headed to the cellar under the stairs to get the dustpan and brush.

'I love living here,' said a voice, and she saw Denny still sitting on the stairs, eyes fixed on his phone. When she gave him a fierce look – *Don't mess with me right now* – he thumped upstairs.

Sasha heard a cork pop in the kitchen and saw Connie doing a little shimmy. 'Let's get this party started.'

28

The following morning, Sasha packed a bag for her and Kev's night away at the hotel, while Angel helpfully looked through the wardrobe.

'What about these?' Her daughter took a pair of six-inch heels from the shoe rack.

Sasha liked those shoes – they were very stylish, and she had purchased them from an expensive boutique in Soho – but they were very uncomfortable, she found them nearly impossible to walk in, and had only worn them once. 'I think three pairs of shoes for one night is more than enough.'

The overnight bag she was taking was already full. She and Angel had discussed at great length which of three dresses she should take, but neither could decide, so she packed all of them. They'd even talked about what lingerie Sasha should wear, a conversation that was something of a first for both of them. Angel kept rooting through Sasha's drawers and held a swimsuit in front of herself. 'Why don't you take this?'

'We're only going for a night, Angel, I don't think I'll have the time.'

'You don't have to rush home. You might have to check out at noon, that's what happens, right, but that doesn't mean you and Dad can't chill at the hotel for the rest of the day, use all the facilities. You can go for a swim and to the spa, have lunch and then go for a long walk. Don't feel you have to come back Saturday morning.'

That was a nice idea, but Sasha's head was full of the investigation, the death of Andrew Dean and now Tony Gardner, and she wanted to get back home in case there were any developments. Right then, as if on cue, her phone rang. While Angel rummaged around, seemingly determined to force her mother to take enough clothes for a two-week holiday, Sasha picked up her phone from the bedside table.

'I'm on the way in,' she told Ajay quickly, conscious that she was late leaving the house.

'The deceased is Tony Gardner, as we expected.'

'Yes,' Sasha said. 'Vaughn told me last night.'

'What you won't know is that we fast-tracked the forensic investigation, as you asked,' Ajay told her, 'and got a partial match on DNA the CSIs recovered.'

'Partial? What do you mean?'

'It'll be easier to explain when you get here.'

'Okay, I'll be there soon... Ajay, hold on a moment.' She pressed the phone to her shoulder and asked her daughter, 'Do me a favour, sweetheart, and fetch my make-up bag from the bathroom.' When Angel was gone, Sasha said quietly to Ajay, 'I'm supposed to be going to that posh hotel tonight. Am I going to have to cancel?'

'I don't see why. Chances are, we could get this whole thing wrapped up by this afternoon.'

'Okay, I'm on the way in now.' When she had killed the call and stuffed the toiletry bag inside the holdall – 'I've put the spare toothpaste in there, and your toothbrushes,' Angel said helpfully – she zipped it up and lifted it off the bed. With all her and Kev's clothes packed, it was ridiculously heavy for a single night away.

'Maybe I should leave it here and come and pick it up tonight before we go.'

'That's just stupid,' said Angel, and tried to take it from Sasha. 'I'll carry it downstairs if you want.'

Sasha gave her a long look. 'You seem very keen to get shot of me.'

'I knew it,' Angel said, her emotions going from zero to sixty in a heartbeat. 'You don't trust me, you never trust me about anything.'

'I didn't mean it like that,' protested Sasha.

'Yes, you did, you don't ever see the good side of me, and you never will.'

'Okay, I did,' Sasha admitted, because she didn't want to have a row first thing. 'I'm worried about you, and about leaving you on your own.'

But Angel made a face. 'I'm fine now. I'm much better, I really am. You don't have to worry about me, Mum. I'm just going to lie on the sofa and watch Netflix and eat crisps.'

Sasha thought of that poor girl, Sarah Tovey, who had vanished on the streets of Brentwood, and it reminded her once again of Angel's own abduction.

'You're not going to sneak out anywhere while we're gone... to a pub or club or something?'

'I'm not going to leave the house,' insisted her daughter.

'Come here, baby.' Sasha took Angel in her arms, and to her surprise and delight her daughter even returned the hug, which made Sasha immediately feel much better about the whole thing. She kissed the top of Angel's head and said, 'You're sure you're going to be okay?'

Angel tutted. 'I'm sure. Just make sure you and Dad have a great time, and don't get too drunk and embarrass me.'

'Ugh.' Denny came into the room and as soon as he saw them hugging turned to leave.

'Denny,' called Sasha, and he popped his head back in. 'Just because you're on a sleepover doesn't mean you and your mates can stay up all night staring like zombies into your phones. Try and get some sleep, yes?'

'We'll be asleep by eleven o'clock,' Denny told her with a smirk. 'Scout's honour.'

Angel grabbed the bag and they followed Denny

onto the landing. 'Go straight to Harley's house after school,' said Sasha. 'I don't want you hanging around in the town centre.'

'His dad is picking us up from school.'

'Good boy,' she said, still feeling a nameless anxiety at leaving them both while she swanned off to a hotel to drink cocktails and enjoy a night of passionate love-making. Denny was going for a sleepover so he'd be okay, but she still didn't like the idea of Angel being alone. She didn't think anybody would break in and kidnap her, but she didn't want her daughter to have a panic attack. And Sasha still didn't discount the possibility that Angel intended to slip out to a bar, or sit in a park drinking cider with friends, or whatever it was teenagers did these days.

But then she saw Kev standing at the bottom of the stairs, looking very attractive as he ate a piece of toast, and remembered that they would at least enjoy a rare chance to reignite the slumbering fire of their relationship.

'Break a leg in your interview,' she told him, coming down.

'Thank you,' he said and leaned in to kiss her on the cheek. 'I'll get to the hotel as soon as I can.'

She pulled him closer and gently bit his earlobe to get him in the mood for tonight. 'Looking forward to it,' she whispered.

'Yeah,' said Kev, with a mouthful of toast and a distinct lack of passion. 'So am I.'

And before she could say anything else, he turned away to get the kids organized for school. They were all talking at once. Angel was talking at Kev, Denny was talking at Angel, and Kev was talking at both of them, and nobody heard Sasha when she picked up the bag and said, 'I'm off, then.'

29

Being on set again, feeling the buzz and excitement of a TV production, was like coming home for Abs, and he couldn't wait to start filming.

Before the car arrived, he'd spent a lot of time picking out a hoodie, laying several on the bed because he couldn't decide which one to wear – to the uneducated eye they all looked the same, but Abs knew better – and to make sure there were no creases or stains. Then he brushed his favourite white trainers until they were gleaming. He took a long shower, using a tangerine body scrub, and stood in front of the mirror for an hour, blow-drying his hair, and flossing and tweezing and concealing and applying lotions to his face, until his complexion glowed with health and vitality.

Abs wanted to look tip-top for his TV comeback; and he wanted to look his best for Kelsey. But unwelcome thoughts kept crowding into his head – he didn't want to think about Deano or Tony, or that fatal weekend in Wales and poor, poor Rhiannon; he didn't want to think about Jez, speaking to someone in that summer house in the wood behind Bethany's parents' house – and he had to slap himself, and tell himself sternly, 'Come on, Abs, sort your head out, mate.'

Then he jumped into the back of the cab sent by the production team and was driven along the seafront beneath the blazing sun, where they were filming at that restaurant owned by the millionaire chef. In truth, Abs could have walked, it was only a few minutes away, but it had been a long time since someone had offered to send a courtesy car to pick him up and he jumped at the chance.

When he arrived, a young production assistant hurried over to meet him. There were people walking around with clipboards and stopwatches, the camera and sound guys were setting up, and it hit him how much he had missed filming the show.

Laid in Essex! was presented as drama, but nothing was scripted, and cast members were expected to improvise. A lot of actors took exception to reality stars – who were real people, normal people who couldn't afford to go to expensive acting schools, and didn't get a leg-up from well-connected parents – but it was all just sour grapes.

As far as Abs was concerned, what he did, making up his own lines on the spot, romancing the camera and the viewing audience, was even more difficult than learning a script. It meant all he had to rely on was his charm, the force of his personality.

There were a few faces he recognized. One of the sparks who had been with *LIE!* since the first series shook his hand and told him that the show hadn't been the same since he'd left.

Abs felt a lump harden in his throat. 'Cheers, fella.'

The PA took him into the restaurant where all the lights were set up, and a trendy young bloke in a pale-blue leather jacket and cropped peroxide hair greeted him like an old friend. The PA introduced him as the director.

'Hi, how you doing? I've heard a lot about Abs,' – he pointed both forefingers – 'the Total Legend.'

Abs grinned and looked around. He had hoped that the producer would at least have shown his face to welcome him back, but he was nowhere to be seen.

Truth was, Abs was nervous as hell. He'd been given a second chance and he didn't want to blow it.

His mind drifted again to that chalet in the wood, and Jez's shock when he saw him outside.

Knock it off, Abs. Focus.

'Here's my best boy!' Kelsey walked in and came over in a cloud of perfume. 'Come here, doll.'

They held each other in a clinch, while everyone waited in respectful silence. When they had finished, Abs stepped back to get a good look at her – she looked mighty fine, as per usual. But he didn't recognize the whippet-thin young guy standing behind her, looking bored.

'Abs, this is Jay Swift,' said Kelz, remembering the guy was there. 'Swifty is my new boyfriend on the show.'

Abs eyed Swifty, who looked barely older than a sixth-former. He wore a massive quiff with a thin moustache, a garish orange puffa jacket and a pair of elaborate trainers; the left and right feet were completely different colours. Abs glanced down at his own footwear, his trademark white, and wondered for the first time whether he was out of sync with the latest trends. Swifty didn't look much impressed with Abs and mostly stared at his phone, and Abs was filled with a cold dread that Swifty didn't even know who he was.

'So what's the set-up for the scene?' He turned to the director, determined to make the most of his comeback, and win back Kelsey. 'If you want my advice, I think it should just be between me and Kelz.'

The director's eyes dropped to the floor as he considered how to respond, but then Kelsey stepped forward. 'I tell you what, Marcus, why don't I take Abs through it?'

'Sure.' The director looked like he couldn't get behind the camera quick enough, making Abs feel anxious.

'The scene is this, yeah,' said Kelsey, 'Swifty is my new boyfriend on the show—'

'Bit young, ain't he?'

'But then we bump into you here.'

'Yeah,' said Abs. 'Got it.'

He saw what they wanted to do now. Kelsey was

seeing this Swifty guy but then she saw Abs and her love for him was immediately reignited. It was obvious that she still wasn't over him. She remembered the good times they had together, and it was obvious that she still held a torch. The love between him and Kelz was undeniable: red hot, molten. She had to make a choice between Swifty and Abs, the love of her life.

It was no contest.

'We meet and poor old Swifty realizes we're still in love, me and you, and then we get back together.' Abs clapped his hands, looking forward to filming the scene. 'It's perfect, it's a good way to ease me back on the show. I don't need to know any more about the scene, let's just start shooting.' He pumped his fist. 'Yeah!'

Kelsey gave him a strange look and led him to the back of the restaurant, near the toilets. The feel of her long blue nails on his arm was electric. 'Thing is, Abs, that's not how it's going to go.'

'What do you mean?'

'I said I'd get you back on the show as a favour, and that's what this is: a favour. It's going to be a lovely little scene, yeah? We meet and there's a confrontation. I tell you how you broke my heart and you apologize, and we talk about the fun we used to have together. No hard feelings, and all that. But I'm with Swifty now. You know that – you must have read the papers?'

Abs looked over at the kid standing staring at his phone. 'What, you're seeing him in real life?'

'Yeah,' she told him brightly. 'They're talking about us presenting a new series on ITV3. They say it's like Mr & Mrs, whatever that is, but for millennials. Swifty's making all kinds of waves in the biz. He's going places, Abs.'

'But you told everyone at the party the other night that we were soulmates.'

'Oh, babes.' She made a face, like, *Bless*. 'That was just showbiz – I was telling everybody what they wanted to hear. Look, I got you back on the show. It's a guest appearance, a cameo, but if you make a good fist of it, who knows? A producer out there might take notice.'

'I don't care about the show.' His chest was clogged with emotion. 'I thought you wanted me back, I thought you and me would make another go of it.'

'Abs,' she told him, not unkindly. 'I love you, of course I do, and I always will. But not like that, not after…'

She bit her lip and he leaned forward. 'Not after *what*, Kelz?'

'That girl, Abs,' she told him quietly. 'The one who disappeared. It just don't look good.'

He wanted to tell her that it had nothing to do with him, he was asleep, he was in a drunken stupor, it wasn't his fault, but he couldn't say that because he may not have killed her, but he was guilty. Poor Rhiannon's shocked, confused family had no idea what had happened to her, she had vanished off the face of the earth. He thought of the pain they must be in, her dad, her aunt and uncle, all the people who loved her. It was no wonder Davey Jenkins had gone wild with anger; if the shoe was on the other foot, Abs would have too. His heart clenched with grief and disgust.

When he closed his eyes, he saw the mud patter across her face in the shallow grave as her young body disappeared slowly into the ground. She would be gone now, reduced to cold bones.

Abs felt dizzy again, like he did when he'd woken up drunk in the middle of the night at the cottage, and the room had spun around him – *the glass, the ceiling, the floor, the mattress* – all of it churning and overlapping in his vision.

Only Kelsey's love could help save him, only her love could make him feel better. He needed her love. He didn't need to be loved by anyone except her. She would save him.

'I don't care about the show. If I'm not coming back to it, fine.' His eyes filled with tears. 'But I love you, Kelz. I've always loved you.'

Kelsey cupped his cheek, careful not to stab her long nails into his ear. 'You're a sweet guy, Abs, but you're making a scene. Save it all for when we're rolling.'

'Okay, guys.' The director clapped his hands. 'Let's get this show on the road. Kelsey, Abs, are you ready to go?'

'Tell me you love me.' His chest hurt, it was full to

bursting with love and pain, fear and shame – and he needed to hear her say it. 'I don't care about any of the other stuff, just tell me we have a future.'

Kelsey frowned. 'My publicist wouldn't be happy, Abs.'

'*Fuck* your publicist. Say you love me.'

'Are we ready to shoot, guys?' The director stepped forward, but Abs wouldn't take his eyes off Kelsey.

'Please tell me.'

'You're embarrassing yourself, Abs.' Kelsey's mouth was a terse line. 'Let's just film this scene, yeah, and then you better go.'

'Tell me you love me,' Abs shouted.

'Listen to me, darlin.' Kelz pulled him close, and when she spoke her voice was low and menacing. 'I did you a big favour when nobody else will touch you with a bargepole, so do not embarrass me in front of my people, or I'll make sure you *never* work in television again. I can do that, doll, you better believe I can.'

Abs stepped back, as if coming out of a trance.

She had never loved him. They were together because it was good for her career, because they were a stronger showbiz brand as a couple than on their own. But all that was over now.

He had done an unforgivable thing, and nobody was going to save him; an unforgivable thing, which he had to put right.

'So, babes.' Always the pro, a big smile lit up Kelsey's face. 'Shall we get this scene done?'

Abs pushed his way past the sound guy and the lighting guy and the director, and into the blazing sun, and walked quickly away.

30

Three years ago

Everyone stood around the clearing staring at the body, unable to believe what they were looking at. Everyone except Deano, who sat on the stump of a tree with his head between his legs.

'Oh no-no-no.' Tony spun in a circle. 'This isn't good, it isn't good at all.'

Abs wasn't the kind of person who got angry, but he was incandescent with rage and fear right at that moment, thinking of all the ways this terrible thing that had happened was going to ruin everything for all of them. Badly hungover, he snapped sarcastically, 'Really, Tone, you think so?'

Jez went and sat quietly with his legs crossed on the woodland floor, a few feet from the dead girl, looking at her blankly.

'Look what you've done, Deano,' Tony shouted at his friend.

Deano hugged his knees to his chest and wept. 'I'm sorry,' he whined. 'I'm so sorry.'

'Don't give us the sob story, mate,' shouted Tony. 'Just tell us what the hell happened?'

Deano shook his head, as if he couldn't believe it. 'I don't... I just don't remember. We were drinking and then I must have gone into blackout, and the next thing I know, I woke up and she was... dead.' His voice became very small. 'Strangled.'

'You've gone too far this time, mate.' Tony jabbed a finger. 'Way too far.'

'Wait.' Abs stepped forward. 'Too far? What are you talking about?'

'Deano's got previous for violence. He attacked an old girlfriend once and there was a restraining order.'

'Great.'

Abs raised his face to the clouds drifting across the sky, the tips of the trees forming spidery fingers at the edges of his vision. It was so quiet in this wooded place, so different from the hurly-burly of his usual life, the noise and frantic pace of town. It was still silly o'clock in the morning. Back home, he'd be blissfully asleep beneath expensive cotton sheets, or on his way to film *LIE!*, flying across Essex in a cab, sipping a soya latte from a KeepCup as he watched the shuttered shops and empty offices flash by. His headache, born of drink and magnified by panic, pounded behind his eyes. He shut them, trying to ignore Tony's angry voice and Deano's sobs, and the sight of that poor girl on the floor, to try and think.

They had to get a grip on the situation or he was going to lose everything.

'Okay.' He opened his eyes and said, 'What are we going to do about it?'

'Do?' Tony looked at him as if he'd lost his marbles. 'We're going to call the police, is what we're going to do.'

'Now wait, let's think about this.'

Abs held up his hands, playing for time. Fact was, he had more to lose than Tony and Jez, a lot more. Tony had a wife and kids, and Jez had just got together with a girl called Bethany, and they both had jobs, yes, but it's not like either of them were famous.

Abs suspected Deano would try to drag them all through the mud, and Abs especially, as he was the last person other than him to see the girl alive. Deano's lawyers would be sure to throw suspicion in his direction.

As a much-loved celebrity, Abs would be crucified in the press. Instead of strangers greeting him in the street like an old mate, they would shout cruel and untrue things at him. *Murderer! Scumbag! Killer!*

He'd lose Kelsey forever.

He had never looked for trouble in his life, he had never hurt a fly. All Abs had ever wanted to be was a nice guy, to be liked and loved, but the universe had played this nasty trick on him. Oh God, that poor girl. Abs would do anything to turn the clock back and make Rhiannon safe again, but it was all too late, because she was dead. He couldn't bear to look at her body, especially because of what he was about to say…

'We can go to the police, yes, or we can do something else.'

'What are you talking about?' Tony placed his hands on his hips. 'We have to call the cops.'

Deano let out a little groan of despair.

'We could do that, of course we could,' Abs said carefully. 'Or we could take her body somewhere else, somewhere far away, so it looks like she got lost and fell in a ditch or something.'

'She's been strangled,' said Tony. 'Of course she didn't fall.'

'Or… or…' Abs had no choice but to say it outright. 'We could bury her. Find a spot up a mountain or in a river, somewhere that even if they do find her eventually, all the evidence will have long eroded away.'

Tony stared, incredulous, and Jez looked up sharply.

'Think about it.' Abs moved around the clearing, maintaining eye contact with them all. 'We all have lots to lose here. Careers, family, loved ones. Jez?' He knew that his best friend would be the toughest nut to crack. Jez was the most upstanding person Abs had ever met, and he needed him on board to have any chance of making this work. 'You'll lose Bethany, she won't want to be with you. Is that what you want?'

Jez's gaze dropped to the floor. 'Abs—'

'Let me finish, mate. If we tell people what happened,

we'll all be held responsible. We'll all likely go to prison for something *we* didn't do.' He gestured at Deano. 'For something this idiot did.'

Brittle-skinned Deano would usually bite back at being insulted, but this morning – devastated, wracked with guilt and shame – he dropped his head.

Jez shook his head. 'Maybe it's not what it looks like.'

'Not what it looks like?' Abs nodded at the body. 'What does this look like to you? The girl is dead. *But.*' He held up his hands, making the biggest pitch of his life. 'Nobody knows she's with us. We were seen talking to her in the pub, sure, but so were loads of people, and she left on her own. Nobody saw us with her outside the pub, and nobody knows she came here.'

Everyone was quiet – the only noise came from songbirds chirping in the trees – and Abs thought he'd failed to sell his plan.

But then Tony nodded. 'Alright. I don't see why we should all have to suffer. I've got a wife and kids, I can't go to prison.'

'Deano?' Abs needed him to agree, to convince Jez to buy into the idea. 'You're gonna go along with this, right? Don't you dare say no, because we're trying to do you a massive favour right now.'

'I don't remember.' Deano rubbed his eyes. 'Not any of it, I just don't—'

'*Yes* or *no*?' snapped Abs, losing patience.

'Yeah.' The big man nodded. 'Sure.'

'That's three of us for the plan.' Abs turned to Jez, who stared at the body. 'Come on, mate, don't let your own life be ruined because of someone else's mistake. We all need you to agree to this.'

When Jez looked up at Abs, his eyes were blurred with tears and his face twisted in an agony of indecision.

'She's dead,' he said quietly.

'Yeah, she is.'

'Maybe it's not what it looks like.'

Abs crouched in front of Jez and said softly, 'We have to decide now because we ain't got much time. Are you with us?'

Shamefaced, Jez nodded.

Abs cupped his friend's neck – *Good lad* – and stood.

'We've got forty-eight hours till we're expected home. So we're going to find some place the police will never look, and we're going to bury her there. Then we're going to scrub and wash our clothes, and we're going to clean up here, inside and out, to make sure every single trace of the girl is removed.'

Everyone looked past him at Rhiannon's body. Abs didn't want to look at her – it was the last thing he wanted to do – but he forced himself, and in his mind he begged for her forgiveness.

'Come on, guys,' he said, finally looking away. 'If we stick together, we can do this. You know what I always say, teamwork makes the dream work.'

31

'Tony Gardner was killed several hours before you and Lolly got there. You'll see from the report that the pathologist estimates that was around mid-morning. The body is very badly burned. Acid was sprayed in his eyes – he was blinded just like Andrew Dean – and he suffered severe head trauma, which is what killed him.'

Sasha and her team sat listening as Ajay brought them up to speed on Gardner's death, and looked at photos taken of the crime scene inside the house. Ajay dropped his notes on his desk.

'He was hit multiple times on the head, we believe by a brick taken from the stack in the front garden, which was left by the body. Then the gas was left on, or a pipe tampered with – the fire investigators are still looking into the exact details of that – causing the explosion.'

'The attack could have been a spur of the moment thing,' said Craig. 'There's an argument on the doorstep.

The killer picks up a murder weapon close to hand, a brick, and bashes him on the head with it.'

'But they just happened to have acid in their pocket?' Lolly made a face. 'They were watching the place, more like. They knew the bricks were there all along. They knock on the door, Gardner opens it and gets a face full of acid.' She mimed throwing it. 'While he's rolling around in agony, they walk in calm as you like, shut the door behind them and bosh, it's easy enough to finish the job.'

'This is all very interesting, Ajay.' Sasha stirred a coffee. 'But I'm still waiting for this bombshell you promised.'

'Lots of DNA would have been obliterated in the fire but an interesting sample was found on the handle of the front door, which blew out. It's a partial match for somebody we found in the database.' He paused dramatically.

'For goodness sake, Ajay,' said Sasha impatiently. 'This isn't a quiz show, just tell us.'

'The DNA is a partial match for Jeremy Weston.'

'Wait, that's it?' Craig frowned. 'It's not beyond the realms of possibility that Weston visited Tony Gardner.'

'No,' Ajay told him. 'That's not what I said. The DNA is a partial match with Jeremy Weston's, but it's not his. It's a fifty per cent match, and the profile has two X chromosomes, so it's female.'

Sasha lifted her teaspoon from the mug, surprised by the unexpected left turn the briefing had taken.

'What are you saying?' asked Vaughn, who had been listening at the back of the room and now stepped closer.

'It's familial DNA, guv,' Ajay told him, 'suggesting a close female relative.'

'In Tony's house?' asked Lolly.

'And we have Weston's DNA, how?' asked Sasha.

'Weston gave a DNA sample for a traffic offence a few months back,' Ajay said.

Sasha nodded at Craig. 'Let's see if we can find a match on the offender database.'

'Andrew Dean is killed, and then Tony Gardner. Both are blinded with acid, most likely to make them vulnerable, and then murdered. Both men went to a holiday cottage with Jez Weston and Abs three years ago, and were questioned about a girl who went missing. Then familial DNA, suggesting a female relative of Jeremy Weston, turns up at Tony Gardner's home.' Ajay looked around the room. 'What does it mean?'

'We know zilch about Jez's background other than he spent much of his childhood in foster care with Abs,' said Craig.

'Then it's time we found out.' Sasha thought about the tense conversation at Jez and Bethany's house. 'Lols, you remember yesterday when Jez told Abs he was the only family he'd got? Abs looked a bit taken aback.'

'Yeah,' agreed Lolly. 'He did.'

Craig leaned forward in his chair. 'Should we talk to Jez Weston?'

'No.' Sasha tapped the spoon, which was still warm from the hot coffee, against her cheek. 'If he thinks his sibling is worth keeping a secret, let's hold back.' She flicked through her notebook for a number, plucked the phone from its cradle and lifted a finger to encourage everyone to remain quiet as she made a call.

A moment later, the phone was answered.

'Hello, Abs, it's DI Dawson.' She pressed the speaker button, then placed the receiver down so everyone could hear. 'How are you today?'

'Yeah, I'm good.' He didn't sound too good, he sounded fed up, but – typical Abs – he quickly recovered his poise. 'You've got a great phone voice – husky, low.'

'Thank you,' Sasha said. 'It must be all those Rothmans.'

'What's happened?' he asked quickly.

'The investigation is ongoing,' Sasha told him blandly. 'And, of course, we will keep you informed as soon as we have any new information.'

'Great.' Abs hesitated. 'Then why are you phoning?'

'We're just trying to clear up some background details. Do you have any brothers or sisters, Abs?' she asked.

'Me?' She heard the confusion in his voice. 'No, why?'

'And what about Jez?' she asked lightly. 'Does he have any siblings?'

'Siblings?'

'Brothers or sisters,' said Sasha.

'Why ain't you asking him this?'

'I will be, but I thought I'd ask you while we were on the phone.'

She looked at her team as they all waited tensely for Abs to answer. 'He has a sister, but he ain't seen her in years.'

Sasha pointed a finger at Craig – *Bingo!* – and he spun his chair round to tap at his computer. 'What's her name, Abs?' she asked casually.

'Lauren.'

'Oh,' said Sasha, as if the thought had only just occurred to her. 'It's just that when Jez called you his family yesterday, you looked surprised.'

'I was, yeah,' said Abs. 'He never mentions her, really.'

'Older or younger, Abs?'

'She's a year older than him, something like that.'

Craig was already running the name through various databases, and Lolly rolled her chair close to watch.

'You don't happen to have an address for Lauren?'

'No,' said Abs cautiously. 'As I say, they ain't seen each other for years, since they were kids. I don't think he thinks of her as family, really, not since she...'

Sasha's shoulders tensed. 'Since she what, Abs?'

'She beat him up when they were kids, pretty badly he said, and that's why they were separated. This was before he met me, so I don't know much about her.'

'So you have no idea where she would be?'

'No,' said Abs. 'Why would I? She moves around

a lot, I think – she's one of them crusties now, into squatting and that. Look, what's this about?'

'As I say, we're just doing a little fact-checking, filling in some background.' She pulled a face at the obvious lie. 'Thanks so much, Abs, that was very helpful.'

As soon as she disconnected the call, by picking up the handset and dropping it again, the members of her team drifted back to their desks. Craig continued tapping gingerly at his keyboard, looking up Lauren Weston on various property and vehicle databases.

Sasha tried to catch up on some other work, writing reports about a fraud case that had been limping along for months, and an attempted murder in Benfleet. At lunchtime, she popped out to get a sandwich and a Diet Coke, and when she returned, Craig walked over with a tablet computer in his hand.

'Lauren Weston,' he said. 'She's been charged with a number of public order offences, at climate change and animal rights protests. She chained herself to railings at a fashion show and was arrested during scuffles at a demo against intensive farming, an anti-meat thing.'

'No match on the DNA database?' she asked hopefully.

He eyed her sandwich. 'Not a sausage, but there's a Lauren Weston on social media, Twitter and Instagram, although she goes by the name of Lore now. She posts a lot of political stuff. Refugee and environmental issues, squatters' rights, stuff like that.'

She took the tablet from him, spreading her fingers on the screen to increase the image on Lauren Weston's Twitter profile page, @LoreWez123; but it was of a pink koala bear. 'You think it's her?'

'The age fits with what we know of Jez and his sister, and the squatters' rights thing is a red flag.'

'What about an address?'

'A woman called Lauren Weston applied for social security benefits, and put her address as a house in Colchester, which is currently being used as a squat. I'll mail you the address.'

'Thanks, Craig,' she said, and went back to trying to compose a mail requesting that she be excused from a departmental health and safety seminar, held over a whopping three days, which was planned for the end of the year. She had attended something similar last year at Vaughn's insistence, and had emerged from it none the wiser about critical health and safety issues, but a couple of kilos heavier from eating all the biscuits. When she looked up, Craig Power was hovering.

'If you're going to see her, I'll come with you,' he said.

'No.' She saved the draft of the email, would take another bash at it later. 'I want you and Ajay to find out what you can about Jez Weston and his sister, and I'll take Lolly to Colchester. Abs said Lauren attacked Jez, so let's see if social services have any record of what happened.'

'Unlikely – we're talking something that happened

well over two decades ago. The easiest thing would be to talk to Jez.'

'Hold off on that for now. When we speak to him, at least let's be armed with all the facts. I want to know why, if she hasn't seen her brother for years, Lauren's DNA would turn up in the home of a murdered man, a friend of her brother's.'

'Lolly.' She called over the office to where her DC was in animated conversation with someone. 'Come on, chatty chops, let's go.'

Ajay glanced up from his desk. 'Do try not to get blown up.'

'Chelmsford phoned,' said DCI Vaughn, striding over. 'They still haven't received that statement from the cousin of Sarah Tovey.'

Sasha blushed. 'I'm sorry, Vaughn, it completely slipped my mind.'

'I said I'd get it done asap,' he told her shortly.

She and her team were working on so many things alongside the investigation into the deaths of Andrew Dean and Tony Gardner, she was juggling so many balls, that she hadn't even opened the email from Chelmsford. 'Where are they with that?'

'Not very far. They're chasing all possible investigative leads, but have had no success.' Vaughn gave Lolly a piece of paper. 'That's her cousin's address. Ring Chelmsford, get the background on the girl's disappearance and go get a statement. Straight away, please.'

'Will do, guv.' Lolly flashed Sasha an apologetic look and rushed off.

Vaughn stood awkwardly with Sasha. She wanted to say something about last night's disastrous get-together at her house but didn't know how to broach the subject.

He saved her the trouble, when he said, 'Last night was fun.'

'Yes.' She hoped he meant it ironically. 'It was eventful.'

'Connie's ex – Barry – is a character.'

There were other descriptions she could think of that nailed Barry's essence more accurately, but she said, 'He's certainly that.'

'I'm sorry.' Vaughn led her towards the photocopier, away from the nest of desks where they could be overheard. 'I should never have allowed Connie to convince me to come.'

'Oh, don't be silly, it was lovely to see you there,' Sasha said cheerfully, lying through her teeth, and she was careful not to stare too closely at the dark circles beneath his eyes. He looked shattered. 'You're welcome any time, Vaughn.'

'After we left your place, we went for a couple more drinks. Connie knows a place with late opening hours. She seems to know all the angles.'

'Hmmm.'

'She's full-on, your sister.' When she smiled blandly,

he nodded at the overnight bag beside her desk. 'Going anywhere nice?'

'Me and Kev are meant to be going to a hotel tonight.' There was realistically little they could accomplish in the office on a Friday night, but she added quickly, 'I'll still be available, if anyone needs me.'

'Nobody will need you,' he told her. He meant it in a nice way, she was sure. As in, *In the event of an emergency, we've got everything covered.* But, to her mind, it still sounded unnecessarily blunt.

32

Sasha drove to the Dutch Quarter of Colchester, the small Essex town that, many centuries ago, was the capital of Roman Britain.

Trying to find the squat, Sasha drove her Spider along a street near the town centre, squinting at the door numbers of the elegant Edwardian three-storey terraced houses, with their tall windows, converted basement kitchens and wrought iron railings. But then she passed a house where the windows were hidden behind colourful throws, banners and flags, all covered with slogans and demands for the overthrow of the political system. One poster sellotaped to the inside of a downstairs window proposed violent world revolution immediately, which must have delighted the mortgage payers of the other homes in this middle-class area.

Sasha parked further along the street and climbed out. As she approached the door of the house, she heard music thumping inside, but nobody answered when she knocked, which wasn't a great surprise. Squatters would be wary of answering the door; bailiffs could turn up on the doorstep at any moment.

Looking through the letter box, Sasha glimpsed dirty white floorboards on the stairs, and could just about make out the top of the landing. The music blasted. What was that, grime or drum and bass, or drill? She didn't know, despite once having both her children try to explain the difference to her. Sasha went back to her car, angling the driver's side mirror to keep an eye on the front door of the house while she made a phone call to her team, catching up on the latest developments in the investigation, all zero of them.

She took a notebook out of her bag, considering whether to leave a note for Lauren Weston. Jez's sister was an unknown quantity in the investigation. Her DNA had turned up at a crime scene. That didn't necessarily make her a suspect at this stage, but if she was in any way involved in the murder of Tony Gardner – and Andrew Dean – there was a strong chance she could flee. Most squatters were suspicious of law enforcement and there was an extensive network of activists across the country; Lauren could literally disappear off the grid if she chose to.

Sasha's phone buzzed in her bag and she saw a message from Kev.

Can't wait for tonight xx

That made her smile. Her fingers hovered over the touchscreen. She thought about sending a dirty response, something to get his pulse racing. But then she remembered he had to keep his wits about him for the job interview later, and wrote instead...

Me too. Love you xxx

The message flew from her phone with a *whoosh* just as the front door of the squat opened and a guy came out. As he left, he placed a pair of massive headphones over his ears and walked off in the opposite direction.

But Sasha's attention was caught by the way the street door began to close very slowly behind him. She was only parked a few yards along the kerb and if she was quick, she could probably slip inside before it closed.

Which was probably a very bad idea.

'What the hell,' she told herself, and she threw the pen and notebook into her bag, shoved it over her shoulder, and climbed out. She raced to the door and caught it just as the edge was about to kiss the frame.

'Hello?' She peered along the shabby hallway, which was littered with dumped boxes and black plastic sacks. The music, with its throbbing bass and angry lyrics, pumped down from the floor above. 'Is anyone there?'

Sasha moved further into the hallway. A doorway on the right led into a gloomy front room, which was hidden from the street by the covered windows, and now she could see why. Because it was filled with boxes of electronic equipment and appliances. Stacked in neat piles around the room, there were dishwashers and state-of-the-art stereo systems, televisions and computers of all shapes and sizes, all in pristine condition. Distracted by the discovery – there was no way all these electronic goods had arrived here by legal means – she moved further into the room. She should call this in straight away, she should –

'Who the hell are you?' said a voice behind her and she spun round to see two men in the doorway. Wearing tee-shirts and jeans, and with long hair and scruffy beards, they stared at her angrily. The one in front was tall and powerfully built, and had blonde dreads, which tumbled down his back. His fists were balled at his sides, the pupils of his eyes bulged; he was off his face on something.

'I'm not here to make trouble.' Sensing danger immediately, Sasha tried to sound calm, but her voice was almost lost beneath the music thumping from upstairs. 'I'm not interested in anything here.'

'Who are you, then?' The man's snarling voice matched the angry expression on his face. 'Because you look like filth to me.'

'Liam.' The other man placed a hand on his shoulder. 'Don't—'

'Shut up.' The man called Liam shrugged him off and stepped forward. 'Who let you inside?'

'The door was open,' Sasha said. 'I'm not interested in any of this stuff, I'm just looking for someone.'

'What stuff?' Liam said in a goading voice. 'I don't know what you're talking about.'

There was a set of double doors at the back of the room, but boxes were piled all around them, blocking her escape. There was only one way out and that was through the door behind these two men, and the one called Liam was in no mood to let her just walk out.

'Her name is Lauren Weston.' Sasha held up a hand, trying to placate him, but she could hardly hear herself think above the *thump whoomp, thump whoomp* of the bass and the blood pumping in her skull. She appealed to the man. 'Can we turn the music down so I can explain?'

'You're taking the piss, just walking in here.' Liam was tense and sweating. 'And now you've seen all the gear.'

'I haven't seen anything,' she tried to reassure him.

'Are you blind, or thick, or what? You're a liar,' he spat.

Sasha knew that the last thing she should do was admit that she was a copper. The situation could take a very dangerous turn.

'I'm sorry, I made a mistake coming inside.' She made sure to keep eye contact with Liam. 'But the door was open and I—'

'She's seen us now,' Liam shouted at the other guy. 'If we let her just walk out of here, we're totally screwed.'

The only thing she could do was appeal to Liam's mate. 'Tell Liam this isn't… we don't need this situation to escalate.'

'You'll come back with other pigs.'

'I'm not going to do that.' She glanced around the room for something to defend herself with, but there was nothing, just boxes of stuff, and her police baton was in the boot of her Spider.

'Lauren Weston,' she repeated. 'I'm just trying to find Lauren Weston.'

Liam came towards her and Sasha stepped back, felt the hard bulk of the stacked boxes behind her. As a police officer, she had been given self-defence training, but she didn't stand a chance against this very big, very angry man, who looked strung out on something.

'Liam.' Panic rising in his voice, the other guy tried to calm his friend. 'She's just some random bitch, dude, you need to dial it down.'

'She's seen what we're doing, bruv, she's gonna run out of here and then the pigs will be on us in minutes.' His hands clapped together with a loud smack. 'In seconds.'

'I'm looking for someone.' All she could do was repeat it again and again. 'If she's not here, I'll go.'

Liam snatched the bag from her shoulder, and started rifling through it.

'Give that back, please,' Sasha told him and held out her hand, but he was already pulling items out. Her notebook and pen, a tampon, a lipstick, a tube of concealer, keys. Her phone clattered to the floor. He snatched her purse from the bag, and took the few notes inside, then threw it on the floor with the rest of Sasha's belongings. Then he found her warrant card and held it in front of her face.

'I knew it.'

He threw it at the other man in triumph.

'That's right.' Sasha made her face a mask of anger, trying to conceal the very real fear she had that this guy was at any moment going to assault her, or worse. 'I'm Detective Inspector Sasha Dawson of Essex Police and if you touch me, if you lay a single finger on me, *Liam*, you will go to prison.'

He jabbed a finger in her face. 'You're police.'

'Step back,' she commanded and looked urgently towards the man at the door. 'Tell your friend to move back before this goes any further.'

In the back of her mind, Sasha registered that the music had turned off. Other faces appeared at the door. 'What's going on?'

Sasha appealed to them. 'If any harm comes to me, officers will be straight here to arrest every single one of you, and I guarantee that they will turn this place upside down. I'm looking for a woman called Lauren Weston. That's all I want to do – find Lauren.'

But Liam grabbed the lapels of her jacket. Sasha was lifted off her feet and her shoulders slammed against the boxes. Stars exploded in her vision and she felt her knees buckle, more from shock than anything else, but then her feet landed back on solid ground as Liam was dragged back.

There was a commotion in the room. Everyone was shouting, there was pushing and shoving. Sasha staggered along the wall of boxes, getting her breath back. All her stuff was getting kicked about; the lipstick flew across the floor. Liam managed to grab her again, a snarl on his face, eyes blazing with rage. She lifted her arms, ready for the blow.

But someone pushed in front of her and shoved him away.

'Back off.' The woman was tall and muscular, but Sasha only saw the back of her head, which was shaved down one side. 'Like to threaten women, do ya? Then take a swing at me, and see where that gets you, yeah?' Liam pulled back his fist, but he hesitated. 'Come on, then, Liam,' she goaded him. 'Give it a go.'

And then he was dragged away by the other people in the room. Liam kicked and screamed, squirming in the grasp of the men who pulled him out of the door, but Sasha sensed that he wasn't trying very hard to escape their grip.

The woman turned to Sasha. 'Are you alright?'

'Yeah,' she said, trembling.

'Good.' The woman bent over to pick up Sasha's bag and shoved it at her. 'Then you can tell me just what the hell it is you want to talk to me about.'

33

Sasha sat at a table in an attic bedroom, which was almost entirely white. The chair she sat in and the table beside her were painted white; the duvet, the floorboards. The only splash of colour in the room was the bulbous gold frame of a distressed mirror that hung above the bed, a crucifix hanging from one corner, and the dark clothes she glimpsed behind the frosted glass door of the wardrobe.

Sasha held out a hand, which was steady now. She sipped the camomile tea that Lauren Weston had brought her, and listened to the thrum of the traffic in the streets far below; a door slammed somewhere in the house. The peace in the room was in stark contrast to the pandemonium downstairs a few minutes earlier.

Moments later, the door opened and Lauren came back in. She was a powerfully built woman with bleached hair, which was long and spiky on one side of her head and shaved to the scalp on the other. A pair of bars threaded through her left eyebrow, dark eyeshadow surrounded her grey eyes and her bottom lip was pierced. She wore a military-style coat, all epaulettes and brass buttons, with black leggings and Dr. Martens boots.

She dropped thirty quid on the table, the amount Liam had snatched from Sasha's purse. 'Don't worry, it's all there.'

Lauren took a straight-backed chair, flipped it around in one swift movement, and swung a leg over to sit with her arms resting on the backrest, *Cabaret*-style.

She considered Sasha for a moment. 'You're either very stupid or very brave just walking in like that.'

Sasha sipped the tea. 'Let's err on the side of stupid.'

'Liam is moving on, which is no great loss. He's always been the most disagreeable member of our community, even when he's clean and sober, which isn't very often. He'll be gone by the end of the day, and good riddance. But let's be clear, policewoman, we're not in the habit of handing people over to the filth. And the boxes downstairs are being removed as we speak. One of our people was doing someone a favour by keeping them here for a couple of days, which was a stupid thing to do, but by the time we're raided, if that's your plan, it'll all be long gone, I can promise you that.'

Sasha hadn't even thought about the hooky gear; she was just interested in warming her hands on the mug. The yellow liquid inside was hot and fragrant.

'Thank you,' she said. 'For… stepping in.'

'You're welcome.' Lauren picked up the warrant card that was placed on the table with the other contents of Sasha's bag and read it. 'Just what are you doing here, Detective Inspector Sasha Dawson?'

'You're Lauren Weston,' said Sasha.

The woman chucked the card down. 'I haven't been called Lauren for years, I'm Lore now. What do you want with me?'

'A friend of your brother, Jeremy, a man named Tony Gardner, was murdered in his home in Hadleigh. We took DNA from the crime scene that closely matches your brother's. It's familial DNA, from a close female relative.'

Lore nodded at Sasha's white hair. 'Is that dyed or what?'

'It's all natural.'

Lore made a face 'You must have had a hard life.'

Sasha smiled. 'Just lucky genes, I guess.'

'I have no idea who Tony Gardner is.'

'But we found DNA in—'

'In his house, yes. When did this happen?'

'He was killed yesterday morning.'

'I didn't get out of bed till two o'clock in the afternoon, and I wasn't alone, so I have an alibi. I don't know what familial DNA is, I don't know this Tony Gardner, and I've never been to Hadleigh, which means you need to give your forensic' – she made quotation marks in the air – '*experts* a firm kick up the arse.'

'Tony Gardner is Jeremy's—'

'I heard what you said,' snapped Lore. 'But I ain't seen Jezzer in years. He's got his fancy life now, ain't that right? He don't want anything to do with me, he's made that clear, and the feeling is mutual.'

'Then we'd like to DNA test you,' said Sasha.

'Yeah,' said Lore sarcastically. 'Good luck with that. I don't know any of the people Jez hangs around with these days, so whoever's DNA that is, it ain't mine.'

'Do you have other brothers or sisters?'

'No, as far as I know, there's just me and Je— Oh Lord.' Lore's eyes widened as a thought struck her.

'What?' asked Sasha.

Lore blinked. 'She's *back*.'

Sasha asked the next question quietly, but blood raced in her veins. 'Who's back?'

Lore shook her head, smiling grimly, and Sasha waited for her to continue. 'Let me tell you about Rachel Weston, my darling mother. Me and Jez were put into care because she went to prison for bashing the brains out of one of her shitty boyfriends.' Lore narrowed her eyes, trying to get the time frame right in her head. 'This was back in the early nineties, when I was eleven, and Jez was, what, nine or ten.'

'What were the circumstances?'

'The lucky fella was called Alan Hart, a really odious character, even more so than the usual sewer rats she brought home. Men used to come and go in our house, they didn't stick around for long. They were unreliable chancers, and Mum had a temper on her. So before long there were screaming fights, things getting hurled everywhere. And let me tell you, Ma could take care of herself, the men always came off worse. The police were always coming round, and social services – it wouldn't surprise me if Child Protection kept their own teabags at our house, they were in and out so much.

'But this Alan was something else entirely – she bit off more than she could chew with that one. He cracked her head, broke her collarbone, she was in and out of A&E. They fought nearly every night. But she clung to him because he had deeper pockets than the others, and she was desperate to give Jez a good start in life.' Lore leaned forward and smiled. 'Notice I said Jez, not me – he was the apple of her eye. Darling Ma couldn't care less about me. Anyway, she let Alan move in for a while, but then he started creeping into Jez's bedroom at night and… well, you can guess the rest.'

She shook her head. 'He never touched me, I don't think he would dare – even at that age I was a handful. Anyway, Rachel found out what he was doing. She didn't confront him or anything, that wasn't Ma's style. Instead, she bided her time and chose her moment carefully. One morning she went to the off-licence and got him paralytic. I was at school, but Jez was at home, off sick, and saw it all happen. The way I heard, when Alan passed out on the couch she took a saucepan and smashed him over the head until his skull caved in. Then, just to be sure, she shoved the business end of a kitchen knife into his chest three or four times.' Lore blew out her cheeks. 'Alan was a bit of a mess when the cops turned up, but I never saw the body, not like Jez. I never went back to that house.'

She paused, thinking about what she said. 'And I've never had a home since, not a proper one, somewhere I've laid down roots. I've moved around, squatting here and there, mostly.'

'She was protecting you,' said Sasha.

'She was protecting Jez.' Lore's boots tapped anxiously on the floor. 'I'm not sure my well-being ever entered her mind – she always loved him more than me. Sometimes I wonder if she even knew I existed. I don't say that with any bitterness. It hurt me at the time, of course it did, but I just came to accept it. Rachel dressed Jez up nice for school – he got a new tie and blazer and everything, paid for by money she stole from her boyfriends – but there never seemed to be any money left to spend on me, so I'd go to school in scruffy hand-me-downs. I was always being sent home because my clothes were literally falling apart. Rachel killed Alan to protect her precious boy. If he sneaked into my bedroom at night, I'm not sure she would even have thrown him out.' Lore shrugged. 'Anyway, Ma ended up behind bars for nearly twenty years.'

'So she's out now,' said Sasha.

'I guess she is, but it's not my concern. As young kids in care, Jez and I were encouraged to write to her – she was our mother, after all – so I dutifully wrote her a dozen letters or more.' Lore snorted dismissively. 'Guess what, she replied to Jez's letters, but not to mine.'

'And your brother, Jeremy, you're not in contact with him?'

'I haven't spoken to him for years.' Lore's voice hardened. 'He's got his supersized life. Money in the bank, the fancy house and Barbie wife. We have nothing in common.'

'When did you last see him?' asked Sasha.

Lore stood and swung the chair the right way round; sat back down.

'I can't even remember. It's not like we were ever close, even as kids.' She twisted one of the laces of her DMs in her hand. 'And we were separated within a year of going into care.'

Sasha smiled gently. 'That's a shame.'

'It was a crazy time, we were kids, and stunned and scared by what was happening. Ma was held on remand and then went to prison. The judge sent her down for the maximum term when he ruled that Alan's murder was premeditated. We dropped with a thud into the system. I was an angry little thing, as you can imagine. I had never been a happy child on account of, you know, my own mother refusing to love me. Despite our shitty home life and the men who came and went every few months, I excelled at school, I loved learning and I was good at it – but then everything fell to bits, and I… I suppose I took it out on Jez.'

'What happened?' asked Sasha.

'He was so bloody quiet and timid, he sucked everything in, just bottled it all up, and one day I came into his room and found him…'

She let out a long, steadying breath.

Sasha waited. 'Found him what?'

When Lore glanced away, Sasha saw a muscle tighten in her jaw. 'It doesn't matter, I got angry and gave him a hiding, and I shouldn't have done it. I was just a wee little girl, but I had a rage in me, and I gave him such a hiding, and the care workers – well, you can imagine what they must have thought, she's a chip off the old block. And so they sent Jez to another home.' She shook her head. 'I was the one with the brains, the one with *prospects*, but Jez has always fallen on his feet, and now he's sitting on a pile of money thanks to a wealthy wife. Funny how life goes, ain't it?'

Someone came into the room without knocking, and Lore shouted, 'We're talking in here. Can we have some privacy just for one bloody minute, please?'

When the guy made a quick retreat, she said angrily, 'Bloody squatters, they never bother to knock.'

Sasha's mind whirled with the possibility that it was Rachel Weston's DNA that was found in Tony Gardner's home. Jez Weston's mother – a convicted murderer.

'When Rachel got out of prison, do you have any idea where she could have gone?'

'Not a clue.' Lore's voice cracked with the bitter emotion of an unloved child. 'And I really don't care. I don't bear Rachel any ill will. I pitied her, I still pity her, wherever she is.' Her head dropped and when it lifted again just a few moments later, her eyes were blurred with tears. 'But it still hurts that she never made any attempt to love me the way she did Jez.'

'I'm very sorry,' said Sasha, and she stood, keen to drive back to Southend.

Sasha reached into her bag to grab a business card, but Lore already had one. 'I found it on the floor downstairs.' She shoved a piece of paper at Sasha. 'That's my number. Next time you want to talk, give me a ring instead of turning up out of the blue.'

34

He rang the bell but no one answered, so he banged on the door. 'Jez, it's me, open up.'

Abs was about to place his finger on the bell and keep it there when the door opened and the housekeeper stared at him. 'What's all the noise?'

'Is he in, is Jez there?' Abs rushed inside without being asked.

'You can't just—'

'It's okay, Pauline,' Jez told her, tightening the belt of a fluffy white dressing gown around his waist. The initials J.W. were embroidered on his chest in fancy writing. 'I'll handle this. Sorry, mate, I was in the shower.'

'I need to talk to you, bruv,' Abs told him.

'Let's go in here.' Jez led Abs into the library. As soon as the door closed, Abs began to pace, feeling the walls pressing in around him.

'I thought you were filming today?'

'Yeah.' Abs couldn't get his thoughts together. 'I was... I mean, no.'

Jez perched on the edge of the sofa, wrapping the hanging flaps of the dressing gown over his thighs. 'What's the matter, mate, something's wrong.'

'We made a terrible mistake, Jez.' Abs paced. 'We did a terrible thing, and we've got to put it right. We've got to tell them where Rhiannon is buried.'

'Wait, slow down.' Jez pulled his fingers through his wet hair. 'What's happened?'

'I've been kidding myself, bruv.' Abs flung his hands in the air. 'I thought if I could just get back with Kelsey, I'd be fixed, but I've been fooling myself. I thought she still loved me, despite everything, but she never did and never will. And because of that, I did the wrong thing, *we* did the wrong thing.'

Jez frowned. 'Aren't you back on the show?'

'Course I ain't.' Abs thought he was going to cry. 'They don't want me back. I was making a cameo, that's all it was, all it was ever intended to be.'

'But that appearance could lead to—'

'I ain't going back, it's over,' Abs snapped. He never lost his temper, never lost his cool, certainly not with Jez, and he felt awful about it. 'There's something else, but I don't understand what it means. That policewoman called me earlier, Detective Inspector Dawson. She asked about your sister.'

'Lauren?' said Jez in surprise. 'Why would she ask about her?'

'She was getting background information, that's

what she said.' He eyed Jez. 'I told her you ain't heard from her for years, right?'

'That's right.'

'Then why's she asking about her, what does it mean? I'm telling you, there's stuff going on that's making me very uneasy.'

Jez looked towards the door. 'Careful, Abs, Bethany is upstairs.'

'We should have told the police about what Deano did to the girl at the time. We should *never* have hidden the body.'

'You didn't touch that girl, Abs.' Jez spoke quietly. 'You didn't kill her. This is all on Deano.'

'Yeah, mate, but we did wrong.' Abs kicked the edge of a rug with a foot. 'And it's not too late to put everything right.'

'Look, you're upset because filming didn't go well.'

'We're going to die for what we did, just like the others. It's, what's the word – retribution.'

Jez looked him in the eye. 'We're not going to die.'

'We've got to tell the feds,' said Abs. 'Before it's too late.'

'Mate, you're being selfish, I've got a *life* now, a wife and home and a nipper on the way, and I'm not – look at me.' Abs lifted his gaze reluctantly from the floor. 'I will not go to prison because you've suddenly changed your mind. You've got to get a bit of backbone.'

Abs looked at Jez, had never seen him looking

so grimly determined, and he guessed he was being selfish. He'd have to try to live with the guilt, make his peace with it. He'd get his career back on track somehow. *LIE!* wasn't the only show in town, and Kelsey wasn't the only girl. He was voted Britain's Sexiest Guy three years on the trot – that had to count for something.

But when he closed his eyes, a familiar image spun in his head, and he didn't hear the doorbell ring.

'I keep having this… it's like a waking dream, Jez. I see the room in the cottage and—'

'Abs, try to forget what happened. Deano is dead, it's over. Get on with your life. You've had a bad day, you've been knocked back by Kelsey, but it's not the end of the world. I'll always be here for you, mate,' Jez said. 'We all feel like this sometimes. I was the same the other night at the party, but I'll be here you for, just like you've always been here for me.'

'Yeah.' Abs pressed his fingers into his eyes to try to stop the bed – the ceiling – the glass – the blade of light – the mattress – all whirling in his skull. 'I know that, Jez. Thanks.'

'No problem, mate.'

Then the door opened and Bethany came in and told them both tersely, 'That police officer is here.'

'Again?' Jez cinched the dressing-gown belt. 'I'm not exactly dressed.'

'Oh, don't worry,' said Sasha Dawson, walking into

the room. 'Believe me, I've seen people in all states of undress.'

Abs nodded warily at the policewoman. 'I'd better go.'

'No, Abs, please stay. You'll want to hear this too.' She glanced at Bethany. 'The both of you.'

'Is it about my sister?' asked Jez.

'In a fashion.' The detective's eyes flicked to Abs, who had obviously told Jez about her. 'We did a forensic sweep of Tony Gardner's home and DNA turned up that was a close match to your own.'

Bethany's diamond wedding ring seemed to flash with agitation when she lifted a hand to her forehead. 'Good God.'

'I haven't been to his house in years,' said Jez.

'It wasn't your own DNA, Jeremy, but a match with a close female relative of yours. I presumed – wrongly – that it was your sister Lauren's DNA. But now I strongly suspect it's the DNA of your mother, Rachel Weston.'

Abs couldn't believe what he was hearing. Jez's shoulders sagged a little, but he seemed to take the news calmly enough.

'We know that your mother was sentenced to fifteen years for murder.' Sasha Dawson perched on the edge of the sofa. 'And that term was increased following an assault she made on a prisoner during her sentence. We know she left prison two years ago. But what we don't know is where she is now. Do you have any idea, Jeremy?'

Jez kneaded his knees. 'No. I haven't seen her since I was a kid,' he said. 'I've never wanted anything to do with her.'

'Your sister told me you were in contact with your mother when she was in prison. That you wrote to each other.'

'Yeah, we were encouraged to, but we both stopped writing to her after a couple of weeks. I've never wanted anything to do with my mother. Why would I?'

Abs looked sharply at his friend. He remembered that as a kid Jez was always sitting in his room writing letters to her, and was very protective of his mother's reputation, would get upset if any of the other kids teased him about her.

He recalled with alarm the conversation he thought he heard Jez having in the chalet in the wood behind Bethany's parents' house, and bit his lip so hard it stung.

'That's typical of Lauren, or whatever ridiculous thing she's calling herself nowadays,' said Jez, annoyed. 'Telling lies, making trouble for me.'

'You think Jez's mother killed his friends?' Bethany asked, incredulous. 'And now she's coming after Jez?'

It seemed to Abs that when she finally spoke, Sasha Dawson chose her words very carefully.

'Rachel Weston is a person of interest in the investigation. At this stage, it's important that we find her

as soon as possible to eliminate her from our enquiries.'
A phone rang in her bag and the detective lifted it out as
she said, 'The first thing we need to understand is why
her DNA has been found at a crime scene, and the only
way to do that is to talk to her.'

Abs paced, throwing glances at Jez, who pressed his
fingers into his pale knees, leaving red marks. His friend
seemed weirdly calm, considering the bombshell they
had been given: that his mum, a convicted murderer,
could be responsible for the deaths of Tony and Deano.

'Excuse me.' Sasha Dawson frowned at the screen.
'It's my office, I'm going to have to take this.'

They all listened tensely as she spoke on the phone.
'Yes, send me over the address... thanks, and tell DC
Chambers to meet me there. I'll get some photos...
Okay, will do.' When she put the phone away, the
detective told Jez, 'A colleague just told me your mother
stayed at Approved Premises in Basildon when she was
released from prison.'

'Approved Premises?'

'A bail hostel,' DI Dawson told Bethany. 'Some former
offenders are obliged to stay there for a period of time
under the terms of their release.' The leather cracked as
she lifted herself from the sofa. 'I'm going to head over
there now to see if I can find out where she went after
that. But before I go, Jeremy, do you have any images
of her I can take with me? We have a mugshot photo of
your mother, but it's twenty years old now.'

'No.' Jez shook his head. 'I had a couple of photos of her when I was younger, but I tore them up. They were... too painful.'

Abs vaguely remembered Jez showing him photos of Rachel Weston when they were kids, but he couldn't for the life of him remember what she looked like. 'Are we in danger?'

'Our advice hasn't changed,' said Sasha Dawson. 'There's no reason to suggest that you're being actively targeted. Tony and Andrew Dean were long-time friends. We know Dean had a number of run-ins with the police, and violent altercations with other people, and both their deaths may well turn out to have nothing to do with either of you.'

Abs nodded tensely, but he felt in his gut that what happened to those men – torn apart by a train, bludgeoned to death – had everything to do with the secret that he and Jez shared.

'Detective...' It was on the tip of his tongue to tell her that secret. That Deano had killed Rhiannon Jenkins and they had buried her body in the wilderness. He was *this close* to getting it off his conscience once and for all, and damn the consequences, but when he spoke, all that came out was a strangled whimper.

'I'm sorry, Abs, did you say something?' asked Sasha Dawson.

'Frog in my throat,' he told her.

'I'll get Pauline to see you out,' Bethany told her.

'It's okay, I can see myself out.'

When she had gone, Bethany stormed to the door. 'That's it.'

'Where are you going?' asked Jez.

She turned angrily. 'I'm pregnant, Jez, or had that slipped your mind? I really don't need this kind of stress. People getting murdered, the police marching in and out of our house 24/7, and now your insane mother popping up on the radar. My parents are going away for the weekend, and I'm going with them.'

'I'll pack,' he told her.

'No, you'll stay here and watch the house, just in case any of your mad relatives try to break in.' Her eyes blurred with tears. 'It's not good enough, Jez.'

Abs felt sorry for Bethany and understood why she was so upset. She didn't deserve any of this. When she left the room, slamming the door behind her, he wanted to ask Jez why he had lied to DI Dawson about his relationship with his mother. As a kid, Jez had always seemed to look forward to the day when she was released. His sudden cold attitude to Rachel Weston didn't make sense.

He thought again about that chalet in the wood, and the conversation he heard inside, and a frightening thought popped into his head.

Jez was protecting his mother, maybe even keeping her safe.

'Mate—' he started to say.

'Do you mind making yourself scarce, Abs?' His

friend took him by the arm and led him to the door. 'I should try and talk to Bethany, she's hurting.'

Abs hesitated, reluctant to go, but he said, 'Of course, bruv, I understand,' and left the house.

35

The Approved Premises that Sasha visited housed female offenders who were on bail, or who were obliged to stay there when released on licence from prison.

This particular hostel sat on the end of a terraced street in Basildon. An ugly red-brick building, it hunkered behind a metal fence intended to help it blend in on the residential street, but which only succeeded in making it look even more of an eyesore.

When Sasha arrived, the fierce late afternoon heat smothering her as soon as her Spider came to a stop, Lolly was locking up her own car. Travelling north to Colchester, then back to Southend and now to Basildon, Sasha had clocked up a fair few miles already this afternoon, and she still had to drive to the posh hotel to meet Kev. She was chomping at the bit to start her night of luxury and romance, after what had been a long and difficult week, but she worried whether it was feasible for her to get away.

They stood at the door of the hostel, beneath the black bulb of the CCTV camera, waiting to be buzzed in. When the door unlocked with a heavy click, they let themselves into a bare hallway with dirty beige walls, given an even more sour aspect by the glare of fluorescent strip lighting. A laminated sign taped to the inside of the door instructed visitors to ensure it was shut properly at all times. And there were other notices on the walls, curling public information posters that warned against STDs, drug-taking and alcohol abuse. Sasha heard laughter coming from a front room, the chatter of daytime TV. One of the key workers, a large middle-aged black woman, introduced herself as Deborah Franks and got them to sign in.

'You've very neat handwriting,' she observed when Sasha handed back the pen. 'I understand you're here about Rachel Weston.'

'That's right.' Sasha rolled her shoulders to try to circulate some air beneath her shirt and jacket. It was stifling in the house; for some mad reason, the radiators in the hallway were warm. She took out her notebook to check the dates. 'I understand she stayed here following her release from HMP Bronzefield two years ago.'

'We get a lot of women passing through here.' Deborah took them into a tiny, windowless office where there was just enough room for a desk with an old computer, a noisy hard drive beneath it, and a towering stack of files. 'But I do remember Rachel. I was her key worker.'

Sasha's ears pricked up. 'Oh?'

'Rachel was a very… feisty lady.'

'What do you mean by that?'

'She was older than a lot of the women who pass through this hostel, in her late fifties or early sixties, I can't remember off the top of my head.'

'She was fifty-nine when she was released from prison,' said Sasha, 'which would make her sixty-one years old now.'

'There you go, then.' Deborah sat at the desk and Sasha and Lolly crowded in front of it. 'Many of the women who come here tend to be younger. A lot of them have spent much of their adult life behind bars, and have nowhere else to go. We get fewer older residents because they tend to have stronger family ties, but Rachel didn't seem to have anyone.'

'What do you remember about her?' asked Lolly.

Deborah gave a little snort. 'That she was very argumentative. Honestly, Rachel could start a row in an empty room. She didn't give a fig who she upset, and we had to watch her very closely. To look at her, you'd think she was very unassuming.'

Lolly looked up from the notebook in which she had been writing. 'Unassuming, how do you spell that?'

'Put "quiet",' suggested Sasha.

'I believe Rachel had a number of altercations in

prison because of her confrontational nature, and we had a lot of trouble keeping her from causing a disturbance. It became a problem.'

'She got into fights?' asked Sasha.

'It never got physical, at least – she could have gone back to prison under the terms of her licence if it had. But everyone was always on high alert where she was concerned, and staff here had to step in a couple of times.'

'What kind of arguments?'

'Some of the residents would be watching the TV, for example, and Rachel would walk in and turn the channel over without asking.' She stabbed at the air with an invisible remote. 'Or she would report a minor infringement of the rules by other residents, like if they didn't wash up after themselves. She walked around like she owned the place and it didn't make her popular. It's a shame she didn't follow her own high standards of behaviour.'

'What happened?' asked Lolly.

'After she left, we discovered she had defaced a wall in her room.'

'That doesn't sound good,' said Sasha. 'What did she do?'

'She wrote the names of her children in marker pen behind the bed. And it was insoluble ink, too, so the wall had to be repainted. If we had discovered the damage when she was here, she would have been put on a warning.'

'Where did she go after she left here?' asked Lolly Chambers.

'You'll have to ask her Offender Manager at the Probation Service about that. But I do remember she kept turning up for weeks after, asking to be allowed back in – she insisted she'd left something behind, but there was nothing in her room. She was very persistent. I think she just wanted to come back – a lot of former prisoners can get bewildered in the outside world after being locked up for so long. And ex-cons can lead very transient lives – it's been two years now, so she could have moved several times.'

'You said she wrote the names of her children?'

'Yes, that's right isn't it, Joan?' Deborah looked past Sasha and Lolly at an older woman who was carrying bed linen along the corridor.

Joan stopped to cock an ear. 'What's that, love?'

'Rachel Weston,' said Deborah. 'Do you remember her from a few years back? The lady who wrote on the wall of her room.'

'Blimey, it's been a while since I've thought of her.' But Joan's sour expression suggested she remembered Rachel alright. 'She was a real menace, that one, defacing the walls and so forth. Always moaning, never happy about anything. She'd complain if she was put up at The Ritz.'

'What names did she write on the wall?' asked Sasha.

The old woman craned her neck forward. 'What did she what?'

'What did she write?' Sasha asked again, more loudly. 'Was it the names of her children?'

'Children?' Joan looked at Sasha as if she had lost her mind. 'She only had one, I think. She wrote his name again and again. Jeremy, Jeremy, Jeremy. The bed was pushed against the wall so you couldn't see what a terrible mess she made, it was all smeared. I tried to clean it, but in the end we had to get it repainted, didn't we, Deborah?'

'We did. As I say, very feisty.'

Joan's nostrils flared. 'That's one word for her, I suppose.'

When Joan had gone, Sasha asked, 'Would it be possible to see the room where she stayed?'

The duty manager blinked. 'The wall was cleaned a long time ago – you won't see anything of interest.'

'Why don't we have a look, anyway?' Sasha smiled. 'While we're here.'

Deborah took them along the corridor and up a flight of stairs. All the fire safety doors clanged shut behind them on spring-loaded hinges, and were covered in more laminated signs, which warned residents not to smoke, not to run, not to litter, not to bully other residents, and to ensure they attended key working sessions.

'The rooms are not designed to look very comfortable, I'm afraid.'

Small and square and overlooking the street, the room was nondescript. The early evening sun had passed over the roof of the building and the light was fading. A single bed was placed up against the wall and there was a listing wardrobe. A pair of thin curtains framed the double-glazed windows and a threadbare rug on the floor covered painted floorboards. The skirting was lumpy from where it had been painted down the decades. Deborah pointed at the side table beside the bed. There was a lamp, a folded newspaper and an empty mug with a teaspoon inside.

'This room is occupied,' said Deborah. 'A new resident arrived this morning, so I'd ask you not to poke around in the wardrobe or drawers.'

When the bed was pulled away from the wall, one patch of paint was noticeably whiter than the rest.

'That's where she wrote her son's name on the wall, but it's gone now. Actually, there's something else.' Deborah stepped off the rug and flipped it over to reveal scratches on one of the floorboards. Sasha saw the initials JW scraped deep into the wood. 'She must have used a set of keys, or a knife from the kitchen.'

Sasha crouched down and touched rough gouges at the end of the floorboard. She reached into her bag for her phone and turned on its torchlight, which was intensely bright in the gloom of the room. Dropping to her knees, she pointed the light at the floor.

Deborah leaned over. 'What are you doing?'

'There's something down there.' There was a sliver of a gap between the floorboard and the one beside it, and she glimpsed something red underneath. When she prodded the floorboard with her fingers, it rattled slightly, so she shuffled inelegantly on her knees to the end of the plank. 'And there's no nail here.'

Lolly lifted the rest of the rug to reveal the other end. 'Or here,' she said.

Sasha took the teaspoon from the mug and placed the handle end under the edge of the floorboard, using it as leverage to lift the wooden plank. It popped up easily.

'Do you have any disposable gloves?' she asked Lolly, who took a pair from her pocket.

Sasha snapped them on, reached under the floorboard, and lifted out a red notebook. She flicked through the stiff pages to find photos of Jeremy Weston. Jeremy as a baby, as a toddler, and as a little boy of six or seven years old. Every page contained photos of Jeremy Weston as a child.

'Notice anything?' said Sasha to Lolly. 'They're all of her son, they're all of Jeremy, there's not a single one of Lauren.'

She turned to the last pages. There were more photos,

stuck in with glue, of Jeremy as an adult. They were all taken in the street, and he seemed oblivious to the camera. One of the shots was taken outside a shop: Jez was inside, half hidden by the reflection of the street in the glass, looking at something on one of the shelves. A caption written in a small, careful hand said, 'Jeremy in shop!'

In another image he sat at a table outside a pub, laughing with friends or work colleagues, a pint halfway to his lips. The caption below it said, 'Jeremy at pub!' On the next page was a photo of Jez and Bethany walking hand in hand. The caption said, 'Jeremy and Lady!'

'Jeremy and Lady?' asked Lolly. 'Is Bethany posh?'

'It's an old-fashioned way of saying woman, Lols,' said Sasha. 'I guess that when she took this photo, Rachel didn't know who Bethany was.' She got to her feet and said to Deborah, 'Would Rachel have taken these while she was here?'

'We have a curfew, and we ask residents to account for their movements, but they're not prisoners here, they can come and go as they please during the day, so it's entirely possible. But we certainly don't allow cameras or camera phones.' She eyed the notebook over Sasha's shoulder. 'This is quite a surprise. I suppose it's what she wanted to get her hands on when she kept coming back.'

Sasha placed the notebook in a plastic bag and took

it outside. It was gone six on a Friday night, and Lolly told her she'd take it back to Victoria Avenue, but Sasha was reluctant to hand it over. She stared at Lolly for a long moment, thinking.

'Lore told me her mother was devoted to her son. What if she's killing his friends in a twisted attempt to win back his love? Or maybe it's some kind of reverse Oedipus complex...'

Lolly looked lost. 'Edie...?'

'She wants her son all to herself.'

'But why Deano and Tony Gardner? As far as we know, yeah, Jez hasn't seen either of them for years.'

'Rachel was stuck in prison, she probably had no idea who her son's closest friends were. But Deano, Tony and Abs were all named in the national newspapers, along with Jeremy, when Rhiannon Jenkins went missing.'

'It's about time you started enjoying your special night, lady,' Lolly scolded. 'You've got to get to the hotel to make sure you're looking gorgeous for your sexy evening with Kev.'

Sasha rattled the bag. 'We should take a closer look at this.'

'But what does it even mean? A lonely woman comes out of prison and takes photos of the son she hasn't seen for years. It ain't a smoking gun, is it, Sash?'

'At the very least, it means she's been watching him, keeping tabs on his movements.' Sasha moved towards her car. 'I'll see you back at the office.'

'DCI Vaughn said you're not to come back.'

Sasha stopped in her tracks. 'He did?'

'He reckons you need to step back. We all do, Sasha. We all know you like to lead from the front, it's why we love you so much, but give yourself permission to take a night off. Get a bit tipsy, you and Kev, get all snuggled up.' Lolly winked. 'Know what I'm *saying*?'

'There's a murderer on the loose, Lols.'

'And lots of good people working hard to find her. The world ain't gonna fall apart just because you've put on the out-of-office.'

Sasha felt anxious at getting away, when she sensed they were tantalizingly close to a breakthrough in the investigation, but it was also true that she was excited by the prospect of a night in a luxurious spa hotel. A meal in the highly rated restaurant, drinks at the bar, a rare chance to light a flame under the cold embers of her marriage...

'Okay then.' She handed Lolly the notebook. 'But someone needs to warn Jeremy Weston, and Bethany, that his mother may be watching them. Tell them to stay alert, and Abs too.'

'Will do, Sash,' said Lolly.

36

Sasha sang along to A-Ha on Magic as she sped along twisting green lanes towards the hotel up near Saffron Walden. The day was mercifully cooling, the sun hanging just above the treetops, red and bloated and spent.

Her Spider Veloce churned noisily when she shifted gear, the chassis straining on sharp bends. Sasha sensed the days of her little car were numbered, and she would surely miss it when it was finally laid to rest in the great scrapyard in the sky. She would probably end up replacing it with something more sensible and appropriate, a vehicle with four doors, a roof that didn't leak, and air conditioning, and she was determined to make the most of the breeze lifting her hair, the sun on her face. As soon as she got to the hotel, she'd check in, maybe fix herself a drink from the minibar and try to relax in the bath while she waited for Kev to arrive.

Pulling up at a junction, she glanced at the time on her phone and saw it was gone seven. She thumbed a number, placing the call on speaker, and let the phone ring on the passenger seat. Sasha loved her Spider, she really did, but she wished she was able make a hands-free call. Also on the wish list for a new car: a dashboard full of widgets.

'It's me,' she told Ajay.

'We're all here, Mrs Dawson,' he told her drily.

'I'm not checking up on you, honest,' she said. 'But I wanted to make sure that you—'

'Rachel Weston's probation officer won't be back from holiday until Monday,' he told her. 'So we won't be able to get a forwarding address for her until then, at the earliest. We're doing benefit, phone and vehicle checks but coming up with diddly squat. We haven't found any trace of her so far.'

'She could have changed her name, her entire identity. We need to find her as a matter of priority.' Sasha lingered at the junction, because once she started driving again she wouldn't be able to hear a word he said over the roar of the engine. 'The DNA of a convicted murderer has been found at a crime scene, a woman who is seemingly fixated on her son. The more I think about it, the more I think we should advise Jeremy Weston to get out of town for a few days, until we find his mother.'

'I called his house, but the housekeeper said they'd gone away for the weekend with his in-laws, she doesn't know where.'

'Well, there's that.'

'And he's not answering his mobile. In the meantime,

we're getting the court transcripts, paperwork and interview tapes from Rachel Weston's trial sent over. But some of that stuff is archived all over the place, so it's going to take a few days. According to newspaper reports at the time, she had family in Cyprus, so there's a chance she may have escaped there.'

It was possible, but Sasha didn't think so. She suspected Rachel would stay close to her son. Watching him, maybe stalking him.

'We've got to find her, Ajay,' said Sasha, who was in half a mind to turn around and drive back to work.

'Look, we've got everything covered at this end. Chill, eat nice food, drink wine, try to forget about it for a few hours, okay?'

'Yes, you're right,' she told him reluctantly. 'Have a good weekend, Ajay.'

She killed the call, and was about to release the handbrake and get moving when the phone rang again.

When she saw the call was from Kev, she asked excitedly, 'How did the interview go?'

'Don't be angry with me,' he said quickly. She could tell he was at a train station, Liverpool Street most probably; heard the boom of a tannoy, the clip-clop of feet on the concourse. 'There's been some kind of power outage.'

'Which means what?' she said. When a car pulled up behind her at the junction, she ignored it.

'All the trains are severely delayed. It's absolute chaos here.'

'Get a cab,' she said.

'I'll try. But there are thousands of people all trying to do the same thing.'

'Kev, this is a one-night thing,' she told him. The car behind beeped impatiently, and she waved it past, ignoring the rude gesture the driver gave her as he drew alongside.

'We'll do it again soon,' he told her. 'I promise.'

'We can't afford to do it again.' She knew she sounded petulant, but she was almost there now, and pissed off that their night together was spoiled.

'Don't be like that,' he said, but his voice was almost obliterated by the sound of the tannoy. 'Go and enjoy yourself and I'll do my best to get there. But the taxi queue is about a mile long and—'

'This is meant to be our special night, Kev, I thought we could use this time to sort through a few things... I should have stayed at work.'

'We can still make a night of it,' he said tensely. 'Or if we can't, I'll take you somewhere nice tomorrow. I'd better go – the longer I'm on the phone, the less chance I'll have in the scrum.'

Sure, it was a Friday night, but she had left work during a double murder investigation, against all her better instincts, and was in half a mind to head back to Southend. After a few days in which she had nearly been beaten up, blown to kingdom come and mown down by a car, it really was the icing on the cake.

'Why does this always happen?'

'I said I'm sorry,' he told her.

'Don't be sorry,' she snapped. 'Just get here.'

She threw the phone down just as another car beeped behind her.

'Okay,' she complained over her shoulder. 'Keep your hair on.'

Accelerating hard, pushing her Spider's knackered engine to the limit, she turned the radio back on. Dead Or Alive was playing, and usually she wouldn't be able to resist singing along to 'You Spin Me Right Round', but her mood had soured and she switched it off in irritation.

Fifteen minutes later, she pulled up outside the hotel, which looked very grand and historic in its beautiful landscaped grounds, and swung into a parking place.

Sasha pulled her holdall from the boot and went into the large reception hall. A wide staircase with dark banisters snaked upstairs, sinister suits of armour stood guard, and a gallery of sombre seventeenth-century dignitaries stared gravely from huge paintings on the wood-panelled walls. Sasha heard piano music coming from the bar to the right of Reception and saw men in smart suits and women in expensive dresses heading in for pre-dinner cocktails. She felt self-conscious in her M&S trouser suit.

'I'd like to check in, please,' she told the man at the front desk.

'What's the name?'

'Sasha Dawson.'

The receptionist's fingers clacked a keyboard. After an age, he said, 'Mr and Mrs Dawson, you're booked into one of our suites.'

'It's just me,' she told him. 'My husband is caught in London – there's some kind of problem and no trains are running. It's a nightmare, apparently.'

'Really? That's the first I've heard of it.' The man raised an eyebrow. 'I just checked in some other guests who've come down from London.'

'Good for them,' said Sasha shortly, and felt immediately churlish.

Sensing that he may not have said the most tactful thing, the receptionist smiled. 'I'm sure he'll be here soon. We have such a lovely room for you and Mr Dawson... when he arrives. Maybe you'll want to enjoy a drink at the bar first.'

'No,' she told him, listening to the piano and the laughter and conversation. 'I think I'll go upstairs and relax.'

All the stress of the week made her feel suddenly tired. All she wanted to do was collapse on the bed. If the worst came to the worst and Kev didn't turn up, she could get a good night's sleep, enjoy a nice hotel breakfast, and drive home first thing.

'Good for you,' the receptionist said.

37

Abs was never a great drinker. He had always tried to keep himself in shape, just in case one of the glossies wanted him to do a photoshoot with his top off, but his chances of getting voted the UK's Sexiest Guy ever again were next to nil, and he needed something to settle his nerves now. Confusing thoughts and feelings careened around the inside of his head like bumper cars at the fair, and maybe a vodka would help him make sense of everything that was happening.

The barman at the pub along the seafront, an Aussie guy, held up a glass. 'Single or double?'

'Make it a double.' Abs got out his debit card as the guy poured a large measure, rang it up at the till and went to fetch the card machine. He drank half of it down in one go, felt the alcohol flood into his bloodstream, taking the edge off his anxiety; but when he tapped his card on the reader, it didn't work.

'Got any cash?' asked the barman.

Abs went through the rigmarole of checking his

pockets, but knew he didn't have any. Spare change caused an ugly bulge in your trousers, and he never carried it.

'I'll go to the cashpoint in a minute and come back, I promise.' But Abs knew that he probably wouldn't be able to get any money out of the ATM. He'd been in denial about how broke he was, just like he'd been in denial about everything else. Every penny he had had gone on this month's mortgage payment on his flat.

He picked up the glass, but the barman took it.

'Are you taking the piss? You've already drunk half of it.'

'Don't you know who that is?' said a voice, and Abs turned to see two blokes standing behind him. There was a short one and a lanky streak, and they both stared at him in adoration. 'It's Abs from *Laid In Essex!* He's like royalty around here, you can't talk to him like that.'

Clapping Abs on the back, the short guy threw a twenty at the barman and told him to line up another drink.

'Don't you worry, fella, I'll pay for whatever you want. My other half loves you, and I think you're an absolute weapon.'

'Thanks,' muttered Abs, who for once in his life couldn't muster the energy to turn on the charm. 'But I just want to be on my own right now.'

The guy didn't listen. 'Those kids they got now on *Laid In Essex!*, they ain't fit to tie your shoelaces, Abs, they're nobodies. It ain't been the same since you left, mate, they need your star power back.'

'Didn't you hear what I said?' Abs snapped. 'Just leave me alone.'

The guy looked surprised. 'There's no need to be—'

'For once in my life, just the once, I'd like to enjoy a bit of peace and quiet, a few minutes all by myself, is that too much to ask?'

'I thought you were meant to be nice,' said the short fella.

'Well, I'm not. You don't know me, you've been misinformed. I'm a fake, I'm a fraud, I ain't nice. It's all showbiz, it's all bollocks.'

'But you're Abs, you're grea—'

Abs slammed the drink down and moved close to the guy, so near that the other man could feel the warmth of his vodka breath. 'You don't know what I've done, you don't know what I'm capable of, so just piss off and leave me alone.'

The man glared. 'You ain't a stand-up guy at all, you're a mug.'

'Just eff off!'

'Watch your mouth, yeah, or you'll be *Laid Out In Essex!* On the floor.' The guy wasn't intimidated by Abs in the slightest, and his mate had to drag him away. 'You wait till I tell the missus what you're really like. Have a good day, you ignoramus.'

'You can get out.' The barman jerked a thumb at

Abs, and went to remove the second vodka off the bar, but Abs grabbed it and downed it in one, slammed the empty glass down.

Moving restlessly along the esplanade, he pulled his baseball cap low over his face so that no one recognized him. He thought about going back to his flat and sleeping off his bad mood, but he couldn't get out of his head the fact that Jez had told Sasha Dawson he hadn't wanted anything to do with his mother, Rachel Weston, even when he was a kid. Abs knew that wasn't true. What's more, it seemed to him that Jez took very calmly the shocking news that his mum's DNA was found at Tony's house.

Something wasn't right, and Abs thought he knew what it was.

He'd heard Jez talking to someone in the chalet in the wood, and knew he wasn't speaking on the phone because Jez had left it in the house. It had dawned on him that Jez was keeping his mum there. The hut was the perfect hiding place, because Jez had told Abs nobody ever went there. For whatever mad reason, he was hiding his murderous mother from the police.

Abs wanted to ask Jez what the hell he was playing at. But this time when the housekeeper answered the door at Jez and Bethany's house, she made sure to stand in his way so that he couldn't just walk in.

'I need to see Jez,' he told her.

'He's not in.'

Abs could tell she was lying by the way she glanced over her shoulder. Jez may even have been standing behind the door, telling her what to say.

'His car is still parked outside.'

'I don't know where he's gone,' said Pauline. 'I'm sorry.'

And then she shut the door in his face. Abs thought about knocking again and giving her a piece of his mind – he was in the mood for it – but reasoned it wasn't her fault. Instead, he walked to the end of the street to phone Jez. The call went straight to voicemail, as he suspected it would. 'Jez, bruv, give me a ring, I need to talk to you.'

What Abs should do is go home and call his agent to start planning the next phase of his career. He was never going back to *Laid in Essex!*, that was obvz. Maybe he could become an actor; he'd already done pantomime, *Behind you!* and all that, and it was easy enough.

He didn't know how long he stood contemplating his future, but it was beginning to get dark. He was just about to go home when Jez's front door opened and his friend came out, carrying a bundle in his arms. It looked like something long and thin wrapped in a tarpaulin. Abs was about to call to him, but something about Jez's demeanour made him hesitate. Jez glanced up and down the road anxiously, and Abs instinctively pressed himself into a doorway so he couldn't be seen.

Making sure to stay hidden, he peeped around the

corner to see Jez place the tarpaulin in the back of his car, and then get in the front. The car roared up the road, then braked hard at the top of the street to wait to edge out into traffic.

Abs raced out of the doorway just as a black cab came down the road. He ran in front of it, forcing it to stop.

Jumping in the back, he pointed up the road just as Jez's BMW was disappearing around the corner. 'Follow that car.'

38

The green light on the mechanism winked when she pushed the key card in the door, and the lock unsnapped.

Sasha dropped her overnight bag to the floor. The room was absolutely exquisite, and huge. A large sofa covered in red velvet and a matching armchair faced each other across a low coffee table of polished oak – neatly stacked with heavy books about Pre-Raphaelite art and twentieth-century design – and an ornate writing desk was set against a wall beneath a circular mirror. The huge picture window, framed by heavy drape curtains, which were tied back, looked out across the manicured lawn. But the centrepiece of the room was the stately four-poster bed with a canopy that stretched almost to the high ceiling, a chocolate placed on both plump pillows. Everything with legs – the bed, the sofa, the armchair, desk and wardrobe – seemed to have those clawed feet beloved of eighteenth-century furniture makers.

She took out her phone and called Kev, but he didn't answer, so she opened the wardrobe and inspected the padded hangers, which jangled softly at the slightest touch. There was an ice bucket containing a bottle of champagne, two fluted glasses on the tray beside it. Sasha slid the bottle out to read the label, making the ice shiver against the metal of the bucket. Cold water raced down her arm.

When she turned on the bathroom light, the soft motor of an extractor fan began to purr. Sasha admired the marble surfaces and polished fittings. The bath, which stood in the centre of the room on shining black and white tiles, was spacious and its enamel dazzling white, and of course it was hunched on clawed feet of dark metal. Beside the sink was a basket of complimentary soaps, body scrubs, soothing lotions and assorted smellies; a fold-up toothbrush, a miniature comb wrapped in plastic, a tiny bottle of mouthwash, even a packet of floss. Angling the movable hinge on the TV screen set into the wall, she kicked off her shoes and climbed into the bath to see whether she could watch it comfortably from there, and the view was perfect.

Going back into the bedroom, she launched herself backwards on the bed and bounced softly on the springy mattress. She lay staring up at the canopy.

It had been a long time since she'd been in such a calm and peaceful room. Even if she managed to wrangle the occasional lie-in at home, she'd hear her

children screeching at each other and stomping all
over the house. Enjoying the feel of the clean, crisp
cotton sheets on her skin, the serenity of the spacious
room, she thought she might have a nap. Or she could
soak in a bath full of bubbles, a glass of champagne
within reach on the bathroom floor.

'This is nice,' she muttered. 'Very nice.'

Sasha closed her eyes, feeling very tired, but then a
peal of laughter lifted up from the terrace below, and
it broke the spell. So she got up and unpacked the bag,
carefully hanging the three dresses she had brought,
and Kev's shirt and trousers, and placed the toiletries
in the bathroom. Then she undressed and stepped in
the shower. The steaming jet of water was hot and
powerful, and she lifted her face to the nozzle, which
was as wide as a dinner plate. She enjoyed the thunder
of the spray on her shoulders, let it burn into her muscles
and ease away the tension of the week – the deaths of
Andrew Dean and Tony Gardner, Connie's hook-up
with Vaughn, her own worries about leaving Angel at
home – and then turned off the shower, took one of the
many soft white towels folded on the heated rail and
wrapped herself in it.

Condensation fogged the mirror and she wiped it
away. To her own surprise, she carefully applied make-
up and realized she wasn't going to stay in the room. It
was pointless being here in this hotel alone, but she was
determined not to let it spoil her night.

She tried to phone Kev again as she got ready – again: no answer – so instead she called Angel. 'Everything okay there?'

'Yes,' said her daughter quickly. 'Why wouldn't it be?'

'What are you doing?'

'Making myself beans on toast,' said Angel. 'Do you want to know every little thing I'm going to do tonight? If you want, I'll text you when I go to the loo.'

'No need to be sarky,' said Sasha. 'I just wanted to make sure you were fine on your—'

'You don't have to constantly check up on me.' Angel's voice was shrill with annoyance. 'Are you and Dad there yet?'

'Your dad is...' Sasha considered her words carefully; she didn't want Angel to be disappointed that Kev may not even get there. 'He's delayed and I'm waiting for him.'

'Well, have fun and, really, you don't need to keep phoning. I'm going to watch that new series on Netflix now.'

'Night, then. Love you.'

Sasha lifted the remote to switch on the TV, and after furiously pressing buttons, eventually managed to find a way to escape the hotel menu and get to the actual TV guide. She hopped up and down the channels until she found one with wall-to-wall music videos from the nineties – Sinéad O'Connor sang balefully into the camera – and then she opened the champagne and poured a glass. At the wardrobe, she chose one of the dresses, the scarlet one with the hem above the knee, and low heels, and put them on. She found the clutch Angel had packed, a glittery thing she had purchased in a moment of madness, and threw in her debit card and phone.

When she was ready, she necked the champagne, grabbed the key card, and headed downstairs.

39

They drove out of town and into the countryside, the taxi hanging back as far behind Jez's car as it could. Abs kept his eyes on Jez's rear lights, but his gaze also snapped frequently to the taxi meter. They had been driving for half an hour, and the cost of the fare steadily ticked upwards in large red numbers.

'We're too far behind, we're going to lose him,' Abs would tell the cab driver anxiously, or, 'You're too close.'

'I'm doing my best,' the driver complained. 'What's all this cloak and dagger stuff about, anyway?'

'Don't you worry about that, mate.' Abs was increasingly certain he knew where Jez was headed. 'Just don't let him see you.'

The driver eyed him warily. 'As long as you've got the money.'

Jez didn't seem to know he was being followed. He certainly didn't speed up, or make any sudden changes in direction. Abs tuned out when the cab driver tried to make conversation.

'I know you,' said the guy. 'You're that—'

'I'm nobody.' Abs pointed ahead of them. 'Eyes on the road.'

'I'm sure I recognize you.' The driver eyed him carefully in the mirror. 'You're that fella off the telly.'

'I get that all the time, I'm always mistaken for him, but I'm telling you I ain't.'

It was very dark now – all the street lights had been left far behind – so there was no way of telling any more if they were even following the right car. And then suddenly the vehicle just disappeared altogether.

'It's gone, I can't see it.'

The cab driver squinted ahead. 'It can't just have vanished, it's around here somewhere.'

'It's gone, mate.' Abs was enraged. 'You've lost it.'

'This is a straight road,' snapped the driver. 'There's only a couple of big houses around here.'

And then Abs realized where they were, on the long road that ran along the edge of Bethany's parents' property. Dark woods flashed by on the left. 'Pull up here.'

The cab eased to the verge. A few yards ahead was the sharp turn onto the drive, the long, winding lane blurring into blackness. The driver turned on the interior light.

'Wait for me,' Abs told the driver. 'I won't be long.'

He went to open the back door, but it was locked.

'You're having a laugh, right?' The driver nodded at

the trees. 'You could just disappear and I'll never see you again. You can pay me right now.'

'I'm not going to be long, I promise.'

The driver gave Abs a hard stare, and his voice took on an ominous tone. 'Get your money out or I drive us back into town to talk to the police.'

'I don't have any... I've not... wait a moment.'

Abs took out his phone and called a number, listened tensely while it rang and rang. Eventually, his agent came on the line. 'Vince, it's Abs.'

'I *knew* it was you,' said the driver in disgust.

'Vince, I need you to pay my cab fare.'

'Abs?' said Vince. 'What are you—'

'Give him your bank details. Please, Vince, it's an emergency.' He handed the phone to the driver through the partition. 'My agent is going to pay.'

The driver took the phone but when Abs tried to open the door it was still locked. 'Let me out.'

'Wait.' The driver turned in his seat. 'Go on, *say* it, just for me.'

Abs wasn't in the mood, but he knew it was always easier to give the public what they wanted, so he gave a double thumbs up and grinned. 'Abs, mate!'

The door unlocked and he trotted down the dark drive.

'Abs,' called the driver. 'Don't you need your phone back?'

The cab was soon out of sight. Abs could barely see his feet, and was only able to negotiate his way by the faint glow of the moon above the treetops. A car sped past on the road behind him, its headlights sweeping through the trees, sending a brief arc of light racing down the curve of the drive.

And then the hulking mass of Jez's in-laws' house appeared against the backdrop of silvery-blue clouds drifting across the black sky. Jez's car was parked on the gravel drive. The back seat was empty, the tarpaulin containing whatever Jez had brought with him, gone. Despite the chill of the night, Abs felt hot and flustered; he pulled off his jacket and threw it to the ground. The burglar alarm light winked above the front door of the house, and when Abs cupped his hands against the windows, he couldn't see a single light on inside. Bethany had gone away with her parents for the weekend, he remembered.

He thumped on the door – 'Jez, you in there?' – but got no answer.

Abs couldn't believe he was completely alone in the middle of nowhere. Friday night used to mean a swanky party, or the opening of a new bar or restaurant, late night drinks in a VIP lounge, catsuits and sequins everywhere he looked; Friday nights meant being the centre of attention. Now here he was, stranded out of town – he got the feeling the cab wouldn't wait for him

– and not a soul knew where he was, or even cared. He slipped around the side of the house and ran across the lawn behind the converted stables.

The dark trees loomed in his vision; he felt the panic building inside of him, and his world began to go on spin cycle again. Familiar images flew out of the wood, fevered memories hurtling towards him, tumbling between the trees like the cheap horrors on a ghost train, so real that he almost flinched. He saw the pint of water on the floor beside his foot; the sword of early morning light burning between the curtains; the damp-stained ceiling; and the mattress on the floor with the sheets twisted on it.

Abs stopped and rubbed his eyes, trying to rid himself of the images, then plunged again into the trees. A twig scratched his cheek just below the eye, making him stumble on the soft, damp earth. Something ran past him in the darkness, its golden eyes reflecting in the blackness, and it scared the shit out of him. He listened to the clatter of his heart, his own stricken breathing, and tried to ignore the rustling and scuttling and hooting of all the invisible creatures in the wood with him. He was totally lost. His gaze whipped from left to right, but all he could see was an army of trees. He wished he had his phone, just for the torchlight.

And then he heard it. Somewhere to his left, the squeak of a door hinge. Abs launched himself forward, and straight into a thicket. Thorns and twigs scratched at his arms and legs, but he didn't care, just ran straight through it and out the other side. The black ground swelled and dipped, and then his ankle twisted in a hole. Abs fell and rolled, dirt and mulch filling his mouth. He felt a slick of warm liquid on his arm, his own blood. He climbed to his feet and ran towards the noise.

'Jez,' he shouted.

And then he saw a glow through the trees, coming from the chalet. The door swung open and Jez's silhouette appeared against the light inside.

'What are you doing here?' Jez said in shock.

Panting, trying to get his breath back, Abs walked to the small porch where Jez stood. His friend closed the door behind him so Abs couldn't see inside.

'She's in there, ain't she?'

'What are you talking about?' Jez laughed nervously. 'I ain't got no one in there.'

'Then what are you doing here in the middle of the night?'

Jez looked around. 'I like to come here sometimes to think. I like the peace and quiet.'

'Don't lie to me, Jez, you've got your mum in there. The police are looking for her, mate. They want to talk to her about the death of Deano and Tony, and all this time you've been hiding her.'

'No.' Jez shook his head, as if Abs had lost his mind. 'I don't know what you're talking about.'

'Mrs Weston!' Abs called, striding towards the door,

but when he tried to move Jez out of the way, his friend stood firm, blocking the door. Abs shoved him, Jez shoved back, and there was a little scuffle, both of them pushing, but not really wanting to hurt each other.

'Abs.' Jez grabbed him by the shoulders, and his face was twisted in dismay. 'Don't do this.'

But Abs gave him a last big shove, sending Jez stumbling off the porch and onto the earth, and placed his hand on the door. 'The police want to speak to her about Tony's death, so we're gonna take her in.'

'If you open that door,' Jez said in a pleading voice, 'things will never be the same. I'm begging you, mate, don't throw away our friendship.'

The wood began to spin again. Abs saw the glass and the curtains and the damp-stain on the ceiling, and the mattress, whooshing and churning behind his eyes, and he felt the panic build inside him.

'Too late,' he said, and turned the handle. Stepping inside, it took a moment for his vision to adjust to the darkness behind the boarded-up windows. 'Mrs Weston? Are you in here?'

When his eyes adjusted, he saw a single bed, with sheets tangled on it. Behind that was a radiator, and he sensed someone on the floor beside it. Abs stepped closer, just as he heard the snivelling sound: someone crying.

'Oh my God,' he said, feeling sick, because a young woman was tied to the radiator. She looked up at him with red, pleading eyes.

'Help me.' Her words were muffled because of the gag tied around her mouth. 'Please help me!'

40

As soon as Sasha walked into the bar, she saw a barman flamboyantly pouring cocktails from a shaker. She looked forward to having a drink: a nice Pinot, a gin and tonic, maybe a pornstar martini.

It occurred to her that she hadn't eaten since lunchtime. She already felt a bit fuzzy from necking the champagne in the hotel room, and it wasn't ideal that she was flying solo – she felt self-conscious in this posh place, but she only intended to have a single drink. Sasha lifted herself onto a stool at the bar. She felt the pull of her phone inside the glittery clutch. It would be so easy to check her emails, or compulsively trawl her favourite news sites, but she was determined – *determined* – to ignore it unless it rang.

The hotel bar was light and airy and sophisticated in a *Country Living* kind of way, with patio windows along one length of it, giving a pretty view of the landscaped grounds. Groups of people sat outside, illuminated in the darkness by the light from the garden lamps, and the soft glow inside the bar made the chandeliers sparkle. The wood-panelled walls were adorned with vast paintings of straight-backed eighteenth-century equestrians and their prancing horses, and the huge room was filled with plump sofas and comfortable armchairs. At the far end was the biggest fireplace Sasha had ever seen. A man in a casual suit played a passable 'Candle in the Wind' on the piano.

There was a raucous group of people who looked like they were cutting loose after a day of meetings in one of the hotel's conference rooms, but mostly the sofas were filled with couples, who looked tanned and healthy from playing tennis all day on the hotel courts.

A barman placed a bowl of nuts at her side. 'What can I get you?'

'I'll have...' She scanned the long menu of wines and saw how expensive everything was. Hell, she was here now, and goodness knows she deserved a decent glass after her long week. Besides, she was only going to have the *one*, and was almost looking forward to getting an early night in that large, comfortable four-poster.

She pointed at a red with an unpronounceable Argentinian name and a ridiculous price. 'I'll have the Malbec, please.'

As the barman poured, Sasha looked up at the mirror behind the bar to watch the room: people ordering drinks or heading into dinner. One handsome guy who came in the door and sat on a sofa in front of the epic fireplace turned her head. When he glanced in her direction, she looked quickly away. Crossing her legs, the hem of her dress rode up her thighs and she tugged it down. The wine tasted like liquid velvet.

But she couldn't shift Rachel Weston from her head, and before she even realized what she was doing, she took the phone from her bag and dialled Ajay's number. Something, a question, a nagging feeling, played across the edge of her mind, but it was elusive. It was something that needed checking, and she hoped that speaking to Ajay might jog her memory.

'Mrs Dawson,' he said, hearing the ambient sounds of the bar. 'How's the High Life?'

'It's a dirty job, but someone's got to do it.' She sighed. 'Kev's delayed in London, so I'm sitting in the bar drinking a glass of wine all on my lonesome.'

'If it wasn't mine and The Husband's anniversary tonight, I'd be there like a shot.'

She popped a nut in her mouth and chewed. 'What's the latest?'

'We're still working on it, but Rachel Weston seems to have dropped off the face of the earth after leaving the bail hostel.'

Sasha chewed a nail. 'I should be there.'

'If it makes you feel better, DCI Vaughn is drafting in more support over the weekend. We'll find her, you can be sure of that. There's one thing you may be interested in – according to background given at her murder trial, she worked at an abattoir.'

He waited till the penny dropped. 'The cattle prod.'

'She'd be familiar with it, and comfortable using it, and she would probably know where to get her hands on one.'

'If you discover anything about her whereabouts, anything at all, let me know, alright?' In the mirror behind the bar, Sasha saw the guy by the fireplace speak to a waiter and point in her direction, and she felt a frisson of excitement. 'Not Vaughn, *me*, got it?'

'Lesson learned, Mrs Dawson. Is there anything else?'

Sasha wracked her brains and eventually said, 'Give my love to Scott. I hope you both have a great night.'

'Don't do anything I wouldn't do,' he trilled.

She was putting the phone back in her bag when the waiter placed a fizzing glass of champagne in front of her. 'I didn't order this.'

The waiter pointed. 'Compliments of the gentleman.'

She turned on the stool to look at the man by the fireplace. He was good-looking, lithe and compact, with a shaved head in that Jason Statham way, and he looked very pleased with himself, lifting a hand coolly off the arm of the sofa in a half-wave.

'Did he now?'

She lifted the glass towards him – *Thanks* – and he

winked: *You're welcome.* When she turned back to the bar, determined not to make it easy for him, she sensed the man continue to watch her. Sasha took a deep breath and climbed off the stool as gracefully as she could manage – the stool was tall, and it somehow took a long time for her toes to find the floor – and walked over to him.

'It's very nice,' she said, holding up the glass. 'Thank you.'

'There's plenty more where that came from.' He grinned and gestured for her to sit opposite. Sasha liked people who smiled. 'I'd be honoured if you would join me.'

She waggled her fingers on her left hand so that he saw her wedding band. 'I'm waiting for my husband, who's stranded in London.'

'Please, I really need help drinking this. I don't know what I was thinking, ordering a whole bottle.' He lifted the champagne from the bucket beside the sofa, and the ice shifted noisily. 'When your husband arrives, you can completely ignore me and I won't get the slightest bit offended.'

'Okay.' She frowned at his self-assurance and sat on the sofa opposite, careful to tug the dress towards her knees. 'I find your terms acceptable.'

'Although if I was your handsome husband,' the guy said, 'I'd move heaven and earth to be with you.'

She sipped the champagne and felt the bubbles flutter in her skull. 'Who said he was handsome?'

'He's got to be, to have a chance with such a beautiful woman.'

She cringed at the terrible line. 'He'll be doing everything he can to get here.'

The man nodded over the top of his glass. 'Sounds like a nice guy.'

'He is, he's...' She thought about it. 'He's one of a kind.'

'I'm sure he's a lot of things – he's just not here. I'm Ian, by the way.'

He held out a hand and when she took it, it was strong and warm.

'Hello, Ian. Sasha.'

Then he winced, as if to say, *Hear me out*. 'Look, I'm famous for putting my foot in it. Tell me to get lost if I'm prying, but I get this vibe from you...' She cocked her head when he hesitated. 'You seem sad.'

'Wow.' Sasha gulped her drink; the glass was half empty now, and the man immediately leaned forward to top it up. 'You don't waste time with the observations. I love him... very much. He's the love of my life. It's just sometimes...'

She shook her head; it would be unwise to continue with the train of thought.

'Tell me,' he said.

She traced a finger around the top of her glass. 'Okay then, I don't think things have been good between us for a while. There, I said it.'

'Let me guess, he's inattentive, a little bit distant. He probably takes you for granted after all these years. You love each other, but you've both let things drift. Your marriage is in the doldrums and neither of you know how to get out of the slump.'

Sasha's phone buzzed and she quickly took it out, hoping it was a message to say Rachel Weston had been found, but it was just a spam mail from one of the utility companies.

'I'm sorry.' She dumped the device back in her bag, annoyed at her Pavlovian obedience to it. 'He's been a bit down lately and I suppose I'm just as preoccupied, what with work and everything, and we need to make time for each other. It's important that we put some fun back into our relationship.' She smiled sadly. 'But it's hard.'

'If your work is important to you, you shouldn't have to apologize for that.'

'Yeah,' she admitted. 'And what I do has real consequences for people. I'm a police officer, a detective.'

'You shouldn't feel embarrassed or guilty.' He planted his hands on the sofa to push himself forward, and she saw he wore a wedding band of his own. 'He should support you in what you do. In fact, I imagine he's very impressed and proud of you, and if he hasn't told you that lately, then he's a fool.'

He was already making Sasha feel better about herself. She liked being here, talking to this man. He was a good listener, and charming, if a little full of himself, and she was excited. Maybe the evening wasn't turning out too badly after all.

He lifted the bottle from the bucket and said, 'How about we get another?'

41

'We're going to get you out of here,' Abs told the woman, trying to undo the ropes that bound her to the radiator. 'Jez, mate, come over and help, some sicko's tied her up!'

But it was dark and his hands trembled, and it was taking forever. She was hysterical now, tears pouring down her face, and she kept saying something, repeating it, so he pulled the gag from her mouth.

'He's going to kill me,' she wailed.

The glass at his feet.

'Nobody's gonna kill you,' he assured her, and impatiently glanced over his shoulder. 'Don't just stand there, bruv, come and do something.'

But the way the girl's red eyes flashed fearfully behind him made Abs blink. Turning slowly, he saw Jez, a still, black shape in the doorway.

'Jez?' he said. 'Talk to me, mate.'

'Please don't hurt me.' Now the girl was looking in terror at Abs. 'I beg you.'

Nobody had ever looked at him like that before, like he was a monster, the worst thing in the world, and his stomach churned. He had to stop for a moment and get his head on straight, in the face of the repulsive truth that had just been revealed to him. When he touched his own cheeks, he found they were wet. With trembling fingers, Abs began to work at the knots once again.

'I'm not with him, luv. Don't you worry, me and you are getting out of here, we're going home.'

'I'm going to die, he told me—'

'Nothing's going to happen to you, you have my word.' Abs was annoyed at his lack of progress loosening the rope, and began to panic. He snapped over his shoulder, 'You've broken my heart, bruv.'

The girl began to weep. 'He's not going to let me go.'

'He's not thinking straight,' insisted Abs. 'He's made a mistake, that's all, a big mistake.'

And then Jez said quietly, 'We can't let her go, Abs, not now.'

'You be quiet, bruv, you've messed up big time. *Big time!*' Tears were pouring down Abs's face, he could barely see what he was doing, and he told her, 'Look at us both, sobbing like babies.'

The blade of light between the curtains.

'Hurry,' the girl pleaded, as he pulled ineffectually at the rope around her wrists. What he needed was a knife, something sharp to cut through it.

'What's your name, darling?' he asked her.

'Sarah,' she whimpered. 'Sarah Tovey.'

'You just stay there, Sarah Tovey.' Because he had words he wanted to say to Jez, the man who had been like a brother, but who Abs now realized he had never really known at all. Or had refused to see what he really was.

The damp-stain on the ceiling.

'Please don't leave me,' the girl cried.

Abs squeezed her arms. 'I'm going nowhere, do you hear me?'

He pulled a sleeve across his sodden face. He was crying because he was angry and disgusted. At himself, more than anything, for refusing to admit the truth about Jez. All these years, he had buried the truth deep inside of him, bottled it all up, giving himself panic attacks. He had stuck his fingers in his ears and gone *la la la*, in order to drown out the unwelcome thoughts.

The mattress.

'We can't let her go,' said Jez.

'Don't keep saying *we*,' Abs told his friend angrily. 'This – what you've done – has got *nothing* to do with me, do you understand?'

Jez stepped forward, holding out his hands in appeal. 'If we let her go, I'm finished, Abs, I'm going to jail.'

The mattress.

'Just stay back, yeah?' Abs held up a hand as Jez came around the bed towards him. 'You're crowding me in, I can't think.'

'You've always been there for me, Abs,' said Jez miserably. 'I promise I won't do it again, but you've got to help me, just this one time. *Please*, Abs.'

The girl sobbed on the floor.

That mattress.

Abs's shoulders sagged, and he felt a sudden terrible calm inside of him, a kind of serenity, like he was standing in the eye of a hurricane. Because he finally had to admit to himself that he'd always known the truth about the events of that night. It's just that he'd spent the whole three years blanking it out, *la la la*, refusing to face the facts, *la la la*, lying to himself that he never knew what really happened that terrible night when Rhiannon Jenkins was murdered.

42

Three years ago

Abs woke with a start at the crack of dawn, and for a few fleeting moments he had no idea who he was, or where he was, or when it was. When he opened his sore eyes, the shabby room was totally unfamiliar. It was only when he lifted his face from the rough sheet, the dried saliva at the edge of his mouth sticky against the rough cotton, that he remembered the drunken events of the night before.

It was insanely early, he knew that much, and his head throbbed; it felt like someone was throwing an anvil around inside his skull, as he swung his legs over the side of the bed and squinted at the blinding light knifing between the curtains.

Abs walked around the mattress on the floor and headed into the kitchen. The walls and doors were all in unfamiliar places, and he seemed to rebound off every single one of them, like the world's slowest pinball. Alcohol burned through his pores and filmed his hot, clammy forehead, but the cold air was chill against his bare legs and the flagstones in the kitchen freezing on the soles of his feet.

He ran the cold tap to pour himself a long, cool glass of water, and drank from it greedily. It soothed his parched mouth and throat. Glancing out of the window, he saw an empty bottle of vodka sitting on the handrail of the porch. Then he took the pint of water to the bedroom. He desperately needed a few more hours' sleep, and knew already that the whole day was going to be a complete write-off. He cursed himself for drinking – *Never again!* – as he placed the water on the floor beside the bed, and gingerly lay back down.

'Jez?' When he stared up at the damp-stain on the ceiling, the room began to rotate again. 'Are you awake?'

The room picked up speed like a fairground ride, and his stomach lurched queasily. Jerking upright, he saw the ceiling and the window whizz past in his vision, and then merge together... the floor, the pint of water beside his foot, the sword of unbearable light between the curtains, and Jez's mattress, the sheets tangled on top of it...

Abs groaned. The contents of his bilious stomach slopped angrily. The ceiling and window tumbled, the floor lurched towards him and the mattress. The curtains and the ceiling... the glass at his feet... the blinding light... the floor... the ceiling... the mattress.

The mattress on the floor.

The empty mattress.

43

'Here's the thing,' Abs told Jez in the chalet in the wood. 'I keep seeing it, our room that morning. It keeps coming back to me, I don't know why – I don't want to see it, it makes my heart beat fast, I can't breathe – but it's like I've been trying to tell myself something all these years. I remember I woke up early to get a glass of water. The whole room was spinning. I saw the glass at my feet and the damp patch on the ceiling and the light coming through the curtains, and they were all going arse over tit. I was so drunk and I desperately wanted to go back to sleep. It's a wonder I never threw up. And I did get back to sleep for a few hours, until we all discovered Rhiannon was dead.'

He spun his hand, recalling. 'But do you know what else I saw before I got back to sleep? I saw your mattress on the floor. But *you* weren't lying on it, Jez, it was empty.' Abs stepped forward. 'So if you weren't in bed when I woke up, where the hell were you?'

'Having a piss, probably,' said Jez defensively.

'Nah.' Abs shook his head. 'Because I went to the kitchen and you weren't there. Where were you, bruv?'

Jez whined, 'Mate...'

'You killed that girl, that Rhiannon. It weren't Deano, *you* did it.'

The girl at the radiator cried out.

Jez shook his head. 'I was asleep.'

'Do not lie to me.' Abs stumbled closer to Jez, fists balled at his sides. 'Tell me the truth.'

'I don't...' Jez looked pathetic. 'Please, Abs, just leave it...'

'What did you do?' Abs grabbed Jez's shoulders and slammed him against the wall. 'What – did – you – *do*?'

'I'm sorry.' Jez's face crumpled in misery. 'I'm so sorry.'

'Tell me,' said Abs. 'I need to know.'

'I did get up to pee,' Jez admitted, retreating into the shadows. 'But then I saw Deano asleep outside and the girl was drunk, and she kept saying she wanted to go home. We argued, I don't remember what about or how it started, but things must have got out of hand, because the next thing I know I had my hands around her throat.'

He held up his curled fingers and stared at them in astonishment, and behind him, Sarah Tovey cried out, pressing herself against the radiator in terror. When he spoke again, he lowered his voice, as if she was intruding on a private conversation.

'She struggled a bit, but it didn't take long, I was surprised at how easy it was to...'

'To what?' whispered Abs.

'To kill her.' Jez's eyes glinted in the deep shadows of the room. 'Deano was only yards away, but he was so wasted he didn't even wake up. And after it was over, and she was lying there, I didn't know what to do. I felt so tired, Abs, so exhausted, and so I just went back to bed. I was going to tell everyone what happened, but I needed to sleep, just for a little bit. And later when Deano said he'd done it, I couldn't believe it. I tried to tell you all, honest I did, but nobody would listen.'

'Why?' Abs couldn't get his head round it. 'Why would you do it?'

'It was an accident, I swear,' Jez pleaded. 'One thing led to another.'

'One thing led to another,' repeated Abs in wonder. 'All these years and you've never told me.'

'Did you want to know, Abs?' Jez met his eye. 'Did you really?'

And he had no answer to that because, of course, he didn't want to know. The last thing he wanted was to discover that his one true mate was a murderer.

'And this poor girl?' Abs pointed at the young woman called Sarah Tovey, cringing against the radiator. 'What's she all about?'

'I tried to tell you the other night at the party about my... my urges, I wanted to tell you, and then... when

I left I saw her walking along and I just... something came over me.'

'Help me,' begged Sarah.

Abs wanted to go to her, but he needed to hear the rest. 'You snatched her off the street?'

'I couldn't help myself.' Jez sighed. 'Trouble is, once you know how to do it, and you make sure you have all the right equipment in the car – tape, something to put over their head, chloroform – it gets easier.'

'Easier?' Abs stared in disbelief. 'There have been others? She's not the only one?'

A look came over Jez's face that Abs didn't like at all.

'No, she's not the only one. When I killed Rhiannon, it released something in me. But I've been careful, Abs, *really* careful. They're here, in the wood, where nobody will ever find them.'

'Those missing girls in the news... that was you?' Abs cried out. 'Jesus Christ.'

'If I'm honest, I've always had these... urges. You remember when you saved me from those two boys when we were kids? They were attacking me because I was hurting their sister.' He laughed dismally. 'Even back then, I couldn't help myself.'

'Listen to him, you have to help me,' cried the terrified girl.

A terrible thought occurred to Abs. 'And Deano and Tony, did you kill them?'

'Of course I didn't.' Jez looked outraged. 'I could never, but—'

'You've broken my heart, mate,' Abs blurted out. 'I don't know who you are.'

'I'm sorry,' said Jez sadly.

Abs had heard enough and he hurried back to the girl, to pluck frantically at the knots of rope at her wrists.

'We can't let her go, she's seen me,' Jez said behind him. 'What can I do to make it better?'

'Go to the police and tell them,' Abs said over his shoulder. 'Admit what you've done.'

'I can't,' said Jez. 'I'm going to be a father, it'll break Bethany's heart.'

'I'm not asking you, bruv, I'm *telling* you. We're going to the feds.' He felt a knot finally loosen and freed one of Sarah's hands. 'We're going to tell them about this poor girl... and you're going to confess... and...'

'Please don't.' Jez wrung his hands. 'I won't do it again, you have my word, but please don't do this.'

'Yeah, and what'll you do with her?' Abs pointed at the tarpaulin against the wall, which was unfurled to reveal digging equipment – spades and forks. 'Planning on doing some night gardening while you're here, were ya? How many are there, Jez, buried around here, tell me that.'

'Two.' Jez wracked his brains. 'No, three.'

'Help me!' The girl clung to Abs.

'You're okay,' Abs told her, getting both her hands free. 'You're safe now.'

'She knows who we are.' Jez hopped anxiously from foot to foot. 'She's seen us, she knows our names, we can't let her go now.'

'You're him,' said Sarah in shock. 'You're Abs.'

He helped the girl to her feet and turned to Jez.

'You ain't touching her, you sick bastard. Trust me on that, you ain't coming near her.'

Jez began to cry. 'Just let me do it, this one last time. One final time and then I promise I'll stop, I won't touch anyone else.' He put his hand over his heart. 'You have my word.'

'You've broken my heart,' Abs told him in anger, and sadness, and he squeezed the girl's shoulders. 'I want you to run, as fast as you can, and don't look back.'

He led her outside, but Jez followed them, saying, 'We've got to kill her.'

Abs picked up a chunky tree branch and held it like a weapon in front of him. 'We're going to let her go, Jez.'

'She knows who we are!'

'Run,' Abs shouted at the girl. 'Just go.'

Sarah Tovey didn't need asking twice and started to move. But as Abs watched her, the branch was grabbed from him. His head exploded with pain and the next thing he knew, he was face down in the dirty mud. He heard Sarah scream as Jez grabbed her.

She thrashed in his grip as Abs got to his feet, his head spinning, and lurched forward, grabbing Jez from behind, pulling him to the ground.

'Go!' he screamed at Sarah, and she fled into the darkness between the trees.

Abs held out a hand to help Jez up. But as soon as he was on his feet, Jez exploded in a furious rage, kicking and punching and gouging. Abs held up his arms, trying to block the angry blows, and somehow managed to kick him away. But Jez kept coming, arms and legs lashing out, and Abs staggered under the furious onslaught. Hunched over, cringing from the blows that rained down on him, he fell to the floor. He grabbed at the branch and swung it as hard as he could. The thick end of it cracked when it connected with the side of Jez's head. He went flying through the air and fell in a heap.

'Jez.' Abs rushed over and knelt beside him, but his friend didn't move. *Oh my days*, he thought, *I've killed him!*

But putting his fingers against Jez's mouth, he felt soft breath. Searching frantically in Jez's pockets for a mobile, he couldn't find one.

He'd have to call an ambulance from the house – if he could even find the house in the dark. Abs began to run, crashing through the undergrowth in the dead of night.

44

'You've asked a lot of questions, so now it's my turn.' Sasha wagged a finger at the guy. She was feeling quite pissed now, and had managed to push all thoughts of Rachel Weston and the investigation to the back of her mind. 'What are you doing here on your own, anyway?'

'Business conference.' He stretched his arms across the back of the sofa, turning them so that she saw tendon and muscle roll beneath the skin. 'I thought I'd treat myself and stay the night in one of the king-size beds they have here.' He grinned. 'And maybe meet a sophisticated lady.'

She nodded at the wedding ring he wore. 'And where's your wife?'

He rolled the ring around his finger. 'Having fun, I hope.'

She shifted forward to interrogate him and when her bare knees touched his, she felt a crack of longing. She took his hand in hers. 'And yet here you are, Ian.'

'It's Duncan,' he told her.

She narrowed her eyes. 'You said earlier your name was Ian.'

He made a face. 'Did I?'

She dropped his hand. 'Maybe you need to get your facts straight.'

He tapped a key card on the arm of the sofa and she felt her own heartbeat pound in her ears. 'So I suppose that now you know I'm a total rotter, you won't want to come upstairs with me.'

She shrugged, but didn't rule it out. 'But what would my husband say?'

He gazed at her. 'I'm positive he'd very much want you to come to my room.'

'You remind me of him, a *lot*.' She lifted her glass to her mouth and considered him over the rim. 'And for that reason I'm going to let you take me upstairs to have your wicked way.'

Kev downed the last of his drink and said, 'Thank God, because I'm too drunk to carry on with this role-play.' He grimaced. 'I wasn't very good, was I?'

'I think we're both a bit rusty, my darling. It's been a long time.' She reached forward to take his face in her hands, feeling the flushed warmth of his cheeks against her fingertips, and gave him a long, slow kiss. 'But, just a note for next time, Ian slash Duncan was far too sure of himself.'

'I thought I'd surprise you,' he said.

'You certainly did that.'

They clung to each other as they headed to the elevator. Stumbling, knocking shoulders, because they were both pissed, but also because they didn't want to let go of each other.

As soon as they got to their floor, Kev took out the key card and clicked it into the electronic lock of their hotel room – but the light stayed *red*. He put it in again – it stayed *red*.

'Hurry up,' hissed Sasha impatiently, and he slotted the key card in the lock and wiggled it. The light turned *green*, the door unlocked, and they practically fell into the room. Pressed against the inside of the door, their hands were all over each other. It had been a long time since they had physically needed each other this badly, and the years rolled away.

'Wait,' she whispered, panting heavily, pulling her mouth from his. 'I forgot to ask, how did the interview go?'

He pulled the dress from her shoulder to kiss the hollow of her collarbone. 'It was a disaster,' he murmured. 'But I didn't want the job anyway.'

'Oh, that's okay, then,' she said, and slammed him passionately against the wall.

'Ow,' Kev said, rubbing the back of his head.

'Are you alright?' she asked in alarm, but already he was reaching for the bottom of her dress, and she raised her arms so he could lift it cleanly over her head, and then his fingers slipped into her knickers, as she fumbled with his belt.

'No,' breathed Sasha when he began to carry her towards the bed. 'Right here.'

'But it's a really nice bed,' he said, laughing, and she was still trying to unclasp his belt, her frantic movements made clumsy by longing, when a phone rang in his back pocket.

'We better get that,' he said, pulling his mouth from hers.

'It can wait,' she said, as his belt finally came undone and she pulled his trousers down.

Sasha groaned in frustration at the insistent ringing of the phone, as Kev tried to reach it. But his trousers were around his knees, and Sasha was trying to drag him to the floor, and he stumbled and fell over, pulling her down on top of him. The phone flew across the floor. 'We had better...' he said breathlessly.

Sasha tried to carry on, he was under her now, just where she wanted him, and when Kev tried to see where the phone had gone, her hand moved beneath the cotton of his boxers and he immediately responded.

He said, 'It could be... We have to...'

'Leave it,' she hissed, but he turned his body so that she rolled off him and crawled on all fours to the phone, while Sasha lay on the floor and let out a roar of frustration.

'Angel?' she heard Kev say, and she remembered that her daughter was home alone, and sat bolt upright.

'I can't...' he said into the phone, and then, 'Slow down...'

Sasha grabbed it from him. 'Angel, darling, what's wrong?'

'Mum...'

Sasha could barely hear her over the blaring music and shouts in the background. 'Angel, is that you? I can't hear you.'

'Mum.' Angel's words were slurred. 'You've got to come home, you've got to...'

'What's happening, what's all that noise?'

'Please come...' said Angel. 'I don't feel—'

The call went dead and when Sasha tried to call back, there was no answer. 'We've got to order a cab, and quick.'

Kev was hopping around like a rabbit, trying to pull up his trousers. 'I'll drive, I think I'm okay.'

She threw the crumpled dress into the overnight bag and grabbed a tee-shirt, pulled on a pair of jeans, then ran to the wardrobe and started pulling the dresses out, making the hangers jangle crazily. It was mad that she had brought so much stuff with her. And the faster she moved, the more the champagne slopped around in her empty stomach, the more unwell she felt.

'We had two bottles of champagne,' she told him, rushing into the bathroom to throw all her make-up bits and bobs, the compacts and containers, into the toiletry bag. 'The last thing we need is for you to be banned from driving.'

When she came back into the room, he was looking wistfully at the enormous four-poster. 'We never got to use that.'

But the passion she had felt only moments ago had gone – replaced by an overwhelming fear for her daughter. She tugged at his sleeve. 'We have to go, Kev, right now.'

While he called down to reception to order a cab, Sasha dropped to her knees to shove the toiletries into the overnight bag. In typical fashion, all the things that had slipped easily into the bag that morning barely fitted back in now.

Her head spun. 'I'm a bit pissed,' she said, by which she meant she was very pissed.

Still on the phone, Kev opened the mini-fridge and took out a bottle of water – 'Drink this' – and then he got down on his knees and calmly packed the bag. 'We've got everything, let's go.'

He picked up the holdall and opened the door, turned to see her standing in the middle of the room. 'You okay?'

'Yeah.' Sasha blinked back tears – of fear and regret. 'So near and yet so far.'

'We'll come back.' He pulled her to him to kiss her gently. 'Ian has unfinished business with you. Or Duncan does, I can't remember which.'

45

Crashing through the wood, Abs had no idea where he was going. He couldn't find his way out and started to panic that he was running around in circles. He called the girl's name, in case she was lost too, but didn't get any answer.

Finally, after what seemed like hours, he ran across the lawn towards the dark house. Jez's car was still there, but there was no key in the ignition. The house was locked up and he considered using some garden furniture to smash his way inside.

Instead, he went to the converted stables and tried the patio door, and to his surprise and relief discovered that it slid open. He crept in, closing it behind him. He couldn't see a thing inside, but from memory he knew that he was in the games room; there was a full-sized snooker table, a pinball machine that hadn't worked for years, a drinks bar shaped like the prow of a ship. Abs dabbed his hands against the wall, but when he found the light switch nothing came on. Somewhere there was a phone, he vaguely remembered that.

There was a pitch-black space at the far end of the room, a door, and he rushed through it, keeping his arms out in front of him to avoid bumping into anything. In the dimness, he sensed he was standing in another rec room. A large dark rectangle hung on one wall, a big home cinema screen. The phone had to be around here somewhere, but Abs needed more light to locate it. He found another light switch and clicked it. The lights went on for a split second – and then off again. There were lots of appliances in this room – Sky boxes and DVD players and sound systems – and not a single one had a light on it that was working.

Which meant the power had been cut.

'Stop being an arse,' Abs called into the dark, sensing that he wasn't alone.

He didn't know if Jez was just playing around, or if he really meant to kill him. Standing against the wall, waiting for his eyes to adjust to the dark and for the features of the room to solidify, he strained to hear movement.

'Jez, mate,' he shouted. 'The girl's gone now and there's nothing you can do about it. She's gonna go to the police, so you might as well talk to me.'

But he didn't get an answer.

'He's lost it,' Abs muttered to himself. Shuffling along the wall, he came to another doorway and saw an obstruction in the gloom, the dark green baize of the full-length snooker table. He needed a weapon – something to defend himself with – and he went to the end pocket and took out one of the balls, which was smooth and heavy in his hand. But it was no good without something to swing it with and he dropped it back in the pocket, where it clunked loudly against the others. He felt his way to the rack of cues on the wall and took one out; twisted the thin metal band in the middle to unscrew the bottom half. He'd use it to whack Jez with if he had to.

A noise came from close by, a scraping sound, and it terrified him.

'Jez,' he called. 'Is that you?'

Sod finding the phone, he needed to get outside where he could actually see something. He'd run up the drive to the road, wait for a car to come along, then go straight to a police station and tell them everything. About Rhiannon's death and his part in the cover-up, and about Jez, who was – the truth made him want to weep again – a total maniac.

So Abs made his way back towards the dim doorway. But suddenly he was slammed into the side of the snooker table. Hands clawed at his neck, fingers tightened around his windpipe and he began to choke. He heard Jez's frantic sobs, and in his terror and surprise, Abs smashed the end of the cue as hard as he could into his ribs. He heard Jez crash into a table and chairs.

Abs wanted to fall to his knees to get his breath back, but he didn't have the luxury of time, and he jumped off the table and staggered to the door. He didn't know if Jez was following him or not, didn't care, just ran as fast as he could. A blue light undulated faintly at the end of a narrow hallway and Abs knew he was heading towards the indoor swimming pool. There were patio doors along the length of the room, and he could let himself out. He ran along the edge of the pool, the surface of the water lapping gently at his feet, its reflection a shimmer on the wall. The smell of chlorine was overpowering.

Abs rushed towards the doors, but when Jez charged at him out of nowhere, he fell through the air.

They hit the water hard and went under, the cold a sudden shock to Abs's system. It poured into his mouth and down his throat. He glimpsed Jez's crazed face underwater, and his arms thrashing, but then he was hidden by a cascade of white bubbles. Jez's arms grabbed at Abs, dragging them both down. Abs lashed out, but Jez's arm was wrapped around his neck. He panicked. Jez was determined to kill them both.

He tried to elbow Jez in the stomach as they sank to the bottom, but Abs was caught in a headlock, and his lungs were filling with water. He was convinced he was going to drown. He tugged at Jez's arm, and when his feet touched the bottom of the pool, pushed off. The back of Jez's head hit the wall of the pool, and the shock made him let go of Abs, who grabbed Jez's head in his hands and slammed it against the side as hard as he could, despite the resistance of the water. When he felt Jez go limp – his friend's eyes stared, his mouth was wide, his hair swaying eerily slow in the water as he began to drift – Abs clawed his way to the surface, feeling that his chest was about to explode. He broke the surface, taking huge gasping breaths. Choking, spluttering, grasping blindly for the lip of the pool. He clung to the edge until he was able to move again, and then dragged himself, sopping wet, onto the tile. He lifted himself onto his hands and knees to throw up water, which slapped onto the floor. Abs let out a cry of frustration and despair, and then he remembered Jez was still in the water. He was probably dead now; he had killed him. He couldn't leave him down there in that watery grave. But when he finally had the strength to stand and look into the pool, he couldn't see him.

Instead, he felt a chill on his wet skin. The patio door was open, and a trail of water led outside.

46

By the time the cab rolled into their street, Sasha was physically sick with worry. Sitting in the front, she gripped the dash as they approached the house. The street was full of young people, teenagers mostly; so many that they spilled off the pavement and stood in the middle of the road, chatting and laughing, drinking and smoking, and oblivious to the ambulance approaching from the opposite direction.

Leaning between the front seats, Kev muttered, 'Holy...'

Sasha slapped the dash. 'Pull over here.'

As soon as she cracked the door, she smelled the pungent aroma of weed. Drops of lager spattered the windscreen as someone sprayed a can over the crowd.

The driver crawled forwards. 'I have to stop the—'

'Just let me out.' She flung open the door and jumped out before he pulled to the kerb. Now she was out of the car, she heard thumping music, a rapper's urgent vocals, blaring from the house. All the teenagers on the pavement ignored her as she pushed her way through. 'Excuse me, excuse me.'

Every single light was on in the house. There were kids milling about on the front garden, drinking and horsing around. Someone had pulled over the recycling bin; its contents were spilled everywhere. A pair of play-fighting teenage boys fell into the hedge.

'Move aside, please,' she shouted. 'Let me through.'

The hallway of her house – her home – was heaving with people all the way back to the kitchen at the rear. Every surface was covered with bottles and cans, and wet with spilled drink. Cigarettes had been ground out on the floorboards, and there were burn holes in the rug she and Kev had bought when they honeymooned in Morocco.

'Please leave,' she shouted over the chatter and music, grabbing shoulders, trying to get people's attention, but nobody took any notice of her. 'This is my house, you have to go now.'

'Who's the old lady?' One drunken kid burst out laughing at her white hair. 'Hey, love, your roots are showing.' Kev took the arm of the kid, who snarled, 'Don't touch me, man.'

But Kev was in no mood and jabbed a finger. 'You and your friends, go home right now.'

Sasha saw a blue light play over the ceiling as the ambulance pulled up outside.

'Out.' Kev forced his way to the door of the living room. 'Out, out, out!'

'Where's Angel?' Sasha asked the teenagers blocking her way.

One of them rolled her eyes. 'Who's Angel?'

'Didn't she invite you?' asked Sasha with incomprehension.

'I heard about the party from a friend and they heard about it on Snapchat.' The kids laughed. 'I've literally no idea who lives here. Nice place, though.'

'Please leave now,' said Sasha, furious.

'In here,' shouted Kev over the top of the heads of the crowd, and she saw him in the kitchen. Pushing her way inside, she found Angel slumped on a chair, surrounded by a group of kids. Her daughter was hunched over, her head lolling on her chest, and there was vomit all over the glittery top she wore.

'Baby,' cried Sasha. 'What's going on?'

Angel's head lifted for a moment, she muttered something, but her hand was hot and clammy when Sasha squeezed it.

'What's she taken?'

'Nothing, she's just had too much to drink, as usual,' said a girl Sasha didn't recognize. 'Somebody called an ambulance.'

'They're here,' said Sasha as a pair of paramedics pushed their way into the room.

The music was finally turned off. Kev kept shouting

for everyone to leave and teenagers started drifting to the door, but not before someone threw a final can of beer into the air, spraying alcohol everywhere. The room was a mess, just like everywhere else in the house. 'Out – now!'

Sasha held her daughter's hand as the paramedics leaned in to treat her.

'Mum,' whimpered Angel.

'I'm here, baby,' Sasha told her. 'I'm right here.'

'I'm sorry,' muttered Angel.

'Let's not worry about that now.' Sasha's heart leaped when one of the kids shoved Kev angrily in the chest – the last thing she needed was for him to lose his temper. But her husband didn't react; he stood his ground, using his height and authority to herd everyone out.

'Tell you what, Angel, yeah?' One girl dumped her cigarette into the dregs of a drink, where it fizzed and died. 'You sure know how to throw a party.'

47

Abs banged on the door of Jez's house. It didn't even occur to him how early it was; the first threads of grey morning light were pulling sluggishly at the darkness. 'Bethany, Bethany, are you there?'

He was cold and damp and it had taken him hours to get here by night bus. By now, the girl Jez had held captive would have gone to the police – if she'd managed to get away, that is. She'd tell them everything and they'd soon be on their way. If Jez knew what was good for him, he would be handing himself in right at this very moment. But Abs didn't want Bethany to find out the truth about her husband from the feds, he wanted to break the news to her himself, about what Jez had done and what he was capable of. She was going to be a mother, she was having a kid, and he owed her that, at least.

Despite the silly hour, he heard movement behind the door. Someone fumbled with the lock, and when it opened, the housekeeper stood in front of him.

'Bethany,' he told her. 'I need to see her.'

'She's not here.'

Abs stared up at the fading stars. In his panic, it had completely slipped his mind that she'd gone away with her parents, and thank God for that. He'd find out where she was and call her.

'Where is she?'

'I don't know, she wouldn't tell the likes of me.' The housekeeper looked him up and down very carefully. 'You don't look too good, and you're wet.'

'Yeah.' He laughed bitterly. 'It's a long story.'

'Is Mr Weston with you?' she asked.

'No.' Jez, his best mate in all the world, was an abductor, a murderer of women, and had even tried to kill him. He let out a sob but sucked it back down. 'I need to call Bethany. Can I use the phone?'

The old woman considered him doubtfully. 'Why don't I fix you something to warm you up – a nice cup of tea?'

'Yeah.' He just wanted to get off the street. 'That would be good.'

She stepped back and Abs went inside, conscious of his damp clothes.

'Come into the kitchen,' she told him.

He looked warily at the closed door of the library as they walked past. 'He's not here, right? Jez, I mean. He's not come home?'

'No, sir, I would have heard him.' In the kitchen, she

poured water from the boiling tap into a cup. 'What's happened?'

'You shouldn't be here in case he comes back. Jez is... he needs help, I think he's... he's killed people... girls.' Emotion surged in him; he knew he must sound like a nutcase. 'You don't believe me.'

She stirred the tea for a few moments and then looked at him. 'I can see you're scared.'

'I should phone Bethany,' he said impatiently as she placed the cup in front of him.

'Drink. You need to warm up, and then I'll find the phone.' He knew she wasn't going to budge until he'd drunk some of the tea, so he blew on it and took a sip. It tasted horrible, but she was right about one thing, the warmth was a welcome relief.

'Right, then,' she said. 'I'll go and find the phone.'

When she left the room, Abs took small, nervous sips of the tea and felt himself relax for the first time in hours. He heard the woman moving about upstairs. Maybe it was the quiet, and the fact that he was pretty sure he had helped the girl get to safety – he had done a *good thing*, finally – but he felt a kind of serenity. In fact, all the stress and anxiety, the discomfort of his wet clothes, his life-and-death fight with Jez, it all slipped away, just as the cup was slipping through his fingers. To his astonishment, the china smashed on the floor between his legs. And then the door opened and the housekeeper came back inside. She frowned at the smashed cup.

'Oh dear, I'm going to have to clear that up now.'

'I'm sorry,' Abs slurred. 'I don't know how it...' He rubbed his head, trying to clear his groggy mind. 'The phone, did you—'

'This phone?' She took it from the pocket of her apron. 'I appear to have had it on me the whole time.'

He squinted at her and at the phone, his head wobbling on his shoulders like one of those dashboard nodding dogs. What he couldn't understand was why she wasn't making any attempt to give it to him.

'I never noticed before,' Abs told her. 'It's the middle of the night and you're fully dressed.'

'I'm glad you didn't notice.' Her smile revealed badly stained teeth. 'I don't like to be noticed.'

Abs felt the world shift on its axis. He sat up sharply, but the action made him dizzy, and the room tipped queasily. 'I don't feel too good.'

She pointed to the smashed china. 'That's because I've drugged you.'

'I've got to go.' Abs's legs trembled with the effort of standing – it was the shock, he supposed – and when the old woman stepped forward and placed a gentle hand on his shoulder, he fell back helplessly into the chair.

'Make yourself at home.' When he tried to climb to his feet again, she pushed him down harder. 'I said *sit*.'

Then there was a banging on the front door and Abs heard a familiar voice shout, 'It's me, let me in.'

The old woman put down her cloth and put a finger to her lips, said, 'You stay there, like a good boy.'

She left the room, the kitchen door spinning in his vision as she shut it, and then the room began to move, too.

Abs heard voices in the hallway, and then the old woman came in, followed by Jez.

'We've no choice now, my darling,' said Rachel Weston. 'He's going to have to die.'

48

'We're going to keep her in for a bit longer, just for observation.' Maybe it was Sasha's paranoia, but she thought she detected mild reproach on the face of the doctor. 'When she goes home, the important thing is to get her to drink plenty of fluids.'

'You mean water, not vodka,' said Sasha, instantly regretting the weak joke.

The man looked down at his notes. 'And, of course, we'll have to refer the incident to social services.'

She knew the child safeguarding procedure. A social worker would visit their home to see if there was an underlying reason for Angel's hospital visit – neglect or abuse – and the prospect made her feel sick. Questions would be asked about why a fifteen-year-old was left alone overnight by her parents.

'Yes, of course.'

'You can probably take her home in an hour or two. Make sure she gets plenty of rest and, as I say, plenty of fluids.'

'Thank you, doctor,' Sasha said.

'She's had a lucky escape,' he told her. 'I've seen young people have a lot worse reaction to alcohol poisoning.'

Through the sliding doors at the far end of the Emergency Department, Sasha saw the sun lift in the sky. She walked behind the curtain of the cubicle at Southend University Hospital where Angel lay with her eyes shut, fell wearily into a chair beside the bed – she'd been awake all night – and took out her phone. It was way too early to call anyone to ask how the investigation was proceeding, but she could at least check some of her favourite news sites.

But then Angel said, 'I'm sorry.'

Sasha peered tensely over the top of her screen and knew to temper her response. The truth was, now she knew that Angel was going to be okay, her frantic worry was curdling into anger. But Angel was still ill and scared, and her harsh words would have to wait. Her first priority was to make sure her daughter was fully recovered, then there would be time for straight talking.

'We all make mistakes,' Sasha said, trying to draw a line under the conversation. 'The main thing, right now, is to get you home. Then we can decide what to do about the damage to the house.'

'It's not my fault,' said Angel.

Sasha sucked down a sharp breath. She was willing to kick her anger down the road for a couple of days, but it was important Angel took some responsibility for her actions.

'Of course it's your fault,' she replied in a strained singsong.

'It was only meant to be a few friends coming round, but then someone must have put it onto WhatsApp or whatever, and tons of people turned up. Suddenly the house was full. I don't even know who most of them were. I was going to phone you, really I was, but I was too scared of what you would say.'

'Let's not talk about it.'

'You're angry with me – you say you ain't, but you are, I can see it in the way your face is all pinched. That's how it goes, when you're pissed off, it gets all...' Angel made a sour face.

'Angel.' Sasha heard the strain in her own voice. 'I don't want to talk about it. Let's just get home. I'm not angry, but I am very, *very* disappointed.'

'And, anyway,' Angel said bitterly, 'what kind of mother would leave her teenage daughter alone all night so she could swan off to a hotel?'

Sasha's jaw dropped open just as Kev came through the curtain and asked, 'Everything alright?'

If he sensed the tension in the cubicle he ignored it, and went straight to his daughter to kiss her on the forehead.

'I think so.' Angel fluttered her eyelids. 'I feel a little better, I suppose.'

'So what's the story?' Sasha asked him. Kev had gone back to the house to assess the damage. He gave a tight little shake of the head. *We'll talk about it later.*

'You're going to tell me sooner or later, so you may as well say it now,' said Angel.

'It's a mess.'

Stuff had been broken and vandalized. There were cigarette burns on the floor and all over the sofa – it was a wonder the furniture hadn't caught fire – and crushed lager cans had been stuffed down the back. Empty bottles were everywhere, and beer stains. Broken glass gouged the floorboards in the living room, the rugs were sopping. There was vomit on the stairs, and discarded nitrous oxide canisters. The upstairs toilet was blocked. A door had been pulled off a cupboard in the kitchen. Kev found a spliff in the bathroom and someone had used a marker pen to tag a couple of the walls upstairs. He told Sasha later that he'd found a bra in their bed. Items had disappeared, including knick-knacks from the living room, Angel's iPad and Denny's laptop. Kev didn't even have time to go through all the cabinets and drawers to find out if other stuff was missing. The damage alone would come to thousands of pounds.

Angel lifted her head from the pillow. 'I want you both to know, I'll pay you back. Every penny.'

'We'll talk about it later.' Kev placed a hand gently on Angel's forehead.

'How are you going to pay us back, Angel?' snapped Sasha, and Kev flashed her a look. *Be nice.*

'I'll get a part-time job, or I'll leave school and work full-time.'

'You're fifteen, you can't leave school. Right now, you couldn't pay for a torn cushion.'

'Let's talk about it another time,' Kev told them both, just as Sasha's phone rang.

Angel pointed to a sign on the wall prohibiting the use of mobiles. Sasha ignored her and answered the call, climbing out of the chair and walking through the curtain. 'Blimey, Ajay, you're in early.'

'Things to do,' he said. 'I'm sorry to interrupt your idyllic sojourn.'

Sasha stood in the busy ED, with its collection of casualties from the night before, the men and women injured in fights or while drunk, or who suffered alcohol poisoning like her own teenage daughter. She stepped out of the way as a girl in a glittery dress and a leg in plaster was pushed past in a wheelchair. She wasn't in the mood to explain the sudden change in her situation.

'Look, we got word that Sarah Tovey has turned up.'

It was early – Sasha was shattered, she had a lot on her mind – and she struggled to recognize the name.

'The girl who went missing in Brentwood,' said Ajay, when she didn't answer. 'She says she was kidnapped and held in some kind of shack in a wood near Danbury. And, get this, she says she was rescued by Abs Cruikshank.'

'Shut the front door,' said Sasha in wonder.

'There was another man, who she said abducted her, but she's traumatized and can't remember his name. They're talking to her at Chelmsford right now. I'll let you know as soon as we get more from the guys there.'

When she finished the call, Sasha could hear Kev talking quietly to Angel on the other side of the curtain. The question that had been nagging at her since yesterday popped suddenly into her head, and she dug out a piece of paper from her bag and rang the number written on it. It was still way too early, six in the morning, but she called it anyway, and to her surprise it was answered.

'Yeah?' There was a gruff rattle in the voice on the other end.

'Lore, it's DI Sasha Dawson. We spoke yesterday.'

A long pause as Lore processed the information: 'Do you know what time it is?'

'It won't take long, I promise.' A doctor frowned at her speaking on the phone and Sasha walked quickly towards the exit. 'Yesterday you told me how you attacked Jez when you were little kids, do you remember that?'

Sasha heard Lore move sluggishly in bed. 'Do we really have to have this conversation right now?'

'Why did you do it?'

'What.' Lore snorted. 'You're going to bring charges all these years later?'

She stepped out of the automatic doors into the cold early morning. 'You said you found him doing something – what was it?'

'Uh.' Sasha could hear Lore trying to pull her thoughts together. 'It was a long time ago, water under the bridge.'

'Please tell me and I'll let you go straight back to sleep.'

Lore sighed heavily. 'He'd caught a bird, it was just a little thing and still alive, and I found him... he was pulling its wings off.' She grunted. 'He was the sicko torturing animals, and I'm the one who got into trouble, but that's lucky old Jez for you.'

'Thank you, Lore.' Sasha hung up and tapped the edge of the phone thoughtfully against her chin. If she went home now, she'd spend most of the day clearing up the mess. At the end of the car park she saw an old woman hanging on to her IV trolley as she smoked a fag.

'May I nick one?' Sasha asked, pointing at the cigarette. The woman nodded at the drooping front pocket of her sagging dressing gown. Sasha didn't relish the prospect of reaching in there, but she really needed a smoke. She'd given up months ago, but the nicotine hit would help her perk up.

'Bless you.' She gingerly lifted the box out and discovered with relief that there was a lighter tucked inside it, so she didn't have to put her fingers in the pocket again. 'I don't smoke. I mean, I have one in a blue moon.' She lit it and inhaled, handing the box back. 'Thank you so much.'

Clenching the cigarette between her lips, balancing her bag on one lifted knee, Sasha tried to dig out her phone again, but the smoke kept getting in her eyes.

'Do you mind holding this?' she asked the old woman, who had finished her own fag. The woman took it and held it away from her body as if she disapproved of smoking, and Sasha finally managed to find her phone. 'I need to make a quick call.'

She turned away to phone Jeremy Weston's number. If he was home, she would make up some kind of excuse about why she was calling.

Someone picked up at the other end, but Sasha didn't hear anything. 'Hello?'

'Can I help you?' answered a woman's voice.

'Is that Mrs Weston? Bethany?'

'No.'

Sasha waited for the voice to elaborate, but it didn't. 'Who is this, please?'

'I'm the housekeeper,' said the old woman.

'Is Bethany there?'

'I'm afraid the lady is away.'

'Do you know when she'll be—'

'She's away,' interrupted the voice. 'For the weekend. Please call back next week.'

'Then can I speak to Jeremy West—'

'He's not here.'

Sasha listened to the dead air of the broken connection. The *lady*, she thought, recognizing the phrase in a different context. It was how Rachel Weston had described Bethany in the notebook they had found beneath the floorboards at the bail hostel. Sasha had thought Rachel used the word as an old-fashioned alternative to *woman* because she didn't recognize Bethany, but maybe she meant it in a more formal way, as in *the lady of the house.*

'Did you want this?' asked the patient, dragging on the nearly finished ciggie.

Sasha crinkled her nose. 'You have it.'

When she got back to the cubicle, her daughter was sitting in a wheelchair, ready to be discharged. Sasha told Kev, 'Do you mind taking Angel home, something's come up.'

'What, is it an emergency?'

She thought about it. 'Something needs my attention.'

He was used to the demands of her job, and familiar with the set look on her face, but this morning Kev said quietly, 'Angel really needs your support right now. Whatever she says otherwise, she wants you to be with her. This, what's happened to our daughter, is the most important thing.'

'Yes, it is, and she's going to get all my love and attention. I've got to check something, or I won't stop thinking about it. I'll come straight home after that.'

Kev sighed. 'Ian slash Duncan understands.'

'Thank you.' She kissed him. 'All of you.'

His nostrils twitched. 'You've been smoking.'

'Yes,' she admitted. 'I was very naughty, but it was just one drag.'

<h1 style="text-align: center">49</h1>

'Jez,' said Abs, slurring. 'What's going on, mate?'

But Jez ignored him as his mother stood on tiptoes to kiss her son on the cheek. She touched his damp clothes. 'Look at you, you'll catch your death.'

'She's your mum?' Abs was shocked. 'And she's been working here the whole time?'

Jez stood against the kitchen counter with his head lowered, unable to look Abs in the eye.

'Well,' corrected Rachel, 'not the whole time, but for a few months. It's taken us a lifetime to be reunited, hasn't it, Jeremy? But here we are, mother and son, back together. I always tried to keep a watchful eye out for my boy, but it was hard when I was in prison. In that place, surrounded by common criminals, degenerates, it was easy to despair. I was grateful to see from a distance how happy he was, and when I was released I plucked up the courage to approach him, and because Jeremy is a good boy, he agreed to see me. It was a blessing to discover that all these years later...' Emotional, she placed her hands on her chest. 'Our special bond was still intact. He asked me to come and work here, because he could see how I was struggling. Jeremy is kind and considerate, even if the lady of the house can sometimes be fierce.'

Abs gave Jez a sharp look. 'Does Bethany know?'

When his friend shook his head at the floor, Abs couldn't help but laugh dismally at the thought of Bethany's reaction if she knew who she was unwittingly harbouring in her house.

'Jeremy has made something of himself here,' said Rachel proudly. 'He has a beautiful home, full of fine things, and the love of a sophisticated woman. And I just know he's going to be a wonderful, doting parent. I've so enjoyed the chats we've had in the months I've been here. I know my little man, I feel his pain, and I could see he was hurting. It has been my great privilege that he unburdened himself to me about... his hobby. One night when the lady of the house was out, we sat at that kitchen table and he spoke about what happened at the cottage the night that little tart died.'

'When Jez killed her, you mean, you sick old bat?'

'Abs, please.' Jez winced. 'Don't talk to my mum like that.'

Rachel Weston glared. 'I also overheard the conversation Jeremy had with that Andrew Dean person when he came here and said he wanted to go to the police, and I knew I would have to act to protect Jeremy. And when that other person came here making threats to Bethany...' She snapped her fingers. 'What was his name, Jeremy?'

'Davey Jenkins.'

'Everything fell into place. I knew he could take the blame. I'd never have a better chance of getting rid of Dean, and that other reprobate.'

'Except Jenkins had an alibi when you killed Deano, and was in custody when you murdered Tony.'

'But Jeremy had an alibi, too, and that's the main thing.'

Abs stared in disbelief at his friend. 'And you let her do this?'

Jez opened his mouth to reply, but Rachel interrupted. 'Mother always knows best, isn't that right, Jeremy?'

'And what about me?' said Abs. 'Was I going to be next?'

'I heard you all muttering and arguing when you and that Tony person came here. I was listening outside the door.'

'I told her not to hurt you, Abs,' Jez appealed to him. 'I begged her.'

'And look where it's got you.' Rachel scowled at her son. 'He came here to tell Bethany about your... late night *activities*. We don't have any other choice now. He's going to have to die, my boy.'

Abs didn't know if it was the shock, a rush of

adrenaline, or the effect of the drug in the tea wearing off, but he felt a little sharper. What he didn't know was whether he could stand, let alone run.

'You ain't gonna get away with killing me!'

Rachel lifted her nose in the air. 'I'll take full responsibility. I'll go back to prison if it comes to it, and gladly so, if it means my son remains free. Jeremy, go to my room. You'll find something under the bed. Bring it down here now.'

It seemed to Abs that Jez looked pale and clammy. 'What is it?'

'Don't waste time, Jeremy.' The old woman's voice lifted in irritation. 'Just go and get it.'

'Yes, Mum,' he said.

When he left the room, Rachel walked towards Abs.

'He's had a hard life, but even as a little boy Jeremy was devoted to me, and he's stood by me through thick and thin. Once you're dead, he'll be free to live his life. There'll be no one left to spread scurrilous lies about him—'

Abs snorted. 'They ain't lies though, are they?'

'There'll be no witnesses to the death of that Rhiannon girl, and now he's got rid of that latest tart, all that remains to do is to kill you.'

Abs grinned up at her. 'The girl got away.'

She gave him a long look. 'You're a liar.'

Abs tried to laugh, but then Jez came in with what looked like a long stick, with a thick handle at one end and prongs on the other, and gave it to his mother. Abs had never seen anything like it, and he made the mistake of asking, 'What's that?'

'This?'

Rachel stepped forward to thrust the double-pronged end of the rod into his shoulder. He felt a sudden, shrieking pain in his bone and muscle, and cried out.

'Bruv.' Abs appealed desperately to his best friend. 'Don't do this, you don't want to hurt me.'

'No talking,' said Rachel.

She jabbed the cattle prod into his chest and the electric jolt made his muscles scream. His heart fluttered dangerously. He cried out, thinking, *This is it, Abs, you're history.*

'Tell her,' he appealed to Jez. 'Tell her what happened to the girl.'

The old woman shoved the cattle prod into his shoulder. 'Shut up, you.'

'Tell her it's true,' screamed Abs.

Jez looked afraid. 'She got away, Mummy.'

Rachel turned to her son in shock. 'Is it true, did she... escape?'

Jez nodded, ashamed. 'Abs helped her.'

Pressing a button on the handle, Rachel angrily thrust the prod into Abs's ribs and he jerked in agony. 'You nasty little man.'

'She knows Jez's name... and where she was held...' Abs panted. 'The police will be here soon.'

Rachel whirled on her son. 'This is your so-called *friend*, the one you pleaded with me not to kill, and look what he's done.' Jez's mother had a face like thunder, and she hissed at Abs, 'Oh, you're wicked!'

She gave Jez the prod and went to a cupboard, took out a pint glass, and slammed it on the counter. Abs watched as she dropped to her knees to reach into the cabinet under the sink, and came out with a bottle of bleach.

Abs blinked. 'What are you going to do with that?'

The old woman twisted the safety cap off and squirted the thick, pungent liquid into the glass. 'You're going to drink it all up like a good boy.'

'I ain't drinking that,' Abs told her, incredulous.

'We'll see about that.' She nodded at her son. 'Jeremy.'

'Mum...' whined Jez, looking conflicted.

'Do it!' she commanded her son.

Jez stepped forward and touched the prod to Abs's collarbone and held it there. Abs felt the shock reverberate up and down his body, making his muscles spasm. He was screaming when Jez held him down. Suddenly he was having trouble breathing. Rachel pinched his nose shut and jerked it up, forcing his head back.

'Open wide.' Pulling down his jaw, she tipped the glass of bleach to his mouth. The ammonia stench made him retch.

'No.' Abs bucked furiously in the chair, but in his

weakened state it didn't take much for Jez to pin him down. Panicking, he felt the bleach burn his bottom lip.

'Down in one!' hissed Rachel, pressing the glass to his lips.

But then the doorbell rang. Rachel froze and looked questioningly at her son. Jez shook his head – *I don't know*. She placed the glass on the table. There was another insistent ring and she went to the counter. Abs heard her rake around in the cutlery drawer. She returned to Jez and handed him a thin skewer, made him press the pointed end to Abs's throat.

'If he screams or shouts or makes any sound at all, put this through his neck.' She touched her fingers fondly to his cheek. 'You're a good boy.'

Jez nodded sadly. 'Yes, Mummy.'

She left the room, closing the door behind her. Abs listened to Jez's quick, desperate breaths. His former friend's eyes were blurred with tears. He looked just like the frightened little kid Abs had met all those years ago. Careful not to move his head in case the point of the skewer pierced his neck, he couldn't help but chuckle.

'Well,' he said. 'You're a chip off the old block, aintcha?'

50

Sasha rang the bell and yawned, feeling tired and hungover. Her phone went off and she took it out, saw Ajay's name on the screen.

'Sasha—' he said urgently.

But the door to Jeremy Weston's house opened, and the housekeeper who stood there was instantly familiar to her.

'I'll call you back, Ajay.' Dropping the phone back in her bag, she smiled at the woman. 'Hello there, I'm Detective Inspector Sasha Dawson.'

Years of incarceration hadn't been kind to Rachel Weston; her face was criss-crossed with deep lines and her greying hair was thin and straggly. There was a stoop in the way she held herself, a slight curvature of the spine. Her hangdog expression pulled down her jowls, but her eyes blazed with fiery impatience.

When she didn't reply, Sasha said, 'May I come in?'

'I told you on the phone, neither sir nor madam are here.'

She tried to close the door, but Sasha held it open. 'Actually, it's you I'd like to talk to.'

The housekeeper looked flustered. 'Me?'

'It won't take a moment.' Sasha didn't wait to be invited in; she walked into the hallway, forcing the housekeeper to step back. 'I'd just like to ask you questions, Rachel.'

The woman scowled. 'Who is Rachel?'

'You are.' Sasha smiled. 'You're Rachel Weston, aren't you?'

'I don't know what you're talking about.' The housekeeper's eyebrows leaped with indignation. 'My name is Pauline Scott.'

'I believe your real name is Rachel Weston.'

'Stop calling me that.' She opened the front door again and gestured angrily. 'You have to go. I have many things to do before my employers get back.'

Sasha had had enough of this dance, and reached into her bag for her phone. She was going to call for backup immediately. 'I'm going to have to ask you to accompany me—'

And then she heard someone cry out. A man's voice, nearby.

'What was that?'

'I didn't hear anything.' Rachel blinked. 'Go, please.'

'It came from inside the house.'

'No, no, *no*, you're mistaken.' The housekeeper shuffled from foot to foot. 'I'm afraid you have to go now, I'm very busy.'

Sasha stepped towards the kitchen, but Rachel jumped into her path.

'You have to go,' Rachel said fiercely.

'Out of the way, please.' Sasha pushed past her, moving quickly down the corridor. 'Hello, is someone there?'

She opened the door to the library – the room was empty – and heard the distressed voice again, closer this time. She walked into a dining room, then, pushing open a pair of internal doors, she saw Abs slumped in a chair in the middle of a large kitchen. Jez Weston was standing over him with what looked like a kebab skewer in his hand. Sasha realized she had no baton on her.

'Jez.' She held out a calming hand. 'Do you mind putting that down?' He looked at the stiletto as if he didn't even know he had been holding it to Abs's throat, and let it drop to the floor. 'Now step away from him, Jez. Over there by the wall, please.'

When he obediently stepped back, Sasha walked to Abs, kicking the skewer out of reach under a cabinet, and crouched in front of him. He was sweating, breathing hard, and there were scorch marks on his neck.

She dropped her bag to the floor and, fumbling for her phone, said, 'We're going to get you to a hospital.'

There were a number of missed calls on the screen from work. From Ajay, Lolly and Craig, among others.

'Mummy said not to let him go.' Stepping forward, Jez's wet eyes were wide and dilated and he spoke in an oddly stilted way, as if he were a child; a little boy. He was in shock, probably, but it was creeping her out. 'I helped her kill the bad man, Alan. She let me stick a knife in him, she showed me how to do it, in and out, in and out, it made a sucking noise, like this.' He made a slurping noise. 'Because I've always been a good boy.'

'Yeah.' Abs nodded at Sasha. 'He's totally lost it.'

'I'm going to have to ask you to go and stand on the other side of the room, Jez,' she said gently. 'Will you do that for me?'

'He killed the girl in Wales,' Abs said urgently. 'And other girls, too, because he's cray cray. But not Tony and Deano, she did that.'

'Who did it, Abs?' Sasha asked, and admonished herself instantly, because she had taken her eyes off Rachel Weston.

She turned quickly, to see the woman coming at her with the cattle prod, which was shoved hard into her side. Sasha felt herself judder, her head filled with pain and static, and her muscles went into convulsion. She fell in a heap.

She must have blacked out briefly, because when she opened her eyes, she was vaguely aware of Rachel

Weston and her son standing over her, arguing. Rachel was pressing the cattle prod into his arms.

'She's police, Mummy.' Jez's mouth wobbled with upset. 'We have to give ourselves up.'

'Nonsense,' she told him. 'You have come so far, I'm so proud of you, and I will not let you throw it all away.'

'Officers are on their way.' Sasha tried to lift herself from the floor, but her limbs were shaking from the shock. 'The best thing for the both of you would be to—'

'You came here alone.' Rachel leaned over her. 'They have no idea where you are.'

'I took a call, just before I came inside.' She grimaced; it felt like her ribs were on fire. 'Trust me, they know all about Jeremy. I strongly advise you to—'

'Be quiet,' Rachel barked, and appealed to her son. 'Once these people have gone, you will be able to live your life. As a husband and a father, as a fine man. Do not give up now, my boy.' She walked to the glass of bleach on the table. 'But we must kill them quickly.'

'The girl who escaped.' Sasha lifted her head to appeal to Jez. 'She identified Abs, which means by now she's identified you.'

'We used each other's names, bruv,' Abs told him. 'Of course they know it's you.'

'Mummy.' Jez rubbed his balled fists in his eyes. 'He's my bestest friend...'

'Not any more I'm not,' spat Abs.

'Do not give up.' Rachel slapped Jez hard across the face and he flinched in shock. 'I did not bring you up to be a quitter.'

'You didn't bring him up at all,' Abs told her. 'Because you were in prison – for murder!'

'We'll kill him first.' Rachel picked up the glass of bleach 'I'll do it right now.'

Abs tried to rise, but Sasha saw he was unsteady on his legs, and when Rachel pressed a hand on his shoulder, he crumpled back into the chair.

'Abs?' asked Sasha, seeing the smashed cup at his feet.

'She gave me something,' he said. 'I'm having trouble standing.'

Holding out the glass of bleach, Rachel told him, 'You're going to drink it, or I will kill you myself.'

Abs looked at the pale, thick liquid slopping inside, and took it in his hand. He placed the glass slowly to his lips, blanching at its acrid smell, and then jerked his hand to throw it in her face. But his reactions were too slow and Rachel grabbed his wrist. The glass fell from his grasp and smashed to the floor, spilling bleach across the tile.

'Very well.' With a terse nod, Rachel marched across the kitchen. The contents of the cutlery drawer shivered when she opened it to look for something suitable to kill him with.

'It's over, Jez, and you know it.' Sasha climbed slowly

onto her hands and knees. When she lifted her neck, she felt light-headed, and knew she wouldn't be able to get up before he could shock her again with the cattle prod. 'Killing us will not help you now. Please stop her.'

Tears raced down Jez's red cheeks. 'Mummy?'

He watched anxiously as Rachel took out potential weapons – knives, a rolling pin, scissors – and threw them on the granite counter. But then she lifted out a long metal needle with a bulbous gauge at its head – a meat thermometer – and held it up.

'Don't listen to her,' Rachel told him as her shoes clipped briskly back across the tile, picking up speed, lifting the long point of the needle above her head, drawing it back.

Abs cried out in terror as she bore down on him, ready to plunge it into his eye, and he threw up a hand in front of his face. The point went through the palm and out the other side. He screamed in agony, but managed to grab her wrist with his other hand, twisting it as hard as he could.

'Get him!' Rachel commanded her son as she grappled with Abs. 'Don't just stand there!' Paralysed with indecision, Jez lifted the cattle prod. 'Get him off me!'

Sasha heard the device buzz as Jez pressed the button on the handle and stepped forward.

'Shock him,' Rachel howled. 'Do it now!'

Abs was using all his remaining strength to twist

Rachel's wrist, keeping the hand impaled with the thermometer out of her reach. With a grimace, he swung her body around—

Just as Sasha grabbed Jez's ankle, making him stumble. The cattle prod shot forward, and the double-pronged tip jammed into the centre of Rachel's chest.

She screamed and juddered. Letting out a strangled yelp, she fell, her body twisting on the tile, arms and legs jerking as she began to seizure.

'Mummy!' Jez dropped to his knees, tried to hold her flailing limbs.

'Don't touch her,' warned Sasha, crawling over and rolling Rachel on her side to keep her airway clear.

There was a furious knocking on the front door, relentless banging – Sasha didn't know how long it had been going on – and Abs stumbled across the kitchen on bendy legs to answer it, leaving a trail of blood from where the thermometer still pierced his hand.

'Is she going to be alright? Is Mummy going to live?' Jez wailed, afraid to touch Rachel as her body jumped and spasmed. 'Please don't leave me again, Mummy, *please* don't!'

51

Following psychological treatment, Jeremy Weston made a full confession to police about the women he had abducted and killed – three, in the years since he murdered Rhiannon Jenkins.

He took Sasha and her team to the chalet in the wood where he had kept them prisoner, and showed them where the bodies of the women were buried. Following DNA analysis, the identities of the three victims – Imogen Owen, Bernadette Dunne, Annabel Kalinik – were all confirmed, and their families informed.

Weston was currently awaiting trial for the four murders, and the abduction of Sarah Tovey, and his mother, Rachel – recovered from her heart attack – for the deaths of Andrew Dean and Tony Gardner, and the attempted murder of Danny 'Abs' Cruikshank.

There was still a lot of work to be done, as Sasha and the MIT pulled together a timeline of Jeremy Weston's movements, gathering CCTV, phone data and GPS information from his car, to connect him to the disappearance of each of the three women. An abundance of evidence – rope, digging tools, chloroform, traces of blood and DNA – had been found at his home, in the boot of his car, and in the chalet.

Based on Jeremy's confession and the abundance of evidence, the threads of the two investigations – the crimes committed by mother and son – came slowly together, and Sasha and her team put in plenty of overtime to build a watertight case.

Rhiannon Jenkins's father was gravely ill – doctors didn't expect him to survive his cancer for much longer – but he had at least lived long enough to learn the truth about the fate of his daughter. Reconciled, Owen and Davey Jenkins held a proper burial for Rhiannon, which was attended by close family.

Immediately initiating divorce proceedings, Bethany Weston had moved back in with her mum and dad. But not at the home near Danbury, yards from the scene of her husband's grisly murders. As the police erected white tents in various parts of the wood, and lamps to flood the space with light, Bethany and her parents quickly arranged to relocate to Cheshire.

One Friday night, five weeks after the arrest of Rachel and Jeremy, Sasha was sitting alone at her desk in the office when she became aware of a hulking figure standing behind her, and she yelped with fright.

'Vaughn!' She put a hand to her chest. 'You frightened the life out of me.'

'I'm sorry.' Her DCI glanced up at the clock on the wall; it was gone ten. 'What are you still doing here?'

'Just finishing off a few things,' she said, eyes fixed on the empty desktop of her screen. She had just closed her documents and email, was shutting everything down. Sasha felt embarrassed at being alone in the office with him. Both of them had kept their relationship strictly professional in the last few weeks, and neither had spoken about the elephant in the room, Vaughn's relationship with her sister.

'No rest for the wicked.' He pulled a chair over beside her desk and slumped into it. Rubbing his face with both hands, Vaughn stretched, his expanding bulk making the chair mechanism creak in complaint.

Sasha placed biros in the pen cup and tidied, to emphasise that she was about to leave, but he said, 'Do you have time for a quick drink?'

'I've got to get home,' she told him, making a little face of regret. The likelihood was, things with Connie had got complicated already – she was probably giving him the run-around about something – and, really, Sasha didn't want to get involved. As her computer powered down, she took her jacket off the back of her chair, picked up her bag and gave him an apologetic smile. 'Another time, perhaps. See you next week, Vaughn.'

'Sure,' he said. 'You have a nice weekend.'

'Don't stay too late.'

'Oh, I'm not staying.' He pointed vaguely at his office. 'I just came back to pick up a couple of things.'

She nodded, pretending to swallow the lie. She felt rotten about it – he had obviously come back to work to talk to her – but for the sake of her own mental well-being she wanted to stay out of his and Connie's personal life. Sasha shuddered at the thought that one of these days Vaughn might even ask for her sister's hand in marriage.

Victoria Avenue was busy as she drove home, and still pleasantly warm at the end of a long summer. Sasha enjoyed the late breeze in her face, hummed to a guilty bit of Boyzone on the radio, and was waiting for the lights to change at the junction with Queensway when she saw a couple walking on the other side of the road. The lights changed and she drove on slowly, making herself very unpopular with the impatient queue of cars behind her, because she couldn't believe her eyes. Connie and Barry were walking hand in hand.

They were too far away for her to call to, heading towards the High Street, so she did a U-turn as soon as she was able and returned to the station.

Rushing into the darkened incident room, she saw Vaughn sitting in a pool of lamplight in his office.

'I thought you were going home?' she said, remembering he didn't have one. 'I mean, leaving the office.' He gestured for her to sit down. 'What's going on, Vaughn?'

He checked that the incident room outside was empty and then opened a drawer to take out a pair of glasses and a bottle of Scotch. He unscrewed the cap and began to pour.

'Not for me.' Sasha held up a hand, but he splashed some into a glass anyway and pushed it towards her. 'Just the one, then.'

Vaughn raised his drink in a toast – 'To your sister' – and slugged it down.

Relaxing back in his chair, he swilled the remaining Scotch around his glass. Sasha wasn't a big fan – she didn't really like the taste – but she showed willing by taking an infinitesimal sip and then setting down the glass, fully intending not to pick it up again.

'So it's over,' he told her.

'I thought it might be,' she said gently.

'She asked me to get her ex, that *Barry*, off a drink-driving charge – he's probably going to lose his licence this time round – and asked if I could just wipe it from the computer. I told her that even if I could, it was perverting the course of justice, and I would get drummed out of the force, and very likely go to prison, but she asked me again, anyway. And then again, and again. She was very... persistent. She almost had me thinking whether I could get away with it.' He drained the Scotch, the tendons in his neck stretching taut as he swallowed. 'And then earlier she phoned to tell me she had made a mistake and... she and Barry were getting back together.'

Sasha blushed. 'Vaughn, I—'

He held up a hand. 'It's not your fault.'

Sasha guessed that was the 'favour' Connie had intended to ask her on the night she had first met Vaughn. Knowing Connie, she was most likely attracted to him, but in the back of her mind she probably also saw an opportunity to get Barry off the hook. It was audacious – and callous – even by her sister's low standards.

'I feel a little silly now.' Vaughn stared into his glass, smiling a little. 'But it was fun while it lasted.'

Sasha blushed, incensed with her sister. 'Oh, Vaughn,' was all she could think to say. 'I'm sorry.'

'I really liked her, you know. She was exciting, unpredictable. It's been a long time since I've felt so... alive. I don't regret any of it, even if she is the wrong person for me. She's a hell of a woman, your sister, a *hell* of a woman.'

She wanted to tell him, *You're well out of it, you had a lucky escape*, but he looked too sad.

'I've got to make a quick call home.' She motioned to her own desk in the dark incident room. 'Do you mind?'

He gestured – *Be my guest* – and turned away to point the remote control at the TV. Sasha hesitated in the doorway, wondering when, or if, he was intending to head back to his hotel, or wherever it was he was living these days.

In the office, where the only points of light came from the various bits of tech, and from the Essex Police badge screen savers bouncing around in the dark, she sat at her desk and rang Connie's mobile.

Barry answered. 'Yeah?'

'Hello, Barry,' she said sweetly. 'It's Sasha. How are you?'

'Yeah,' he said sheepishly. 'Good, as it happens.'

'Lovely. Is Connie there, by any chance?'

Barry didn't waste time handing Sasha over to her sister.

'Hello?' said Connie, coming on the line.

'Hold on a minute, Con,' Sasha said, and went to close Vaughn's office door – he was faced away, staring at the TV – then padded back to her desk.

'So, Con—'

'Are you going to be quick, darling?' said her sister impatiently, and Sasha could hear music and laughter in a pub or bar in the background. 'I'm really quite busy.'

'Oh, don't worry, Con, it won't take long,' said Sasha, who took a deep breath and then turned the air very blue.

52

Sitting on his bunk, Abs listened to the shouts and yells coming from the ping-pong competition on the concourse of the wing. One of the cons, a lifer but a decent fella, stuck his head into the cell to ask if he was going to join in.

'Got something to do, bruv,' Abs told him.

Every few minutes someone popped in to try to convince Abs to join the fun, because everyone in the prison liked him, the inmates and guards alike, and everyone wanted to be his friend. Some of the things the other prisoners were doing time for would make your hair curl, but these violent offenders and armed robbers and drug dealers were always asking Abs for an autograph to send to their missus or girlfriend, and they all wanted to hang out with him. Early series of *Laid In Essex!* were being rerun on ITVBe in the afternoons, and Abs sat and watched them with a group of the fellas, and he'd tell them funny stories about what happened when they filmed such and such an episode.

It weren't no picnic being in prison, but his life there wasn't so unpleasant.

Nobody could even believe Abs was inside, him being a celebrity, but he was convicted of conspiracy to pervert the course of justice for his part in covering up the murder of Rhiannon Jenkins and hiding her body.

In a series of police interviews about what happened in Wales, Abs poured his heart out. He recalled with unblinking focus the events of that night and the following morning; it was a massive relief to finally let the truth emerge. He pleaded guilty, and accepted his sentence like a man. He was serving a seven-year stretch, but could be released in half that time if he was a good boy. Some of his guilt – not all of it, but some – lifted from his shoulders. Abs hadn't had a panic attack for months now.

He thought about Rhiannon Jenkins a lot. It may have been too little, too late, but Abs was happy to know that she was now finally at rest, and that maybe her family could get a little bit of peace knowing what happened to her. And the families of those other poor women too, Jeremy Weston's secret victims, who he buried in the wood near Danbury.

God rest their souls, and – Abs shuddered just thinking about his former mate – may Jez rot in hell for his crimes.

He took from under his pillow the letter Kelsey had written him. Abs guessed it was the first letter she had ever sent, because it wasn't like she could just text or call whenever she wanted.

He put his nose to the thick paper once again – it was drenched in her favourite perfume – and then ran his fingers over the indentations caused by her pen. In clumsy handwriting, she explained that it wouldn't be appropriate for her to visit, as much as she dearly wanted to, because she didn't want to be a distraction to all the other men during visiting hours with their wives.

Babes, she wrote at the end of it, *lets meat up a.s.a.p. when u get out. Theres a coooollll new bar opened in Benfleet and I no u will loooove it. I miss u soooooo much, babes.*

    Yor Kelsey. Xxxxxxx

Abs knew that when they finally did meet, she'd tip off photographers about the location, at a well-known bar or restaurant, so they could capture the big moment for the tabs.

But Abs also knew that Kelsey had recently lost a couple of sponsorship deals, and had heard from Vince that it was by no means a done deal that her contract on *Laid in Essex!* would be renewed. The word on the street was that she'd been acting like a diva on the show and had fallen out with a couple of execs. And Abs also knew that a hot young girl had joined the series, who was dating that posh movie star with the big hair, and she was getting a lot of attention. These days, Kelsey was desperate for press coverage, and was forced to piggyback on Abs's notoriety by trying to rekindle their relationship. She'd given more than one interview hinting that Abs was the love of her life.

He listened to the thwack of the bats, the click of the ball on the ping-pong table, and the laughter of the cons. One of the players scored an unlikely winner – Abs heard the ball skitter across the floor – and someone shouted, 'You lucky wanker.'

Balancing a piece of cheap prison issue notepaper on his knees, he picked up the ballpoint pen. Abs was no great writer himself, and he didn't know what he wanted to say to Kelsey. Once upon a time he would have jumped at the chance of writing her a love letter, grateful for the opportunity to pour out his heart.

But he had already written one letter that day and was exhausted. He had pitched an idea to a TV network for a new reality series called *Celebrity Bang-Up!*, in which famous people were sent to prison and forced to play a series of party games against real cons for privileges. Every time they lost one of the games, the celebs would be locked in solitary confinement. Abs was really pleased with the pitch – he had brainstormed it with some of his mates here, who had enthusiastically contributed ideas – and he hinted in his letter to the commissioning executive that maybe, what with his considerable experience of both television light entertainment and the penal system, he may be just the right guy to present the show, if they could just wait for him to get out of HMP Pentonville.

The point of the pen hovered over the paper as he thought hard about how to respond to Kelsey. But the click of the ping-pong ball and all the laughter downstairs was distracting. Everyone sounded like they were having a good time.

Deer Kelz, he wrote. But couldn't think what to say next. He tapped the pen against his chin, wracking his brains.

One of the cons stuck his head in the door. 'You playing or what?'

'Abs, mate!' he answered, and he threw the pen across the cell, stuffed Kelsey's letter under the mattress, and climbed off the bunk.

'Lads.' Stepping out of the cell, Abs lifted his arms in a rock-star pose. 'I'm coming down!'

And everybody roared.

He'd get around to finishing that letter later, he was sure he would.

Acknowledgements

Sasha Dawson will be back, you can be quite sure of that. In the meantime, let me thank a few people who helped in the writing of *The Woman in the Wood*.

Michael Gradwell and Inspector Kevin Horn are my go-to guys when I need to ask about police procedure. They have patiently answered all my questions – sometimes the same ones – over the course of several books now. And the same goes for Senior Paramedic Jason Eddings, who assists with all the medical detail. In addition, Gordon Staples kindly helped with the chapter about approved premises.

Sharon Harris from Bear Estate Agents helped me find my way around Southend and South Essex. Scientist Kath Mashiter, MBE, kindly shared some of her forty years' forensic experience, as did crime writers Caro Ramsay and Nicola Monaghan. I'm grateful to Robert Stirling-Gallacher, who provided a typical moment of inspiration, and I should also thank Colin Scott, without whom this book would have been written a hell of a lot more quickly.

And, of course, there's the talented crew at my publisher, Head of Zeus. Special mentions go to wonderful editor Laura Palmer, editorial assistant Anna Nightingale, production manager Christian Duck, Vicky Joss in digital marketing, publicist Kate Appleton, marketing director Jessie Sullivan, copy editor Jenni Davis and proofreader Neil Burkey. As usual, Mark Swan has delivered a cover to die for.

Many thanks once again to my unfeasibly tall agent, Jamie Cowen, at The Ampersand Agency, who helped launch me on this crazy writing adventure, and to Rosie and Jessica Buckman at The Buckman Agency.

As usual, friends and family encouraged and supported me as I wrote this book. Fiona and Archie have to put up with me on a daily basis – so extra love and apologies go to them. And my office would be a lonely place without my devoted four-legged writing companions. Gracie and Jason never fail to lift my spirits on the good writing days, and the bad.